RESOUNDING PRAISE

for the breathtaking debut of
an extraordinary new SF voice

SARA CREASY'S

ꙅONG OF ꙅCARABAEUS

"A powerful debut . . . gripping characterization,
non-stop action, fascinating biological speculation, and a dash of romance. Don't miss it!"
—Linnea Sinclair

"*Song of Scarabaeus* is an enjoyable, fast-paced slice of
adventure science fiction, infused with a measured dose of romance. The technological and political background is revealed
with a deft hand, never getting in the way of the action."
—*BookPage*

"This brilliantly conceived debut heralds a significant new
talent. . . . Creasy's convincing scientific speculation, appealing characterizations, and eerie alien landscapes
make this science fiction romance deeply satisfying."
—*Publishers Weekly* (* starred review*)

"Traditionally, readers of fantasy are looking for well-
developed characters while SF fans want plot and action.
Song of Scarabaeus definitely has both going for it."
—Robin Hobb

"Sara Creasy is a new writer to watch, and *Song
of Scarabaeus* is a novel to read and enjoy."
—Vonda N. McIntyre

By Sara Creasy

SONG OF SCARABAEUS
CHILDREN OF SCARABAEUS

*S*carabaeus Children of

SARA CREASY

HARPER Voyager
An Imprint of HarperCollinsPublishers

HARPER Voyager

An Imprint of HarperCollins*Publishers*
10 East 53rd Street
New York, New York 10022-5299

Copyright © 2011 by Sara Creasy
Cover art by Chris McGrath
ISBN 978-0-06-193474-2
www.harpervoyagerbooks.com

First Harper Voyager mass market printing: April 2011

Harper Voyager and ⟩ is a trademark of HCP LLC.

Printed in the U.S.A.

10 9 8 7 6 5 4 3 2 1

For MCP,
who saw me through

ACKNOWLEDGMENTS

Thanks to my friends at Tucson RWA for their encouragement, especially to Cindy Somerville for being my emergency reader; to my agent Kristin Nelson for her support and understanding; to Diana Gill, Will Hinton, and everyone else at Harper Voyager Books involved in the book's production; to Chris McGrath for a couple of great covers; to my wonderful mum for moral support and grandma duties; and to MCP, with love, for everything else.

Children of
Scarabaeus

CHAPTER 1

Edie Sha'nim was dying.

Surrounded by the hubbub of a busy border station, she huddled her knees to her chest and concentrated on remaining conscious. The pressure of sensory overload jangled her brain as the too-bright lights and too-loud shouts of travelers assaulted her from every angle. The molded plaz chair pressed into her spine like a row of knifepoints. As if frozen in blocks of ice, her fingers and toes pulsed with fire each time her heart struggled to squeeze one more measure of blood through her arteries.

Resting her cheek on her knee, she stared across the concourse to the large windows overlooking the jump node. She'd counted four incoming vessels in the hour or so she'd been sitting here. Counting was about all she was up for now—neuroshock had taken over her system, mincing up her brain, stripping her nerves, leaving every nerve ending screaming.

At any moment, the jump node would light up again and the ship that came through would be the one looking for her.

Her eyes flicked to the side—she was too exhausted to move her head—focusing as best as they could on Finn standing thirty meters away in the waiting area of the security checkpoint, talking to someone. He'd positioned himself so he could watch Edie while he talked. His gaze roved around the concourse every few seconds, then back to her and occasionally to the woman with him. She was, Edie presumed, a ship's captain—and with luck, their ticket off Barossa Station.

The concourse stretched out between Finn and Edie to opposite bulkheads, and was bulging at the seams with traders, spacers, and station crew. Some moved with purpose, others milled around the makeshift market stalls or chatted and argued in small groups.

At last, Finn walked back to her. He was speaking on his commlink, but she couldn't pick out the conversation over the background noise and he was done by the time he reached her. He looked grim—but no more so than he had for the past week. Considering her slow slide into catatonia, he didn't ask how she felt. He'd stopped asking four days ago—days that she'd spent disoriented and curled up in pain on a bunk. Flashes of light danced around his short dark hair like a broken halo. Her optic nerves could not be trusted.

"Cat's on her way with her trader pal," Finn told her.

Edie nodded her head once, which made her feel woozy. Her thready heartbeat stuttered with hope and fear. *Cat's on her way*—which meant the deal had gone well: the trader had accepted the payment they'd offered. The only question now was whether he'd stolen the correct drug for her. If he'd made a mistake, Edie was dead.

And the moment she died, the leash that bound Finn to her would break, killing him, too.

Taking the seat next to hers, Finn sat motionless and watched the crowd. The tension written on his face had become a familiar sight during the past week, the leash filling his head with a staticky echo of her desperation and disintegration. She had promised to fix the interference but was in no state to try now.

Through the blurred confusion of holoviz screens and

billboards, Cat Lancer's approach was unmistakable—the elegant slender figure, the dark skin and flashing eyes, the gold flight suit. She walked with a barely noticeable limp, still recovering from a bullet wound. Formerly the navpilot of the rover vessel *Hoi Polloi*, Cat was now helping them. Yasuo trailed behind her—the *Hoi*'s young engineer, as eager as the rest of them to evade their client Stichting Corp. A few weeks earlier, Stichting had organized the forcible recruitment of Edie and Finn by the *Hoi*'s crew, and sent them on a deadly mission. Six of them had survived, but only four remained together. Gia the cook, a freed serf, they'd already shipped home, and Corky, senior engineer, had been cut loose as soon as they arrived at Barossa Station. Having convinced him that Captain Rackham had betrayed the crew, they trusted him not to turn them in—but no further than that. As far as they knew, he was drinking himself into a stupor at one of Barossa's many bars.

Captain Rackham was dead, shot by the least likely member of his crew to wield a gun. It was a fitting end for a man who'd tried to preserve his false war record by murdering his crew.

The *Hoi Polloi* was already on its way to the junkyard, and its scrap price would pay for their ride off Barossa. Even without the Crib plasma bolt that had blown out the ship's rear end, they would have had to dump the vessel anyway. The Crib would be looking for it, as would Stichting Corp, which believed as strongly as the Crib did that it owned Edie.

Beside Cat was a burly man in a smart jacket—the trader-thief Cat had hired to do their dirty work. If he'd done his job, done what Cat had recruited him to do, Edie's lifeline was only meters, seconds away. Anticipation made her limbs tremble.

Finn stood. Edie didn't trust her body to keep her upright, so she stayed put.

Cat introduced the trader as Beagle. "He's seen the goods and he's happy."

Beagle stared at Edie, not acknowledging Cat's statement. "You got the shakes, love?" He looked her over with a measure of disgust, like she was a drug addict in need of a fix.

Finn held out his hand, palm up. "Show me."

From his inside jacket pocket, Beagle whipped out a small box bearing the distinctive insignia of the Crib, a circle cradled by two arcs. He opened it, delicately removed a bright sliver of plaz the size of a grain of rice, and dropped it into Finn's palm.

"Only one?" Finn eyed him suspiciously.

One was enough—*for now*. Six months of life.

Beagle grinned. "It wasn't easy. The only way into that lab was through the front door. Bought myself an expensive ident and posed as a Crib doctor. Got a fascinating tour of the place." He turned the box around to show the contents. "Stole the stuff from under their noses . . ."

Edie wasn't listening. She stared into the box in disbelief—at row upon row of implants, neatly aligned. *Years* of life.

It was impossible. Neuroxin had to be distilled from the native vegetation on her homeworld of Talas, and the drug degraded after a few years. Edie was the only person who used these implants, so the lab manufactured only a few at a time. Why would they make so many at once?

Her heart sank as she realized what it meant. They *looked* right, but . . .

"Too many . . . You made a mistake," she whispered, wrapping her arms around her ribs as a wave of neuroshock ripped through her body. If she hadn't been sitting, she'd have fallen over by now.

"I don't make mistakes." Beagle sounded indignant. "You weren't expecting such a bounty, huh? Maybe we need to reconsider the price." He glanced behind, at Cat and Yasuo, both of whom had none-too-subtly boxed him in.

Finn already had an injector out and slotted in the implant. He turned on the built-in holo and tipped the readout toward Edie so she could read the micro-inscription. The magnified text swam in her vision. *Neuroxin, batch #13-AA3. Crai Institute Research Labs, Talas.* This was genuine. It made no sense.

Her relief lasted only a second, crushed by doubts. What if it *was* counterfeit? What if it was outdated and ineffective? What if the Crib had switched the drug for something else? But what was left of her rational mind knew that couldn't be the case. The Crib—specifically, her boss, Liv Natesa didn't want her dead. They just wanted her back.

Cat's commlink beeped and she glanced at the message.

"We've got three Crib battlecruisers headed this way."

Edie felt like all the air had been pushed out of her lungs. A surge of adrenaline set her heart racing, and Finn flinched as his chip reacted.

"How long?" he asked Cat.

"My buddy in TrafCon just picked them up on a node beacon. They'll be in-system in about three minutes. Then we've got maybe fifteen until they dock. The general alert will go up in a few seconds and I don't think Barossa's guests are going to be happy."

Beagle looked petrified. "They're after me."

"Three battlecruisers? Don't flatter yourself." Finn took Edie's arm and pushed up her sleeve. He gave her a questioning look and she nodded. They had to try it. He flashed a microbial flare across her skin and injected the implant inside her elbow. With alarm, Edie noticed that his hands shook. She tried to calm down to ease the interference along the leash.

Beagle wasn't far wrong. His ship, or perhaps even his body, had been tagged. She'd expected it. The Crib needed Edie, and Edie needed neuroxin. Talas was the only place to find the drug, so the Crib had to simply sit back and wait for her, or someone she paid, to steal it. The trader needn't have bothered with his disguise—Natesa and her cronies wanted him to steal the implants and lead them back to Edie.

The station's PA system chimed. "Ladies and gentlemen, this is TrafCon announcing for your pleasure the imminent arrival of our noble allies, represented today by three warships chock full of friendly milits." There was more than a touch of insolence in the young male voice.

The reaction on the concourse was immediate and dramatic. People ran and yelled. Some pushed their way toward the docking bays, others to the lifts leading to the cargo bays. Many gathered around the windows that overlooked the jump nodes, staring out with disbelief written on their faces. Edie turned in that direction just as the incoming node flared in an arc of light. The light faded and three white dots emerged.

Beagle's face paled and sweat popped out of his pores. "What the hell is the Crib doing out here? They have no jurisdiction."

"Crib Interstellar Patrol has ordered us to shut down the docks," the voice continued over the PA. "It will take us a few minutes to comply."

Cat grinned. "That's Digger up in TrafCon. Barossa can't argue with three battlecruisers, but I asked Digger to give all these guilty consciences time to leave if they want to."

Plenty of people wanted to leave. The concourse was in pandemonium and the docking bays were no doubt even worse. Beagle looked around at the mayhem.

"The box, please?" Cat asked sweetly.

Beagle gave it one more try. "I got you good stuff and lots of it. The price has gone up."

"One implant or fifty—makes no difference." Cat dangled the key to the cargo hold in front of his face. "You can't sell it anywhere else. It's worth nothing to anyone except her. You get paid what we agreed on. Hand it over."

The payment was all the valuable antiques from Captain Rackham's collection on the *Hoi*. Beagle had nothing to complain about—other than the tag on his ship, which would soon land him in a Crib jail unless he could pull off a disappearing act.

Beagle clutched the box to his chest, unwilling to give it up, his face scrunched with indignation. Crib milits were only a few minutes from docking—Finn had no time for games. He grabbed the trader's forearm and twisted it away from his body, then closed his other hand around the box. When Beagle didn't let go, Finn pushed forward suddenly and jarred the man's shoulder, knocking him off balance. Finn easily extracted the box from his fingers, and Beagle, a head shorter than the big man and not in the best shape, didn't try to get it back.

"Is it working?" Cat asked Edie.

Edie had felt nothing when the implant first went in. Now a calm presence seeped through her veins, blanketing and shielding her from the surrounding hyperstimulation of colors, sounds, and movements. The nausea that had been her constant companion for a week was lifting, and she moaned in relief. Her senses dulled but felt more closely linked to reality.

"I feel okay," she said. "I'm *okay*." After having no neuroxin in her bloodstream for days, the sudden surge of the drug had a dramatic effect. Her biocyph-enhanced cells immediately metabolized the chemical—toxic to other humans—and its byproducts flooded her nerve endings. Her muscles relaxed and she sagged in the chair. Finn's warm fingers closed over her wrist as he checked her pulse.

Cat looked over Finn's shoulder at the approaching vessels. When Edie followed her gaze, she saw that ships were already fleeing Barossa and heading to the outgoing node.

"You sorted out our ride?" Cat asked.

"Over there." Finn nodded toward the area where he'd been talking earlier to a ship's captain. Then he leaned over Edie with concern in his eyes and pushed sweat-soaked hair off her forehead, cupped her chin with his hand—a steady hand, this time. "Okay?" Finn's intense gaze burned through her as his thumb dragged along her jaw before dropping away, his expression fading to something lighter and safer.

He pulled her out of the chair, supporting her with his arm around her back, and picked up one of their two duffel bags. Edie felt dizzy and numb but already stronger as the neuroxin pumped through her body. The knowledge that she was not going to die—not from neuroshock, anyway—was enough to keep her conscious and upright.

She turned to Beagle as Finn tried to get her walking. "Your ship's tagged." Her voice was drowned out by the noise of the panicking crowds. She repeated herself, louder this time. "*Your ship's tagged.* They followed you here. Get off the station and pay a good infojack to destroy that tag."

"*What?*" Beagle was furious. He rubbed his wrenched shoulder. "Why is the Crib interested in one lousy box of meds?"

"Just leave." Cat tossed the cargo hold key at him before moving quickly through the crowd toward the security checkpoint.

"*It's you, isn't it?*" Beagle yelled. His panicked eyes bored into Edie's. "They want *you.* Who the hell *are* you?"

The desire to explain made Edie pause. Who was she? The Crib's protégée and pawn, its most successful cypherteck, its least loyal citizen. Unwitting creator of the new face of Scarabaeus, the world she'd tried to save. Abductee, fugitive, Finn's partner in crime and his constant companion until they could find a way to cut the leash.

No words came out of her mouth. Her brain was still sluggish. And this trader was irrelevant, in the end. She'd warned him—there was nothing more she could do.

Finn turned Edie around and they followed Cat, with Yasuo behind them holding the second duffel bag. Finn's strength and heat bled through her jacket and into her bones. Every step was easier than the last, and her senses were settling back to normal. For the first time in a week, her thoughts coalesced into meaningful patterns and she was able to concentrate on more than just staying conscious. The captain up ahead . . . Passage off the station . . . A ride to the Fringe. And then, helping the Fringers with the cryptoglyph locked inside Finn's head—the key to saving the outlawed planets from ecological meltdown.

The concourse streamed with people rushing in every direction. The imminent arrival of three Crib battlecruisers was out of the ordinary on any station. But the lowlifes on Barossa had more reasons than most to consider it an emergency—and hundreds of spacers and dozens of ships did not intend to hang around to find out what was going on. A mass exodus was under way.

The security checkpoint was the barrier between the concourse and the docking bays. It only worked one way—arrivals were checked on their way in, departing spacers were not. Barossa was just outside the border of Crib space and had no interest in following Crib procedures when it came to tracking people's movements. A couple of rovers, an escaped convict, a cypherteck on the Crib's most-wanted list—they should have no trouble leaving.

The woman who'd been waiting for them stood up and appraised the group. She wore clean, faded clothes and a cap on her head stamped with her ship's logo. The no-nonsense, hard lines on her face suggested she was a seasoned space traveler.

"This is Captain Xin," Finn said. "She's agreed to take us to Tallyho Station on the *Medusa*."

The captain nodded a greeting to Finn. "Are you ready to leave? We have company, it seems. The Crib doesn't send Lines unless it means business, and I've no desire to get caught up in Crib business."

"I agree," Finn said. "We're ready."

"Then there's just the matter of payment." She had a thick accent. "I thought you said there were four of you?"

Yasuo had disappeared.

"Shit." Cat looked around frantically. "Thought he was right behind us."

They scanned the crowd. In the hustle it was impossible to spot him.

Finn handed Cat his duffel bag. "I'll go look. You pay up and wait for me."

He didn't have tell them not to board without him. That could mean a death sentence for him. Not only was the chip in his head wired to explode if Edie died, it would also detonate if they were separated by more than two thousand meters. Having recruited him as Edie's bodyguard, the rovers had thought the setup provided a good incentive for Finn to protect her.

"We leave in three minutes," Xin called after Finn.

"Kid's probably buying a souvenir," Cat told her with a tight smile.

Edie knew better. Yasuo had always struck her as a bit skittish. He'd been silent during their plans over the past week, just going along with them, never really saying what he wanted to do. Now he'd finally decided to go his own way. That would've been fine if it weren't for the three battlecruisers about to dock. They couldn't risk him being captured by the Crib. Unlike Corky, he knew their intended destination.

While Edie kept a lookout for Yasuo, Cat completed the payment with Xin. Eager to depart before Barossa shut down the docks, the captain became increasingly anxious as the seconds ticked by.

"Four minutes until the docks are locked down," the PA announced.

"I'm afraid I can't wait any longer. Follow me." Xin looked from Cat to Edie. "Unless you want—" She stopped suddenly, staring at something over Edie's shoulder. Her brow pinched. "We have a little problem."

Edie spun around to see what she was looking at. Every holobill and viz on the concourse showed the same display. *Fugitive at large. Apprehend upon sight by order of Crib Central Command. Reward offered.*

Accompanying the text was a larger-than-life revolving mug shot of Edie.

CHAPTER 2

"Jezus . . ." Edie instinctively ducked her head.

The display cycled to show more faces—Finn's, Corky's, Yasuo's, Gia's, Cat's. *Known associates.* Finn's mug shot came from his Crib serf file. The others were stamped with Stichting Corp's logo. The Crib must have demanded the *Hoi*'s crew roster and personnel files from the company. Now someone on the approaching ships had jacked into Barossa's PA system and stuck their faces on every information board on the station.

Except that Cat Lancer's mug shot was of someone else entirely—a gaunt blue-eyed woman with midtoned skin. The new ident that the infojack Achaiah had set up for Cat had involved using a worm to change Cat's appearance in records across the Reach.

Finn was suddenly at Edie's side, his jacket collar raised in an attempt to hide the lower part of his face. His appearance broke Xin out of her trance.

"The Crib wants you, and that's reason enough for me to pretend I never saw you," Xin said. "But the deal's off. I'm sorry. You might have better luck with—"

Finn cut her off with a quick motion of his hand. He didn't need to hear her suggestions. "Cat, get a refund. Plan B."

Cat nodded. She and Finn must have already discussed this while Edie had been too sick to get involved in their plans.

Finn took Edie's elbow and guided her with purpose toward the security check. With all the bustle and panic around them, no one paid much attention to the wanted fugitives in plain sight. Yet.

"Yasuo?" she asked as they hurried along wide corridors lined with windows overlooking the docks. She had to jog to keep up with him.

"Gone. If the Crib gets him he'll crack on the first question. We need a new ride and a new destination. Turn on your e-shield to minimum. From this point we can't leave a DNA trace."

Edie obeyed, wondering what plan B was and how it might affect their plans once they reached the Fringe. From Tallyho, a midsized Fringe station, they'd planned to find a ride farther out into the Reach. Cat had a few contacts from her rover missions over the last few years, and through them they'd hoped to find worlds that needed their help. They'd never told Yasuo the reason they wanted to go to the Fringe, other than to hide out—only Cat knew about the cryptoglyph—but he could still reveal names and places to the Crib. They had only minutes to change their plans entirely.

It seemed Finn had thought ahead. They'd reached the end of the docks, and the crowd thinned out. Finn turned a corner and swiped a key through a door labeled *Rescue and Tug*.

"Courtesy of Cat's buddy in TrafCon," he said in response to Edie's questioning look.

She followed him down narrow, branching corridors. Behind them, Cat raced to catch up.

"What did you give your buddy for the key?" Edie asked Cat.

"Access codes for the *Hoi*'s cargo holds so he could sell the rigs before the scrap merchants picked up the ship. He's given us more than the key. I just spoke to him—he's clearing as many ships as he can for departure before the Crib shuts the place down."

Cat took the lead, and after a couple more turns stopped at a numbered hatch.

"This is it."

Finn's key snapped open the hatch, which led to a short gangway. They piled inside. While the airlock cycled, Finn rummaged in the duffel bag and pulled out three devices that looked like narrow collars.

"Breathers," he explained. "The ship is pressurized, but not with breathable air. Hold still."

Before she had time to object, Finn drew the collar around the back of Edie's neck and pressed firmly on the clip at the front. She felt a sharp pain above the beetle shell embedded between her collarbones, and yelped in surprise.

"Sorry. You're supposed to apply a local anesthetic first."

"No kidding." Her throat felt scratchy, then cold as air from the storage pouch on the back of the collar began to flow directly into her lungs through the tube piercing her trachea.

Finn attached his own collar with a minimum of fuss. Cat seemed to be having trouble with the injection part of the routine. Her fingers hesitated over the clip on her collar. As the far hatch snapped open, Finn reached over and did the job for her. She scowled but muttered her thanks.

Cat led the way into the cockpit of a cramped skiff. There was barely enough room for all of them to stand, and there was no pilot's seat.

"What is this—a tug?" Edie asked as Cat punched the control panel. "We can't get far in this."

"We're only going a few hundred meters. Usually the tug operates automatically. I can override that," Cat said. She scanned the holoviz readout. "Okay, there are two cargo ships due to depart in the next couple of hours."

"Take the *Lichfield*," Finn said.

"Okay. I'm sending a message to Digger to ask him to clear it ahead of schedule. Once we're on board, the tug will return to this dock automatically and the Crib'll be none the wiser."

"*Cargo?* This is your plan B?" Edie looked from Finn to Cat, expecting answers.

"We're the cargo," Finn said. "We're going cryo."

Edie's breath caught. Cryosleep? She'd spent the last week in a state of near death—and wasn't ready to do it again.

The tug gave a barely discernable shudder as the docking clamps released. Cat opened the front shutter and guided the tiny vessel away from the station, following the pylons that extended from it. Larger ships were docked at the end of the pylons, which served both as tethers and as railings for conveying cargo crates into ships' holds.

"I really hoped we wouldn't need plan B," Cat muttered. "I'd rather take passage on a Fringer tin can than a drone vessel."

"A drone . . . You mean no crew?" Edie asked her.

"That's right. Fully automated. Just a bunch of cargo crates strapped to an engine, really." A navpilot in cryo on a ship with no pilot—no wonder Cat was nervous.

"Listen, this friend of yours in TrafCon . . . you trust him not to turn us in?" If they got out undetected, he would be the weak link.

"Digger? Yes, absolutely. Known him for years. That's one reason we ran to Barossa in the first place. The Crib has no reason to question him. And he has plenty of reasons to avoid talking to them."

Behind her, Finn opened a small shutter at the rear. They were far enough from the station now that its entire curved flank was visible. Dozens of ships were leaving. One by one the larger vessels detached from their clamps or pylons and the smaller ones sailed out of hatches, reoriented themselves, and headed outward to the jump node.

A shadow swept across the side of the station. A massive black-and-silver shape descended from above—a Crib battlecruiser, on approach to one of the docks. Edie cringed, an instinctive reaction. She knew they couldn't see her, but her heart seemed to stop.

Beyond the perimeter of the station, a second Line-class loomed. Was Liv Natesa on one of those cruisers? A week ago, Edie's former employer had caught up with the *Hoi* at Scarabaeus. They'd only barely escaped.

A swarm of fleeing ships streamed past the cruiser's sleek hull in the other direction. Every few seconds, the outgoing jump node lit up in a ring of light as a ship departed.

All those people were reacting out of fear because they didn't understand the Crib was after *her*. Edie felt sorry for Beagle. He'd saved her life, and Finn's, by stealing those meds, and didn't deserve the trouble he was in now. Maybe he was on one of those ships, already safe. More likely he was still loading up all that precious cargo they'd given him. Rackham's antiques and artifacts were worth a fortune, if Beagle could find a buyer for them.

"The ship we're heading for—the *Lichfield*—what's its destination?" Edie tried to stop the tremble in her voice as she contemplated cryosleep. They had no choice. The milits would be here any moment and no one else on Barossa would take them.

"Deeper into the Fringe, making stops along the way," Cat explained. "These automated vessels fly a tortuous route through the nodes, making deliveries and pickups. Cheapest way to ship anything if you don't care how long it takes."

"And the Crib can't trace us?"

"The manifest is confidential, so they'll never know we're on board. Even if they wanted to, the Crib can't afford the legal hassles of checking every courier service, let alone one outside Crib space. And with all these ships fleeing Barossa, a drone ship is the last one they'd suspect."

"Let's hope so," Finn said.

Cat docked the tug flawlessly. "Releasing the *Lichfield*'s docking clamps," she reported. "Digger came through—it's ready to depart. Switching to autopilot."

The tug began its journey toward the jump node, the *Lichfield* in tow.

"Time to get on board," Cat said.

But it wasn't as simple as Edie had imagined. The tug was attached to the *Lichfield* by docking clamps, not by the hatch through which they'd come. That hatch led nowhere. Nevertheless, it was their way out.

Edie listened in stunned disbelief as Finn explained their next move while he reeled out a tether.

"Depressurization drains the e-shield fast, so we need to find an access hatch quickly and break in."

Edie's mind was still fixated on the word *depressurization*. That meant . . . the cold vacuum of space. She shuddered and bit down on a dozen questions about safety and risks. She trusted that Finn knew what he was doing. She had to.

"We have to be inside the ship before it hits nodespace." He attached the tether to her belt and handed the end to Cat. "If something goes wrong, we can't return to the tug because it'll be on its way back to the station by then. Let's keep an open comm line. No sudden moves."

"How long will the breathers last?" Edie asked.

"The shields will die first—we've got maybe ten minutes. You ready?"

She wasn't, but she nodded.

Cat depressurized the tug and Edie felt the buzz of her e-shield as it ramped up power to compensate. As Finn cycled the hatch, Cat leaned forward, her lips close to Edie's ear.

"Time to find out if your Saeth knows what he's doing."

Finn slung the duffel bag over his shoulders like a backpack and climbed out of the hatch onto the stern of the *Lichfield*. He held out his hand to help Edie down. The weightlessness made her stomach flip. Behind her, Cat sealed the hatch.

The long hull of the *Lichfield* rose up in front of Edie. From the corner of one eye she picked up the intermittent flashes from the node, signaling the departure of other ships.

She didn't dare turn to look. She watched Finn, and matched his movements by grabbing on to struts and pulling herself along. Holding on wasn't a problem in zero-g. It was simply the terror of hanging in empty space that set in. Her heart raced, demanding more oxygen. Finn gave her a familiar look that told her to calm down. The breather provided a steady trickle of air into her lungs, but it didn't feel like enough. Fighting back the feeling of suffocation, Edie concentrated on taking shallow, slow breaths.

Hand over hand, the three of them climbed along the hull of the *Lichfield*. Finn seemed to know where he was going. Maybe he'd done this a hundred times before as a Saeth rebel. She told herself that and felt a little more confident. She turned her head in time to see the tug detach and head back to the station. Filling her view was the jump node, normally an invisible portal to nodespace. It was constantly active now as ships streamed out of the system.

She was getting cold. The e-shield kept her body heat in, but it wasn't completely efficient. A tinny beeping sound took her by surprise. She glanced down to see the warning light on her e-shield flashing. A fainter echo trailed the beep—someone else's alarm reached her ears through the open comm line. She craned her neck and saw the light on Finn's shield generator also flashing.

Instinctively she moved her hand to her belt to double-check the readout. Inertia spun her entire body and she fell away from the cargo ship. Too panicked to even scream, Edie clawed for a handhold and instead felt something solid across her back. Finn had reached out to grab her shoulder, his shield melding with hers. He stopped her spin and she hit the hull. He pinned her against the vessel until she found the handholds again.

"I said keep *still*."

"My shield . . ." she managed.

"I know. You'll make it."

Finn moved only one more step and stopped. He pulled a device no bigger than his finger from the duffel bag and attached it to the access panel directly above him. Where did he get all this stuff? Edie had been unaware of his activities while she was sick. During that time he and Cat must have been preparing for all this.

He pulled back slightly as a puff of smoke shot out of the access panel's handle. The panel blew open and the air inside evaporated into space.

Finn reached down and hauled Edie up. As she clambered inside, he detached the tether. She lurched against the walls of a narrow airlock as the gravplating pulled on her. Scrambling inside as fast as she could, she heard Cat climb up behind her.

Edie turned and waited for what seemed like an eternity until Finn pulled himself inside. He shut the access panel and put them in total darkness. She heard him rummaging around in the duffel again. "I need to weld this or the hull breach will set off security alarms."

"Won't it already have done so?" Edie asked.

"No. The toms will investigate first, and transmit an alarm to the company HQ if it's serious." Toms were small multifunctional droids used mostly for maintenance jobs. "I need to fix it before the toms get here." Finn fired up a small torch and swept it over the edges of the hatch. After a few seconds he tapped the panel, and then nodded to Cat. She opened the inner airlock door. Air rushed in.

Cat shone a flashlight down a dark, cramped corridor. "Where does this lead?"

"It's a maintenance tunnel for dockside repairs," Finn said. "Should be a panel in the floor that we can drop through. See if you can find it." He was still checking the welded panel for leaks.

Edie crawled a few meters down the tunnel, feeling with her hands for handles or catches. Her fingers caught on an indentation.

"Got it." She pushed out the panel.

Cat's flashlight illuminated the hole. "Looks like a main corridor."

Finn caught up with them. "Set your e-shields to low, just for warmth. There's no other danger."

They slid through the hole onto the deck. Each of the six walls of the corridor had a railing down the center in a shallow depression half a meter deep. It matched the struts Edie had seen on standard cargo crates. These passages were essentially conveyor belts that moved cargo from the port into allocated bays in the ship, and out again when it came time to deliver.

Finn pulled another mysterious gadget from the duffel bag. It was clear there were no personal belongings in there, only endless Saeth tricks. He turned it on and began walking.

"Echomapper," he explained.

A holo bloomed over the device, showing a blueprint of the corridor they were in and the cargo crates to either side with the indistinct shapes of their contents. One deck above and below were also mapped, their edges fading at the limit of the echomapper's range.

"There should be at least a couple of crates with cryo capsules," Finn said.

A rumbling noise came from behind them. Cat shone her flashlight. A cargo crate was advancing at an alarming speed, filling the entire cross-section of the corridor with no leeway around the edges: it would crush them.

"This way." Finn jogged down the narrow track. He ducked into an alcove, pulling Edie in with him. Cat pressed herself into the small space just as the crate rumbled past. They peered out to see the crate stop a few meters farther along, then it moved sideways into an empty bay.

"Must've been loaded at Barossa," Cat said.

Finn climbed up, and Edie realized the alcove was a maintenance access area. There wasn't much on the ship that was built for humans, but this alcove had a ladder.

On the next deck, Finn walked up and down, mapping as much as his device could register, while Cat and Edie waited, listening for approaching crates. As Finn returned, another strange sound echoed through the ship.

Edie pressed herself back into the alcove. "Is that—?"

"It's the engine," Cat said. "We just entered nodespace."

Which meant they were safe from the Crib, at least for the duration of this jump. Nothing could track a ship in nodespace. And if the node had several exits, as most did, the ship might take any one of them. Its itinerary was flexible—recalculated after every port by the nav computer. As the *Lichfield* moved farther into the Reach, the Crib's search would become even more futile.

"Found what we need," Finn said.

He led the way down the corridor and turned when it branched. They stopped at a crate that looked much like any other, except that instead of the usual loading doors, this one had a tiny airlock, locked from the inside.

"Your turn," Finn said to Edie.

She pressed her fingers into the port and found it to be a standard mag lock. She snapped the airlock open and the three of them crammed inside. The inner hatch cycled and they stepped into the cargo crate. Ghostly blue striplights came on and illuminated the neat stacks of cryo capsules. With the plaz windows misted over, Edie couldn't see the occupants' features clearly. She didn't want to. She shuddered to think she'd soon join them.

Finn checked a panel near the hatch. "We've got atmo." He turned off his breather, and Edie and Cat did the same. The air was freezing and smelled of antiseptic. "The air automatically replenishes and heats a little when the hatch is used," he said, his breath misting the air, "or when the cryo capsules turn off."

Meaning when someone woke up. At least there were safety features.

"Who are they?" Cat asked.

Edie checked the panel, which listed the names and origins of the occupants along with short bios.

"I don't think they're colonists," she said. "No specific destinations listed."

Finn looked over her shoulder. "Migrant workers. They

move from planet to planet until someone decides their skills are wanted and defrosts them."

"So how long have they been in cryo?" Edie scrolled the list and answered her own question. "Fifteen months, nine months . . . *Jezus*, this one's twenty-two months . . ."

Cat examined the capsules. "There're half a dozen empty ones back here," she reported. "They look fine."

Finn went to check them himself.

"So where are we getting off?" Edie asked, still creeped out by the thought of all these sad people—so desperate for work and a home that they froze themselves indefinitely until someone needed them.

"We can't access the ship's route from here," Finn said.

"Then where? Where's the bridge?"

"There's no bridge. There'll be a command center in the heart of the ship, but it's not worth the risk of raising an alarm."

"What are you saying?" Edie felt more uncomfortable by the second.

"We need to hide among these people," Finn said. "We'll create bios like they have, and wait to be defrosted."

"What if that never happens?" Twenty-two months in cryo—or more—was unthinkable.

"We can set a maximum sleep time. Say, fifteen months."

"What?" That sounded almost as bad. "Over a year in cryo?"

"A year for our trail to go cold," Cat said. She didn't look happy about it either.

"The whole point is to get to the Fringe and help people," Edie said. "A lot can happen in a year. Thousands of people will die . . ."

"I know you're impatient to get started," Finn said, "but there's no sense rushing into this and getting caught." He pulled equipment out of a locker. "I need you to dream up some fake stats for us, something that will appeal to impoverished planets. That way, the people who do wake us will be more likely to need our help."

While he and Cat sorted the equipment and read over the capsule instructions, Edie jacked into the panel where all the migrant workers had recorded their stats. She created new bios for the three of them, adding bits and pieces from the other bios so that their names, planets of origin, qualifications, and various details blended with the other workers. There was room to list all kinds of certifications and idents. Many of the workers had written nothing for those, so the omission in Edie's case didn't seem strange. She listed op-teck as her profession, in the hope it would appeal to anyone with biocyph troubles, and grouped them as a family so they would be brought out of cryo together. Then Edie entered the maximum sleep period as fifteen months and authorized port authorities of any Fringe world to wake them sooner if they could provide employment.

Finn brought her a set of biosensors. He placed a cuff around her wrist.

Edie tried not to look at the three cryo capsules that Cat had pulled forward from the rack. They lay open—chilled coffins of white and silver. Cat helped Finn check them over one last time. Edie wrapped her arms around herself, trying to stop the shivering.

Finn beckoned to Edie. For a moment they looked at each other. She wanted to say something to him, in case this was the last time she saw him alive. But no words came. He watched her steadily.

"In you go." A smile flickered on his lips, a wordless acknowledgment that he understood. At least, she hoped so.

She climbed into the first capsule. He hooked up her sensor cuff and fired up the unit. Edie felt a spike inside the cuff slide into her vein. The cover snapped shut over her and locked with a hiss. Through the lozenge-shaped window in the front, she saw Finn checking things again. On the far side of the rack, she watched Cat climb into her capsule and its cover close.

After a few seconds Edie was aware of feeling far less apprehensive and claustrophobic than she should. The spike fed her tranqs, a precursor to the cryo fluids. She no longer felt cold, either. She concentrated on Finn's face as their eyes met through the plaz. The crease between his brows settled into a familiar look of concern. Her blood ran ice cold and her lungs hurt. Her breath misted the window and formed delicate ice crystals across the plaz. As her eyelids grew heavy, Finn's face blurred and faded.

Edie closed her eyes and drifted.

Something was wrong. She was burning up. In a panic, she raised her hands to push open the coffin. But there was nothing there. She opened her eyes and blinked to clear her vision, expecting to see Finn's face, expecting to hear his voice telling her everything was okay.

But the face that looked down at her was young, serious, unmistakably military.

Unmistakably Crib.

CHAPTER 3

Her warmed blood felt like fire as it pumped through her veins. The rest of her was still cold. Edie rolled her head to one side, trying to make sense of her surroundings. She was on a bunk, not in a cryo capsule. In a medfac, not a cargo crate—more of a screened-off cubicle. And there was no sign of her fellow sleepers.

No sign of Finn.

"Where's Finn?" Her voice was a dry croak. How long had she been asleep, anyway?

At her side, a young milit fiddled with the IV bag next to the bunk and checked the readout on a med tom attached to the bunk's railing. "Take it easy. The doc says the effects of cryo will wear off in another hour or so."

"How far away are we?" Her brain couldn't quite produce the question she needed to ask. *Is Finn nearby or is he more than two thousand meters away . . . and dead?*

"You're on the *Peregrine*, ma'am." The milit had the correct professional tone, but he had an awkwardness about him that made Edie think he was out of his depth. As if having Edie on board was a situation he didn't know how to deal with. "I'm Sergeant West. We're heading to rendezvous with—"

"Where's Finn?" Edie yelled. It came out as a hoarse cry. She tried to sit up. West reflexively grabbed her arm and eased her back.

"We retrieved no one else from the *Lichfield*." He sounded taken aback, even a little apologetic.

That didn't stop his words digging into Edie's chest like daggers. A wave of desperation lifted her off the bed and carried her across the cubicle as she threw herself at the sergeant. She didn't know what she screamed. Her lungs ached with the effort. She flailed against West and the faceless milits who came to his assistance from the other side of the screen.

Finn's dead.

She'd seen the bloody result of what happened when a serf's boundary chip went out of range. Since the moment they'd met, she feared this. It was only a matter of time before Finn met that end, too. He was just a serf. No one to mourn him but Edie.

They cuffed her to the bunk, reset the IV spikes she'd pulled free, and tranq'd her. Not enough to make her sleep. She lay listlessly, her mind dull as minutes and hours ticked by. She saw Finn, a lifeless body in a cryo capsule, now a coffin, his skull blackened by the bomb. Blood splatters dripping down the window.

Her logical mind clicked back into place, overshadowing the emotional turmoil: Finn was frozen. No dripping blood.

Could the bomb detonate when it was frozen?

She didn't know its specs. The Crib had put it there. No reason to believe it wouldn't work in freezing temperatures. But the rovers had modified the bomb trigger with biocyph—circuitry that required a biological interface. It was embedded in his brain—and his brain was frozen.

Edie yelled for help until someone finally came to see what the fuss was about.

It took a few minutes for them to track down West. While she waited, Edie listened to the sounds around her. This was a small ship, judging from the engine noise and the proximity of people passing to and fro on the other side of the screen. If not for the restraints, she would have explored it on foot.

The scratch down West's cheek that Edie only vaguely remembered inflicting might have had something to do with his wariness when he finally returned. She'd explained about the leash and the bomb to anyone who would listen, and somehow her garbled ranting had made it back to him in a fairly coherent form.

"I understand you want us to turn this ship around," West said, "and pick up an escaped convict from the *Lichfield*?"

"Yes. Right now. Before he wakes up and dies. If you don't fetch him—"

West shifted uncomfortably. The young man clearly did not relish the assignment he'd been given as liaison to a runaway teck.

"This is the serf who kidnapped you from Talas Prime Station thirteen months ago?"

Edie stared at West. Thirteen months? Assuming they'd woken her up as soon as they'd retrieved her capsule, that meant she'd been in cryo for a year. The revelation disorientated her, momentarily dislodging her thoughts of Finn.

"You guys are slipping. It took you a whole year to track me down?"

West grimaced. "The *Peregrine*'s a border patrol vessel, ma'am. Our assignment in tracking you down, as you put it, started only nine days ago."

"This is a Crib vessel. Milits. You're all the same to me. Do you know how many treaty points you contravened by crossing into Fringe space and boarding a commercial courier ship?"

"Not something you need to worry about. We had authorization from the highest—"

"I don't care," Edie interrupted. Only Finn mattered. "First of all, that serf didn't kidnap me." That wasn't exactly true, but there were extenuating circumstances. "He was tricked by rovers into the whole thing. And second, if you don't bring him back here alive, I won't cooperate. I know Natesa's plans for me and I won't do it. If you force me, I'll sabotage everything." She'd done as much once before, for what now seemed like a far more trivial reason.

"You can't expect the captain to turn this ship around and waste ten hours for a serf. He's dead either way, you know."

Edie stilled, her blood pounding in her ears. West was right. She was safe in Crib hands because they needed her. No one needed Finn or cared about his fate. He'd be charged with kidnapping, or escaping at the very least, and shot.

And refusing to cooperate with Natesa probably meant little to West. It was likely he knew nothing about Project Ardra, anyway.

"Let me speak with the captain."

"Uh—no, ma'am. That's not going to happen."

"Then let me speak to Natesa." She could hear the defeat in her voice.

"That I can arrange. As a matter of fact, she's been requesting permission to speak with you ever since we informed CCU of your recapture."

The acronym sent a shiver down Edie's spine. The Crib Colonial Unit had been Edie's self-appointed benefactor since she was ten years old, her employer since she was sixteen. More specifically, Edie worked for the Special Branch responsible for terraforming new colony worlds and for other projects . . . such as Ardra.

Project Ardra was Natesa's baby, and she needed Edie on the team. Edie had refused to be involved, even talking her way into a three-month reassignment on Talas's space station in a last-ditch effort to avoid the project. Now it looked like Ardra was her only bargaining chip in negotiating for Finn's life.

They set up a comm next to Edie's bunk and mercifully released the cuffs so she could be more comfortable. Natesa was not at the Crai Institute on Talas as Edie had expected. The call trace said she was on a CCU ship, the *Learo Dochais*, and its location was hidden.

Natesa looked as poised and coiffed as ever, and Edie knew from experience that the woman was just as controlled—not to mention controlling—on the inside. The gleam in her eyes no doubt resulted from her glee that her protégée was once again in Crib hands.

"Edie, my dear. Our last encounter did not go as I'd hoped."

That encounter took place a year ago for Natesa. To Edie, it was a very recent memory. There were a dozen smart-mouthed things Edie would like to have said. She bit her lip and kept quiet.

"But let's put all that behind us." Natesa tilted her head with a sad smile. "You disappeared for a year. You can't imagine how that devastated me."

"Because you need me for Ardra."

"Because I *care* about you, Edie."

Were those actual tears welling up in Natesa's eyes? Edie didn't trust them for a second.

"You know how I feel about Ardra," she said.

"You have contractual obligations . . ."

That damn contract. Two years of service for every year of education the Crib had given Edie in training—the standard deal, and it had seemed like a good one when she first left the Talasi camps. Short of another disappearance, though, there was nothing Edie could do to get out of it.

"I know that. And I'll work for you until my contract expires in eleven years—on one condition."

Natesa had visibly relaxed, but now her eyes narrowed. "And that would be?"

"The serf from Talas Prime Station who escaped when I was kidnapped—Finn—is still in cryo on the *Lichfield*. The rovers hijacked his boundary chip to make *me* his boundary, forcing him to serve as my bodyguard. The range of the leash is just under two thousand meters. Beyond that, the bomb in his head will explode. The fact that he's frozen is keeping him alive—at least, I hope so. I want him picked up immediately."

"And what then? Keep him frozen?"

"Find a way to cut the leash without killing him. You have an army of tecks at your disposal."

"What if that's not possible?"

"Then he comes with me. He stays at my side until you find a way. As long as you keep him alive and unharmed, I'll work for you."

"Is that it?"

"Yes."

Natesa shrugged, as if the request was a mere triviality. "Very well. I'll arrange to have the *Peregrine* retrieve him. Meanwhile, you take care of yourself. We're so looking forward to having you join our team."

Edie cut the connection and tried not to think about eleven more years of servitude.

Less than an hour later, Sergeant West was back in the cubicle looking somewhat bewildered, which Edie decided was his way of being pissed off.

"Well, ma'am, you have friends in high places. You have us all intrigued. A few days ago our orders were to board and search the *Lichfield* for an AWOL teck. Suddenly you're important enough to call the shots over a runaway serf."

"He was a POW. He should have been freed four . . . *five* years ago." She had to remember to account for that missing year.

West made a dismissive gesture. "Maybe you can get him a parole hearing." He pulled up a stool and sat, awkwardly, as if someone had told him to be affable. "The captain is curious about you, so I made it my business to check your files—at least those files the CCU has made available."

"Then why isn't the captain questioning me?"

"He thinks I have a friendlier face." West grimaced. "What exactly have you been up to for the past thirteen months?"

"I was frozen for most of it."

"But before that? We know you were in the company of rovers and that they took you to a planet in the Valen Sector. What were you doing there?"

"They were doing what seeding rovers do. Stealing BRATs to sell to the Fringe." BRATs—biocyph retroviral automated terraformer seeds—were the Crib's terraforming machinery, used across the Reach prior to colonizing new worlds. "The rovers had information that the seeds on that planet never germinated—easy pickings. Have you turned the ship around?"

"Yes, we're heading back to the *Lichfield* for your friend. Then we rendezvous with the *Learo Dochais* in two weeks, and you'll be placed in Administrator Natesa's custody."

"Then I don't think we have anything else to talk about, *Sergeant*."

West sighed. And gave up rather too quickly. Perhaps he didn't have the authority to question her, after all. His next statement essentially confirmed it.

"The Crib is sending an officer to the *Learo Dochais* to interview you further."

"Perhaps someone with a little more clout?" she mocked.

West shrugged, and she suddenly felt sorry for him. His manner so far suggested he was a nice guy, and in her experience there weren't too many of those in the Crib.

"Someone you know, apparently. Colonel Theron."

West left her to contemplate the name. Theron—he'd been a commander all those years ago, in charge of the seeding team that went to Scarabaeus. He'd never even gone dirtside, as far as she knew. But at the time she'd held him responsible, as a representative of the Crib, for the plan to destroy that beautiful world. A world she knew they weren't supposed to be standing on. There were rules, and the Crib had broken them. Planets were supposed to have no more than simple lifeforms to qualify for terraforming. Scarabaeus was the first attempt to terraform an advanced ecosystem.

Eight years ago she hadn't been able to stand by and let it

happen. But her solution had only made things worse. The result was the mutated jungle where the *Hoi Polloi* crew had died a year ago.

By the following day, Edie felt strong enough to get up and move about. She was ordered to stay put, which meant she was limited to the tiny med cubicle and the passageway outside it. Her limited exploration confirmed that the ship was only thirty or so meters long, the rear third of the cabin consisting of the medfac and crew bunks slotted into every conceivable spare space. The middle third, from the brief glimpse Edie had caught of it, was the mess and rec area, and the front third must be the bridge and teck stations.

West told Edie she was to eat and sleep in the med cubicle, as there was nowhere else to put her. At her expression of dismay, he found her some entertainment caps—ridiculous toons that she watched in a daze between napping and anxiously awaiting news of Finn.

The *Peregrine* docked with the *Lichfield* while Edie was asleep. The first she knew of it was when West told her, hours later, that they'd retrieved the capsule. They were keeping Finn frozen until they met up with the *Learo Dochais*. She had to believe him, because she wasn't allowed to see for herself. She had to trust that Natesa knew she was serious.

The two-week journey passed monotonously. Stuck in the med cubicle, Edie had plenty of time to consider her future. Escape was an unlikely option. Natesa simply would not allow that to happen a second time. Finn, a highly trained Saeth soldier, had been unable to escape a labor gang for four years, and his eventual escape had only been possible with outside help.

Their only outside help was Cat—still in cryo, unless the *Lichfield* had already reached a dock where her skills were wanted. Eventually someone would wake her and she'd find Edie and Finn gone. Cat was a survivor. She'd be okay. But would she help? She'd have no way of knowing what had happened. Would she think Edie had abandoned her?

Edie decided her first priority, once she was on the *Learo Dochais* and Finn was safe, would be to determine Cat's whereabouts. If Cat could help—if they could escape—they could continue with Edie's mission: to use the cryptoglyph in Finn's head to save the Fringe worlds from Crib domination.

CHAPTER 4

Edie sat on the edge of the bunk and waited impatiently. From snippets of crew conversation earlier, she knew they had docked inside the *Learo Dochais*'s hangar a couple of hours ago. She felt rested and strong—in body, anyway. Her mind was another matter—boredom and anxiety did not sit well together.

When Sergeant West showed up, she eagerly hopped off the bunk, ready to see Finn again and suffer the unpleasant but inevitable task of facing Natesa.

The ship's central narrow corridor was abandoned, as were the bunks and rec area. The crew must have boarded the *Learo Dochais* to stretch their legs. Without explanation, West led Edie all the way forward until the corridor widened into a room with a large oval desk—some sort of briefing area overlooking the empty bridge. At the head of the table sat a man with an angular face and expressively arched brows that made him look eternally patronizing.

She'd been expecting this moment. Still, she shivered now that she was face-to-face with him again. The failure of the Scarabaeus mission obviously hadn't affected Theron's career. He'd had plenty of missions since. One failure was hardly exceptional in an industry where a twenty percent success rate was considered good enough.

"Good morning, Ms Sha'nim. I'm Colonel—"

"—Theron. I remember."

"—of the Weapons Research Division."

"Where's Finn?"

"Please, take a seat." He waved a hand toward a chair fitted into the bulkhead on the other side of the desk. Behind her, a semi-transparent screen moved across the corridor to enclose the area.

Edie sat and fumed. She was tired of the delays, but she couldn't avoid Crib bureaucracy. Best to get this over with quickly.

Two med toms scuttled into new positions on the bulkheads on either side of the room. Attached to each, in addition to the normal physiological tracking devices, was a camera.

"This interview is being recorded and biomonitored," Theron said. "Edie Sha'nim, I'm here to inform you that you're under arrest for piracy, treason, and murder."

Edie was in no mood for Crib grandstanding. "I haven't killed anyone."

Theron raised an eyebrow. "So, the rest is true?"

She hesitated. Was this the time to ask for a legal rep? Well, it really didn't matter. No one was sending her to jail—she was too important to the Crib for that, surely.

"From a certain perspective." She indicated the box of neuroxin implants on the desk that someone must have retrieved from her cryo capsule. "You forgot grand larceny."

"Indeed. Are there any other charges you feel I've overlooked?" The colonel may have been attempting a joke, but his face was deadpan.

"Who am I supposed to have murdered?"

Theron glanced down at the notes on his palmet. "A serf by the name of Bryden Ademo." That was Finn's fellow convict, the one she'd been unable to save when Cat took them all for a joyride beyond the boundary of Talas Prime Station.

"He wasn't murdered. He escaped and his boundary chip killed him."

"If you engineered your so-called kidnapping, as some of my colleagues are inclined to believe, you are responsible for his death."

"That's not what happened."

"The circumstantial evidence is damning. You asked for, and were granted, a three-month reassignment to Talas Prime, giving you certain . . . opportunities. Shortly before that time was up, you went AWOL. A few weeks later, you were found in the Valen Sector in the company of rovers. The rover ship was boarded by Crib milits, but you overpowered Crib Administrator Natesa and refused to surrender."

"Be sure to add felony assault and desertion to that list."

"I'll make a note. However, for the moment, my interest lies—"

"Is Finn alive?"

Theron looked mildly annoyed by the interruption. Edie didn't know him well, but she guessed he was that military type who suffered mild annoyance whenever he had to deal with civilians.

"He is indeed alive. He's a former Saeth, isn't he? That's trouble I'd rather not have to deal with." Before Edie could demand to see him, Theron continued. "I have every intention of handing him over to Natesa when you report to the *Learo Dochais*. You'll have your way, Ms Sha'nim. Now my interest lies in the planet VAL-One-Four. I understand you call it Scarabaeus, and the name seems to have stuck around here."

Edie's fingers fluttered to the beetle shell at her throat, the remains of a creature she'd found on the planet before human technology destroyed it. The beetle had inspired her name for the planet and the rovers had adopted it. The Crib must have confiscated the *Hoi Polloi*'s archives before the ship made it to the junkyard—otherwise they wouldn't know her private name.

"What about it?" Edie tried to sound innocent. But she knew what had happened, and her stomach sank. She knew that when Natesa had caught up with the rovers near Scara-baeus, a probe had been sent. Even if Natesa hadn't been interested, reports of the planet's strange development had found its way to Theron. Edie knew the direction his military mind would have taken: bioweapons.

Edie's hopes that Scarabaeus would be left in peace evaporated.

"You'll recall that I was in charge of the seeding operation eight years ago," Theron said. "I'm now in charge of the exploration of the planet and I have a team stationed there. When I heard you'd been found, I immediately traveled here to meet you. Over the past few months, we have observed some very strange activity on Scarabaeus. The rate of evolution is two orders of magnitude faster than it should be. In theory this should lead to widespread ecosystem collapse, but that's not happening. In addition, our attempts to control the biocyph have been met with violent defensive reactions."

"What does this have to do with me?"

"I need your help in understanding exactly what's happening."

He'd asked no questions, but waited for Edie's input nonetheless. She quickly ran through her options. His cyphertecks probably already knew far more about the planet's current state than she did. She'd spent only a few hours there—a year ago.

She attacked. "You illegally tried to terraform an advanced ecosystem. Are you so surprised by the results?"

Theron gave a thin smile and sat back in his chair. "Ah, but it's not that simple. The BRATs dropped on Scarabaeus by the initial team failed to germinate. We sent an unmanned probe one year later to confirm this. Yet clearly they *did* germinate at some point after that. And now we have this bizarre ecosystem, highly mutated, evolving at an alarming rate under the control of distorted biocyph that seems to have forgotten it's supposed to be making a Terran-like world."

"I was only a trainee on your team," Edie reminded him. "You're asking the wrong person."

"And the right person would be . . . ? Your team's cypherteck was killed by a stowaway eco-rad on the trip home."

Bethany had been her friend as well as her trainer. "Whatever happened, it wasn't her fault. It was probably some faulty biocyph."

"Well, let's not play the blame game. You're the Crib's top cypherteck, Edie. You tell me why the terraforming got out of hand over the past few years and turned the planet into a nightmare jungle."

"How would I know?"

"You were there. We know your rover team set foot on the west side of the large southern continent. According to the statement of a certain"—he checked his notes—"Mitchin Yasuo, the rover we have in custody, you barely escaped." He straightened sharply, making Edie involuntarily shrink back in her seat. "How *did* you escape? Yasuo claims a flash bomb wiped out your shields. You would have been infected by retroviruses. You should be dead."

"Most of us *are* dead. Captain Rackham planted that bomb and he killed his own crew. He was bribed into making those runs by Stichting Corp—the company that funded the rovers."

"We investigated Stichting and found no connection—"

"Of course not." It wouldn't be the first time a Crib investigation had failed to find a Crib-based megacorp guilty. "Eco-rads threatened to expose Rackham's faked war record unless he sabotaged the missions. You know how rads feel about biocyph teck, whether it's rovers or the Crib using it. Rackham betrayed the *Hoi Polloi* to them and had their previous cypherteck killed. So Stichting kidnapped me to replace her. This time, Rackham tried to wipe out the entire team once we were dirtside. The bomb killed almost everyone else and damaged our shields. I managed to reconfigure a BRAT seed to ignore me and Finn, so we could pass through the jungle without it changing us."

"I see. What about the physical attacks? My men have had

no end of trouble just getting close enough to the BRATs to jack in. They're almost completely inaccessible. We've been unable to establish a dirtside base. We can only find out so much using remote monitoring."

Edie and Finn had been attacked, too, but Edie felt compelled to defend the planet's innocence. "If Scarabaeus attacked them, it's because they attacked it first."

Theron pushed a palmet toward Edie. Above it hovered a holo of a xenocritter, something Edie had never seen before—yet it looked familiar. Flat-bodied with crablike pincers and short thick legs. The scale showed it to be almost a meter long.

"This creature comes from the region where your team landed," Theron said. "Any idea how something like this could evolve?"

"This is from Scarabaeus? There's nothing there bigger than a rat."

"There *was* nothing. Now there's this. They tell me its lifecycle is five weeks. It evolved before our eyes in only a few generations into a creature that spews toxic mucus. It can crush a man's leg with those jaws. And it has a taste for human flesh."

Edie shuddered. Was this really descended from the small slater creature she'd encountered? Small, but deadly even then—dozens of them had stripped the dead bodies of her crewmates in minutes. The massive increase in size seemed impossible in only twelve months. But Scarabaeus was like no other planet. Its BRAT seeds weren't working toward a Terran ideal. They'd lost that programming years ago. They were doing something else entirely.

"I don't know what to tell you. Without examining the ecosystem's specs . . ." Edie felt sick. She didn't want to become involved in Scarabaeus again. She'd left that world to rot. But seeing this mysterious creature . . . Edie felt herself being dragged irresistibly back in.

Theron observed her reaction in silence before he spoke again. "As part of your debriefing, you'll write a report for the Weapons Research Division on how you reprogrammed the biocyph so you could *pass through*, as you put it."

"A report. You guys always want reports. I work for Natesa now. She'll have enough reports for me to write, thank you."

"Ultimately we all work for the Crib. You will do whatever the Crib requires of you."

He made it sound like a threat, and Edie had no response. She was just another good Crib citizen now. Still, he really didn't have the authority to make her do anything for him. She knew that much about the Crib's hierarchy.

"Here's the thing, Edie." Theron leaned forward for emphasis. "Something is guiding the evolution of increasingly bizarre and aggressive lifeforms on that planet. And we've found your signature in the code."

Edie stopped breathing for a moment, uncomfortably aware of the toms recording her every move, every heartbeat and breath. If Theron found out about her kill-code, which had caused the ecosystem to mutate in the first place, he'd want to duplicate its effects on other worlds. A nightmare vision flashed through her mind—dozens of advanced alien ecosystems under Crib control, mutating according to Theron's whim, manufacturing bioweapons to satisfy his military ambition.

"Mine and Bethany's signatures, yes," she said carefully. "I was her trainee—she let me handle some of the routine stuff."

From Theron's unwavering glare, she knew he saw she was hiding something. "Can you replicate it?"

"Replicate what?"

His expression turned hard. "Don't play games. Your loyalty and integrity are not exactly rock solid, and while you still have defenders at Crai Institute, I personally suspect sabotage. I know you did this. *Somehow* you did this, and it's created a unique situation we've never seen before in over a thousand years of terraforming. VAL-One-Four was an advanced ecosystem, analogous to the Paleozoic—"

"*Late* Paleozoic." Edie felt her frustration rising as fast as his. "We shouldn't even have been there!"

"In all other cases, attempting to terraform planets at that advanced level of development has resulted in total ecosystem collapse. Why was this planet different? It's because you interfered."

Edie hadn't even known they'd made other attempts to terraform advanced worlds yet—that was Project Ardra's objective. But that project was new. As unwelcome as the revelation was, it did not surprise her. She shook her head.

"Let me tell you something, young lady. I have enough information at my disposal to know for certain that you're lying. Holding back. Rest assured, I will find a way to extract the information I need."

"*Extract* information?" Edie almost laughed in his face. "Are you going to *torture* me? The Crib doesn't torture its citizens."

"No. No, it does not."

Despite that assurance, his tone filled her with dread. In the silence that followed, Edie struggled to get her thoughts together. Theron's cryptic intensity was too much. Finally, she managed to speak.

"I'd like to board the *Learo Dochais* and start my work with Natesa." It galled her that Natesa was now her ally, at least against the military might of the Crib.

"In due course." Theron considered her gravely for a few more seconds. Then he hit a comm switch on the desk.

The screen drew back and two people entered the area. Edie was relieved at first that one of them was Sergeant West. He held a small unit in his hand, which he placed on the desk out of her reach. The other milit was a young woman and from her hands dangled a pair of restraints.

"Hey—" Edie made to get up. The woman wrestled her back into the seat with West's help, and cuffed her wrists to the arms of the chair. "What the hell are you doing?" She was too shocked to be scared.

Theron watched impassively. "Jogging your memory."

Ignoring Edie's struggles, the woman clamped Edie's head between her hands and West attached a line to her temple. The other end of the line was attached to the unit. It looked like a simple conduit with few controls and no holo. That meant the control board was somewhere else, remotely jacked into this one. Through the hardlink she explored the unit quickly and found nothing unusual, just a transmitter/receiver.

A flutter in her skull told her someone had jacked into her splinter—the wet-teck interface grafted to her cerebral cortex—via the unit. Edie clamped down on the intrusion. It didn't take long for the unseen person on the other end to skirt around her security protocols. This was a cypherteck, then, and a good one.

"What do you want?" she demanded of Theron, who had come around the desk to perch on the corner, only a meter away. "There's nothing in my wet-teck that can help you."

"I think perhaps there is."

Theron nodded to the female milit, who lit a large holoviz on the wall before moving behind Edie to join West.

Edie stared at the screen and a chill slid through her veins. It was Finn, very much unfrozen. He paced a small cell in what must be the *Learo Dochais*'s brig. From what she could see, he looked healthy and unharmed. The feed was a high-angle vid only, no audio. Why would they transfer him to the bigger ship, but not her?

"That man has a few interesting things in *his* head," Theron said. "A Saeth comm chip that the Crib hijacked to create a boundary chip, hooked into a nasty little bomb. The leash that connects his chip to yours. And some kind of . . . discipline device."

Edie jerked her gaze away from Finn to glare at Theron. "No . . ."

But Theron was looking at the screen. Edie turned to watch it again, forgetting for the moment about the other cypherteck's connection. Before she could register what was happening, the cypherteck had found the trigger in her splinter and jolted Finn.

CHAPTER 5

Finn dropped to his knees, clutching his head, and toppled over.

"No!" Instinctively, Edie tried to stand. The restraints held her and the seat did not budge. The line attached to her temple slapped against her cheek. She shook her head, trying to dislodge it, but it was no use.

Edie clamped down on the connection and forced the cypherteck back. In a matter of seconds, he returned. As fast as she could put up barriers, he tore them down. Edie watched as Finn slowly started moving again. He staggered to his feet—one hand on the wall for support, the other clamped across his forehead.

"We found your code buried deep in the start-up routines on Scarabaeus. Somehow that code has affected the planet's evolution, and now we can't control it. Tell me what you did."

Edie had forgotten Theron was even in the room. She ignored him and put her entire focus on protecting the trigger. But the cypherteck was skilled, in a haphazard sort of way. Brilliant, in fact. He sent seekers through her wet-teck to gnaw at the barriers, breaking them apart until—

The trigger fired again. Edie couldn't stop herself from

watching. Finn hit the wall as if he'd been punched, then slid down and lay unmoving on the deck.

"Damn you, Theron. Stop it!" Her hands balled into tight fists, her fingernails cutting into her palms, and lines of cold sweat trickled down her face.

Theron came over to the chair, planted his hands on the arms and leaned over her. "You did something. What was it? We found a toxin all over the planet's ecosystem, a substance my tecks tell me is a derivative of neuroxin. Neuroxin only comes from two places: Talas and your blood. Is that what you did, Edie? Did you poison the planet all those years ago?"

"I put Haller out of his misery!" Edie fired back, not caring if he understood what she was talking about. Haller, executive officer of the *Hoi Polloi*, had been captured by the jungle and she'd found him being slowly digested. She'd killed him with her neuroxin implant, but the jungle had sucked the implant dry and left her in neuroshock.

Talking was a mistake. The cypherteck used the momentary lapse in her concentration to break through, and triggered the jolt again.

Edie cried out in anguish as Finn, who had barely begun to rise after the last jolt, collapsed on the deck.

"Get this fucking teck out of my head!" she screamed, her face inches from Theron's. She kicked out sharply and her boot connected with Theron's shin. His mouth hardened into a thin line. He grabbed her chin and twisted her face toward the screen. Her breath caught on a sob at the sight of Finn's unmoving body. Edie willed him to stay down. Perhaps they'd stop if they thought they'd injured him. Perhaps they *had* injured him.

"Tell me what you did, Edie, and this will end."

"Why are you doing this?" she yelled. "The deal was you wouldn't harm him."

"I've made no deals with you. And he's just a serf."

Edie kicked out again, repeatedly. This time Theron backed away until he was out of reach.

Finn had pulled himself upright again. For a brief moment he looked directly at the camera in the upper corner of his cell, his face creased in pain and confusion. Blood trickled from his nostrils. Edie wept, ashamed of herself for doing so in front of Theron, even more ashamed that crying took her concentration away from what the cypherteck was doing.

"Stop it!" She screamed it over and over until her throat was raw and all she could do was whisper. "Please . . ." She hated how pathetic she sounded. Pleading for mercy wouldn't have any impact on Theron.

The trigger fired again. Finn crashed against the bulkhead, his mouth open in an unheard scream of pain, and he crumpled into a heap.

Theron's relentlessly calm voice broke through Edie's misery and helplessness. "We can keep doing this for as long as it takes. The doc informs me it will knock him out eventually, but there's always tomorrow. Now, you meddled with Scarabaeus all those years ago. Tell me what you did to that planet. And tell me how I can control it."

Edie sank back in the chair as defeat rolled over her. She'd spent her life coming to the slow realization that the Crib was using her. She'd prepared herself, over the past two weeks, to return to that life. But that had nothing to do with Finn. He'd been illegally and unfairly incarcerated by the Crib, and now it was torturing him because of *her*.

She closed her ears to Theron's continued cajoling and increasingly demanding questions. Breathing hard, she stopped screaming and stopped struggling. Instead, she concentrated on the cypherteck. Blocking the next attack wouldn't be enough. She had to stop *him*. Wipe him out.

He scuttled around her barriers, nudged between the tiers that she'd riveted together, and ripped them apart. Edie had to jump all over the place to fix the gaps. Her brain felt raw, ready to split open as it pounded with every rapid heartbeat. The cypherteck searched for another way in. He'd find it soon enough. Edie had never battled a cypherteck in her head before, but she recognized this as one of the best—as good as she was, if less rigorously trained. She got the impression he ran more on instinct, which made him unpredictable. Where had Theron found such a naturally skilled teck?

Where had *Natesa* found him? Perhaps the cypherteck was on the *Learo Dochais*, someone working with Natesa on Project Ardra.

Edie sent a trace down the link to assess the box at her side. It had storage capacity she could use. As she formed a plan, her body shivered uncontrollably with the effort. She cut off that awareness. Only two things mattered: stopping the cypherteck from triggering the jolt, and cutting the connection altogether.

There was only one way to do the latter. She needed to catch him off guard, and that meant letting him do it one more time. For a few seconds after each jolt, he'd eased back a little.

Edie sorted through her splinter and gathered together the biggest, fattest chunks of random data she could find. She tagged them and lined them up—and then, with a concerted effort that tore out her soul, she dropped her guard and let the cypherteck have the trigger. He slammed a shrill cacophony into Edie's splinter that seemed to set it vibrating at a high frequency. Disoriented, she could have done nothing to stop the next jolt even if she'd tried. The cypherteck triggered it.

She didn't watch the screen. She couldn't bear to see Finn stumble and fall again.

With the cypherteck off guard, she let the data chunks flow down the link and into the box, where she amplified them to the limit of the device.

"Come on, Edie. Don't let him suffer. I know you care deeply about him. I know you want this to be over."

"It *is* over . . ."

Edie forced the data packet out along the remote connection in one nightmarish jolt, and fired it directly into the cypherteck's brain.

Instantly, the intruder was gone.

The box lit up with a flashing red telltale to indicate the

broken connection. Theron noticed immediately. His gaze swooped on Edie as she slumped back into the seat.

"What happened?" he demanded.

His voice sounded distant and fuzzy. The female milit rushed over to Edie and lifted her head to check the link connection. She checked the unit as well.

"I don't know, sir. The connection overloaded. I think—"

Theron's commlink beeped, an insistent clear signal above the sound of rushing blood in Edie's ears. Shaking uncontrollably, she lifted her head to meet Theron's furious glare.

"Get her out of here," he barked.

West looked confused. "Sir?"

"I don't care where! Take her to the brig on the *Learo Dochais.*" His comm beeped again. "Dammit." But he didn't answer it.

West reset Edie's restraints to cuff her hands in front of her, and pulled her out of the chair. She regretted her earlier conclusion that he was a nice guy. He was Crib. She must never let down her guard with the Crib. Stumbling on weak legs, she went docilely now only because she was emotionally exhausted, and because Finn was in the brig. She would get to see him at last.

West took her down the exit ramp into the hangar of the *Learo Dochais,* catching the woman on duty in the control room off guard.

"Is she sick?" the woman asked, rushing along the catwalk and down the steps as West and Edie crossed the deck.

Edie knew she must look a sight—exhausted, soaked in sweat. She was roiling in so many emotions, she couldn't speak. The woman's comment reminded her of the leash, and that Finn sensed her strong emotions as an irritating white noise through his chip. That could only have made his torture worse. If he was conscious again now, for his sake she had to clamp down on those feelings.

"She's not sick. Colonel Theron interrogated her." From West's tone, Edie realized he was angry with Theron but holding it back. Perhaps he hadn't known what was in store for her when he was ordered to participate. In any case, her opinion of West rose marginally. "He's sending her to the brig until Natesa's ready to take over."

"Uh, I don't think that's necessary." The woman checked her palmet. "She's been assigned quarters on Deck D. Ship time is oh-five-hundred. Administrator Natesa will be available in three hours."

"Perhaps you should wake her immediately—"

"No. I want to go to the brig," Edie said. Her voice was scratchy, her throat raw from screaming. "Take me to Finn."

"Who?" The woman looked genuinely confused, which filled Edie with sick worry. Was Finn's presence on the ship so trivial that it was unknown to the dockmaster?

"Permission to visit the brig?" West said.

To Edie's relief, the woman nodded.

West led Edie to the lift, where he undid her restraints. For a few seconds they stood in silence as Edie rubbed the red marks where she'd bruised the skin while struggling.

Then West spoke, not looking at her. "I'm sorry, ma'am. Colonel Theron told us the man was a Saeth. I thought . . . I didn't know what was going on. I didn't know you would suffer."

Edie didn't trust herself to answer. The Saeth were fair game to the milits. The milits had been fair game to the Saeth, in their time. She stood in silence as the lift ascended, and the doors opened.

The lean lines of the *Learo Dochais*'s corridors brought back unwelcome memories. Edie had spent half her adult life on Crib ships like this. Spotless black gravplating, reflective blue bulkheads, and gleaming silver trim forming endless parallel lines. Security and maintenance toms skittered along the edges of the deck.

The brig was little more than a small annex that led to a couple of even smaller cells. In the annex, a medic was in conversation with the guard on duty. The workstation showed a holoviz display of the interior of one cell, the same view Edie had watched from the *Peregrine*. Finn lay on his side on the deck, a med cuff on one wrist.

"Why haven't you taken him to the infirmary?" Edie demanded.

The medic glanced from West to the guard, as if waiting for permission to speak. When neither said anything, he answered, "I'm not sure exactly what happened to him. His vitals are stable. We have a far more serious problem in the infirmary. I have to get back there." He spoke to the guard as he left. "I'll monitor the prisoner from my station."

"Let me in to see him," Edie said.

The guard was not happy with the request, but West gave him a look and he snapped the hatch. Edie pushed past the guard and went inside.

"He's sedated," the guard said.

Edie knelt to touch Finn's hand. Someone had wiped some of the blood from his face, and the med cuff displayed promising vital signs. Edie kept herself calm, forced down a new wave of tears and anger, not wanting to fire up the leash.

"Finn . . ."

He stirred and turned his head toward her voice. She leaned over to press her forehead against his, willing him to forgive her.

"I'm sorry. I'm so sorry."

As she pulled back, his eyes opened. Where they should be white, they were blood red. Edie gasped and gripped his hand. He looked at her, recognition slowly dawning.

The guard stepped forward. "Uh, that's temporary, the doc says. Burst capillaries, nothing serious."

Edie could think of half a dozen angry things to say to the others in the room. She kept them to herself. Natesa was the one who had to answer for this.

"I won't let them hurt you again," Edie told Finn.

He closed his eyes without speaking.

The cell walls closed around Edie as she felt the Crib tightening its grip on her life. Natesa had promised not to harm him, but here he lay, tortured and near unconscious in the brig. That woman had a lot to answer for.

A commotion outside the cell drew her attention. What now?

Liv Natesa burst into the cell. Her hair was pulled back hurriedly into a ponytail, and her face was scrubbed clean of makeup. Her face was taut with anger, but in her eyes was a stricken expression that Edie had never seen before.

"What did you do?" Natesa cried.

Edie's composure dissolved. "You promised he wouldn't be hurt!"

As she rose, West jumped forward and took a firm grip on her arm to hold her back. "Don't make me regret taking off the restraints," he muttered.

"What's going on here? What did you do to her?" Beneath Natesa's anger, Edie saw fear and shock rising to the surface. She wasn't used to such a blatant display from Natesa, whose poise was legendary.

West started to explain. "Colonel Theron questioned her on the *Peregrine*—"

"I'm not talking about *her*." Natesa glared at Edie. "I was just informed that you put my . . . one of my cyphertecks into a coma."

Edie found it hard to care. Especially when Natesa didn't care about what she and Finn had just been through. "I had to stop them. They tortured Finn. We had a deal—"

"I assure you, I did not authorize any torture." Natesa's voice was flat, cold. Her sudden calmness seemed to take great effort. She glowered at West. "Your crew is to return to the *Peregrine*. I want your ship out of my hangar—immediately."

West shifted his feet stiffly. "I'll relay your message to Colonel Theron," he countered with a touch of insolence. Natesa wasn't a milit, or the captain of the *Learo Dochais*. She didn't have the authority to throw around such orders.

Natesa's lips settled into a hard line. "Just stay out of my way. *You*"—she jabbed a finger at the guard—"Have someone escort Ms Sha'nim to the infirmary for a physical, and then to my office by oh-eight-hundred."

"Wait!" Edie cried as Natesa turned to leave. "Finn's the one who needs to be in the infirmary."

Natesa cast a glance at the motionless man on the deck as though he were an irritating complication. As she brushed past the guard on her way out, she said, "Fine, take him. Keep him under guard."

CHAPTER 6

One bay in the infirmary was the subject of a good deal of activity. Edie couldn't see the bunk or its occupant, but medics wandered in and out giving each other terse orders and reports. It must be the cypherteck behind those screens. She wanted to ask how the woman was, but pride held her tongue. She refused to feel guilty—she'd only done what she had to, to protect Finn. Still, she'd intended only to stop the cypherteck, not put her in a coma.

After a long wait, Finn was brought up to the infirmary on a stretcher and sequestered in another bay, also out of Edie's sight. Soon after that, a middle-aged doctor finally arrived to do her physical. Dr Sternhagen had just come on duty and knew nothing about the condition of the other patients. Edie complied with the questions and examinations to get the ordeal over with as quickly as possible.

"I'm finding no residual effects from the cryosleep," Dr Sternhagen said as she slipped her hand into the dataglove at her console to make notes. "The team on the *Peregrine* did an excellent job in resuscitating you. I've seen the results of rushed awakenings from cryo and it's not pretty. Unbalanced salts, clogged lungs, permanent cell damage . . ."

She stopped babbling to concentrate on what she was

writing. As Edie looked around the infirmary, wondering if they'd let her see Finn, something familiar caught her eye. She slipped off the bunk and went to the cabinet across the room. Half a dozen identical boxes were stacked behind a clear plaz door. They were the same size and color as the box of implants Beagle had stolen for her.

All these neuroxin implants just for her? Or were there other Talasi on board? It was hard to see why there would be. As far as Edie knew, she was the only Talasi ever taken from the camps. The Talasi had no formal education system so it was unlikely any of them were qualified for this mission. So why all these implants?

Edie put that puzzle aside for now. What this really meant was a renewed hope for escape. If she could steal a supply, she could survive without the Crib's help for a few years at least, until the drug degraded.

She returned to her seat as the doctor returned.

"Overall, you're in excellent health," Dr Sternhagen announced with a professional smile. "Get some rest today, and I'll declare you fit for duty tomorrow."

"What about Finn?"

"I haven't examined him myself. I'll consult with the medic on his condition. Administrator Natesa has asked me to investigate the link between your interface and his boundary chip."

"The leash—don't try to disable it. You'll kill him."

"Rest assured, his health is my primary concern."

"And I don't want everyone here knowing about it. People have tried to use it against us." She was thinking of the *Hoi*'s XO and the way he'd manipulated them.

"I understand. There's no need to worry about that."

They were back in Crib hands on a heavily guarded ship. That was reason enough to worry.

Two silent milits escorted Edie to Natesa's office on Deck A, the admin suite. Unlike the bland, uniform Crib décor on the other decks, the admin rooms were plushly appointed and accessorized. Edie recognized Natesa's touches everywhere, from the custom-framed portholes lining the corridors to the large stone water feature in the main annex. This deck was designed to impress. Why Natesa needed to impress anyone with décor was something Edie could only guess at.

Stepping into Natesa's office, Edie saw that no expense had been spared here, either. The curved rear wall of the room was a transparent window that overlooked a vast chamber. The chamber housed a lush indoor garden bursting with exotic greenery. Stylish woven rugs covered the deck.

The woman herself stood behind a large polished desk that was positioned exactly in the center of the room to give the appearance that it was partially surrounded by the garden. She was a good deal more composed than before, now wearing a fitted gray suit with her hair twisted into a tight bun, and her lips a dark streak across a pale face. Her staid appearance was in stark contrast with the overly appointed office.

"A few examples of Prisca's native flora," she said, noticing that Edie's attention was drawn to the garden. "Prisca is the planet we're orbiting—the first candidate world for our project."

"In other words, these are examples of the native flora you're in the process of destroying."

Natesa's thin mouth formed a half-smile. "Not destroying, Edie. Changing, recreating, molding into something more useful. And after I prove the validity of the project here, we'll move on to other worlds." She moved around to the front of the desk and sat in one of two high-backed armchairs angled in front of the desk. "Sit. We have a lot to discuss."

"No one will tell me anything about Finn."

"He'll be released soon from the infirmary. In return for his safety, you promised me your cooperation. So let's talk about—"

"After what just happened to him, don't expect me to cooperate with you."

"As I told you before, I am not responsible for Colonel Theron's actions. I'm as horrified as you by what he did, not only because of the deal we made but because of the consequences of his little interrogation." She paused, as if distracted. Presumably she was referring to the cypherteck Edie had injured.

"So will Theron have to answer for it? I mean, are there any consequences at all for torturing an innocent man? Or does he get away with it because he's a high-ranked officer of the Crib?"

Natesa gave a helpless shrug. "This is all out of my hands, I'm afraid. I'm not the military."

"I hope you don't expect me to write him a report about Scarabaeus."

"Is that what he told you to do? You don't have time for that. You work for me."

"He said I was under arrest."

"He exaggerated. No formal charges have been laid against either you or Finn. Not yet." The way Natesa leaned very slightly on the last word only magnified the threat. "However, your behavior when we caught up with you a year ago, when you refused to return with me, not to mention the curious events surrounding your so-called kidnapping—all this has put you in a precarious position. Here's the problem—I have no idea how far I can trust you. But I do value your expertise. Project Ardra needs you. We need to come to some arrangement."

Edie could see where this was going. "So, I behave myself and you lay off the criminal charges?"

Natesa bobbed her head in acknowledgment. "That goes for Finn, too."

"Finn should never have been incarcerated in the first place. When he was arrested five years ago, the treaties were already signed."

"That's hardly my concern."

"Well, it is my concern. I want you to put things right. Get

Achaiah to cut the leash." Achaiah was the infojack who created the leash in the first place. Natesa's people had picked him up near Scarabaeus a year ago. "Where is he, anyway?"

"To my knowledge, he's in a prison camp somewhere in the Rutger System. Not far from here, actually. But I thought he said he couldn't cut it."

"It's a place to start. Even if he can't, he might know someone who can." Infojacks maintained wide-reaching networks. "And I want freedom papers for Finn. I don't want you throwing him back on that labor gang as soon as he leaves the ship."

"Again, that's nothing to do with me."

"But you can petition for it."

Natesa shifted uncomfortably, like she was annoyed at being dragged into all this. "Very well. I'll see what I can arrange."

"And there's one more thing. I want to talk to Lukas Pirgot."

"Your old bodyguard? Whatever for? I told you some time ago, he's a traitor who—"

"I don't believe that story. In any case, you promised me contact with him if I came back to work for you."

"You broke that deal when you assaulted me, threw me off your damn pirate ship, and disappeared for a year." Natesa kept her voice level, but her tone was deadly nonetheless. "It serves no purpose to bring him back into your life. He's yet another irrelevant distraction and a bad influence."

"When has Lukas ever been a bad influence on anyone?"

"He was convicted of treason. I've no doubt he'd tell you all kinds of things to make you doubt me and CCU. You need to see him for what he really is—a sick old man with a grudge."

"Wait . . . Lukas is sick?"

Natesa faltered, as if she realized she was only telling Edie things that would make her even more determined to contact him. "Don't concern yourself with Lukas Pirgot."

"Why are you putting up barricades? If you let me talk to Lukas, if you free Finn, it'll go a long way toward making me more interested in Project Ardra."

Natesa drew a tight breath. "If you *dare* do a thing to compromise the secrecy or success of Project Ardra—"

"Believe me, if I was going to compromise the Crib in any way, I'd set my sights higher than Ardra." Such as saving the Fringe worlds from Crib oppression. Edie felt her face warming and cursed herself for saying too much. She couldn't let Natesa rile her.

But Natesa was too worked up over Edie's many requests to notice. "There will be no contact with Lukas. As for Finn, I'm watching him closely. It seems you're unduly influenced by such men. And an ex-Saeth, of all things!"

Edie gritted her teeth but kept her mouth shut. On the rare occasions when Natesa worked herself up like this, speaking only made things worse.

"I'll allow him to remain here only because I'm forced into it by that wretched leash. As a civilian and an ex-convict, he can't be allowed access to any sensitive material. We have restricted areas on the ship, and other . . . considerations. I will allow him relative freedom to pursue his own interests while on board. There is plenty of supervised work available, if he would like to earn some creds."

Edie liked the sound of *pursue his own interests*. He might be able to find Cat, even plan an escape so they could get to the Fringe. But Natesa wasn't done.

"Even if I find this infojack and the leash is cut, I can't say I'm comfortable with him roaming about the Reach knowing so much about Project Ardra. We could never trust him."

Edie felt a shiver of fear down her spine. "What's that supposed to mean?"

"Don't be naïve, Edie. Ardra is far too important to trust to a Fringer lag."

"If he does leave, and mysteriously vanishes, I'll know what you've done. And you'll have lost me forever." Adrenaline pumped through Edie's veins as she recognized the precarious position Finn was in. Natesa wanted Edie's willing cooperation. But at some point, perhaps her desire to control Edie would override that consideration. Perhaps she'd just hire an assassin.

Something in Natesa's expression changed—so subtly that Edie almost missed it. Her eyes widened slightly as if she'd just realized what Edie was thinking. Then her face softened. "You have nothing to fear. Good heavens, I'm not a monster and I don't appreciate the insinuation. All I've ever asked of you is that you do your job."

"Listen to me, Natesa. Finn has no interest in spilling your precious secrets about Ardra. As far as I know, all he wants is to go home."

"Let's hope that's true. As for your role here, you've joined us at a critical moment in Ardra's implementation phase. After your recent . . . *excursions* over the past year, I'm in two minds about giving you full access to the project. You will have no unsupervised access to the lab. You'll begin with routine testing under the chief cypherteck, Caleb Chessell, until you prove yourself to me."

Edie knew the name. Chessell was an award-winning Crib cypherteck with three decades of experience, renowned for his innovative approach and a terraforming record that was probably second only to hers. He was also a notorious control freak and egomaniac. Edie had never met him, but she'd heard a few stories.

"You have so much to offer CCU, and in particular this project," Natesa continued with a bland smile. "More than anything, I want my faith in you restored. Now, rest today. Report to Chief Chessell in the labs, tomorrow morning at the start of the shift. He'll explain your work." She stood up and walked behind her desk, her attention on her holoviz, effectively dismissing Edie.

"I don't know why you think Ardra stands a chance," Edie said. "Terraforming advanced ecosystems won't work."

Natesa tilted her head, her eyes sly. "That's not an attitude I appreciate, Edie. Chessell has developed some groundbreaking code that's helping us on Prisca. And we have an elite cypherteck team on board. Our new training program has been extremely successful—these tecks are the best in the Crib."

"Including the one in the coma?"

Natesa's expression stiffened. "She is a member of the team, yes."

"How is she?"

"Her condition is unchanged."

Edie swallowed another unwelcome pang of guilt. *It's not my fault. It's not my fault.* She repeated the words to herself, but the mantra wasn't working very well.

From the moment Edie stepped into her quarters, she had the feeling Natesa was trying to win her over. A VIP stateroom, better even than the officers got. A spacious, comfortable sitting area led to a tastefully furnished bedroom, the two rooms linked by a small hallway that led to a bathroom. After spending her life on ships where everything was built for functionality first, it might take some time to get used to the fine fixtures and decorative touches.

Despite the accommodations, Edie would rather have spent the time with Finn, but her guard had made it quite clear she was to stay in her quarters for now. More than anything she wanted to explain to him what had happened. She could only hope he understood that she'd never have done it deliberately, that she'd never break the promise she'd made—what seemed like a lifetime ago—after that first terrible time when Haller had forced her to jolt him.

Edie showered and changed and returned to the sitting room to open the shutters covering the viewport. Her eyes were drawn immediately to the planet floating below the ship, a white-and-blue beach ball on a sea of black velvet. The *Learo Dochais* was in high orbit.

She lay on the backless couch and studied the streaked surface of the planet. Her brain was crowded with too many thoughts to really consider where she was or what would happen next. Helpless frustration rose to the surface. She had felt this way before, after learning that the rovers had jacked Finn's chip to force him to be her bodyguard. The Crib was no better than the rovers, just as willing to punish an innocent man in order to get what they really wanted. *Her.*

Sleepy from the residual effects of cryosleep, Edie dozed.

When her door chime woke her, it was hours later. She stumbled to the hatch and snapped it open, eager to see Finn again. And he was there, standing behind two milits. So was Natesa.

"I've brought your friend for a visit," Natesa said, walking uninvited into the room. "To reassure you of his good health."

Edie wouldn't have described Finn as looking particularly healthy. As he entered the room, glancing at her only briefly, his expression betrayed no emotion. He looked tired and gaunt. The blood in his eyes had mostly subsided, and he'd been given a change of clothes. He sat on the couch she'd just vacated, leaning forward to rest elbows on knees. She wondered what he'd been told, whether he'd been threatened.

She wanted Natesa to leave so she could talk to him alone.

Natesa was conferring with the milits. Edie overheard enough to realize Natesa was asking them to organize quarters for Finn on a lower deck.

"Finn is staying here," Edie said, interrupting their conversation.

Natesa turned. "Here? Is he your lover?"

Edie felt her face warming at the bold question. Without meaning to, she looked quickly at Finn. He raised his gaze to meet hers but didn't seem perturbed. And he left it up to her to answer.

"The leash . . . we have to stick together," Edie said evasively.

"We've been over this. This ship is much smaller than the leash's range. You're in no danger of separation, and his services as a bodyguard are not required. We'll find a job for him and he'll reside on the workers' deck." Before Edie could object, Natesa added, "No arguing, Edie. It's not possible for him to remain in VIP quarters. However, I'll allow him to stay here for a day or two until something else can be arranged."

As Finn didn't seem interested in joining the conversation, Edie spoke for him. "You said Finn could pursue his own interests. He has friends in the Reach. He'll want to find out what happened to them."

Natesa arched a dubious brow. "You want me to give him access to communications?"

"Why not?"

"Well." Natesa's lips thinned. "We'd have to keep an eye on that, of course." Hopefully Finn had a few tricks up his sleeve to get around Natesa's monitoring. "Now, please remember our arrangement, both of you. Consider yourselves on probation." Natesa extracted two crew keys from her pocket and dropped them on a console near the hatch. "One for each of you, with individualized access parameters. If your key doesn't open a door, you're not allowed to be there. The mess is on Deck E, or you may call the galley for food—I wouldn't make a habit of that, though. The staff has quite enough to do without running around the ship answering room service calls."

Finally, Natesa and the milits left. Edie locked the hatch, leaning against it for a moment to get her thoughts in order. When she looked at Finn, he was watching her. He looked immeasurably calmer than she felt.

"Are they listening in?" he asked.

Edie hadn't considered that. "I don't know. It's a possibility. But generally, the Crib is too arrogant to be paranoid." She swallowed nervously, still unsure of what Finn thought of all this. "Are you okay?"

Instead of answering, he said, "What's going on?"

She walked over to the viewport, feeling his eyes on her, and looked at Prisca. She could explain what the Crib was doing here and what her role would be, but she knew that wasn't what he was asking. As she thought about what Theron had done to him, her anger resurfaced. Glancing at Finn, she saw him rub the back of his neck slowly, a gesture she knew meant her emotions were firing up the chip in his skull.

"I'm sorry about this, about everything. You felt my . . . panic when they were jolting you. I should've tried to stay calm but I couldn't."

"No, I'm glad I could sense you. Made it easier."

"Easier?"

"It felt like you were with me, in a way." His dark eyes hid the horror he'd suffered. "Did they hurt you?"

"No, they wouldn't do that. They only hurt the things I care about."

He held her gaze a moment longer. Edie chewed her lip and wished she had the nerve to go to him. They'd shared one brief moment of intimacy on the *Hoi*'s skiff before she'd pushed him away. And later, one kiss. Did that count for anything now? He'd been given a choice between freedom from the leash, or retaining the cryptoglyph so they could help the Fringers. He'd chosen the latter. Now those plans were in ruins. Did he blame her? Edie didn't want to find out.

Finn straightened, drew a deep breath, and changed the subject. "Natesa said something about food?"

Grateful for something else to think about, Edie called the galley. By the time someone arrived with a tray, Finn had figured out the entertainment caps and turned on some loud music. Just in case a bug was already in place.

"Does everyone usually eat in the mess?" Edie asked the kitchenhand, a skinny lad with lank blond hair.

"Yes'm. Deck E. Supper starts at eighteen-hundred hours, breakfast at oh-six-hundred. Tomorrow's pancakes."

Finn had other things on his mind. "What's the crew complement?"

"Sir?"

"How many milits, how many officers? And the rest of the crew?"

"Well, there's Captain Lachesis and his first and second officers. There're four of us in the galley, including me and the cook. I'm Nevill, by the way. Five or six maintenance tecks, I think. And a whole lot of workers on the skyhook project and the terraforming, of course." He topped off his report with an emphatic nod and a grin.

Finn winced at the sketchy information and Edie felt embarrassed for the boy.

"Nevill, do you know about the seeding team?" she asked him, eager to extract more information although not for the same reason as Finn. "How many cyphertecks?"

"Oh, the tecks don't come to the mess," he said, contradicting his earlier statement. "They stay on Deck C. Sometimes their teachers come by."

"Teachers?" A curious word to use.

"You know, their trainers and the op-tecks."

"Oh." She smiled her thanks and Nevill made to leave. "Wait, who should I ask about supplies? We need a few things."

"The quartermaster is Mr Kensee. I'd do it now rather than tomorrow morning because he's real grumpy before noon."

"Thanks for the advice. And for bringing lunch."

Nevill gave a shy smile and left, snapping the hatch behind him. Edie and Finn settled cross-legged on the floor and ate off the low table between the couches.

"Natesa suggested you get work. I guess she'd rather you stay busy. I'm going to be in the labs ten or twelve hours a day."

"Forget Natesa." Finn lowered his voice so that Edie had to lean forward to hear him over the music. "This is what we should be concerned about, right?" He tapped his skull—the cryptoglyph.

"There's nothing we can do about that here."

"Then we need to not be here."

She should've guessed his thoughts had already turned toward escape. "But how . . . ?"

"I don't know yet. Opportunities always come up, eventually."

"I saw boxes of neuroxin implants in the infirmary. If I could steal some, they'd keep me alive a few years."

"That's a start."

"Cat's out there. She'll help us."

"Most likely she's still in cryo."

"Then who? The Saeth?"

Finn gave a small shrug. "The war's been over for years. I don't know how many survived, or if they've disbanded. I don't know how to find them. But we'll get out of here, Edie. I just need to know you haven't forgotten the mission."

Edie put down her fork. "I haven't forgotten." She sounded defensive, which wasn't what she'd intended. "Finn, I'm on your side."

"I know." His lips quirked into a quick smile that disarmed her. The intensity in his eyes reminded her of the first time they'd met, when he'd trusted her to save his life—and of all the moments since then, the connections they'd forged because no one else had been on their side.

Silence between them stretched several seconds too long as those moments flashed through her mind. Looking away, she fumbled with the tray and pushed her plate aside.

"I'm exhausted," she said, "and you look worse than I feel. Let's get some blankets for that couch. Um, you can take the bedroom if you want." On the *Hoi* he'd spent weeks cooped up in a tiny annex next to her quarters. Here there was no reason he couldn't have a proper room, at least until Natesa threw him out.

"The bed's yours." He thumbed over his shoulder, toward the window. "I'll take the view."

CHAPTER 7

They found Mr Kensee's supply room on Deck E. He was an older man, probably a retired milit judging from his bearing, and despite Nevill's warning he gave the appearance of being perpetually jolly.

"Take what you want. And call me Ken."

They piled changes of clothes and other supplies onto the countertop. Everything down to the underwear and toothpaste was stamped with the CCU logo. Edie wished for Cat Lancer's feminine touch as she selected a heap of bland tees, slate-blue pants, and unscented shampoo.

"If you need anything special," Ken said, "you know, out of the ordinary, I've got a nice little supply in the back. Nice prices, too."

Edie gave him a polite smile without comment. She didn't want to tell him she had no creds. She was expecting that her account would be set up soon. As for Finn, he was no longer a serf toiling at the Crib's pleasure, and if he took on work here, they had to pay him, too.

Ken didn't comment on their choices, although he seemed a little disappointed they didn't want anything from his special stash. He noted everything down on his inventory list and organized a couple of toms to haul the stuff. The toms tugged a pallet behind them, dutifully following Edie and Finn back to their quarters.

Edie was ready to crash without even putting anything away, but it seemed rude to leave everything lying around in the sitting area, which was now Finn's room. While he disappeared to take a shower, she sorted the clothes. Her limbs moved mechanically as sleep became a more and more desirable goal. With an armload of clothes, she took a step into the corridor between the rooms and caught a quick glimpse of Finn's silhouette behind the semi-opaque shower screen before pulling back. The last thing she wanted to do was treat him like everyone else did, like a serf who had no right to respect or privacy.

Returning to the sitting room, she dropped her clothes on the couch, changed into loose-fitting pants and a tank top in preparation for bed, and sat to wait for Finn to finish. After a few moments, her head was on that soft pile of clothes and she stretched out on the couch and closed her eyes.

A comforting warmth radiated along Edie's body. When she pulled herself out of sleep, she found herself looking at the viewport with its breathtaking vista of the planet. The clothes she'd used as a pillow lay scattered on the deck. The warmth was Finn's body, curled around hers. His skin touched her skin at a few distinct places. Her shoulder blade against his bare chest. Her lower spine against his stomach. And his hand resting on her hip, burning through the fabric of her pants. His breaths, rhythmic, disturbed the hair at the crown of her head—Edie remained still, enjoying all the sensations.

She wanted to turn toward him. More than wanted—her body thrummed with the need for contact. But it sounded like he was asleep, and if awakened, he might pull away. Or worse, send her away.

The effort to remain still and calm was too much for her. It was hardly fair—she may have fallen asleep on his bed, but he was the one who'd chosen to join her.

"Finn?" she whispered experimentally, quietly.

"Yeah?" he answered, fast enough to suggest that he'd been awake all along.

Feeling brave, she turned onto her back, relishing the feel of his hand sliding across her hip and coming to rest on her stomach. He remained on his side, his cheek lying on the bicep of his other arm, which he bent so that his fingers could play with her hair where it flopped over her forehead.

"Are you cold?" he asked.

"No."

"You're trembling."

Because I want you. Edie clenched her fists and reminded herself of all the reasons this was a bad idea. She'd resisted all feelings of desire for Finn, telling herself he couldn't do his job in protecting her if he was distracted by a sexual relationship. Years ago, her trainer Bethany had died in that very situation when she and Lukas had fallen for each other.

But they weren't on a rover ship now. Her life was no longer in danger, and no one was forcing him, or even paying him, to watch over her.

"You're in my bed," he said.

"You're taking liberties . . ." She kept her tone playful.

He slid his fingers out of her hair and made a show of lifting his other hand off her stomach. Now no part of him touched her. She turned her head to face him. He wore an easy half-smile, like he already knew what she would do. She waited a breathless moment, feeling the anticipation build as her skin cooled where his hands had been and the rest of her body heated up, starving for contact.

"I want you to touch me," she said.

His hand returned to her stomach, this time underneath her top, making her flinch and then relax. She released a shaky sigh as his fingers and thumb stroked parallel paths down the sensitive skin on either side of her navel.

He was taking his time about it. She rolled onto her side and into his embrace. Lips crushed together before limbs had time to adjust. Then she was on him, hungrily, while his hands slid around to cup her bottom. She pressed against him, overeager in her desperation, and sensed him holding back. He rolled her onto her back, not breaking the kiss, and straddled her but held his body away from hers.

That gave her other opportunities. She dragged her fingers down his chest, feeling his stomach muscles tense under her fingernails, and tugged at his waistband. He groaned and broke the kiss. Reaching down, he grabbed both her wrists and pulled her hands away. He lowered his forehead until it almost touched her chest, breathing hard, his body tense.

Only then did she understand.

The leash. Her arousal was firing up the leash and causing him pain.

Frustration drew an anguished moan from her throat. Anger followed quickly, forcing hot tears to her eyes. She blinked them away before they spilled, untangled her legs from his and slid off the couch. He caught her hand briefly but she pulled away and stumbled across the deck toward her room.

"Edie—"

She didn't want to face him, didn't want to talk about it. Of all the reasons she hated the people who'd jacked Finn's chip to enslave him, this one suddenly felt like the cruelest of all.

Somehow he caught up with her before she made it through the door, pulled her against him and held her while she tried to calm down. She *had* to calm down. Her anger was as tumultuous as her sexual arousal had been. The leash didn't distinguish. Either way, it blasted his head with static.

Warm in his embrace, the raw emotion subsided but the outpouring hadn't doused her desire. She pulled back a little, leaning away as his embrace loosened.

"I will fix that," she said. In truth she had no idea how to, and was terrified to try. Interfering with the leash might cause it to detonate.

He gave an understanding smile while his eyes gleamed with a hint of mischief. "That would be . . . terrific."

"I still need to give it some thought first."

He nodded and let his arms slip away, and she went to her room alone.

It was early evening when Edie awoke. She hadn't meant to sleep that long and realized with annoyance that her diurnal rhythm was completely reversed from that of the ship.

Her clothes, everything she'd collected from the quartermaster, were piled up on a console near the door. Finn must have brought them in while she slept. She could hear him moving about in the next room. Her mind replayed their last encounter and she wondered how he felt. Embarrassed, perhaps? Frustrated, no doubt. He'd wanted her, and that alone made her feel better.

She leaned in the doorway, feeling as if she needed an invitation to step into his space. He was pulling on running shoes.

"Did you sleep?" she asked.

"A little. Going for a run."

"You sure you're up for that?"

"Yeah. May as well find out where that crew key will take me. Besides, I need to get the blood moving." He looked up. "D'you want to come?"

"Where is there to run?"

"Deck F has some long stretches, according to the schematics I pulled up." He nodded toward the console in the corner, where the holoviz displayed some basic information about the *Learo Dochais*.

"Sure, I'll come along." After two weeks cooped up in the *Peregrine*, a year in cold sleep, and a week before that bedridden with neuroshock, her body was ready to heal itself. She returned to her room to dig out running shoes, then clipped back her hair.

Outside their quarters, a couple of twists in the deserted corridor brought them to a lift. Alone in the car as it descended, Edie finally had the courage to look Finn in the eye. He gave her such a sweet, sad smile that she felt tears threatening again. And had to look away. This was no good. They had to find a way to be together without the tension and drama.

The lift doors opened on Deck F. A short corridor branched into a longer one that curved to the left in the distance and looped all the way around the outer bulkhead.

Finn set off at a brisk pace and they ran loops in silence. To keep pace with Finn, Edie ran a longer stride than felt natural. Her legs began to ache, not unpleasantly, and the endorphins kicked in. But after five loops she fell back and slowed to a stop to catch her breath. She expected Finn to continue without her, but he turned and walked back.

"Had enough?" he said.

"I need a moment."

"Let's go back. No point in pushing it."

"Okay. I'm hungry, anyway."

They headed toward the lift. Edie rounded the corner a pace ahead of Finn and saw a flash of movement as a small figure darted into a side corridor.

"Hey . . . there's someone . . ."

Edie jogged to the corridor but there was no one there.

"I saw someone," she told Finn. "A child."

"Are you sure?"

"Yes, I'm sure."

Edie checked for unlocked hatches and alcoves along the corridor. Something clattered up ahead. Finn heard it, too, and strode off in the direction of the sound. They turned another corner and pulled up sharply.

A boy stood there in white PJs. His dark hair stuck out in all directions and he had a grin frozen on his face, like he'd been caught red-handed. His grin vanished as he stared at Finn and Edie and realized they weren't anybody he expected to meet on this deck. He started to back away.

Edie held out a hand. "Hey—don't run. What's your name?"

The boy looked around for an escape route. Failing to see one, he boldly drew himself up and crossed his arms.

"What are you doing out of bed?" he said.

Edie held back a laugh. "Don't be cheeky. Tell me your name and I won't tell anyone *you're* out of bed." Maybe he was the child of one of the workers on board. But there was something disconcertingly familiar about his features—she couldn't put her finger on what it was.

"I'm Galeon." The boy jutted his chin defiantly. "I know who you are. You're Edie Sha'nim. I've seen you on the holoviz."

That took her by surprise. "How did you know?"

"Miss Aila told us all about you."

"Who's Miss Aila?"

"Our teacher, of course."

Our teacher? "How many children are on board?"

"Me and three others. The girls. They're all asleep in the dorm. Well, not Pris. Pris is sick and didn't even come to school today. Anyway, the others don't know how to sneak out like I do. Who are *you*?" He shot the question at Finn, who had relaxed against the bulkhead.

"That's Finn," Edie said distractedly. What was it about this child that made her so uncomfortable?

Galeon approached Finn and stood his ground when Finn straightened a little. He stared up at the big man. "How come you don't say anything?"

"I'll say plenty if you ask the right questions."

Galeon liked that. He grinned. "How old are you?"

"Twenty-eight."

"That's exactly four times how old I am! Are you a milit? Do you have a rifle?"

"No, and no."

"Do you play Pegasaw? I bet I can beat you."

"I wouldn't count on it," Finn said, amused.

Galeon liked that, too. He beamed for a second, then turned to Edie with a frown. "What about you?"

"What about me?"

Wrong response. Galeon lost interest immediately, and

stepped up closer to Finn to scrutinize his face. "Why are your eyes red?"

Finn didn't miss a beat. "Someone hurt me."

"Oh." The boy looked confused, like he'd heard something too grown up for his ears. As his forehead crinkled into a frown, Edie knew what it was. He reminded her of herself. Something about his dark hair, his facial features, his delicate chin . . .

Galeon was Talasi.

Her stomach sank as she put the pieces together. So this was Natesa's new team of skilled cyphertecks—these four children on board. It made sense, in a twisted way. Natesa had taken Edie from the Talasi camps at age ten, trained her with biocyph, and turned her into the Crib's most successful cypherteck. The biocyph in her blood, put there by her ancestors to enable the Talasi to survive on a toxic planet, made interfacing easy for her. It was only logical for Natesa to seek new talent from the same source.

Four Talasi children, all needing neuroxin to survive away from their homeworld. The boxes of implants made sense now.

Galeon cocked his head suddenly. "Someone's coming."

He raced past them and disappeared down a different side corridor in a streak of white. Seconds later, someone strode past the end of the corridor—an off-duty meckie, probably. He glanced disinterestedly at Edie and Finn as he passed.

Edie set off after Galeon, Finn trailing behind. "Dammit, Finn. She's using children."

"What?"

"Galeon is Talasi. Natesa's using Talasi children on her new improved cypherteck team." Her head filled with questions. How long had these children been in training? Why did the Talasi elders relinquish them to CCU? What kind of life did they have? And why had she never heard of any of this before?

Finn caught her arm and pulled her to a halt. "Wait, Edie. What does this have to do with us?"

"How can you ask that? I can't stand by while—"

"The plan is to get out of here." He dropped his voice in case anyone else was near. "Take the cryptoglyph to the Fringe. Cut the leash. Not run around after children. Besides, that kid seemed fine."

"He's fine now. He'll grow up to discover he's being used to feed the Crib's greed. And that he has no other options. I know what that feels like."

"What can you do about it, anyway?"

"I don't know."

"Specifically, what can you do about it that doesn't interfere with our plans?"

Nothing. He was right. She was furious and brokenhearted about Natesa using children, but she couldn't stop her. She couldn't refuse to participate or make a fuss—she was bound to cooperate until she and Finn managed to escape.

CHAPTER 8

The mess at breakfast time was noisy, crowded chaos. Edie counted fifty people, at least, gathered around long tables. At one table, everyone wore work coveralls and the conversation was particularly lively. Half the seats were empty. Edie wasn't tempted to join them. Lively people tended to ask questions and demand participation.

She carried her tray to a small table in the corner and waited for Finn to join her. They ate in companionable silence until a thickset older woman with curly ash-blond hair got up from the meckies' table and came over to theirs.

"Winnie Tanning," she announced. To Edie's surprise, she addressed Finn. "Mr Finn? I was asked to find a job for you."

"It's just Finn." He put down his fork.

"Okay. What can you do?" Winnie sat down beside Edie and folded her arms on the tabletop.

"I'm versatile. What's on offer?" Finn matched her no-nonsense approach.

"Well, we have a new group of workers arriving and I'll have to assign them. But it seems you get first pick. Let's see . . . Bernie Kunek over there is in charge of the ag-teck processing rigs. They're setting up half a dozen of those on the surface and doing some preliminary tests."

"He can't work dirtside," Edie said. At least not while she was on the ship and well beyond the leash's range.

"Okaaay." Winnie flicked an annoyed look at Edie, who felt suitably chastised for butting in. The woman didn't ask for details. "So, my project is the beanstalk and we have shipside and dirtside teams."

"A skyhook?" Finn said over the rim of his water glass.

"That's it. A series of space elevators to pull goods out of the gravity well, once the ag-teck comes online in a few months. We already have one skyhook in operation. The *Learo Dochais* serves as its counterweight. We're building three more. I can always use an extra hand if you know your way around a toolset. What are you—a meckie?"

"Near enough."

Winnie gave a brisk nod. "I think we're going to get along well, Finn. Report to my office, Deck G, soon as you're finished here." She hesitated a moment before adding, "Most of the guys don't know you were a Saeth. I'd keep it quiet, if I were you."

He returned the nod and she left.

"I bet that's the shortest job interview you've ever had," Edie remarked.

"It's the *only* job interview I ever had."

It was a strange feeling to part ways with Finn as he left for the lower decks and she made her way to the labs. She was used to having him at her side.

As she entered the lab through a small foyer, a man and a woman were bent over a holoviz, studying readouts. They wore official CCU tunics, which made Edie wonder if she was supposed to have picked up similar garb at Ken's.

The wiry woman with a shock of cropped black hair and dark bright eyes straightened and held out her hand. "Morning. I'm Ming Yue Huang, chief op-teck for Ardra."

Edie shook her hand but her gaze drifted to the man. When he half turned to stare at her, she recognized him from news-caps. He was in his midfifties, of average build and average looks. There was nothing average about his reputation, however.

"This is Caleb Chessell, chief cypherteck," Ming Yue said.

He didn't offer his hand, so Edie didn't offer hers. Instead he went back to his work without acknowledging her.

"Friendliest face on the ship," Ming Yue muttered. "Just to get this out in the open, he's a little worried about being usurped."

Edie couldn't tell if she was joking. "By me? I'm not exactly employee of the month."

"I'm just glad to have you on the team," Ming Yue said, and she sounded genuine about that. Perhaps she was grateful for the opportunity to work with someone other than the revered Chief Chessell. "I supervise the day-to-day logistics of the seeding project. You'll work mostly with Caleb. He can bring you up to speed."

Caleb didn't look like he wanted to do that. He gave a tiny shake of his head that made his stringy hair shiver.

"What about the other cyphertecks?" Edie asked. "The children?"

Ming Yue cocked an eyebrow. "I didn't think . . . Natesa told me you didn't know about the children yet."

"I know about them."

"I'm supposed to take you to the training lab tomorrow to meet them. The classroom, we call it. We don't have a lot of contact with the kids. They can be challenging to work with, as Caleb can confirm."

"Are they all Talasi?"

"Yes. Natesa set up a school for Talasi children outside Halen Crai six years ago, to train them as cyphertecks."

Edie had spent her teens in Halen Crai, Talas's only city—built inside a sealed mountain to protect its inhabitants from the toxic ecosystem. Six years ago she was eighteen years old, a newly qualified cypherteck, already disillusioned after stepping foot on Scarabaeus two years before that and witnessing the beauty the Crib intended to destroy. Six years ago . . . also when Lukas, her bodyguard, vanished without a trace, without saying goodbye.

Natesa had told her Lukas was a traitor. Edie didn't believe that. But was his imprisonment linked to the opening of the school? Had he known about it, and perhaps raised objections? He'd always been loyal to the Crib and it was hard to imagine he'd go against them, but the timing seemed more than coincidental. Edie filed away the information for now.

"Strange that I never heard about a Talasi school," she said.

"It's a classified project. I don't know all the details—"

"CCU learned from you," Caleb broke in. He tipped back in his seat at an alarming angle and glared at Edie. "They knew the Talasi kids would have the talent, because like you they inherited biocyph in their cells. So they developed tests to assess the children's affinity for biocyph. They can pick the good ones at age two or three."

"Are you saying those children have been in training since they were babies?" Babies in the Crib's care . . . It made Edie shudder. She'd been ten years old when she went to Crai Institute, thirteen when CCU took over her education and her life entirely. How much more brainwashed must these children be? "How many are there, other than the four on board?"

Caleb shrugged. "All I know is, they brought along the best ones on this mission."

"They're quite remarkable," Ming Yue said eagerly, clearly hoping to diminish Edie's objections. "They have a unique way of interfacing with the biocyph and they're fascinated by it. A little undisciplined, but they get the job done."

Edie would have liked to throw in a sarcastic question or two about what kind of childhood they were having, and what kind of future they could look forward to, but this wasn't the time. These two tecks had nothing to do with it, really.

Ming Yue left Edie with Caleb, who laid down the ground rules in brisk tones.

"You only have level-two clearance right now, so I won't be showing you most of what I'm working on." His tone held undisguised arrogance. She tried to forgive it. Perhaps his attitude was warranted, especially considering he was dealing with a disgraced junior. She listened politely as he ran through some basic stuff as though he felt she needed a primer.

"Natesa told me you'd developed some new code that's proving useful," she said, to take the focus off herself and onto him, which was where he no doubt felt it belonged.

"Yes. I wrote the regulator code that we've implemented on Prisca. Without it, we'd be using regular boosters on the planet, and we all know what a disaster that would've been."

Boosters were notoriously unstable. They sent the biocyph into overdrive, usually resulting in ecosystem meltdown. The gray organic sludge that tecks called mash was the result, and it was irreversible.

"I'd like to look at it."

"Not until you have level-five clearance."

"Then what can I look at?"

"Follow me."

He led her into the adjoining lab, a smaller room where two tecks were working, holoviz displays spinning around their heads. Both of their CCU tunics displayed a cypherteck logo. Counting herself and Caleb, one teck in the infirmary, four children and presumably at least one on the planet's surface, took the total to eight cyphertecks on the team. It was unheard of. Most seeding teams had only one.

Caleb lit a new display and nudged it toward Edie. "These are the specs from Prisca's primed BRATs, ten months ago, shortly after the planet was seeded. A good place to start."

"Wait—the BRATs came online ten months ago, and Winnie's team is firing up the ag-teck in only a few months. Your code boosted the biocyph *that* much?" Usually it took a decade or more to terraform an alien world to the point where it was suitable for colonization and farming. Longer, surely, for more complex worlds like Prisca.

"I won't toot my own horn, but"—he did anyway—"my code is proving revolutionary."

"And the evolution on Prisca is stable?"

"My sim projections show excellent results." He gave a small shrug, as though Edie could not possibly understand the extent of his work. Which was more or less true. Studying his innovations had been part of her training, but she hadn't studied his work on this project. She did, however, find his overconfidence worrisome. Boosters of any kind were bad news.

"I didn't ask about your *sims*," she muttered. "So where do the children fit in?"

"Well, we get the usual errors, of course. The ground crew downloads data directly from the BRATs. From that raw data we create error logs."

He flashed up a series of logs from the previous day, too quickly for Edie to see much, but one thing was clear.

"These are just from one day? That's a helluva lot of errors." And that didn't bode well for Prisca.

"Not really," Caleb said evasively. "Normally the biocyph would self-correct, but this ecosystem is evolving so fast that many of the errors have to be fixed manually using sim extrapolations. Not something you or even I could handle. But the children have a unique way of working together to interface with a supercomplex datastream. They don't understand the biology. They're just trained to pop those glitches back into place."

Caleb returned to the other lab. Edie was interested in analyzing how the children handled the error logs, but apparently level-two clearance wasn't sufficient for that. Instead she was stuck with data that was ten months out of date and really didn't tell her anything. As she filed through it, her gaze wandered around the lab. Racks of biocyph modules lined the bulkheads. She knew from the CCU seal on each unit that this was stock biocyph, not yet primed. It was almost too much to believe—each module was worth more than she could earn in a lifetime, and there were dozens of them.

She had to check for herself. Casually, she got up from her console and wandered over to the nearest rack. The other tecks were too engrossed in their work to notice her. She pressed her fingertips to the port on one module and heard the tuneless buzz of stock biocyph, just as she'd guessed. What the Fringe worlds wouldn't give for these resources! They relied on preprogrammed biocyph handouts from the Crib, because only the Crib had the templates to construct stock biocyph like this. It could be turned into ag-teck or med-teck or environmental jigglers, even used to repair BRAT seeds.

Could she steal the modules for the Fringe? Her mind spun in a new direction. If she had free access to the modules, what could she create? The possibilities seemed limitless and the temptation to meddle was overwhelming. Could she use the cryptoglyph from Scarabaeus to program the biocyph? Right under the Crib's nose . . .

But she didn't have free access to the modules. She could do nothing with them during work hours because other tecks would always be around. And if she used her crew key to enter the lab outside her shift, the entry would be logged as a security breach and she'd be found out immediately.

One of the cyphertecks gave her a suspicious look. Fortunately she'd already drawn her hand away from the port. She moved back to her console and pretended to be engrossed in Caleb's useless data.

When Edie was summoned to the conference room on Deck A that afternoon, foremost on her mind was confronting Natesa about the children. Righteous indignation had helped her develop an outraged speech, and she was intent on delivering it. Instead, she walked onto a battlefield where Natesa and Theron were engaged in combat, and her personal objections were irrelevant.

Natesa stood at the head of a long table, her mood black as the Reach. Theron sat stiffly at the other end, as far from her as possible. Clearly they'd been at it for a while, so wrapped up in the conflict that neither acknowledged Edie when

Natesa's assistant showed her in. Between them sat a thin man with captain's stripes on his uniform. Edie remembered the kitchenhand had called him Captain Lachesis. He wore a slightly apologetic look, as if embarrassed by the display of emotion going on before him.

"This isn't a case of martial law," Natesa was saying. "There's no war going on here. Edie works for CCU, and you simply don't have the authority to reassign her to your team."

"Yet *you* had Caleb Chessell reassigned from my team to yours last year."

"Ardra requires the best cyphertecks in the Crib and the project is important enough to demand them. Your pet project with its senile BRATs can hardly compare."

"You're delaying the inevitable, Ms Natesa," Theron shot back. "I *will* get the permission I need—it's only a matter of time. I don't believe you have as many friends in the Crib as you think, especially not while Prisca flounders."

"Prisca is not floundering. Everything is going as expected."

"That's not what I hear."

"Who have you been talking to? Read my official updates. CCU is perfectly happy with the way things are going."

"Pardon me for not quite believing your *official* updates."

"This is ridiculous. Prisca has been online for less than a year, and you're judging the entire project on the basis of a few wild rumors. There are people who want to see me fail. That's no secret." Natesa sent Captain Lachesis an appealing look, as if he should speak in her defense. The captain remained silent, staring at his interlocked fingers on the tabletop. "I've implemented a process that speeds up terraforming a hundredfold. There will be medals all round, no doubt. It's no wonder others are trying to drag me down."

"*You* implemented it? *My* cypherteck created it! You owe me a huge favor."

"You have some nerve, after *you* put a member of my team in the infirmary—"

"You don't even intend to use Sha'nim's talents here. Instead you've relegated her to menial tasks."

"That will change in time. I know Edie won't disappoint me."

"She can serve the Crib far better by working for my research division."

Edie caught her breath. Work for the Weapons Research Division? "I refuse to work for you," she said.

Theron and Natesa swiveled to face her, their expressions mirror images of shock, as if they'd only just remembered she was in the room. Her comment was addressed to Theron. He seemed unperturbed by it.

"You'll work where you're told to work." Theron jabbed his finger on the table to emphasize his words.

"You tortured Finn. I refuse to work for you," Edie repeated.

Natesa looked smug, at what she must have perceived to be a sign of her protégée's loyalty. "That's right. You work for me," she told Edie. "The colonel is getting ideas beyond his jurisdiction."

Lachesis cleared his throat as he prepared to intervene. Theron got there first.

"You'd better hope that Prisca is recoverable." His expressive brows grew thunderous as he pushed back his chair and stood. "You were only given one shot at this, Adminstrator. If Prisca collapses, as my sources think it will, this discussion is moot and Edie will join my team. Now, if you'll excuse me, my schooner is ready to leave and I'm eager to get back to my *pet project.*"

He left the room with a generic nod of respect to the captain.

"Damn arrogant sonofabitch." Natesa fumed. "The audacity of that man! He's been insufferable ever since he made colonel. Does he have any idea—" She stopped herself and turned to Lachesis. "Surely there's something you can do about this. This is *your* ship and Edie is assigned to *this* crew."

"And Theron's a colonel," Lachesis replied. He still seemed embarrassed by the whole thing.

"I demand that you take this to CCU. We've been friends a long time, Jeremy."

Lachesis squirmed at the emotional blackmail and gave a painful shrug. "I need to get back to the bridge."

Natesa closed her eyes, taking a few deep breaths until Lachesis was gone. Then she turned a hard look on Edie. "The higher-ups at CCU headquarters will sort this out. *Nothing* comes before Project Ardra."

"Not even four childhoods?"

"What? Ah, yes. Ming Yue told me you'd learned about the children. That's why I wanted to see you." As Edie drew breath to deliver her speech, Natesa held up a hand to silence her. "Spare me, Edie. I know what you're thinking. But you don't know what's really going on. These are desperate times and we must use all available tools."

"The only desperation I see is you attempting to bolster your career. Is it really that important to have the best, fastest terraforming team in the Reach?"

Natesa gave a weary sigh. "As I said, you don't know everything. How did you find out about the children, anyway?"

"Someone let it slip." She didn't want to get the boy into trouble.

"Well, tomorrow afternoon we'll visit the classroom and meet them. I want you to watch them work."

"Are they really as good as you say? Theron said Prisca was floundering."

"Nonsense. Teething problems. Prisca will be a glorious success, and it's all because of my children."

CHAPTER 9

"Edie!"

Natesa's sharp tone from the next room sent a stab of annoyance through Edie. Finn stopped what he was saying midsentence—he'd come into the bedroom to find out if she was ever getting up—and Natesa stepped into the doorway. Her glare fell on Finn and then, inexplicably, to the rumpled bed that Edie had just vacated. Edie didn't care what Natesa thought, and the woman had no right to barge into her quarters. They always kept the hatch locked—she must have a master crew key.

Before Natesa could launch into whatever she'd come to say, Finn made to leave.

"I'll meet you in the mess," he told Edie. He strode across the room and angled his body to slip past Natesa in the doorway without touching or looking at her.

Natesa turned to watch him with a smirk of distaste. Edie heard the hatch snap as he left.

"You used to be an early riser," Natesa said. "I couldn't find you in the mess hall."

"So you barge in here without permission? Please don't do that again."

Natesa raised her brows, surprised by the outburst but not at all offended. "My apologies. I have some good news that I wanted to share." Her face stretched into a smile as fake as the crimson stain on her lips.

Edie was dubious that anything Natesa had to tell her would ever be good. She sat on the edge of the bed and waited.

"I've tracked down the infojack who created the leash. He was indeed incarcerated in a labor camp in the Rutger System, for kidnapping and high treason, among many other things. I've received permission to transfer him here temporarily, with orders to cut the leash."

Edie's immediate reaction—a sense of dread—caught her by surprise. Cutting the leash had always been her number one priority. Now the real possibility was on the table—and she was terrified. Achaiah might kill Finn in the process.

"Does he really think he can do it?" she asked.

"I spoke to him at length. He has a few ideas on how it might be accomplished. I think it's worth trying."

"*Trying* isn't good enough. He can't do it unless he's absolutely certain it's safe. You have to let me be there."

"I'll see if I can arrange that. In the next few days you'll be very busy getting your head around Project Ardra."

"I don't care. I have to be there to make sure nothing goes wrong. For that matter, you'll need Finn's consent before you start messing with his head."

"I hardly think he'll object."

"Why did you let him leave the room, anyway?" Edie asked. "This concerns him."

"I'm not responsible for his comings and goings." Natesa picked an imaginary fleck off her lapel. "Speaking of which, I'm not happy with this arrangement." She waved her hand around, her gaze again lingering on the bed. "He shouldn't be in VIP quarters. I have important guests from Central arriving in a few days and I don't want them seeing a meckie wandering around on this deck. Winnie Tanning will get him a new room on the lower decks. Your relationship with him is no doubt distracting you from the work you're legally required to perform here."

Edie pressed her fingertips to her forehead, massaging the ache forming there. "This is so far from being any of your business, Natesa. No one has complained about my work. I'm doing everything you asked."

"I don't like him," Natesa enunciated. "The best thing for everyone is to cut this leash so I can throw him off the ship."

Edie didn't like Natesa's choice of words, but what she said made sense. This was a classified project that Finn wasn't cleared for, as if a former Saeth and ex-con would ever be cleared for such work. He wasn't supposed to be here.

Her heart squeezed at the thought of him leaving. Leaving *her* behind. Would he come back for her? After all they'd been through together, he'd find a way—wouldn't he?

When Natesa was gone, Edie curled up her legs and hugged her knees as self-doubt crept in. With the leash cut, everything would change. Finn had spent the last few years just surviving, and now he'd have the chance to truly live. She couldn't compete.

Colors erupted like lava from the projector on the floor, forming a holosphere filled with tiny lights. The lights gathered together in a complex pattern and danced in formation. On closer inspection, Edie could see the pattern was divided into smaller clusters, and the lights in each cluster repeated the patterns of the larger formation. And within each cluster, again, tiny groups of lights repeated the same dance. The whole effect was that of a spinning, whirling fractal starscape pulsing to an unheard beat. A heartbeat. This was no computer simulation. Its rhythms were ever so slightly off—human, not machine.

The entire structure was being controlled and choreographed by the three children sitting around the projector.

Edie stood at the back of the classroom, amazed. Whatever she thought of Natesa's school, she couldn't deny that this display was beautiful. And that it took not only skill but coordination. Three minds working in harmony in the datastream, three young faces frozen in concentration as they stared up into their composition of light. Edie had never seen anything like it. Everyone knew cyphertecks worked alone.

Edie glanced at Natesa at her side. The woman gave a smug smile, knowing that Edie was impressed by what she saw.

The children's teacher, a forty-something woman with short curly hair and a pinched face, walked slowly around the outside of the trio, alternating her attention between the light display and the children. Edie recognized Galeon, the boy she and Finn had met. With him were two girls of about the same age.

As the lights cascaded in a waterfall of color and faded out, the teacher came up to Edie and Natesa.

"This is Aila Vernet," Natesa said. "Aila, this, of course, is Edie Sha'nim."

Aila regarded Edie with down-turned eyes that gave her a sad expression even when she smiled, as she did now. "It's an honor to meet you. The children have been looking forward to this. They've studied your techniques rigorously as part of their training."

Three pairs of young eyes were now focused on Edie. She could tell Galeon was suppressing a grin, and was doing a pretty good job of it.

"Is it normal for them to coordinate in a group like that?" Edie nodded at the projector.

"Oh, yes," Aila said. "They do their best work in teams. We could never manage the complexity of an ecosystem like Prisca's without their efforts."

"Do they understand what they're doing?"

"Not exactly. They know nothing about biology and ecosystems. And this visual interface is only for show. They don't appear to need visual cues once they're jacked in together. We've developed an interface that allows them to assess and modify the datastream without understanding the specifics. They look at the alien eco-specs and nudge them toward the Terran ideal, but to them it's just a datastream."

"You don't trust the biocyph to do this by itself?" That was how it worked on normal terraforming projects.

"In extensive sims, we tried it that way," Natesa interjected. "With complex ecosystems like this, we find the biocyph is less able to learn from its mistakes. One mistake can take the terraforming down an irreversible path of evolution, and then the Terran ideal can never be reclaimed."

"That's why we need constant monitoring." Aila displayed a series of worksheets on the nearest holoviz. "In the lab we have Caleb Chessell collecting data from the planet to create error logs—evolution paths that deviate too far from the Terran ideal. Then the children work through each log to nudge the errors back on track before it's too late."

"Fixing mistakes on the fly?"

"Exactly."

It was an unusual approach. Biocyph usually worked best when left to fix its own errors. Human intervention was only required during the setup phase.

Edie glanced around the sparse classroom. It seemed to her remarkably bare and lifeless for a children's workspace. It was simply a lab stacked with consoles. Natesa worked in luxury while the children spent their days in this sterile cell.

Natesa excused herself and Edie settled into a seat to learn more. As the children worked quietly, Edie had the chance to find out more about Aila. She was a Crib cypherteck with twenty years' terraforming experience, and had been brought in from Crib Central to train the children at Natesa's school when it first opened. She didn't appear to have any real affinity for the children, but they didn't seem to care. They wrapped themselves up in the biocyph. Their enthusiasm and concentration amazed Edie. She'd never particularly enjoyed her training—perhaps because it had been a lonely endeavor. For a while she'd attended a regular school where she had classmates, mostly the children of milits doing their tour in Halen Crai. But when cypherteck training intensified, the institute had isolated her.

From then on, Edie's companions had been her tutors and

the datastream. She'd done what she was told—most of the time—because she hadn't known there were options. Her sheltered life there had stripped away all the other pathways her life might have taken until only Natesa's plan for her remained.

Would these children come to view the Crib in the same way as she did? Or would they remain loyal citizens, devoted to Natesa's cause, never questioning their so-called duty?

The children broke for lunch, moving to an informal seating area in the corner of the classroom to eat from bento boxes delivered by the kitchenhand. As Aila engrossed herself in work at her console, Galeon sidled up to Edie and tugged on her sleeve.

"Where's your friend?"

"Finn? He works on Deck G."

"That's where they're making the beanstalk."

"That's right."

"I hope they let us visit Prisca. I want to ride that beanstalk."

"It's rather dangerous. The planet, I mean." With active BRAT seeds on the surface, constant shielding would be necessary to prevent the retroviruses from altering human DNA. Edie had to trust that the dirtside base was adequately protected, because there were already people stationed there. She didn't share Galeon's enthusiasm to go down to the surface.

"She's not dangerous," Galeon retorted. "She's not well."

"Who's not well? The planet? What makes you say that?"

"She sings the wrong tune. That's what all these are for." His arm swept across the room to encompass the consoles and holoviz displays from Prisca's eco-specs. "Can't you feel how sick she is? All out of balance."

This world had, of course, evolved in a perfectly normal manner before CCU arrived and planted biocyph all over it. Galeon's description helped her understand the children a little better, however. They saw an ecosystem in flux as damaged, and the Terran ideal as the cure. It made sense that, to them, bringing the planet into balance meant creating a Terran environment.

"Finn said he would play Pegasaw with me," Galeon said suddenly. "You should bring him here."

"I don't think that's what he said, was it?"

Galeon stared at her, his soft brow furrowed. "I'm the only boy. Did you notice? Everyone else here is a girl, even you. You should bring Finn up here so we can hang out."

Hanging out with Galeon was the last thing Natesa would allow Finn to do. Edie felt for the boy, though.

"What about Caleb Chessell?"

Galeon ducked his head, leaning toward her to whisper. "We don't like him much. Prisca doesn't, either."

"He's very . . ." Edie searched for an appropriate word. "Clever."

Galeon wrinkled his nose. "Listen, you tell me where Finn's room is and I'll bring Pegasaw and we'll have a match."

"We're— His room is on Deck D at the moment. How will you sneak out?"

"Which room on Deck D? How many doors from the main lift?"

"Uh, you turn left out of the lift and then it's the second on the right," Edie said, curious to see if Galeon could actually make it to their quarters.

"Tell him I'm a very good player, so he'd better practice."

Edie couldn't help smiling. "I'll tell him."

"Raena," Aila called to one of the girls as the children put away their lunch boxes. "Why don't you show Edie what you've been working on today?"

The girl gave a shy smile and waited for Edie to join her.

"Raena didn't do a very good job of it," Galeon declared.

"Galeon! Please return to your own work," Aila scolded.

"Where's Pris?" he demanded. "She was supposed to partner with Raena."

"Pris is still not well enough for school today."

"He's right," Raena said quietly. "I had to partner with Hanna and she makes the biocyph angry."

The other girl tossed a mop of straight black hair out of her eyes and scowled over her shoulder.

"All right, everyone. Hush now," Aila said. "Back to your exercises. Raena, go ahead."

"Hanna didn't like this one much, and it didn't like her," Raena whispered to Edie as her console lit up. "But we finished it on time."

The holoviz that bloomed over the console no doubt made little sense to the girl. Edie recognized the representation as a subsection of an ecosystem's physiology—the pathways of a few proteins and their interactions across every species in the ecosystem.

Edie jacked in. The datastream flooded her splinter and she felt her senses cave inward as her concentration turned toward the music. Ignoring the visuals, she followed Raena riding the crest of the melody, dashing from one tier to another as if looking for something.

"There it is," Raena said. She snagged a tiny riff, a jagged sequence that was clearly out of place. It had leaked through from another tier. "Can you feel it?"

Raena turned the riff around and shuffled it back into place with surprising agility—Edie couldn't have done much better herself.

"See? It feels much better now."

"Feels?" Edie repeated.

"You don't think so?" Raena shut down the holoviz abruptly and stared at her.

"I'm not sure what you mean."

"That's how they talk about the biocyph," Aila explained, looking at Raena proudly. "They always refer to its moods, its feelings. It's quite remarkable. The other cyphertecks were as confounded as you, but it seems to work for them. The biocyph is 'happy' when the team works well together, or 'upset' when they fail to fix a problem, that sort of thing."

So this was a game to them, and the biocyph was their playmate, complete with personality and moods.

"I understand you experience the biocyph as music?" Aila said.

"Yes. But most cyphertecks I've met describe it in visual terms. My trainer would talk about patterns and numbers—it meant nothing to me."

"I suppose emotional responses are as appropriate as any other interpretation. After all, human brains can't deal with the raw data. It's not surprising the Talasi experience it differently from other cyphertecks. The biocyph in their . . . *your* cells helps bind the wet-teck interface more intimately to the cerebral cortex."

Aila spoke so matter-of-factly about taking children from their home, grafting wet-teck to their brains, and training them to be dutiful workers for the Crib. Edie would never get used to that. And yet, looking around the classroom, the children didn't appear to be unhappy.

"How many children are in the training program?" she asked.

"You mean at the school? Twenty-four, not including the four here on the *Learo Dochais*. We brought the most promising group with us. They miss Pris's input right now. She's the eldest girl."

Snippets of conversation flashed through Edie's mind. *Pris is sick . . . not well enough for school today . . .*

"What's wrong with Pris?" She heard the tremble in her voice.

"I'm not exactly sure." Aila looked uncomfortable. "They won't tell me."

Edie knew. Suddenly, she knew. Muttering an excuse, she stumbled out of the classroom and fell against the bulkhead outside, struggling for air. It hadn't even crossed her mind that Theron would use a child to torture another human being. Now it made sense. He could have told the girl anything, made it into a game—she didn't know what she was doing. And now she was lying in a coma.

CHAPTER 10

Edie found herself outside the infirmary before she'd consciously made the decision to start walking. Maybe she was mistaken. Maybe . . .

A screen surrounded the only occupied bed. Edie couldn't bring herself to step inside. She viewed the scene through a crack where the screen was slightly open. Despite what she'd braced herself to see, it took her a moment to comprehend. An unconscious child. The waifish face and dark intense brows were all too familiar. As was the faint circular scar on her temple.

A monitor display arched over the girl's head. A med tom in one corner blinked in silent surveillance. As Edie moved closer, Natesa came into view, sitting at the girl's side and holding her hand.

"Hey, you can't be here," someone said behind Edie.

Natesa looked up and locked eyes with Edie. Her expression changed from concern to annoyance—but the concern had looked real. Perhaps Natesa really did care about this child.

Natesa's gaze flicked to the medic coming up behind Edie. "No, it's all right," she said. "Edie, you may come in."

Somehow Edie managed to step behind the screen without her legs giving way. She felt hollow inside, like all the emotion had been sucked out of her.

"Her wet-teck overloaded," Natesa said quietly. "We're still not sure how serious the neural damage is."

Edie didn't know what to say. *I did this.* How could she continue pushing away the sense of guilt with her victim right here in front of her?

"She's my daughter," Natesa said to break the silence. "My adopted daughter—or she will be, when the final paperwork comes through."

That struck Edie as incongruous. Natesa had never displayed any maternal inclinations.

"How did you persuade the Talasi elders to give her up?"

"You know how those people live, Edie. How they treated you. Legally, it wasn't hard to remove those children who displayed exceptional talents that the Crib needed. We compensated the Talasi by helping to reforest their lands. And why do you care? You've told me time and again that you don't consider yourself one of them."

True enough. The Talasi had rejected Edie even before she was born because her mother, a visiting anthropologist from the Crib, had "seduced" one of their men—an act they viewed as a betrayal of trust.

Noting Edie's scowl, Natesa added, "You have no grounds to question my judgment or the actions of CCU." She stroked the child's arm. "Pris was one of the first students at the school, and the most promising. She's had a much better life in state care. When you disappeared . . . that was very hard on me, Edie. I felt like I'd lost a daughter."

"I don't believe you."

Natesa gave a take-it-or-leave-it shrug. The woman had certainly paid a lot of attention to Edie's health and education, but only to further her own career. She'd never shown love. And now Pris was Edie's replacement—not that Edie was jealous. Much as she'd fantasized as a child that her own mother would come back for her some day, she'd never wanted Natesa to step into those shoes.

At least, she'd never consciously wanted that. The way Natesa doted on Pris stirred deep emotions that Edie struggled to keep down.

"What kind of childhood are you giving these kids?" she asked. Because it was easier to deal with generalities than confront her personal feelings.

"I realize you've never appreciated the opportunities I gave you, but don't assume these children will be so ungrateful. After the difficulties you had—and continue to have—in adjusting to a new life outside the camps, we decided it would be better to raise these children in our care from the start. They will be happy and productive Crib citizens. They'll traverse the Reach a hundred times in their working lives, to the benefit of all citizens." Natesa seemed oblivious to the fact that her choice of words demonstrated exactly the attitude Edie so resented.

"And their entire worth as human beings will be measured by this talent, which *you've* developed and honed. You have no idea what that feels like—to be a pawn instead of a person. Dammit, you even named this planet after her. Do you know what a burden that must be?"

"I'm sorry you feel this way," Natesa said with a sigh. "But I understand. I really do. I tried to protect you, but there were some things I couldn't control. Bethany's violent death. Your bodyguard Lukas—I know he was like a big brother to you, but in the end he let us all down. You used to run away all the time, do you remember that? Even before this whole debacle with the rovers, your loyalty was in question. You caused me many a sleepless night. Colonel Theron's sadism notwithstanding, I intend to avoid that sort of drama with these children. No distractions. No unnecessary outside influences."

Edie read a warning into that. "Is that what you think Finn is? An unnecessary influence on me?"

Natesa's look turned shrewd. "It's clear you've formed a strong attachment to that man. Considering his background, I can't imagine why. But from my perspective, and for the sake of the project, he's an impediment to the mission. If it comes to my attention that he is distracting you, or otherwise undermining your work here, I'll have him thrown in the brig."

"You don't need to threaten us. Finn's not stupid. He'll do his job and stay out of trouble." At least as far as Project Ardra was concerned. The cryptoglyph—that was another matter.

"I do hope so."

Natesa angled her body away from Edie, dismissing her.

"Will you let me know if her condition changes?" Edie said.

"Yes, of course. I don't blame you for this, Edie."

"I don't blame me, either." Her voice sounded oddly flat.

Edie went looking for Finn.

Deck G was built on a scale three times the size of the rest of the ship. The cavernous area accommodated room after room of ag-teck machinery and equipment for building the processing plants and skyhooks.

Edie wandered down noisy corridors and peeked into open hatches. The atmosphere was in stark contrast to the spotless labs where the only sounds were quiet conversations and the whirring of biocyph. Here she dodged oversized machinery and skirted crates and tools lying on the deck.

Just when she thought she might truly be lost, she ran into Winnie, who pointed Edie in Finn's direction. She found him hunkered on the deck surrounded by greasy machinery parts. He looked up sharply, surprised by her sudden entrance.

"Having a bad day?" He must sense that she was upset.

Edie's guilt bit at her, stronger than ever, and stopped her from telling him about Pris. He'd probably call the child a casualty of war, something he had faced a thousand times, and she didn't want to hear that. She drew a breath and tipped her chin at the parts scattered around him.

"What's that?"

"An oscillator from a free-electron laser system. They use it to power the skyhook's climbers."

"What are you doing with it?" Her voice still sounded shaky from lingering emotions.

"Putting it back together. I think Winnie's testing me." But he looked contented enough, surrounded by tools.

"So, is this something you can handle?"

"The work? Sure. It's something to do." He had to raise his voice over the clanging of work going on. "What's wrong?"

She felt like an idiot, bringing her personal hang-ups to him. She put Natesa out of her mind for now.

"Um, can we talk here?"

Despite the activity all around them, Finn's work area was several meters from anyone. Nevertheless, he stood and drew her toward a more private corner behind a bank of floor-to-ceiling consoles.

"Go ahead."

"The lab where I'm working—they have some biocyph equipment that I think I can use with the cryptoglyph."

"To do what?"

"The same thing we planned to do on the Fringe, but remotely." Her mind had been working on an idea for hours. "Create a key that unlocks the BRATs—essentially a piece of crack code that we transmit across the Reach. We fix them all in one fell swoop."

"*That* would be quite an achievement."

"It'll take some time to work out. I need after-hours access to the lab, but I can't use my crew key. If we can steal a crew key from one of the meckies . . ."

Finn looked interested but wary. "Is it worth the risk of being caught?"

"It seems too big of an opportunity to pass up. We have no plan of escape. Natesa's looking for the first opportunity to throw you in the brig. If she does bring in Achaiah or someone to cut the leash, I don't trust her not to break her word and send you back to a labor gang. Anything could happen. At least this way we'll have done what we set out to do—complete the mission."

She knew she was talking his language now. As a soldier, the mission was all that mattered. Still, he looked less enthusiastic than she'd have liked.

"We may have a plan of escape," he said.

"Such as?"

"I was going to wait until this evening to tell you . . ." He looked around, checking for listening ears. Satsified they couldn't be overheard, he said, "There are two Saeth on board this ship."

Edie's jaw dropped. "How do you know?"

He touched his temple. "My chip's giving me a proximity alert. A new group of workers boarded this afternoon and the Saeth were with them."

"Can you communicate with them?"

"No. The Crib destroyed most of my chip when they hijacked it."

"So where are they?"

"I don't know exactly. They must have infiltrated the project. They'll reveal themselves when the time's right."

"Assuming they're here for you."

"I'm going to assume they are. But let's keep our options open and explore your idea of making a crack from here." He looked at her carefully. "Are you okay? You came in here worked up about something."

"I'm fine. There's something else I want to do. I want to contact my old bodyguard, Lukas Pirgot."

"Do you have access to long-range comms?"

"I doubt it. Can you help?"

"Maybe. We can piggyback a call on the ship's routine transmissions."

A short bell sounded in the distance.

"Shift's over," Finn said. "My new buddies here invited me to join them for supper in the mess. Come with me."

She nodded and followed him out.

A dozen or more meckies were all heading in the same direction—to the lifts that took them to the mess on Deck E. Edie stuck close by Finn, wondering at the strange looks she was getting and starting to regret she'd agreed to eat with him. In the mess they walked to the table occupied by Finn's colleagues, and it became even more obvious she didn't belong. She slid onto the bench beside Finn, knowing she was breaking some unwritten rule about teck staff mingling with workers from the lower decks. Still, the looks the workers gave her were mostly friendly curiosity.

While Edie was politely ignored, they talked readily to Finn. He was as laconic as ever and they didn't seem to mind. Edie admired the easy way he slotted into this group.

"How do you do that?" she asked him on the walk back to their suite. "You didn't give them a straight answer to anything. Even I still don't know where you come from. But they treat you like one of them already."

"I am one of them. In that line of work—as long as you get the job done they respect you."

"Why did they ignore me?"

"You're a celebrity."

She hadn't expected that. "I am?"

"Yes. And you're under Natesa, which makes you doubly important. They don't want to say the wrong thing. They don't know what to say."

Edie tried to picture herself from an outside perspective—a highly trained Crib teck using mysterious technology to reshape worlds for colonization . . . Perhaps she'd think cyphertecks were celebrities, too, if she wasn't one.

When they reached Edie's quarters, she was eager to set up a call to Lukas, who resided, at the Crib's pleasure, in a prison camp on Anwynn, a Crib outpost. The disinterested staff member on the other end of the line politely explained that the prisoners' rec time wasn't for another six hours, and that was the only time calls could be received. Edie sent the prison a line of credit so Lukas could call her back.

"What's your boss going to think about this?" Finn asked.

"I already know what she thinks. But it's not a crime to call an old friend."

For the second time in as many minutes, the tom access panel near Edie's bedroom door moved. The first time, she'd ignored it, thinking it was a trick of the light filtering through from Finn's room. Now she wasn't so sure. Sitting up, she tapped the headboard to turn on the wall light-strip. Then the access panel bowed as if pushed from the other side. Perhaps a maintenance tom was stuck inside the tube.

Before she had time to get out of bed, the panel suddenly flipped open and a tiny foot appeared, followed by a thin leg clad in white PJs.

"Galeon!"

The boy climbed out of the access tube and straightened. "Where's Finn?" he demanded. "You told me second door on the right. I counted the panels. So where is he?" Galeon strode over to her bed and pulled back the sheet.

"Hey!" Edie hissed. Much as his behavior amused her, it was hardly appropriate.

Galeon spied the doorway and went for it, and she had no choice but to get out of bed and follow him.

Finn's viewport was open, bathing the room in reflected light from the planet. Finn was already out of bed—he must have heard the commotion and figured things out—and he stood waiting, arms folded. His imposing presence filled the room.

Galeon didn't heed the warning stance or the stern look. "It's time for our game." He pulled a small flat box from his pocket, set it on the table, and switched it on. A holo expanded to reveal a playing board and colored pegs.

Finn looked at Edie, not Galeon, as if waiting for her to fix everything.

"You shouldn't be here," Edie said. "You'll get into trouble."

The boy ignored her, and she glared at Finn. Galeon liked him. Maybe he'd listen to him.

Finn said nothing.

Edie tried again. "Galeon, please. You'll get *Finn* into trouble."

"No, I won't. It's just Pegasaw. One game." He sat cross-legged on the deck and thumbed the controls to set up the board.

"Did you crawl all the way here through the tom access tubes?" Edie asked.

"Not all the way. There's crawl space under the gravplating," he said matter-of-factly. "And there's ladders between the decks, if you know where to look." He glanced at Finn looming over him. "You can go first."

"No. Galeon, I mean it," Edie said. "You have to go back to bed. If anyone—"

"Wait a minute." Finn dropped to his haunches on the opposite side of the table and tapped a peg on the holoviz to shift it into position, which put a wide grin on Galeon's face. "You can get anywhere on the ship from the crawl spaces and access tubes?"

"I don't know about *anywhere*. But lots of places. Except for the top deck."

"How about Deck B? The labs?"

Edie saw where this was going. "Finn, we can't ask him to . . ." Her voice trailed away as Galeon turned a bright-eyed look from Finn to her and back again.

"Ask me to what? I'll do it! I can do anything."

"Why not?" Finn said over the boy.

"That would be using him . . ."

"He knows what he's doing. It's a perfect solution."

"What are you talking about?" Galeon's voice rose in pitch as he tried to get their attention.

Edie bit her lip, shaking her head as she tried to come up with another objection. But those biocyph modules were calling her name. Surely they should take every opportunity.

"Come on, tell me," Galeon whined. "Tell me now or maybe I *won't* do it."

Finn gave Galeon a long appraising look. "I don't know. Maybe you're not the right man for a secret mission."

"I am! I can do a secret mission!"

"Really?" Finn said dryly, and moved another peg. "A *top* secret mission?"

Galeon put on a serious face. "I won't tell *anyone*," he breathed.

"Finn—"

Finn held up his hand to silence Edie. "Let's do a test run, okay? It's worth trying."

Edie ran her hand through her hair, appalled with them both for even thinking of involving a child in this. But if Galeon could get them into that lab, no one would ever know she'd been there.

Edie capitulated. "Okay. Galeon, there's some . . . secret work I need to do at night, in the main lab on Deck B. Can you get there and unlock the door from the inside?"

"Yes, I can do that. When?"

"How about tomorrow night, at about this time?"

"What are you going to do there?" Galeon had lost interest in the game.

"That's need-to-know," Finn said.

"What does that mean?"

"It means it's so top secret that I can't tell you until you need to know."

"But I do need to know!"

"As leader of this mission, I get to decide what you need to know," Finn said. "It's your turn."

They played out the game, Galeon tense with excitement. Edie stared unseeing at the holoviz, paying no attention to the moves. She was ashamed of herself, using Galeon like this, and struggled to accept her justifications.

Finn won a resounding victory, and Edie expected Galeon to sulk about it. But he shook Finn's hand with a grin.

"You're good at this game," Galeon said.

"You played pretty well. Watch your peripheral defense strategies."

"I will. I'll practice."

"Time to go," Edie said, hoping Galeon wouldn't make a fuss.

Galeon tucked the holoviz projector into his pajama pocket and trailed Edie back into her room, then disappeared into the access tube and pulled the panel shut behind.

Edie turned to Finn, who was watching from the doorway. "This is wrong. Using children is what Natesa does."

"We played a game and gave him a fun adventure. According to you, that's not what Natesa does to children."

"Don't you ever look beyond the immediate mission, Finn? You need a job done so you find the most direct way to do it. Don't you ever wonder how the job fits into the big picture?"

"I'm a foot soldier, not a general," he said, as if that explained everything.

"Saving the Fringe worlds is a job for a general."

His eyes narrowed. "There are no generals on the Fringe. That's why our Liberty War turned to shit. Until the Fringers figure out a way to act together, foot soldiers are all they've got."

"I would just like to know if I'm doing the right thing. If the end justifies the means."

"Freeing billions from oppression? That end doesn't need much justification. And your means aren't hurting anyone. The kid will be fine."

CHAPTER 11

Edie's console beeped for her attention.

"That's the call from Anwynn." She slipped into the seat and waited for the sat network to hook up. As she waited, she thought about Finn's attitude. His philosophy didn't quite sit right with her. Galeon might be fine, but Pris was not. Edie couldn't just forget that. Finn's extreme focus on the mission was a useful skill for a Saeth, but he was in the real world now. The plight of the Talasi children, the fate of hundreds of Ardra worlds . . . These problems, under Edie's nose, weren't as easy for her to ignore.

Finn left the room just before the call came through. She was grateful that he respected her privacy. At the same time, she wished he and Lukas could meet. She wanted Finn to know what Lukas had meant to her. She wanted Lukas to know that even though he'd disappeared, she wasn't alone anymore.

A minute later, Lukas came on the line. Edie had a smile ready for him. It failed to materialize when she saw his appearance. He looked dreadful, his gaunt skin pale and tinged with yellow, and around his eyes were purple rings.

"Thought someone was having me on," he said, an eyebrow quirked. "But it's really you." He sounded the same, his gentle gruffness taking her back almost ten years to a time when she was an unreliable teen in awe of Bethany and somewhat afraid of him. He'd been a solid wall of muscle then, even in his midforties. Now his prison garb hung loosely from his shoulders.

Edie swallowed and tried to sound cheerful. "Yes, it's really me. They finally told me where you were."

She didn't have to explain who "they" were. Lukas knew. He'd been a loyal Crib citizen all his life, and a decorated milit, but he knew Edie's feelings about the Crib.

"So, here I am, missy," he said.

"Lukas . . ." Edie's voice cracked from the strain of seeing his desperate situation. "*Why* are you there? They told me you'd turned traitor. I know it can't be true."

Lukas shifted in his seat. "Where are you? The trace here's telling me you're on a Crib ship."

"Yes. I had a little adventure over the past year, but I'm back with CCU now. Tell me what happened."

"Well, I raised some objections all those years ago, and your boss Natesa didn't like that."

"Objections to what?"

"After Bethany died . . ." He cleared his throat, started again. "After I took over guarding you, I guess I took more notice of what the program was doing to you. I made . . . complaints. They hired me to protect you and I tried to do that. Seems they didn't want me to be anything more than a bullet-stopper. Natesa didn't want to know. Then I found out she was going after the Talasi kids. Wanted more cyphertecks just like you for her big project. That was the last straw."

"So they got rid of you to shut you up?"

"That's about it. Called me a traitor and shipped me here."

"I was afraid it was something like that. I only just found out about Natesa's school, and realized they set it up about the same time you disappeared. At the time they told me you'd retired. It all happened so suddenly. One day you were just gone."

"Sorry it turned out this way. But it's not so bad here, you know. I got married."

"Really?"

"Three years ago. Her name's Beria. She takes care of me."

Edie had to ask the obvious question. "Are you ill?"

"Some degenerative thing. I have good days and bad." Edie didn't want to ask which today was. Lukas looked barely strong enough to hold himself upright in the chair. "They've got me on meds and it helps. Doc says I'll be around for a good many years."

"Are they going to let you out?"

He lifted his shoulders in a shrug. "I don't know. But I've got Beria. Life is good."

His perspective was incomprehensible to Edie. While she fumed at yet another Crib injustice, his entire world had shrunk to one woman.

"Don't give up, Lukas."

"Me? Of course not. But I've accepted things." He leaned forward. "What about you, missy? Are you staying out of trouble?"

Possible answers flooded Edie's head. She'd been kidnapped, run with rovers, turned a distant planet into a mutated disaster, and now she planned to undermine the Crib by liberating the Fringe worlds. No, she hadn't stayed out of trouble.

But Lukas didn't need to know any of that. The last thing she wanted was to make him worry. He'd protected her, and now she'd protect him.

"Trying to," she said. "Natesa has me working on an experimental project to terraform advanced ecosystems."

"Project Ardra. I knew about it from Bethany."

"Seems to be yet another way to feed the Crib's greed."

"Is that what you think Ardra is?"

"What do you mean?"

Lukas looked away, troubled, as if waging an internal battle over whether to say something. When he didn't respond, Edie changed the subject.

"I have a new bodyguard, Finn." Not strictly true—Finn wasn't her bodyguard anymore, but she wanted Lukas to know she was safe.

"Hmm. A milit?"

"No." Feeling bold, and because she thought it might appeal to Lukas's sense of humor, she added, "He fought for the other side."

Lukas's face grew animated for the first time and his brow rose with interest. "How did that happen?"

"Long story."

"I've got something to say to him. Put him on."

Edie bit her lip. She didn't want to force Finn into this, but she couldn't deny Lukas. "Hang on."

She got up and put her head around the doorway. Finn lay on the couch in the dark. His face was turned toward her and he was awake.

"Lukas wants to meet you."

Finn frowned, but followed her back to her room. He leaned over the console to put himself in Lukas's view.

"So you're her bullet-stopper now," Lukas said brusquely. "She said you fought in the Reach Conflicts. Who'd you fight for?"

It was the same question as *What planet are you from?* The Fringe worlds had never really managed to put together a cohesive allied force during the Reach Conflicts, so for the most part each planet fought for itself. Except for the Saeth, of course, and Edie didn't imagine Finn would reveal that.

"You mean *what* did I fight for. I fought for independence in the Liberty War," Finn said, using the Fringers' term for that conflict. He managed to inject some bitterness into his words, a reminder to Lukas that they'd been enemies over that goal.

Lukas's eyes narrowed, as if he was deciding how to put the younger man in his place. Edie was relieved when he kept his tone light. "Well, congratulations, son. You won."

Edie knew that wouldn't go down well. Despite the treaties that guaranteed no Crib interference, the Fringe worlds would never have real independence until they no longer had to rely on Crib technology to maintain their worlds.

Finn had cast his eyes down, formulating a response. Eventually he looked up and said, quietly, "I would say I'm still fighting for it."

Lukas looked grim, but to Edie's surprise there was understanding in his eyes. Like her, he surely felt disillusioned by the Crib after what they'd done to him. Edie had the sudden urge to tell him about the cryptoglyph, to explain her grand plans to help the Fringers and dismantle the Crib's stranglehold. To make him proud of her. But she couldn't be sure this conversation wasn't being monitored. If the Crib found out about the cryptoglyph, they'd destroy it. The lives of billions of people—current and future generations—depended on keeping it secret.

"Okay, I've got two things to say to you," Lukas said to Finn.

"Go ahead," Finn said warily.

"Come to think of it, I guess I don't have to tell you this first one. Don't trust the Crib."

"Never have."

"There's more going on than they've told her."

"Such as?"

"No," Edie broke in. "Lukas, I don't want you getting into trouble."

"More trouble than this?" He grinned, revealing a gappy row of yellowing teeth. "I'm not afraid to speak out, you know that. Here's what they won't tell you. There's widespread famine across the older Central planets. That's why the Crib relies increasingly on resources from the Fringe. It's not greed so much as necessity."

Edie stared at the holoviz. "Famine? That's impossible. Those are the richest, most abundant worlds in the Reach."

"They *were*. Listen, they'd talked about this around Bethany years ago, when you were just a kid, Edie. Something's been going wrong with the biocyph on the Central worlds. The way Bethany explained it to me, biocyph just can't maintain the Terran ideal for more than a few centuries. It picks up too many errors. Failure is inevitable. Their ecosystems are falling apart. The older the world, the worse it's affected."

"How is Project Ardra supposed to fix it?"

"It doesn't fix it. It provides resources to prop up those worlds. That's all. And no one really knows there's a problem, see. The Crib manages to cover it up by extorting resources out of the Fringe worlds. When crops fail, the government imports food. When the air degrades, they install expensive environment jigglers. Ardra will provide a new influx of resources."

"But that means . . ." Edie's mind raced ahead. "Lukas, they're using accelerated biocyph to terraform Prisca, the first Ardra world. If failure is inevitable, the Ardra worlds will fail a hundred times faster. They'll only get a few years' use out of those worlds before they turn to mash." If the biomass of an entire Ardra world turned to mash . . . Edie shuddered at the thought of a planet covered meters-deep in the gray sludge of rotting biomatter.

Lukas's expression settled into a deep frown. "If you want advice from me, I can't give it. I'm just a simple soldier. Served the Crib for twenty-five years. Then I said the wrong thing to the wrong 'crat and I ended up here. I don't want to see you heading the same way. Now I didn't tell you about this so you can get yourself into trouble trying to fix it. I just want you to be aware that they lie."

"I knew that." She just hadn't expected Natesa to keep her quite so much in the dark. Not just her—billions of Crib citizens were being deceived, unaware that their future was so close to being extinguished.

"I have to get going, but I'm going to tell you the second thing." Lukas returned his attention to Finn while Edie dragged herself up from depressing thoughts. "You're a soldier like me, so I know you'll understand. Keep your mind on the job. You got that?"

Edie winced. Lukas was talking about himself and Bethany, about their relationship that distracted Lukas and—as far as he was concerned—resulted in Bethany's death. Edie and Finn had already started down that path. Only the leash was stopping them.

But Finn said, "Yes, sir," without a hint of shame.

"And you take good care of her." Lukas's voice took on the gruffness that Edie recognized as coming from deep-seated emotion. "She was a touch delinquent as a kid. Looks to me like she turned out okay. Don't let her out of your sight."

Finn gave a curt nod while Edie's eyes welled up at the familiar refrain. During the years Lukas had protected Bethany, and then Edie, it had been his way of reassuring them they were safe in his care.

"Do you need anything?" she asked him. "Creds? Anything at all?"

Lukas waved a mottled hand in a dismissive gesture. "I'm doing fine. Working half-shifts right now. I've got watered-down beer twice a week and I've got Beria." His face flickered with pain—physical or emotional, Edie couldn't tell. "Don't you worry about me. And don't call again, missy. This time-out's using up my rec chits and I need 'em to pay for the beer."

She smiled at his admonishment. "Okay. I won't. Not for a while, anyway. Good luck, Lukas."

He nodded and cut the link.

"What am I supposed to do?" Edie said, more to herself. She felt more helpless than ever. The more she found out about Ardra, the worse it got.

Finn straightened. "The fate of Crib worlds isn't your problem."

"It's not just Crib worlds. Humans have based their expansion into the Reach on doomed technology. The Fringe worlds are a few centuries younger, but eventually their biocyph will fail, too."

Finn had nothing reassuring to say. "I'm a little too preoccupied with my own survival until tomorrow to worry about humanity's survival centuries into the future."

* * *

Natesa had her reasons for keeping the truth from Edie, and Edie didn't want to reveal that it was Lukas who had told her—despite his assurances that he didn't care, she wasn't going to risk Natesa's wrath or give the woman a reason to check her comm logs. But there was a way to "discover" most of the information for herself. She accessed Caleb's sims and spent the morning running one in particular. It showed how the terraforming should proceed, using his new regulator code. It showed the installation of ag-teck and the billions of kilos of food the planet's biomass would create at a rate of several crop yields per standard year. She forced the sim to cycle through several years until . . .

There it was. Beyond ten years, the sim predicted increasingly erratic biocyph behavior, critical errors so pervasive that a ship full of cyphertecks could never hope to keep up with them, let alone the BRATs' own self-correcting programs.

Every planet touched by Project Ardra was doomed.

She slapped her palmet on the desk in front of Caleb, its holo showing a late-stage sim of the planet below them.

"How long is this sustainable?" she asked, her voice tight with anger.

"Ah, you've found my sims. Those are the pinnacle of a lifetime's work, you know."

"I'm sure you're very proud of them. How many people can one planet feed before it rots forever, Caleb?"

"A world with Prisca's biomass can feed ten billion people."

"There are over two hundred billion people on the Central planets. You'll need to terraform twenty Ardra worlds every decade. Even assuming they all work, which is unlikely, where will you find all these planets? The project's specs have only identified two other suitable candidates."

"Two planets *in this sector*. We start local. In theory there are almost a hundred planets within a suitable distance that should have the required level of ecosystem complexity for—"

"A hundred planets? That's only fifty years of food, not allowing for any population increase. Then what? What happens after you've turned every living planet in the Reach into mash? Where will we live then? What will we eat?"

Was this really the future for humanity?

"Fifty years is a long time. We'll have come up with a more viable solution by then." At Edie's incredulous scowl, he added, "People are dying *now*, Edie. Perhaps you don't realize this is an emergency situation. Okay, not your fault—the Crib has hushed it up to avoid panic. But we've already had fifty years of decreasing output across Crib Central planets, each year worse than the last. We had to do something now. Especially with the Fringe worlds closing in."

"What do you mean?"

"Why do you think the Crib was so keen to sign those independence treaties in the end? They'd just found out that the Fringe worlds were affected by the same problem."

"But those worlds are newer. Some of them are centuries newer. Why is their biocyph already failing?"

"We don't know. All we can say is that the output indicators we use to measure productivity are declining there, too. And a lot sooner, in relative terms, than happened on Central planets. The point is, the Crib didn't want to be saddled with the responsibility of taking care of the entire Fringe. It was happy to cut them loose."

"Just as long as they were forced to keep providing resources, under threat of extermination."

Caleb shrugged. "You come up with a better solution to this entire mess, I'm sure there's a 'crat somewhere who'll listen. Just remember, most Crib 'crats sit around pretending it's not happening. Natesa spent years convincing Central to give Ardra a shot, and they're still looking for any excuse to shut down the program because it's too expensive or too ambitious or just because they don't much like Natesa."

"What happens if Ardra fails?"

"If this world fails, most likely they'll cancel the entire program. There isn't enough support at Central to get a second chance. And if the program's canceled, the Crib will keep doing what it's always done—it'll take what it needs from the Fringe worlds."

CHAPTER 12

As Edie made her way to the classroom, she gave Caleb's words serious thought—for perhaps the first time, she was seriously considering the other side of the argument regarding Ardra. There must be another solution. There had to be. But until then . . . was this the best option? If the cryptoglyph freed the Fringe worlds and the Crib could no longer extort resources from them, the Central planets would need Ardra worlds in order to survive.

That the Fringe worlds were also suffering the same output decline was the most worrisome part of the whole situation. Unlocking the BRATs wouldn't solve that. The Fringe worlds were apparently still doomed to suffer ecosystem degradation and famine in their future. The cryptoglyph would free the Fringers from oppression and make the next few decades more bearable, but it couldn't ultimately save their worlds.

Aila was pleased to see her. She wanted Edie to jack in with the children to look at some recent problems they'd been tackling. She directed the children to the projector in the center of the room.

"Take your seats, everyone. Edie is going to work with you this afternoon."

"But we need Pris for that," Raena said.

"Edie can take her place."

The children looked at her with expectant faces, and Edie forced a smile.

"I'll hook up the holoviz, although the children don't really use it," Aila said. "It's the only guide I have to assess what they're doing."

Edie nodded. She, too, didn't need the visuals but understood that most cyphertecks did.

The holoviz extruded a coil of lights that swirled in a treacly tornado of data, representing a subsection of Prisca's ecosystem. The children paid no attention to it. Sitting in a circle around the projector, they touched their fingers to the ports and closed their eyes. Edie sat in the empty spot in the ring and jacked in with them.

The datastream flowed through the wires in her fingertips, up her arm, along her spine, and into her wet-teck interface. Her instant impression was that of losing her footing. She slipped and tumbled into the datastream, and chaos closed in from every side. She concentrated on making sense of the cacophony. Somewhere deep beneath the noise, a high-pitched note sang out. She raced between the tiers and followed it. It nudged her away, as if trying to redirect her. Other similar notes, all the same pitch but with different frequencies mixed in, surfaced above the hubbub.

Three notes. These were the children, and they didn't want her following them. They wanted her to take her assigned place. She observed them for a few seconds and realized where she belonged. Each child moved in a different tier, and as soon as she dropped into place on her tier, the notes blossomed into a rich chord.

The tiers had ragged edges, representing the areas of Prisca's ecosystem that had not properly evolved toward the target ideal. Had she been working alone, she'd have tackled each tier one by one. But she could see the impossibility of the task: there was too much to keep track of in an ecosystem this complex. Fixing one tier would cause a rip in another, and no cypherteck could work fast enough to tidy everything up.

The children hopped from tier to tier, swapping places to maintain control of each one while helping one another patch up the broken areas. They composed riffs to slot into place and tied loose areas together with glyphs to stop the cracks spreading. Edie was fascinated as she listened to their music.

She opened her eyes and found Galeon staring at her from his opposite place in the circle, through the colored lights swirling between them. He was frowning. Edie's first thought was that it had something to do with their encounter last night. Then Raena, beside her, nudged her with her elbow and Edie concentrated again on the datastream. They were annoyed that she wasn't doing her part.

She closed her eyes and tried to join in, jumping from tier to tier to see what needed to be done. It wasn't working. The children curved away from her, like repelling magnets. She was being too assertive. She had to work *with* them. She relaxed and let their music flow through her splinter.

Now she saw how they aligned themselves around the datastream to form a diamond-shaped funnel. From these positions they plucked at the edges of the datastream as it flowed past, like a piano tuner listening for bum notes. Edie had been resisting taking up her position in the diamond formation because it didn't feel right to her. The fourth vertex—hers—was bent out of shape, making the funnel waver.

She fell into place to form a perfect diamond, and heard that pure chord chime again. She sensed the buzz of excitement among the children as they recognized the change. What had felt like a disorganized jumping around between the tiers was now a single machine with four cogs turning in unison, each moving its neighbor and being moved in turn by another to create a circle of motion.

Edie lost her sense of time. The music no longer moved with beats and rhythm. Now it flowed as a continuous stream and she was part of the structure holding it together. The diamond melded together the ripped tiers, dropped notes into the broken chords, perfected the melody as it cascaded along.

When it was completed, she felt the diamond disintegrating. The children pulled away and jacked out. Edie wanted to hold on to it. Her mind couldn't maintain the shape and the diamond wilted and crumbled. She had no choice but to let it go.

She opened her eyes and pulled her hand clear, and the datastream dripped away. Galeon grinned at her.

"She figured us out," Racna said. She sounded a little peeved but was smiling.

"Amazing," Aila said. She'd watched the visual sim of the datastream. "That's very promising."

The other girl, Hanna, didn't look as pleased as the others. "I want Pris to come back."

"*She's* just as good," Raena scolded.

"Pris's better," Galeon said, a challenge in his voice.

Edie sensed the tension among the children and felt like an intruder. They'd only known such harmony while working together, without an outsider—and had created an us-against-them mentality. They were only children, but it was their source of power.

She understood that. She'd been one of them, years ago. The only Talasi in the seeding program—the only child, in fact, and the only cypherteck with a perfect record. That elitism had imbued her with a certain power, which forced Natesa to overlook her attitude problems, her running away, and later, her refusal to cooperate on Ardra. Natesa had no choice but to find ways around her reluctance.

Edie saw no apparent evidence that these children abused their position as vital parts of the seeding team. It was unlikely they even understood their importance to the project, yet they must have recognized that no one else could do what they could do. Until now.

"After what I've seen today," Aila said, "I'm going to ask permission from Administrator Natesa for you to spend the afternoons in the classroom. You can sit in for Pris until she's well again, and help the children with the error logs."

"Are you sure I have the clearance for that?" Edie said, trying to keep the sarcasm light because the children were listening.

"We'll work something out."

Natesa stood behind her chair, fingers clasping the back of it in a white-knuckled grip. "I'm granting Aila's request. I can't say Caleb's happy about it, but we need your help in the classroom for a while."

"Why would Caleb be unhappy? He'd rather grind me under his heel than accept I have something to offer the project?"

"Caleb is something of an eccentric. I make it my business to ignore his personality quirks as long as he gets the job done. Besides, his happiness is not the issue. We do need your help. I will upgrade your clearance accordingly."

"It's about time. I already figured out a few things you've been keeping from me. Such as the famines on Central worlds. And the declining output indicators across the Crib *and* the Fringe."

"Well!" Natesa sighed. "I don't have to remind you that that information is highly sensitive. The last thing we need is mass panic. But at least now you understand how serious things are, and how important Ardra is."

"What I understand is that Ardra is a band-aid solution, and you don't have a clue about the root cause of the problem."

"We have entire departments at CCU devoted to solving exactly that mystery. However, our job at Project Ardra is to feed the people."

"And in the process, destroy every living planet across the Reach."

"We're doing what we must." Natesa fiddled with a pile of datacaps on her desk. "As for what *you* must do, it's important that you get up to speed on the children's work. The error logs generated by the biocyph on Prisca are increasing. Caleb Chessell can't explain it. He assures me it's nothing to worry about, but we need to nip it in the bud."

"Maybe his regulator code that's boosting the biocyph is the problem. I'm sure he hasn't considered that, but have you?"

Natesa all but rolled her eyes at Edie's heavy sarcasm. "There's nothing wrong with his code. For twenty years his sims have been lauded by CCU for their predictive accuracy. Those sims with this new code are perfectly adequate for our purposes."

Perfectly adequate—it wasn't exactly a stellar commendation.

"But you're saying Theron's sources are correct—there are problems with the terraforming."

Natesa turned to gaze at the garden held captive behind a plaz wall. Edie got the sense she was avoiding eye contact—avoiding Edie altogether, which was highly unusual behavior from this woman. "Areas of the ecosystem on certain continents are not as healthy as we'd like," Natesa said. "But Theron is seriously misinformed. Naturally he wants to magnify the problem and shut us down, regardless of the importance of the project. He believes military might can solve everything. But rifles and battlecruisers don't increase harvest yields, do they?" She spun around, her lips a tight line as if she wished to take back what she'd said. "There's nothing to worry about. I'm sending Chessell dirtside to oversee operations there. I have every confidence in him, and in the children's ability to handle the increased workload."

Edie wasn't so sure. Boosted terraforming was just a bad idea. But she wasn't going to sweat over it. She wasn't here to make waves. She was here to work for Finn's safety and freedom.

"Have you applied for Finn's freedom papers yet?"

Natesa closed her eyes for a moment and drew a lungful of air in through her nostrils. "Any other loyal citizen of the

Crib with a binding contract wouldn't dream of trading her cooperation for these little personal favors."

"Don't minimize this, Natesa. Freeing Finn isn't only personal. It's justice."

"And it means nothing in the grand scheme of things!" Natesa closed her eyes again for another deep breath, calming herself down. "I have set things in motion. It takes time. I assure you that if and when the leash is cut, he will be immediately removed from this ship. Meanwhile, you have work to do helping to make this project a success."

And Edie had work to do on her own project, too.

Edie pulled a biocyph module off the rack and set it on the lab counter. Across the room, Galeon had already engaged Finn in a game of Pegasaw. The boy had come through for them, finding his way to the lab that night to unlock the hatch from the inside.

As Edie's hand brushed the port of the module, she was again struck by the immense potential at her fingertips. She'd never even dreamed she'd have access to stock biocyph. The plan had been to journey to the Fringe with Finn, visiting each planet one by one to use the cryptoglyph. Stock biocyph would enable her to use the cryptoglyph remotely. With this unit, no bigger than a football, along with the algorithm stored in Finn's chip, she intended to create a master key that would forever change the political and economical structure of the Reach.

And could start a war. *Another* war. Finn had warned her about that, but they'd decided to go ahead and use the cryptoglyph anyway. And when she'd told Finn of her discovery that the Fringe worlds' biocyph was failing just like that on the Central worlds, his response had been to reassure her that this was worth trying.

"You can only do what you can do," he'd said. "You don't have to save the galaxy."

There was no hesitation on her part. It wasn't just the

plight of the Fringers that motivated Edie. The opportunity to thumb her nose at the Crib was tempting in its own right.

She jacked in. The biocyph's orderly tiers hummed with expectation. She'd thought long and hard about how she was going to do this, and now it was time to try. The tiers flowing through her splinter felt slippery. She used glyphs to pin them down, working on instinct because this was new to her. She'd never worked with the untrained, meandering music of stock biocyph before. Time stood still, as it always did when she was immersed this deeply in the datastream. Her mind grew used to the rhythms so that her intense concentration became automatic.

The first stage was relatively simple—create a generic biocyph lock that mimicked those of the Fringe BRATs. Edie tapped into the *Learo Dochais*'s archival files for that. But something was wrong. As she tried to code the lock into the datastream, the tiers slid out from under her. She complexity of the lock wouldn't mesh with the empty tiers.

If she couldn't get this right, there was no hope of continuing.

She tried again, emptying her mind of distractions and focusing on the biocyph as it buzzed through her mind. When the datastream fell away yet again, like water trickling through a sieve, she grunted in frustration.

She opened her eyes and found herself looking into Finn's. He sat opposite her, and she had the feeling he'd been watching her for a while. The nape of her neck was hot and damp, and her legs were cramping.

"Something wrong?"

She nodded. "It's too much for me to handle. I can't set up the biocyph lock. Without it, there's nothing for the cryptoglyph to crack."

"Try again."

"I've tried. The problem is that stock biocyph is empty. It's like trying to attach a lock to a nonexistent door. It won't stick."

"Do you have to use stock biocyph?"

"Yes. If I put the lock on programmed biocyph, the cryptoglyph will simply unlock it, and only it. I'm trying to make a master key here. I didn't realize the stock biocyph would be so slippery." Edie sat back in her seat, feeling defeated. "*Damn.* I don't know how to make this work."

Galeon wandered over. "Are you working on the top secret mission?"

"Yes." Edie put a finger to her lips. "And we can't talk about it, okay?"

"Are we going to play again?" He thrust the holo under Finn's nose, showing that he'd been working through some moves by himself.

"In a minute," Finn said with infinite patience. "So what next?" he asked Edie.

She stared at Galeon until the boy grew uncomfortable and pulled a face at her. "Maybe I need some help," she said. "I have an idea."

CHAPTER 13

Edie set the biocyph module on Aila's desk. "I'm curious to see what the children make of this."

Aila didn't bat an eyelid that Edie had the expensive equipment—after all, it came from the lab where she worked. Edie was counting on her lack of curiosity. Every day, Caleb sent the children a new set of tasks. Today, Edie's first official day working with them in the classroom, she had slotted in one of her own.

The children tackled Caleb's work with their usual disciplined enthusiasm. They were more accepting of Edie this time when she joined in, and that made her feel guilty. Not because she intended to deceive them—they would no more understand the biocyph lock than they understood Caleb's isolated data from Prisca. In any case, it was Aila and CCU she was deceiving. No, it was because their single-mindedness forced her to realize that this work, the datastream, was all they had and it fulfilled them. Edie hadn't wanted to become emotionally involved with the children. There was nothing she could do to help them. But as she watched their young minds being shaped and harnessed by the Crib, already to the point that they could imagine no other life, the desire to save them grew stronger with each passing hour.

"It keeps running away!" Raena said with a giggle.

They'd reached Edie's task at last. Jacked into the biocyph module, which itself was new territory for them, they spent a few minutes jumping across the tiers as though it were a fascinating new playground. They found the tiers slippery just as Edie had, and she corralled them into their diamond formation to funnel the datastream. The biocyph lock floated free where Edie had left it, impossible to pin down. Now she had help. She nudged the lock into place and sensed the children examining it, prodding it, trying to figure it out.

"We need to embed it in the tiers," Edie said. "Let's see if we can do it."

"What *is* it?" Hanna said, poking at the edges with a quickly constructed seeker. "I can't see inside it."

"It's ugly and mean," Galeon declared.

"Is it broken? Should we fix it?" Raena, asked.

"Yes, we need to fix it," Edie said. She spun the biocyph lock to show them the glyphs she'd attached to it. "Grab the glyphs and attach them to the tiers."

Edie felt the difference as soon as they made the attempt. With the datastream under control this time, the lock was easier to hold as they aligned it to the tiers. The lock shuddered in their grasp when it touched the tiers, sending out jagged notes that distorted the perfect hum of the raw biocyph's untainted song. Then it slotted into place, spiraling around the tiers in a brief moment of chaos and cacophony. It froze in formation, an insoluble jumble of code that held captive the empty stock biocyph.

Raena looked unhappy. "Did we fix it or make it worse?"

"What's it for?" Hanna asked. "It doesn't do anything."

"You did great," Edie said. "And it's not meant to do anything. It was just an exercise."

Just an exercise . . . As Edie left the classroom, module tucked safely under her arm, she wondered what Aila would say if she knew what the children had just done. Or more specifically, what Edie intended to do with what they'd just done.

* * *

She'd barely had time to return the module to the lab when her palmet signaled she had an incoming call on her personal console. From Anwynn.

She raced back to her quarters, only to find it was a prerecorded message. And it wasn't from Lukas.

A middle-aged woman with kind, sad eyes and weathered skin peered into the holoviz.

"Edie, I'm Beria, Lukas's wife. I'm so sorry to have to tell you that he died last night."

The simple words struck Edie like a bodily blow. She staggered into the seat at her console. *He died . . . he died . . .* Her mind repeated the phrase, washing out all other thoughts, until she realized Beria was still talking.

"He talked about you often, Edie, and he was so thrilled to hear from you." Beria looked down at her tightly clasped hands resting on the console on the other side of the Reach. "He was sick, as you know. He seemed to be doing well on the meds, but . . . he had a sudden seizure. It's never happened before. It was very quick."

Beria still hadn't looked up. Edie felt like her blood had turned to icy sludge, like it was struggling to push oxygen through her body. *It's never happened before.* Now those words started repeating in her mind.

Beria composed herself and looked up. Her eyes had taken on a desperate, haunted look that broke Edie's heart.

"Edie, take care of yourself. He told me before he died that he wanted the very best for you."

Beria's face faded as the message ended. For a few minutes Edie could only sit slumped in her seat, riding out the shock.

He had a sudden seizure. It's never happened before.

She felt the truth to the core of her soul: Natesa had had Lukas killed. Because he'd said too much, or because Natesa resented his influence over Edie, or . . .

A second realization hit at the same time—she could never prove it. Natesa would never admit it. And accusing

Natesa would get her nowhere. Lukas was dead and there was nothing she could do to get justice for him.

And if Natesa could kill Lukas that easily, she could kill Finn, too. There were so many ways. An "accident" with the rigs where he worked. An "accidental" separation beyond the leash's boundary that triggered the bomb in his head. Execution for kidnapping a Crib citizen—Natesa had made it clear that was still on the table. Or if the leash was cut, she could send him away and hire an assassin and Edie would never even know. Finn would disappear, and she'd never know if he was dead or alive.

She had to warn him.

She ran though the busy, noisy workrooms and alcoves and hangars on Deck G, pushing past workers, winding her way around equipment, barely seeing the organized chaos around her, ignoring shouted warnings to *slow down* and *watch out*. She couldn't find him. Reason kicked in at last and she stopped at a general access console to check the scheduling. Finn was assigned to the loading bay today. She was going the wrong way.

She backtracked, forcing herself to walk at a steady pace. It was only then she noticed that she was being followed. The same stocky man in utility coveralls always seemed to be nearby, a few steps ahead of her or a few steps behind. Checking equipment, clearing walkways, greeting other workers with brief words . . . He was always there.

Immediately her thoughts went to her illegal activities with the crack. Her guilty conscience heightened her awareness—more than likely making her paranoid. How could a utility worker know what she was up to? She'd returned the biocyph module to the lab, moving it to a rear rack so no one would use it for a long while. She'd carefully timed her visits to the lab and was certain no one had seen her with the module—but even if they had, Aila had remained unsuspicious, so her story about a random exercise for the children should hold.

No, this man must be coincidentally going in the same

direction. He was simply taking his time, pausing to chat along the way. When she took a deliberate wrong turn and he didn't follow, she breathed a sigh of relief.

But when she looked back again, she saw that he'd headed down the corridor leading to the loading bay. Was he after Finn instead? Alarm bells went off in her head, tensing every muscle in her body. Natesa had dealt with Lukas . . . now she was after Finn.

Edie turned on her heel and hurried down the same corridor. She heard a man's voice, low and accented, and Finn's reply. She followed the sounds around another corner.

Finn and the man clasped forearms in a manner that signified more than just a formal greeting. It was a show of comradeship. Despite their physical differences, this man and Finn were mirror images. The same bearing, the same expressions of mutual respect even though they appeared never to have met before.

This, then, was one of the Saeth. Edie hung back, feeling silly for being paranoid, feeling ill equipped to deal with this moment while Lukas's death was so fresh in her mind.

As she watched the men interact, the truth unfolded before her eyes. Finn belonged with the Saeth. Lukas's future had been stripped away years ago, as had hers, but Finn had a life to return to. Their two worlds had nothing in common. For one ridiculous, selfish moment she hoped the leash would never be cut and she could have him near forever, whether in her world or his.

She caught Finn's eye over the man's shoulder. He, noticing Finn's attention was elsewhere, turned quickly. He didn't seem surprised to see Edie.

"She's with me," Finn said.

The man nodded, and Edie could see he already knew that.

"We wanted to catch the two of you together," he said. "That's why I followed you here."

"We?"

As the query left her lips, Edie sensed someone coming

up behind her. Finn's expression changed as he saw who it was. A tall woman brushed past Edie, her confident stride exuding both power and sensuality as she approached Finn. All Edie saw from the back was shiny auburn hair, neatly bobbed, and the same meckies' coveralls that everyone else on the deck wore—she somehow made them look like high fashion.

"Jaron Solfinn Atellus," the woman murmured.

For a moment Edie thought she was addressing the other man. But she had eyes only for Finn. *Jaron Solfinn Atellus.* Finn's real name. Edie had never heard it before.

Finn drew in a breath and let it out shakily. Edie felt the emotion pouring off him as surely as if the leash's interference worked in the opposite direction. As she watched the two of them greet each other with the same handshake, she knew at once who this was.

There was a woman, Finn had once told her. *Because of her, I took up a cause.*

Edie remembered the pang of jealousy she'd felt when he first told her, and now it returned with a vengeance. This woman was the reason Finn had joined the Saeth. This was his former lover, who had held so much influence over him as a younger man. Even ignoring her physical perfection, which wasn't easy, Edie sensed a seductive charm rolling off the woman. No wonder Finn had followed her, and fallen for her.

"It's just Finn now." There was a tightness to Finn's voice that Edie had never heard before. She couldn't tell if it was nerves or wariness or something else—in any case, it signaled a deep emotional response.

"Finn. Short and sweet. I like it." The woman turned to include Edie in the group, her dark-rose lips still curved in the affectionate smile she had bestowed on Finn. Her clear aqua eyes, highlighted with a smudge of black makeup, were mesmerizing. "So this is Edie Sha'nim."

Finn jerked his head at the woman. "Edie, this is Valari Zael." His eyes were narrowed in concern as he looked at

Edie. Her shock and grief, transmitted down the leash as indefinable white noise, were making him uncomfortable.

The other man watched the reunion with interest. He had an easy smile on his face where Edie felt her own expression had frozen. He held out a hand to her.

"And I'm Corinth."

Edie drifted forward a couple of steps, feeling out of her depth among three Saeth. She shook Corinth's hand in the normal manner, and then Valari's. She wanted them gone. She wanted to tell Finn about Lukas and warn him about Natesa. But these two people were their only hope of rescue.

"How did you find Finn?" she asked, because she couldn't think of anything else to say.

"The Saeth picked up a signal from your chip a few weeks ago," Valari said, turning back to Finn, "when you passed through an area of space that we routinely monitor. Blind luck. By the time we got to the *Lichfield*, they'd taken you. But we noticed a woman listed as part of your group, so we took her and—"

"You found Cat?" Edie broke in.

"Caterina Carmel, yes." That was Cat's new ident. "We thawed her out and got the full story from her."

Cat under a Saeth spotlight. That couldn't have been pretty.

"Is she okay?"

"She was somewhat uncooperative at first. Rather abrasive, actually."

"She's not *that* bad," Cornith said, addressing Finn. "Anyway, she wants the same thing we all want—to get you out of here."

"Once we figured out where they were taking you, we used our resources to infiltrate Project Ardra," Valari explained. "I volunteered for the assignment, of course, and chose Corinth as my second. And here we are, a couple of meckies with the appropriate security clearances. I work here on Deck G. As a utility teck, Corinth has wider access on the ship." Her startling eyes went from cool professional to soft concern in an instant. "We thought you died with your men five years ago."

"The Crib put me on a labor gang as a lifer, tied my chip to a boundary marker to keep me in place," Finn explained.

"Yes, we could tell from our remote scan there was something wrong with your chip. That's why Corinth is here. He's the best teck we have."

"Edie's a cypherteck," Finn said. "She broke the boundary link—that's not the problem." He looked at Edie, signaling her to continue by tipping his chin.

Edie pushed back thoughts of Lukas for now, as well as questions about Cat. "Rovers kidnapped me and forced Finn along for the ride with a leash," she said. "They linked his chip to mine to turn him into my bodyguard. If we're separated by two thousand meters, his chip explodes."

"Have you tried cutting that link?" Corinth asked.

"No. It's a biocyph lock. Unbreakable."

"I have some biocyph experience. I'll give it a shot."

"You have a wet-teck interface?"

He shook his head. "I use a dry–wet interface. I know that doesn't impress you," he added quickly, "but I'm pretty good."

A dry–wet interface was like using a fork to eat soup. Sometimes it gave you a different perspective on a problem, but it couldn't in and of itself come close to what a cypherteck's wet-teck interface could do. Edie doubted it would work when she'd failed.

"I did make an attempt. The bomb is integrated into his chip," she said. "Messing with it could kill him."

"I understand." Corinth looked at Finn. "It's up to you, of course."

Finn was still focused on Edie. He nodded slowly. "Can't hurt to take a look."

"I want to be there. To help. To make sure nothing goes wrong," Edie said. To her ears, her voice sounded lame. Desperate. She wondered if it was obvious to the others how she felt about Finn, and how ridiculous and irrelevant those feelings now seemed to her. She wasn't Finn's future—these people were.

Valari laid her hand on Finn's arm. "Well, let's not count on anything. We don't leave a brother behind—we're here to get you out." And because of the leash, Edie, too. Edie wasn't at all sure how Valari felt about that. "Now, we may be undercover but we signed a couple of those lovely Crib contracts. Walking out of here means going AWOL, and there are a bunch of milits on this ship ready to stop us doing that. But we have back-up out there."

"How many of us are left?" Finn asked.

"Perhaps more than you might expect. We've kept a low profile and we haven't been idle—there's a great deal of work to do. Largely incognito, of course. It's still the case that almost no one trusts the Saeth. I'm heavily involved in relocating refugees, which is actually more PR work than anything."

"You took your time coming forward," Finn said, without accusation. He just wanted to know why.

"Because of Edie," Valari said. "We knew the Crib picked you up together. Then we found out she was a cypherteck for the Crib. We weren't sure what the connection was between the two of you. To be honest, we didn't realize at first— didn't *expect*—that she was on your side."

"I'm on his side," Edie said firmly. "And I'm not here because I want to be."

Valari nodded. "We know that now. We spent a few days gathering information."

"So what's the plan?" Finn asked.

"We have a ship, the *Molly Mei*, two jumps from here. We're in contact via a scrambled link, waiting for the right moment."

"I can't leave without a supply of neuroxin," Edie said, self-conscious of the fact that her presence in the equation, thanks to both the leash and her dependence on a rare chemical, would complicate Finn's escape.

"My crew key gives me access to the infirmary," Corinth

said. "We'll take the drug at the last possible moment—otherwise it'll be missed."

And Edie would be the obvious suspect in the theft.

"By the way, your friend Cat is on board the *Molly Mei*," Valari said. "To put it bluntly, she insisted on coming along, although letting her join us on the *Learo Dochais* was out of the question."

Edie suddenly felt a whole lot more optimistic. Cat was out there, close by, and apparently itching to help.

"Can I talk to her?"

"I'll arrange it."

Edie felt the need to defend her in front of Valari, who had obviously experienced a personality conflict with Cat. "She'll be useful on the Fringe. She has contacts."

"So do we," Valari said bluntly.

"What Edie means," Finn said, "is that we have valuable information we need to get to the Fringe. We need the Fringers to trust us. Cat can help."

"Well, now I'm curious." Valari exchanged a look with Corinth. "Exactly what are you talking about?"

"Meet us at the main lab on Deck B, oh-two-hundred tonight," Finn said. "We'll show you."

CHAPTER 14

Edie sat with Finn at a tiny table in the mess. Valari and Corinth sat some distance away, eating with a bunch of meckies, not wanting anyone to connect them with Finn, at least not for now. Edie had waited until this moment to tell Finn, knowing that doing so in a public place would help her keep her cool. She needed him to take her seriously. If she fell apart, he might believe she was overreacting.

"Lukas is dead." Her voice shook, but only a little and it was mostly from anger. "I think Natesa had him killed—poisoned his meds or something."

Finn swallowed a mouthful of soup. "What? Why?"

"To remind me that she controls my life." The lump in her throat made talking difficult. "She must've tagged my external comms. Maybe even listened in. In any case, she knew I spoke with him. She does that. She takes away the things I care about."

"Maybe she just didn't like what he told you. She didn't want you to know the Crib's secrets."

Edie stared at her untouched food, feeling herself drowning in a sudden wave of despair. She waited for it to pass. "Natesa will kill you, too. An accident with the leash or . . . something."

"Let her try." Damn his belief in his own invincibility. They'd butted heads over this before. "Listen," he said with less heat, "maybe Corinth knows a way to cut the leash. Maybe he knows someone on the Fringe who can, once we're free."

"What if Natesa gets there first?"

"If she values your cooperation, she has too much to lose by killing me now."

"She killed Lukas!"

"You don't know that for sure. I'll bet she's counting on plausible deniability." He watched her for a moment. "Edie, we *will* beat them. We'll get out of here and we'll be fine."

She nodded, trying to look encouraged by his words. Trying to *feel* encouraged, instead of sick with worry.

Edie spent the evening working through a sim of what she needed to do that night in the lab. She'd already arranged with Galeon to meet them there. A couple of whispered words in the classroom, a quick smile and a wink in return, and the next phase of Galeon's "top secret mission" was under way.

And her guilty conscience was back to haunt her. She was using the boy. The consequences for him if they were caught would be incomparably minor in comparison to the consequences for her and Finn, of course. Especially with Natesa looking for any excuse to be rid of Finn. What could the Crib do to a seven-year-old boy who'd been duped by treasonous adults?

Still, Galeon might not see it that way.

She found Finn sitting on the floor in his room, leaning against the couch and fiddling with something. On the table was an assortment of junk—tiny pieces of tubing and wiring and broken bits of plaz.

"What's all this?"

As she went over to him, she saw he was twisting wire. On one corner of the table were four finished pieces. Edie recognized the size and shape. She picked one up.

"Are these for Pegasaw?"

"Yeah. Figured I'd make the kid a real set."

Edie examined the pegs. They were identically shaped, and set into the top of each was a nub of red plaz.

"How many do you have to make?"

"For a full set—ten red, ten black. And the board."

"Where did you get all this stuff?"

"Around. It's just junk."

Edie sat down beside him to watch, fascinated. He used his fingers to warm the wire before twisting it into a peg, set the red stone in the top and secured it with a final loop of wire. Then he carefully pressed the peg into shape to exactly match the others.

"I hope he appreciates it," Edie said. "Maybe he prefers the holoviz."

Finn smiled without looking up. "Then I'll have to teach you how to play."

Edie couldn't take her eyes off his strong and sure hands. The news about Lukas had gnawed at her all afternoon. It was good to focus on something else, something so mundane—a reminder of how life was supposed to be. Watching Finn, she wondered if he craved the same sense of normalcy to balance their strange and stressful lives. In any case, she understood this aspect of him—that he liked to keep busy, even on a meaningless project like this.

"We need to be at the labs in a few minutes."

"Okay." He started clearing up the bits.

"I'm glad you're making him a gift. Maybe it makes up for what we're making him do."

A frown flickered across Finn's face. "You make it sound like we're corrupting him. He doesn't understand what he's doing."

"One day he might. If he grows up to be a loyal citizen, what will he think of the fact that he committed treachery?"

"If your life with the Crib is any indication, he's got all kinds of disillusionment in store for him—even without our help."

Still, she hated the idea of Galeon becoming disillusioned with Finn, in particular.

"Is there any chance . . ." She wasn't sure if she dared ask the question, but he looked at her expectantly. She had to ask. "Any chance your friends would agree to rescuing the children as well?"

Finn's mouth compressed ever so slightly. It made Edie think he'd bitten back what he was going to say. Instead, he asked, "What makes you so sure they need rescuing?"

"Because I'd have wanted to be rescued at age ten if I'd known what my life would become."

"The kids are fine, Edie."

"Pris isn't fine—she's in a coma!" Her voice rose, louder than she'd intended. "Galeon's life is reduced to crawling around the ship at night for fun—"

"Wait—who?"

For a moment, Edie had forgotten she'd never told Finn about Pris. "She's the cypherteck they used to torture you."

That got his attention. "They used a *kid*?"

"That's what they do, Finn. They'll use them any way they want to. They can justify anything when they claim the future of humanity is at stake."

Finn jammed the pegs he'd made into a tiny pouch that he slipped in his pocket. "Can we ask Valari and Corinth to put themselves at risk abducting these kids on the grounds that you don't like how they're being raised?" She wondered if he was playing devil's advocate. "Anyway, how do you propose to grab a kid in a coma without anyone noticing?"

"I haven't thought it through completely, I admit," Edie said. "Let's talk about this another time." She'd planted the idea in his head. Maybe he needed time to mull it over. "So what about these Saeth—do you trust them? With our secret, I mean."

"Yes, absolutely."

She wanted to ask about Valari—wanted to ask *something* about Valari. What the woman had meant to him, what she meant to him now. How exactly to put that into words? She had no right to delve into his past and his feelings when their own relationship was barely half formed. In any case, he was not a man who talked freely about such things.

They headed for the lower decks. A crew member in casual clothes joined them in the lift, nodding a greeting. He got out on Deck C, to Edie's relief. Finn stared at the lift door as it closed, his eyes unfocused. The lift ascended.

"You seem distracted," she said.

He snapped his attention to her, hesitated a few seconds, then said, "No, it's nothing. Not compared to what you're going through right now."

"What is it, Finn?"

"I guess I never expected to see her again." His lips quirked in a quick grin. "I must be in shock."

So, he was thinking about Valari. Edie's stomach sank but she rallied a brave face. "In shock? I thought you loved her."

He gave her a strange look. "I never said that."

"Did you love her?" May as well find out.

"I was nineteen years old and infatuated. She made me feel . . . Well, it doesn't matter. I was a stupid kid and it took me a long time to realize that I was just one of many similarly stupid kids."

"Do you feel manipulated?"

"Not exactly. I agreed with her ideals regardless of our relationship. Through her I found the Saeth. Something to fight for that went beyond the politics of individual worlds."

His low tone and refusal to meet her eyes told Edie he didn't want to talk about it further. Fair enough. Despite Edie's burning curiosity, any personal history between Valari and Finn wasn't her business.

But this wasn't just personal. She sensed the lure of his wartime comrades pulling him away from her. What if the leash was the only thing holding him at her side?

By the time Valari and Corinth showed up at the lab, Galeon had long since returned to his dorm, following two more rounds of Pegasaw with Finn. Edie explained the boy's involvement, assuring them he could be trusted thanks to his friendship—more like hero worship—with Finn.

"Good thing you have help," Corinth said, glancing around the lab with the professional eye of a teck. "My crew key gets me into a lot of places, but not here." He gave a low whistle as he scanned the modules. "Is this stock biocyph? Incredible. This could make enough med-teck to save a million lives. *Ten* million lives."

"We have something that could save billions," Finn said.

Valari's eyes lit up with interest. She had sidled close to him. "Tell us."

"I'll let Edie explain." Finn moved away from her and from the group, and for the third time checked that the hatch was locked. He remained at the door as if standing guard, although his stance was casual. One look at his face told Edie that he was still working through some emotions. She, on the other hand, had taken some effort to push her grief aside for the moment.

"It's an algorithm," she said, "a cryptoglyph that can permanently break the biocyph lock on terraforming seeds. It removes the need for the annual Crib renewal key."

For a moment Valari seemed dumbfounded. Then, her voice thick with doubt, she said, "Does it work?"

"I think it will, yes."

"I've heard of rovers selling keystone BRATs to Fringers. They never perform as advertised, if at all."

"This is different. Those keystones are patches and the biocyph learns to work around them in a couple of years. This isn't a patch, it's a permanent solution because it destroys the lock."

"Where is this cryptoglyph? Did you write it?"

"No. I . . . found it, and stored it in Finn's chip."

"Is there some reason we can't transmit it to the Fringe right now?"

"It's integrated into his chip. Can't be downloaded."

Corinth had been listening carefully, leaning against the console with his arms folded. If he thought it was too good to be true, he showed none of Valari's suspicion. "So we're talking about a new long-term mission—visiting each planet on the Fringe, jacking into the BRATs, and breaking the locks one by one."

"Yes. But there might be a much quicker solution."

Edie pulled a palmet off her belt and called up an encrypted file she'd prepared, a file she kept isolated from the ship's databases. A holo bloomed over the device, showing a sim of the biocyph module she'd appropriated.

"You managed to embed a biocyph lock in stock biocyph?" Corinth looked suitably impressed, and Edie was pleased he knew enough to recognize what he was seeing. Maybe he could help with the leash after all.

"I intend to crack this lock with the cryptoglyph," she explained. "Because the lock is embedded in stock biocyph, its form is essentially generic—"

"—so cracking this should create a master key. A key we *can* transmit. Holy fuck." Corinth looked at Valari, excitement gleaming in his eyes.

Valari was evidently bewildered by the holo display. When it came to the technical details, she relied on his reaction to determine how she should react. Now she looked cautiously enthusiastic. "Let's not get ahead of ourselves. Are we jeopardizing our escape plan in any way by doing this?"

"I've already configured the biocyph module," Edie said. "I need an hour or so to create the crack, which I can store in my splinter. Then I wipe the module and leave it on the rack—eventually someone will come to use it and discover it's a dud. They'll never know why."

"As for the transmission," Corinth said, his enthusiasm gaining momentum, "once it's out there, it's out there. Can't be pulled back."

"Can we send it from here?" Edie asked.

"Well, there are two issues," he said. "First, we can't encode the message, else the Fringers won't be able to read it. Second, if we do it from here, we'd have to hide the origin of the transmission. We'd use a scrambled line, and that would be enough if it was just a single site-to-site transmission. But we're talking about blasting the entire Reach with this thing. If anyone did manage to track it back, we're in trouble. My suggestion is to send it to the *Molly Mei* on a scrambled line, and have them send it out."

"There's a third issue," Valari said. "Convincing the Fringers that the code isn't some snippet of a hacker's biobomb, or a Crib trick. They won't upload it to their seeds unless they trust it."

"We need a guinea pig," Corinth said. "A world that does trust the code, to show the way. Once word gets around that it works—assuming it does work—the other planets will be happy to use it too."

Valari nodded slowly, deep in thought. She threw a glance in Finn's direction. He was still at the hatch, listening in silence. "I'll find a suitable world. You get this master key made," she told Edie. "Corinth, help her."

Edie felt her hackles rise at Valari's tone. When had the woman decided *she* was in charge of Edie's project? She couldn't let it slide.

"I don't actually need his help." She took a moment to enjoy the look of surprise on Valari's face. "I just need Finn."

Valari had the good grace to incline her head in acknowledgment. "I'll leave you to it, then."

"I know you don't need my help," Corinth told Edie, "but I'd like to jack in and watch you work, if that's okay."

"Sure." Edie reeled out a hardlink from her belt, handed it to him, and moved the biocyph module into place between them. She pressed her fingers to the port while he plugged in the hardlink and attached the other end to a tiny device behind his ear—the dry–wet interface that allowed him limited access to biocyph circuitry.

Valari wandered over to Finn and engaged him in quiet conversation. Edie found herself watching them both, searching for visual clues that might tell her where their relationship stood. When she realized Corinth was observing her, she looked away sharply, swiveling her seat a few degrees to hide her face, which felt so hot it must surely be flushed.

It was a relief when Finn came over at last. "Ready for me?"

"Yes."

He sat beside her. She connected their temples with a hardlink and the familiar cadences of his chip filled her mind. His chip was a miniature version of the biocyph module, a single thread of biocyph that the infojack Achaiah had grafted to his existing chip in order to link its receiver to Edie's splinter. Most of the thread was empty matrix, and Edie had used that to store the cryptoglyph.

The cryptoglyph could not be copied or downloaded, so the work now had to take place in Finn's chip, with her splinter serving as a bridge. She gathered together the knot of notes that formed the biocyph lock and fed them into his chip. Finn stirred beside her, frowning as he sensed the added load of data. She was aware of Corinth hovering in the background, interpreting the datastream in whatever manner his interface allowed him.

The lock formed an input shelf, a query awaiting code. Normally, the Crib provided that code—at a price. Now the cryptoglyph in Finn's chip flowed around the lock, not to fill the input but to change its actual structure. The two datastreams pressed together like lovers at a dance, moving at first out of time with each other, but quickly falling into step.

The lock shifted suddenly, unfolding and refolding into a new configuration. The cryptoglyph melted away to leave behind a perfectly tuned string of notes.

"That's it? That's the crack?" Corinth murmured.

Edie copied the string to her splinter and ran a series of checks, looking for flaws in the code. Once she'd satisfied herself that it was perfectly formed, she disconnected the link.

Only then did she give herself permission to feel satisfied. She met Finn's gaze, and his hand closed over hers on the top of the console and squeezed it. She knew he was remembering those fifteen hours of hell on Scarabaeus, its night-mare jungle that had almost killed them, the seed where she'd reprogrammed the biocyph to save them, and, in the process, found the algorithm.

The twisted, mutated ecosystem on Scarabaeus that her kill-code helped to create was surely a small price to pay for the freedom of billions of Fringers.

They stayed in the lab another three hours while Finn and the two Saeth discussed possible rescue scenarios. Edie felt excluded from the discussion. These were professional soldiers, while she was tagging along for the ride. She kept her grief over Lukas tamped down. She kept quiet about the children, too. One thing at a time.

Before they left, Corinth examined Finn's chip. He grunted a few choice words at the way its original Saeth comm capacity had been "hijacked and mutilated," and mapped what he could to a datacap for later review. As for the leash, he wasn't willing to do anything more than look over it for now.

"I've a few contacts I might ask about this," he said. "Maybe we can generate some ideas."

Edie hoped his confidence was warranted. "Just don't do anything without me."

CHAPTER 15

Edie rolled over, exhausted and heavy-limbed, as her alarm beeped. It felt like only seconds ago that she'd climbed between the bedsheets and it was already time to get up. She was used to hearing Finn moving about in the next room, but he'd been banished to the workers' quarters. She rolled over again and dozed.

Hours later, she awoke feeling groggier than ever from too much sleep. No one had called to ask where she was. On her way to the lift, she passed new faces in the corridor—two smartly dressed women with Crib medallions emblazoned on their suits. They nodded a synchronized greeting without breaking their conversation. Natesa's guests must have arrived—Crib 'crats visiting Project Ardra to see how their money was being spent.

"Rough night?" Ming Yue asked when Edie entered the lab.

Edie made a noncommittal noise and pulled up the latest reports Caleb had sent her from base camp. Natesa had finally upped her clearance, and while Caleb had a tendency to downplay the situation, as if any problem was a direct reflection of his professional abilities, Edie knew it was because he was worried about the way things were going dirtside. She'd seen the error logs the children were dealing with. Things were not running smoothly.

"When is Caleb coming back to the ship, anyway?" she asked Ming Yue. She knew the conditions at base camp were uncomfortable and imagined Caleb was not enjoying himself.

"Last I heard, he was working on presentations for our visitors. The VIPs arrived on the *Fortitude* during the night, so Natesa's in full-blown hospitality mode and dragging Caleb into it. He's thousands of klicks away but still can't avoid it."

Edie intended to avoid Natesa, and it looked like that was going to be easy enough for a while. She didn't trust herself not to accuse her of having Lukas killed. She had to constantly remind herself to stay quiet, keep the anger at bay, do her job. She and Finn had a rescue option now. No point making trouble.

"I bet he hates that," she said.

Ming Yue gave twisted smile. "Actually, he's often better at it than she is. He loves to show off, and the Crib 'crats love to be wowed."

"I hope Natesa doesn't want me wowing them, too."

"Not sure. She dropped by this morning but when you weren't here, she said it was okay to let you sleep in."

That was a little odd. Allowing Edie to shirk off was very unlike Natesa. "Why would she say that?"

Ming Yue shrugged. "She was preoccupied with something else. Some guy was transferred under guard from the *Fortitude*."

"Under guard?"

"Yeah, he was picked up en route and brought here. That's all I know."

Edie knew more. She'd been expecting the arrival of this criminal. She just hadn't known until now that he'd be coming in on the VIP ship.

Achaiah.

Edie left her work without a word of explanation to Ming Yue and raced to the infirmary. She'd made it clear that she wanted to be there when Achaiah made the attempt to cut the leash—and Natesa had deliberately gone behind her back.

Expecting to find milits blocking her path, her pulse hammered with the instinct to fight her way through. Instead, she found the infirmary quiet and orderly. One milit, a young man, stood in quiet conversation with the medic assistant on duty at the front desk. In the room beyond, Edie saw the vague outlines of two figures through the frosted screen.

She was about to charge through when the screen drew back. One of the figures was Finn. His expression sullen, he grabbed his jacket from the back of a chair and stalked across the room. When he saw Edie, he gave a slight jerk of his head to signal her to follow.

As soon as they were outside the room and a few paces down an empty side corridor, he thumped his fist against the bulkhead in an explosion of anger. Startled, Edie stood back. She'd never seen him so agitated. He leaned against the bulkhead, forehead pressed into his forearm, taking deep breaths. She waited it out.

"They knocked me out," he said at last. "Did something to my chip, I'm sure of it." He looked at her, realized she didn't know what he was talking about, and started again. "They called me up here for a physical—said it was a prerequisite for the job. They went through all the usual stuff, and then next thing I know there's a spike in my neck. I saw that infojack in the room, I swear . . . When I came to just now, the medic told me it was for a routine check of my chip. Since when does that require me to be unconscious?"

"Achaiah was there to cut the leash—"

"If it was cut, the interference would be gone, and it's not."

"So maybe he tried and failed. At least you're still alive." She was furious, though, that Natesa hadn't let her be present. That's what they'd agreed to. "Let me take a look, see if I can figure out if he messed with it in some other way."

He acquiesced, turning toward her. She touched her fingertips to his temple and programmed a quick seeker to search his chip for signs of tampering.

"Dammit," he hissed. "We're so close—another couple of days and we're free. Except that they could've reset the boundary for all I know. I leave and I die." His body was tense with frustration and . . . *Fear?* It felt like fear to Edie, though she'd never seen him come even close to showing that emotion before, and it terrified her now.

Questions ran through her head—nothing she needed to voice, because she knew he was asking himself the same questions. Achaiah was nothing if not unpredictable. Evil one moment, inexplicably generous the next. What might he have done while jacked into Finn's chip? Something Natesa had ordered him to do? Something on his own whim?

Or had he done exactly what he'd been brought to do—attempt to cut the leash, nothing more?

She knew Natesa would smoothly deny anything else was going on. And she'd never get to Achaiah, who was probably already in the brig awaiting transportation back to prison.

"Okay, listen," Edie said, forcing calm into her voice. "I'm not finding any new programming in here." Achaiah's aftertaste was thicker through some tiers than others, leaving a trail of his linkup. "He examined the leash pretty thoroughly."

"Why? He created the fucking thing."

"Maybe to refresh his memory before trying to cut it. Maybe to check if I've tampered with it." She withdrew her hand, satisfied with the examination. "As far as I can tell, he didn't try to cut it. I guess he was telling the truth when he said he didn't know how."

"Then why the hell is he even here?" The venom in his voice made her wince, even though she knew it wasn't directed at her.

"He probably convinced Natesa there was a chance, just so he could enjoy an excursion out of his cell for a few days."

"Earlier you tried to convince me Natesa wants me dead. Why didn't she just ask Achaiah to trigger the bomb by accident?"

"Because she knows I'd never forgive that. She'll be more subtle, so I can never really be sure. So I can never blame her."

Finn spanned his forehead with one hand, massaging his temples as though doing so might erase the lethal chip from his skull. "I want this fucking bomb defused. I'm tired of being *owned*."

He pushed away from the wall and headed for the lift. Edie had to jog a few paces to catch up to him. As the car descended to the lower decks, she kept quiet, unable to gauge his mood until he looked directly at her and she saw a calm determination had returned to his eyes.

"Sorry, Edie," he said quietly. "Didn't mean to take it out on you."

"It's okay. Didn't think you had."

She would have said more, something about understanding how it felt to be owned and trapped and afraid. But he pulled her against him then, in a tight embrace, burying his face in her shoulder. His chest moved against hers as he breathed, deep and slow.

"I'll ask Corinth to try and cut the leash," he said.

Considering Lukas's death and now this, it was time to make a definitive effort of their own.

Edie was summoned to the admin deck that afternoon. She found Natesa in the conference room of the admin suite, which had been transformed into a reception area. Gone was the long heavy table. The walls had been opened up to adjoining rooms to create a large open space. Around the outer bulkheads were large holo displays, each projecting a different aspect of Project Ardra and the terraforming efforts on the planet below. The entire effect was, presumably, to convince the visiting Crib 'crats that all was well on Prisca, and that Crib citizens were safe in Natesa's hands.

Natesa was deep in conversation with her assistant Darian as they went over schedules. Edie hovered near the door until Natesa finally noticed her.

"Ah, Edie. I'd like you to prepare a short presentation on Prisca's progress for our guests during the reception and banquet tomorrow night."

Edie hadn't expected that. "You want me to explain how things are going horribly wrong?"

"Don't be ridiculous. Chessell's latest data from the surface is quite reassuring. He tells me the new adjustments he implemented are going according to plan."

"He planned for large areas of biomass degradation? Because I'm betting that's what's going to happen. Already *is* happening in some localized regions—"

"Degradation is a very strong word. My understanding is that we have contained regions of instability, which is only to be expected as the planet's complex ecosystem adapts to the accelerated retroviral interference."

"There's no such thing as a *contained* region when it comes to BRAT seeds. They talk to each other constantly. And if that instability, as you call it, can't be reversed, we're going to end up with complete ecosystem collapse."

"Nonsense. We're talking about a few small problem areas."

"We're talking about a domino effect once the collapse begins."

Natesa pursed her lips and shooed Darian away. "Your negativity is the last thing I need at this function," she hissed. "I need a nice upbeat report on our new regulator technology. Nothing too technical. These guests are VIPs from Central. They support Project Ardra, and we need that support to continue. They need to see the project working, and working well. They'll tour the dirtside facility, where Chessell is ready to show them our amazing results so far. I can't have you contradicting the expert opinion of my team down on the surface."

"Then you want me to lie?"

"I want you to emphasize the enormous progress we've made in terraforming technology with the implementation of the regulator code. I want you to explain the children's role in handling the error logs, and how their unique teamwork enables us to monitor and adjust the terraforming process in a way that's never been done before. I want you to present a united front as we demonstrate these successes we've worked so hard for."

Edie chewed her lip as she glanced around the room, surrounded by the ridiculous hype of Ardra that whitewashed all problems. If she were a 'crat from Central, eager to hear good news, she might be convinced by the flashy, reassuring holos. But she'd seen data they never would. There was a chance she was wrong about the degradation already taking place, but she didn't think so. She and the children had spent hours on Caleb's error logs. They couldn't work through the logs fast enough—and their solutions only patched up a disaster waiting to happen.

Still, this wasn't her problem. She could toe the line for Natesa. She had to, because she was only biding time.

"Okay," she relented, "I'll do what you want. My warnings about impending degradation still stand, though. I don't think Caleb is being cautious enough."

"Please don't think I'm discounting your opinion," Natesa said. "First and foremost, we must allay any doubts our visitors may have. However . . ." A glimmer of that nervousness that Edie had noticed at their last meeting was back. "I appreciate your concerns about our chief cypherteck. Ming Yue Huang has raised the same concerns—she feels his ego may be affecting his scientific impartiality. Now that he's dirtside, I want you to double-check a few things in the lab."

"I don't have the clearance to look at his files."

"I will authorize it."

"What exactly should I look for?"

"There's a possibility that he's being . . . overly optimistic in his reports."

"You mean less than honest?"

"No, that is *not* what I mean." Natesa regarded her through slitted eyes. "You know what? I've changed my mind. I'll have Aila give the presentation. She's not quite so good with the technical details, but she knows enough to satisfy our audience."

Edie shrugged. "Fine. So do I still have to attend this function?"

"Of course. Everyone knows the famous Edie Sha'nim has returned to my team. You'll put in an appearance. And wear something nice."

You must be kidding. Edie bit back the words. Instead, she approached another touchy subject.

"Finn told me about Achaiah attempting to cut the leash. Why wasn't I told about it?" She masked her anger behind a forced offhand tone.

Natesa gave a tight smile of apology. "I didn't want you involved. If something went wrong, you'd only blame yourself." How considerate. Natesa seemed oblivious to the fact that Edie would like to have been given the choice. "In any case, it's a great pity Achaiah failed," Natesa went on. "What I wouldn't give to remove that man from this ship and from your life for good."

The words were benign at face value, but they sent a chill through Edie. Again she found herself holding back a response.

Natesa started to move away, ending the conversation. Then she suddenly turned back. "Oh, you'll be happy to know that Pris woke up last night. So far, she seems to be recovering well."

Then she did walk off, beckoning to Darian, who rushed over obsequiously, and Edie was left standing there to absorb the news.

CHAPTER 16

"I'm doing an excellent job," Galeon announced when he opened the hatch to the lab that night. "You should find more top secret missions for me."

Finn followed Edie into the room and snapped the hatch shut behind them. "I'll think about it."

"Come on, then," Galeon said, producing his little holoviz and turning expectantly to Finn. They would have to indulge him for a while, then send him off before Valari and Corinth arrived.

"Wait, I have something for you," Finn said.

He handed over the pouch Edie had seen earlier. The boy tipped its contents on the tabletop.

"What are they?" He picked up a peg in his fingers and turned it over to examine it from all angles.

From his pocket Finn withdrew and unfolded the board he'd fashioned from sheets of plaz and polished to a high sheen. "This is a real Pegasaw set."

Galeon's eyes lit up. "For me?"

"Yes. Do you have somewhere safe to hide this stuff?"

"Of course! I've got lots of treasures in the dorm that no one knows about."

Edie watched awhile as they played. She could tell Galeon

enjoyed the feel of the pegs between his fingers. Was it really that simple to please the boy? She tried to remember herself at that age—an outcast among the Talasi, living in the Crib relocation camps with milit guards for friends because they were the only ones who'd talk to her. One of them, Ursov, used to tell her about the stars he'd visited. He would talk about his son. Looking back, she hardly remembered the things he'd said. She realized now it was the attention she'd relished. The knowledge that someone cared, that she wasn't invisible.

Did Galeon feel anyone cared for him beyond his role as a teck?

He was particularly talkative tonight. He wanted to know who taught Finn to play Pegasaw, what else he was good at, if he liked coco-rice. Whether he'd ever owned a dog. Even Finn was surprised by that last one.

"I grew up on a farm. There were dogs around," he said.

"But did you have your own dog?"

"My sister sort of adopted one once."

"What did it look like?"

"A stringy mutt with hair flopping in its eyes. We taught it to fish."

"Dogs can fish?"

"This dog could fish. There was a stream at the bottom of our property and we fished for flat guppy."

Edie listened in fascination. She'd never managed to extract this much information from Finn about his past.

"I want a dog," Galeon said.

"A dog is a big responsibility," Finn said, while Edie's heart twisted at the yearning in Galeon's voice.

"A lizard, then. Or a spider."

"A pet spider?" Finn smiled indulgently. When he glanced at Edie, the smile faded. He must sense something coming through the leash—she felt unhappy enough to set it buzzing—and now he must see it on her face.

"Yes, a pet spider would be cool," Galeon was saying. "But they won't let me have one. I asked." He moved a peg decisively. "Maybe you could ask for me?"

A grim expression came over Finn as he looked at the boy. Edie could tell he was affected by Galeon's innocent request.

"Can't help you there," he said at last.

Galeon hid his disappointment well. "That's okay. It would frighten the girls, anyway."

Ten minutes later they were done with the game and Edie sent Galeon back to bed via the access tubes, new Pegasaw set in pocket.

"I can't bear the thought of leaving him here," Edie said. "He just needs to be a little boy."

Finn was still sitting at the table where they'd played, lost in his thoughts, and acknowledged her words with a barely perceptible shrug of one shoulder. The gesture seemed to say, *What am I supposed to do about it?*

"That childhood you talked about," she went on, determined to make him see. "Dogs and fishing and . . . I didn't even know you had a sister! That childhood, that's what these children will never have." She slid into the seat opposite him. "You told me you were tired of being owned. I understand that. I'm tired of being pushed around, too. We'll send out this crack tonight, make sure it works, then transmit it across the Reach—and our Fringe mission will be complete. After that . . . Finn, escaping the Crib isn't enough for me anymore. I want to help these kids. I want to take them with us."

His expression didn't change. "Even if it goes against our best interests?"

"We can figure out a way. Galeon will do whatever you tell him to."

"If you take away these kids, Natesa will just bring in a new batch."

"Probably not. They're saying this planet is her only shot at proving herself with Project Ardra. But even if she does bring in more, I'll still have saved *these* kids."

"Valari won't go for it."

Jezus, didn't he see she wanted him to persuade Valari on her behalf?

The Saeth arrived a few minutes later as planned, and Valari didn't go for it.

"If this remote crack idea of yours doesn't work, we need Finn on the Fringe. That humanitarian mission far outweighs your personal concern for some kids. We can't risk the rescue operation. I won't risk it."

"You said you don't leave brothers behind," Edie said carefully. "These are my brothers and sisters, and I won't leave them behind." She waited for Finn to jump in, but he remained silent.

"Then let's hope Corinth can cut the leash," Valari said, "and I won't have to worry about the children *or* about you."

So, she'd leave Edie behind. That wasn't entirely unexpected.

"And if he can't?"

"I can't imagine it's that hard to force the issue." Valari made a deliberate visual sweep of Edie from head to toe, as if assessing how hard it would be to take her down. There was really no question—of course she and Corinth could force Edie to comply. A little manhandling, one spike of tranq, and there was nothing she could do about it.

"You won't force her," Finn said so firmly that Valari was compelled to back down. "We've been forced around enough, both of us."

"Finn . . . *Jaron* . . ." Valari turned from soldier to seductress in a flash. "This is not why we're here."

"I'm not saying I agree with her," Finn said. "But you won't force her. It's up to Edie what she does."

Valari blinked and swallowed hard, stunned into silence. Corinth was no help. He sat drumming his fingers on the console, waiting to see what would happen next.

Edie decided to act as if they'd come to an agreement. "So let's come up with a plan to take the children. They need a supply of neuroxin implants, like me. The infirmary has dozens, enough to last several years. Corinth, you said you had access to the infirmary?"

"Uh, yes. But the infirmary is always manned, right?"

"We don't need to walk in the front door. We just need to get to Dr Sternhagen's office. That's where I saw the box. The kids' dorm is on the same deck. I imagine there's some sort of security posted."

"You said this kid Galeon uses the access tubes and crawl spaces," Corinth said, ignoring Valari's glare. "Could he persuade the others to follow him to a rendezvous point?"

"That should work. Where are you with your rescue plan?"

"Our ship is pretty much ready to go once we give the signal. It'll enter the system with engine trouble—say, a neutron leak. Something they can't fix without docking for emergency repairs. The *Learo Dochais* is required to render assistance. With the *Molly Mei* docked, we just need to sneak on board and depart before we're missed."

"There's a VIP event tomorrow evening," Edie said. "Is that too soon? Almost the entire staff and crew will be in one place that evening—Deck A. Should make it easier for us to move around and ultimately to disappear."

"Twenty-four hours is enough time."

"Okay. Finn, you deal with Galeon. I'll steal the neuroxin using Corinth's crew key. You two"—she looked from Corinth to Valari, who stood tight-lipped in the background—"clear the way for us to get to the *Molly Mei*."

"And what's the contingency plan?" Valari spoke up suddenly, sharply. "What if the kids don't show, for example? Do we wait around until the whole thing falls through? We only get one shot at this. The *Molly Mei* will be escorted out of the system as soon as it's fixed, and your ride to freedom will be gone."

"Then let's all hope the kids *do* show," Edie said. "Because I won't leave them here."

It felt good to take charge, to be decisive. It felt good to be the one standing up for these children, to step into the role Lukas had filled for her.

Valari looked like she wanted to squeeze out more objections. Instead she said, "I've been looking for a world we can persuade to try out the crack. Some place that trusts me despite the crack's unknown source. Some place that needs our help." She gave Finn a cautious look. "The best option is Fairbairn."

Beside her, Edie felt Finn tense. Edie had never heard of Fairbairn, but in truth any Fringe world name meant equally little to her.

"Since when did Fairbairn need this sort of help?" Finn asked.

"It isn't the most desperate world, that's true. Still, we're heading in a bad direction. Despite our government taking a neutral stance during the Liberty War, since then the feeling has turned largely anti-Crib. Not a bad thing in itself. In fact, it's helped me bolster the reputation of the Saeth to the point where I no longer have to hide my identity as one of them. But it's led to five years of unrest, bordering on civil war."

Valari's choice of pronouns made it clear that Fairbairn was her homeworld. As she continued to explain, Edie realized something else. Valari had recruited Finn as a young man . . . on Fairbairn? Was Fairbairn his homeworld, too? She absorbed each new detail about him and filed it away.

Finn looked a little surprised at the information as Valari continued.

"Our economy is wrecked. We've struggled to pay the Crib's renewal fees for years, and now we're several months late. The BRATs have shut down and our ecosystem is stumbling."

"If it's only been a few months," Edie said, "then this planet sounds like an ideal candidate for a demonstration of the crack. If it works, you'll get quick results—an immediate reversal of at least some of the damage."

Finn didn't look particularly happy, which confused Edie. Valari seemed to understand.

"I can see you have mixed feelings about this," Valari said. "Just think, if it works, you can return home a hero."

"That's unlikely," Finn said. "We have to maintain

anonymity. Otherwise Edie becomes a target for every desperate Fringer out there."

Valari shrugged. "So where should I tell the authorities on Fairbairn I got the crack?"

"I don't know," Finn said. "And here's another problem—if you use it on Fairbairn, you'll be seen as playing favorites, saving your own world first. The Saeth don't do that."

"Then use Cat," Edie said. "She comes from Cameo, a Crib world, but for years she ran with rovers. She'll be seen as neutral. She has contacts on the Fringe who will believe any tale she spins about how she acquired the crack."

"So, Cat approaches Valari with it," Corinth said, "perhaps indirectly via these contacts of hers, and Valari vouches for her in order to convince the authorities to upload it."

Valari thought about it for a moment. For the first time, she actually looked pleased. "It just might work," she said at last.

"You've got one helluva bunch of buddies, Finn." The scrambled line rendered Cat in tiny distorted cubes of light that lent a bluish tinge to her dark features. "So polite. So friendly. Jezus. I might just invite them to join my book club."

"Nice to see you again, too," Finn said with half a smile.

"So—the Saeth got me, the Crib got you. Who's better off, huh?" Cat had fought for the Crib during the Reach Conflicts, and her opinion of the Saeth was based on Crib propaganda. Still, she and Finn had just about been on speaking terms by the end of their adventure on the *Hoi Polloi*. Hopefully, her opinion was changing.

"I know how you feel about the Saeth," Edie said. "Please take my word for it that you were misinformed about them. I need you to trust them, work with them."

"I promised I'd help you, Edie. Bring it on."

Cat already knew about the cryptoglyph. Edie explained about the remote crack she'd made, and that they wanted to test it on Fairbairn.

"So you want me to get the word out to my contacts," Cat

said. "I'll dangle the carrot, give them enough specifics that they inevitably suggest Fairbairn and put me in touch with that woman Valari Zael."

Cat couldn't see that Valari was standing in the room, to one side of the holoviz. The way she said *that woman* spoke volumes about how the two of them had got along.

"Yes," Edie said. "We need this to look like Fairbairn is the most obvious choice. And it is. With Valari's help, it's also the one place we're virtually guaranteed they'll listen."

"Okay. Send me the crack."

"Wait!" Valari stepped into view, put her hand on Edie's arm and shook her head, concerned. "I would rather send that code to Fairbairn myself. I don't want it out there, out of our control."

Cat caught on fast. "Ah, there you are, Valari. You don't trust me? I thought we were best friends."

"If the crack doesn't work properly," Valari said, "if there are side-effects we haven't considered . . . It's safer to keep it under control until we're sure."

"As soon as we give it to Fairbairn's authorities, it's out of our control," Edie pointed out.

"I'll make sure they don't spread it around if it's faulty."

"You can't guarantee that. Besides, Cat won't spread it around if it's faulty, either." Edie spoke over Valari's objections. "I made this thing. I decide who gets it."

As Edie spoke, she surreptitiously pressed her fingers to the console's port, connecting her splinter to the comm system.

"Got it," Cat said with a grin.

Valari scowled, her lips tightening. This woman was just not used to someone else making the decisions.

"Find a way to persuade Fairbairn to use it," Edie told Cat. "If their tecks say it worked, send it across the Reach and get the word out."

"Will do."

"Thanks, Cat. It's good to know you're out there and on our side."

"I'll let you know how it goes. Give Finn a big kiss for me."

That made Finn smirk and Corinth chuckle. Edie cut the link.

"On to the next order of business," Corinth said. "The leash."

"I'll leave you to it," Valari said. "I'm heading back to my quarters to write a proposal for my contacts on Fairbairn."

When she'd left the lab, Corinth pulled up a seat to the console and continued. "I have a pretty neat idea on cutting the leash. Actually, more like tricking it into accepting a new input in lieu of transmissions from Edie's chip."

Finn didn't hesitate. "Let's do it."

"Not so fast," Edie said. "Explain exactly what you intend to do."

"I create a recorded loop of your brainwaves and code it into his chip's receiver," Corinth said. "Then, as far as it knows, you never leave his side."

Edie took a moment to absorb it. The leash was a line of communication between their chips that transmitted and received her brainwave signature, combined with a biocyph lock that connected his chip to the bomb in his skull. As long as her brainwaves were being received, the bomb would never detonate.

Finn was looking at her expectantly.

"It makes sense," she said, feeling hope tickling at her heart.

"If it works," Corinth said, "we can thank my friend on Minehead. She's the one who suggested it."

He placed his palmet on the table and the three of them sat around it. Recording the brainwave signature took only a few minutes. Corinth uploaded it to Finn's chip via a hardlink.

"Imprinting now."

He used his palmet to code the commands while Edie followed his work by riding the hardlink. She had no direct access to Finn's chip but she could hear its echo, the clench of the leash, the locked tiers containing the detonator. She had to push back a sense of frustration, knowing she'd have done the job ten times faster using a direct link between her wet-teck interface and Finn's chip. But Corinth was good— he could only scratch the surface of the biocyph in Finn's head, but it was enough. And he was meticulous and careful. She felt confident he'd do the job right as he integrated her brainwaves into the chip's circuitry.

"Now we just have to switch over the connection," Corinth said.

He made it sound benign, but it sent a bolt of panic through Edie. Finn gave her a quick look and she tried to force a smile, but her nerves killed it. They'd made a new connection, now they had to cut the old one—the true leash, the one connected to her splinter.

If it worked, she told herself, this would be the last time Finn would ever suffer the discomfort of feeling her emotions buzzing across the leash.

If it didn't work . . .

"Let me do it," she said.

Corinth looked at her with surprise. "Are you sure? Finn—?"

Finn said nothing. His eyes locked onto hers and she saw no fear there, no uncertainty. Only trust. Then he nodded. *Yes*, he was sure.

Edie was terrified, but she knew she had to be the one to do this. If Finn was about to die before her eyes, she wanted to know she'd tried everything she could to prevent it. Even if that meant being the cause of it. And she didn't want it to happen in this cold impersonal lab, in front of a stranger.

"Not here," she said. "We'll find somewhere else, just Finn and me."

CHAPTER 17

The garden was open access for all crew. Finn's crew key wouldn't get him anywhere else on Deck A, but he could get into the garden. This was the one place in Crib territory where he got equal treatment.

Edie had only seen a tiny wedge of the garden through Natesa's office window. In total it was a hundred times bigger, with several windows from the admin deck overlooking it. A ribbon of light outlined each window but the rooms beyond were dark—the admin staff kept regular hours and it was the middle of the night. The garden, too, was in its nighttime phase. The narrow, raised walking path was lit with dimmed striplights marking its edges.

The soft light made Finn's dark hazel eyes shine, and his hand closed around Edie's, warm and reassuring. The warmth spread up her arm and filled her chest. It squeezed her heart and stole her breath. She had to think to remember how to breath. In and out, in and out.

They stepped onto the path, treading on scattered stray leaves, green with purple undersides. No doubt someone would sweep the debris away before it died and turned brittle, especially with important Crib guests on board. The vegetation surrounding them stood still and silent, the only sound a calming trickle of water somewhere nearby. This was no natural world. Plants had been carefully positioned to create pleasing silhouettes, with species artfully mixed together in contrasting colors and shapes.

The path branched and at random Edie chose the left. They came to the water feature, a simple waterfall flowing over stacked river stones into a small pool. Their approach triggered a sensor and the bottom of the pool began to glow.

Edie knelt on the ground beside the pool, drawing Finn down with her. She disentangled her fingers from his and pressed her palms against her thighs, feeling the skin grow clammy.

"Are you sure?" she asked him.

"Yes."

"We don't have to do this right now."

"Then when?"

"When we're safe. When we're free."

"If you're right about Natesa, I'll be dead before that happens."

"Or I could kill you right now, attempting to free you."

"I can live with that."

They shared a smile at his joke.

"Finn, I'm scared."

"I'm not. It's okay, Edie."

He laid an arm across her shoulders and pulled her gently toward him, until she was leaning against his chest. He'd been scared of what Natesa had the power to do to him—she'd felt his visceral fear at being manipulated and controlled. But this time, she was the one with his life in her hands. He wasn't scared of dying, she realized. A soldier expected death. He was scared only of being powerless to choose how he died. Natesa's games weren't the battles he'd chosen to fight.

Cutting the leash, right here and now, was the choice he'd made. Whatever the consequences.

Tilting her face, she saw his eyes were closed, his expression peaceful. She rested her cheek on his shoulder and pressed her fingertips against his left temple. The contact made her skin tingle. She'd done this before—it felt like a lifetime ago—meddled with his chip to save his life. Then he'd been a random unknown serf, and if she'd failed then, she'd have surely forgotten him already. But now . . . Flashes of the man passed through her mind—his strength and loyalty, his touch, his smell, his sense of honor and fairness. If she failed, would the rest of her complicated life even matter? The children, the Fringe worlds, least of all Ardra . . . She couldn't imagine any of it mattering if Finn wasn't at her side.

If she failed, Achaiah would pay. He was on this very ship, wasn't he? She'd find him and kill him.

She pushed aside the flush of hatred and concentrated on Finn's chip. Its datastream washed over her, a song she knew well. She checked Corinth's imprint again. And again. The leash appeared to have transitioned to the new input. It looked good. That was really all that could be said about it. She and Corinth were both working in unknown territory. But it looked good. It had better be good enough.

She drew a deep breath and cut the old connection.

Her breath came out in a shaky gasp.

So did Finn's. His arms closed around her a little tighter. Then, "I can't feel you anymore."

No interference. The leash was cut.

And he was still very much alive. His body radiated heat that soaked through her skin as they huddled together. Her heart pounded, and though he might feel it against his chest, he would no longer sense the emotional turmoil that went with it. Edie had to clear her mind to assess why she felt so agitated. For the first time since she'd met him, his life did not depend on hers. He could leave this ship—leave her, at any time. In fact, even though he was officially still a serf, Natesa would throw him off one way or another as soon as she found out the leash was cut. Edie had to trust he could take care of himself when that happened. Her obligation to him was over.

Would he take her with him? Why should he, and risk both himself and his comrades? Natesa would never give up on tracking her down, especially if Edie stole the children . . . if that was even possible. More than likely, her obsession with rescuing the children would doom their entire escape plan.

She had to refocus. She had to put Finn first and not be sidetracked by what she perceived to be a tragic injustice against the children.

She realized she'd pulled away from him, and her forehead ached with tension. He didn't need the leash to know she was troubled. He grasped her chin and turned her face toward his, until their eyes met.

"Don't leave me behind," she said.

"I won't."

"If Natesa finds out the leash is cut, she'll make you leave."

"Then we won't tell her." He made it sound like the most obvious decision in the world.

"Valari will leave me behind if there's any chance your escape is compromised."

"I won't let her. I will never leave you behind."

She believed him with a certainty that shocked her. She'd never expected to be so sure of him. But she knew him well enough to know that once the words were said, his honor depended on making them true.

He'd given up his freedom once before, because of her plan to help the Fringers. That mission was accomplished—with the crack safely distributed, the Fringe worlds didn't need the cryptoglyph. They didn't need her or Finn anymore. She couldn't ask him to risk his freedom again over her emotional entanglement with the children.

"The children . . . Finn, we can't risk it. I understand that now. Maybe one day, somehow, we could come back for them. But we can't take them with us."

His eyes narrowed. "If that's what you want."

"Yes, it's what I want." It wasn't. But it was the best solution to her conflicting objectives. "Thanks for sticking up for me, though."

"I want to give you what you want."

She released a shaky sigh. "You've no idea how good that sounds. Nobody has ever . . ." Her throat closed over and she couldn't finish.

"I know that. I'm on your side, Edie."

Finn lay back on the hard ground, pulling her close so they were lying side by side, facing each other. He kissed her gently and she responded, and they explored each other with lips and hands—unhurriedly, like they had all the time in the world, rather than with the intention to arouse passion. After the tumultuous emotions of the past few days, his quiet embrace was exactly what she needed.

Despite Natesa's change of heart about Edie giving a presentation to the VIPs, she hadn't changed her mind about Edie investigating Caleb's files. In the morning Edie found a new set of files available to her at her console in the lab— Caleb's work over the past few months, ever since he joined the project.

Edie's thoughts were on the planned escape, which was scheduled for late in the evening. She could've postponed looking at the files, claimed she was too busy, and then by tomorrow she'd be gone. But in truth she was curious. Exactly what was Caleb hiding? Her innate feeling about the situation on Prisca bore little resemblance to the glowing reports Caleb was handing Natesa every day.

She went straight to the most recent sims of Prisca's BRATs. She was used to dealing with the error logs that Caleb generated from this data, so with those fresh in her mind, any discrepancies should stick out.

It didn't take long to find an unusual command in his code—an instruction to ignore a certain persistent glitch in the datastream before generating the daily error logs. Edie followed the glitch back through time, but she already knew what it was before she traced it to its source. She knew exactly what Caleb had done, and why.

Natesa proved impossible to track down, as she was too

busy entertaining her guests. Edie wrote her a quick report and then called Caleb on the planet's surface. He was outraged to learn she'd been going through his files.

"I've spent years building my databases," he spat out, wild-haired and red-faced. "Don't you dare trawl through them to pilfer my subroutines. My professional reputation depends on the innovations I've developed, and I don't need the so-called top cypherteck in the galaxy stealing my ideas."

"I'm not interested in your secrets. Not those secrets, anyway." Edie kept speaking over his next barrage of accusations. "I found a rogue protein in the mix. It was introduced only days after the BRATs came online."

"Contamination? That's unlikely. We were very careful."

"You can never be careful enough. You have equipment and workers on this project from a dozen worlds. Any one of them could have carried exotic DNA with them and contaminated the ecosystem."

"And what if they did? A certain level of contamination is acceptable, and irrelevant to the biocyph calculations."

"On a regular terraforming project with primitive lifeforms and low biomass, maybe. When things are going slowly, the biocyph has time to code around a hiccup like this. It self-corrects. But thanks to that regulator code you installed, everything is evolving too fast. The biocyph was unable to integrate this protein into the Terran ideal. It went rogue, established its own path of evolution, and the error snowballed. And you deleted it from the error logs."

"Because it's irrelevant!" he said between gritted teeth, like she was an upstart with no right to challenge his superiority. "The point is that the process *is* working on Scarabaeus, where the pace of evolution is even faster. You walked around on that planet without e-shields, contaminating everything, yet it shows no signs of ecological degradation."

"I can't explain it. Yes, there must be something different on Scarabaeus, a control mechanism that Prisca's missing."

"I'm telling you, there's nothing wrong with Prisca's

control mechanisms." He pushed his fingers through his tangled hair. "Have you told Natesa about this?"

"Of course."

Caleb groaned. Well, if he wouldn't accept there was a contamination problem, Edie wasn't going to push the issue. Let Natesa sort it out. With luck, Edie wouldn't be around to see the rubble bounce.

"I don't see the point of keeping this from her," Edie continued. "And what about the VIP tour of the compound? You can't hide what's going on forever."

"We have severe storms blowing in. I'm working on Natesa right now to cancel the dirtside tour. And keep your mouth shut tonight at that function. Theron's bound to have sent his spies to dig up dirt."

"I've already had this speech from Natesa. I don't—" Her palmet beeped with a message from Finn. "I have to go," she said abruptly, and cut the link. Thoughts of Prisca and Scarabaeus fled as she read a room number on Deck E and a brief text message:

Good news.

The room was Valari's, in the meckies' quarters. Valari sat at the console and Finn stood over her, leaning on the desk with one hand. As Edie approached, he slipped his free hand into hers and squeezed it. She smiled, marveling at how she could manage such a normal expression considering the way his unexpected touch jolted her.

On the holoviz was Cat's grinning face, distorted by the scrambler.

"It's a recorded message," Finn said, giving Valari a quick nod.

Valari replayed the message.

"Listen up," Cat said, "the crack worked! It's only been a few hours, but Fairbairn reported that their BRATs came back online with no sign of the biocyph lock remaining. Amazing! You guys are gonna be heroes. Well, not quite." She grinned again. "Couldn't name names, see. So, basically, I'm the hero. I got the okay from the captain here to transmit the crack through the commsat network, so I'm just waiting on your word."

"I've already sent the message to go ahead," Valari told Edie. "I hope that's all right by you," she added quickly.

"Yes, of course." Edie exchanged smiles with Finn, entwining her fingers with his. She wasn't going to let Valari's arch tone dampen her elation. This was what she and Finn had hoped for, ever since that night they'd huddled together inside a cold BRAT on Scarabaeus, when she had dared to hope she could take on the Crib with a single piece of code.

"Our navpilot Navin Ganesh on board the *Molly Mei* is a comms expert. He'll ensure the transmission gets out, and that no one can trace it back," Valari was saying. She sat back in her seat, her gaze falling briefly to Finn's and Edie's interlocked hands before drifting away. "I think we have reason to celebrate. And there's even a party tonight—well timed!"

"The meckies are invited to that?" Edie had assumed the VIP function was only for admin and technical staff.

"Yes. We were warned to dress up and behave ourselves," Valari said. "Celebrations aside, tonight we make our exit. The *Molly Mei* is about to make the jump into this system as soon as Cat has sent that transmission."

"We're ready," Finn said. "Until then, we carry on as normal. I need to get back to work. My boss has assigned my team to clean up the workshops in case there's an inspection."

"I have a few things to do as well." Edie started to follow him out. One thing she needed to do was visit Ken's store and see if he had anything she could wear for the function.

"Edie, wait," Valari said. "A word?"

Edie hesitated at the hatch, wondering what Valari would have to say to her that she didn't want Finn to hear. Finn left without comment.

As soon as they were alone, Valari said, "Assuming the *Learo Dochais*'s captain allows our ship to dock, the only remaining problem is these children you insist on rescuing."

So that was all. Edie wondered why Finn hadn't already told Valari of her decision. "It's okay. I realize now it's unrealistic to take them. And I'm okay with it."

Valari looked surprised but quickly recovered her poise. "I appreciate your change of heart. I failed to persuade Finn to take a stand, so I thought I had a real job ahead of me persuading you."

Edie wondered exactly what means of persuasion Valari had intended to use. Emotional blackmail? It didn't matter now. She'd decided to put Finn's freedom first, as she should have done from the start.

"I'm glad I made things easy for you," she said.

"You're very close to him, aren't you?"

The question took Edie by surprise and she stammered a response. "Y-Yes . . . well, not exactly. I mean, we've been through a lot together."

That sounded so weak. Finn and Valari had no doubt been through much more. She felt awkward discussing this with Valari, who was so much more alluring and self-assured than she'd ever be. Especially when her relationship with Finn was at a crossroads. They'd never directly discussed how they felt. They'd never made love. They'd never talked about a future together. And once they were free, it was likely their lives would head in different directions. He had the Saeth to return to. She had to make her own life out there, and the single skill she possessed was so powerful, so sought after on the Fringe, she'd have to hide it if she didn't want to be hunted for it.

"Listen to me, Edie. He is very attached to you. For some reason . . . well, I don't know. He's not the same young man I used to know. He feels very protective of you. More than that, he would do anything for you. I hope you won't take advantage of that."

Edie drew a deep breath, preparing to tell Valari it was none of her damn business. Then she breathed out in a rush, her protest dying on her lips, because Valari was right. She had already taken advantage of Finn by convincing him to kidnap the children—not because he thought it was a good idea, but only because she wanted it.

Well, that was over. She and Valari had both made Finn sign up to their causes. Whatever happened to them or to the children, she wouldn't do it again.

CHAPTER 18

Edie had once made a promise to Finn—that she'd wear a dress for him if he grew out his buzz cut and combed his hair. Well, the buzz cut was gone. Now that she knew Finn was going to be at the function, maybe it was time to wear the dress. She'd be pandering to Natesa's request at the same time.

She spent the rest of the day mentally preparing herself for a visit to the quartermaster. By the time she left the lab she was ready, and detoured to the supply room where Ken was closing up. He was already dressed for the evening's occasion in creased pants, a collared shirt, and a purple waistcoat.

"You've left it a bit late," he said. "You want a frock for the party tonight, am I right?"

"Uh, just something simple. I have no idea about this stuff."

"That's what I'm here for."

He looked so eager, she half expected him to rub his hands together with glee. He scrutinized her for a full minute, circling her slowly, then yanked open a closet, pulled out a few clothing items, and dropped them on the low shelving unit in the center of the room. Sorting through them quickly, he selected two and handed them to Edie.

"These will fit."

Apprehensive, she picked them up. The dresses were made out of smooth sheer fabric, one dusky pink and the other dark shimmery blue. Did people really wear these things?

Misinterpreting her look, Ken said, "Go on, they'll fit. I'm never wrong. Which one?"

"I can't wear these." She put them down.

"Nonsense." Ken selected the pink dress. "You'll look pretty as a rose in this."

"*No one* will ever get me to wear pink."

He raised a thick brow at her and relented, replacing the dress. He held up the blue dress against her. It was a little shorter than she'd have liked, reaching halfway down her thigh, but the color was more subdued and the neckline not quite as outrageous.

"Perfect. Now—shoes?" Ken waved at the footwear selection lined up at the bottom of the closet.

"Forget it. I mean, thanks for your help, but who wears pumps on a starship?"

"Stick to the center strip in the corridors so you don't catch a heel in the gravplating. Here we go."

He found a silvery-gray pair. Reluctantly, Edie pulled off her right boot and stuck her foot into the stupid thing. It was too big.

"Hmm. I've got more that might be your size." Ken found a pair of black strappy sandals with ridiculously high heels.

Edie had had enough. "Sorry, I'm not wearing those. Just . . . no way." She glanced at the dress, trying to imagine herself in it, and failing. "Let's forget the whole thing. Just find me a tee with glitter on it, something like that."

She put her boot back on while Ken watched. "You're not leaving my shop without a nice frock. Take the blue one. I'll rent it to you for half price."

He was very persuasive. She did manage to resist his

imploring when it came to the shoes and matching accessories, but handed over creds for the dress and got out of there as fast as she could.

"These storms are giving our base camp a real battering," Caleb reported that evening. He'd made a direct call to her quarters while she was getting ready for the evening's function. Natesa had told her to be there in ten minutes for something called cocktails. "Finally got Natesa to agree to postpone the VIP tour until the weather improves."

"As if sunshine and rainbows are going to make Prisca look any better."

"If you think Prisca is unsalvageable," he said, sulking now, "just say so."

"I think Prisca is unsalvageable. More precisely, I don't think it was ever viable." She sounded more phlegmatic about it than she felt. Her years of working with alien ecologies had given her an appreciation for the creativity and beauty of nature. Three billion years or more of unique evolution were about to be destroyed on Prisca. Not just altered and redirected, but wiped out—turned into organic sludge. "Look, I really have to go," she told him.

She signed off, took a quick shower, and yanked a comb through her damp hair—then stepped into the dress. She had to move slowly to avoid ripping the fabric, so flimsy and soft, with a sheen highlighting the neckline and bodice. The back was cut rather low, and the halter-style top exposed her shoulders and framed the inlaid shell between her collarbones. All in all, she did not feel like herself. In the mirror, she didn't look like herself, either. But she did look pretty good. Her reflection gave her a boost of self-confidence.

She started wishing for the sandals Ken had shown her. But those heels . . . there was no point tottering around feeling insecure all evening. In any case, it was too late now. She freshened up her work boots and pulled them on. Who looked at a person's feet, anyway, when there was cleavage up top?

Outside her room, a couple of admin staff headed to the lift in front of her. Edie stepped into the car with them. The man wore a smart sport jacket, the woman a scarlet-and-gold dress that was much fancier than Edie's. She'd taken some time with her hair and makeup, too. Edie tucked stray stands of hair behind her ear, feeling mousy by comparison. Then the man gave her an appreciative look, which helped.

The admin suite, cleared of office furniture, was set up with lounge chairs and trestle tables laden with finger food. Bland music wafted through the air. In one corner, a few meckies had assembled around the drinks table. They wore colorful scarves and bracelets, and chinked glasses with exaggerated mock manners. Finn was nowhere to be seen. Edie had never found a reason to wear a dress before and now she had one—but couldn't find him. Winnie gave a tipsy shrug and claimed not to know where Finn was.

Edie already wanted to leave. She hated crowds and speeches—especially Crib 'crats giving speeches, and there were bound to be plenty of those coming up.

The VIPs were easy to spot among the milits and the regular crew because their attention was focused on the children, who sat in a small circle in the center of the room. A globe of dancing lights surrounded them—a glamorous demo, not a meaningful example of their Project Ardra work. But it served its purpose, which was to impress the guests. The children's stifled yawns, indicating it was past their bedtime, were perhaps not quite so impressive.

She noticed Pris among the children—she hadn't realized the girl was well enough to attend. Edie could tell which of the four patterns in the holo was hers. It wasn't quite in sync at times, causing the other children to throw her irritated looks. Not enough for the audience to notice, but it was clear Pris was having trouble with her interface.

Natesa stood nearby, wearing an emerald-green sheath with a slit up the side. She nodded in bored acknowledgment to the elaborately dressed man chatting in her ear. From his uniform, Edie realized he was the captain of the

Fortitude, the ship that had ferried the VIPs to the *Learo Dochais*. Natesa kept her eyes on Pris. Her hard expression told Edie exactly what she thought of Pris's performance, and Edie knew the woman well enough to know what was going through her head—she may not blame the child for her mistakes, but she was sorely disappointed. And Pris would suffer under that disappointment. She would be made to feel it was her fault, however subtly, because she'd been brought up to believe that her value as a human being lay solely in her ability to perform as a cypherteck.

Pris already knew that. She looked devastated, and Edie's heart went out to her. How could she abandon these children to such a life? She alone was uniquely able to empathize with them, and she was going to walk away.

Through the tumbling lights of the holo, she noticed Finn at last, watching her from the other side of the circle. He wore his regular work clothes—no party dress-up for him. She was grateful he could no longer sense her emotional state because at that moment she could barely breathe. Anger and guilt congealed into a solid lump in her chest. She turned away from the children and pushed blindly through the crowd. She needed to get out.

She was going the wrong way. Whirling around, she headed for the exit. Someone brushed her arm as if to slow her down, and she pulled away sharply before realizing it was Finn—he'd moved to follow her. The concern etched on his face did nothing to alleviate the heaviness dragging at her heart.

Natesa was suddenly at her side. With her was an older man in a black tux and an absurd silver bow tie. Natesa wrapped her bony figures around Edie's upper arm, firmly enough to force her attention away from Finn.

"Edie, this is Administrator O'Mara. He's interested in your work with the children." Natesa gave a charming smile as if she and Edie were best friends. Then she moved off with a meaningful look that Edie interpreted as a warning to start parroting random boasts about CCU's wonderful protégées.

"Lovely to meet you, Ms Sha'nim. Call me Eric." O'Mara's grandfatherly manner put Edie somewhat at ease as he corralled her toward the drinks table. Edie looked around for Finn, but he'd faded into the background noise and motion of the party. "What'll you have?"

She looked at the colorful assortment of bottles arranged on the table and swallowed, confused. O'Mara smiled, further eroding his image of a fearsome senior 'crat.

"Try this."

He mixed a clear liquid from one bottle with fizzy water from another, and added a squirt of amethyst syrup. He dropped in a couple of frozen glowing spheres and handed her the glass. Edie took a sip. The bubbles stung her tongue with a vaguely fruity taste and then the alcohol burned her throat. She nodded with a smile and took another sip to please the attentive old man.

"What do you want to know?" she asked. May as well get this over with. Then she would leave this wretched party.

"You probably don't know this," O'Mara said, "but I was a biologist for Crib Central, stationed on Talas for several years while you were at Crai Institute. I oversaw the resettlement camps and unofficially advocated for the Talasi during that difficult period."

"No, I didn't know." Edie wondered why he was telling her. She'd had no involvement with the Talasi since Natesa removed her from the camps as a child.

"Tragic situation." O'Mara stared into his drink. "Still, I understand things are looking up. Detoxification of the forests is proceeding well, and several tribes have moved back to their ancestral zones."

The alcohol in her stomach emboldened her. "Perhaps you can tell me how Natesa managed to convince the elders to take custody of dozens of Talasi children, to be raised by the Crib."

"I'm sorry, that was after my time. I'm also a former cypherteck with great admiration for your talents. When I retired, I was so very proud of my thirty-five percent success rate with terraforming. Then you came on the scene and I realized my self-assessment had been somewhat generous." He gave a self-deprecating smile. "I've followed your career with some interest. I've always wanted to meet you. When Colonel Theron contacted me on his way back to Scarabaeus and asked me to join this little tour, I jumped at the chance."

So this was one of Theron's "spies," as Caleb had put it. And apparently Natesa didn't realize who he was or she wouldn't have introduced him to her.

Edie modified her original question. "What does Colonel Theron want to know?"

The look in O'Mara's eyes told her he understood that she understood what was going on. He was good enough not to play games. He guided her into an adjoining room, someone's office that had been given over to yet more displays extolling the success of the project, before asking, "What's the latest word on Prisca?"

"The lab produces daily reports with all the updates you need to know."

"We just learned that the tour of the planet's base camp has been canceled. Why?"

"Not canceled . . . postponed."

"Not postponed. *Canceled* entirely."

"Well, there's a storm."

"Storms come and go. We were scheduled to stay for three days. Now Natesa's shipping us out tomorrow and fobbing us off with a detour to some state-of-the-art science station on Port Trivane, on the way back to Central."

Things must really be bad. "I don't have an explanation for you. I didn't know any of that."

"Could it be that she doesn't want us to see firsthand what's happening on Prisca?"

Edie was tired of the charade. In a few hours she'd be on Valari's ship and none of this would matter. "Look, if our pretty displays and demos don't convince you that everything's wonderful, my platitudes won't change your opinion."

"I don't want platitudes. I want the truth."

"I know what you want. I know what *he* wants—me, on his team."

"Yes, we'd love to have you on the team. How would you feel about that?"

"That's a strange question. Don't I have to go where I'm told?"

O'Mara gave an awkward smile. "Make no mistake, Theron has the authority, backed by the Weapons Research Division, to order you to Scarabaeus. But there have been . . . problems in the past with your compliance."

"So that's why he sent you—to find out if I'd *willingly* join him. He tortured an innocent friend of mine for no reason. There's your answer." Edie jerked away from O'Mara, intending to leave.

"So let's take it as given that you don't want to work with the colonel. But what about the planet itself?"

She stopped in the doorway. What about Scarabaeus? Its lure was inescapable . . .

"The reports coming from Theron's team are remarkable," O'Mara went on, seeing he had her attention. "The complexity of the biocyph, the unnatural behavior of the aggressive organisms it creates as if on a whim, changing daily. This is well outside the biocyph's programming, no matter what mutations have accumulated. These developments are surely the result of some sort of emergent property."

She shook her head. She wouldn't get dragged into this. She couldn't. By tomorrow she'd be light-years away. They'd have to figure out Scarabaeus for themselves.

"It sounds like you're trying to say Scarabaeus has evolved sentience, which is impossible," she said brusquely. She meant it. Stating the idea aloud sounded ridiculous to her ears. "No sims have ever predicted anything approaching that outcome."

O'Mara produced a datastick from his pocket and snapped off the top cap. He held it up between thumb and forefinger. "I think you'll find this interesting. It's a download from a BRAT on Scarabaeus."

"I thought Theron's people couldn't access the BRATs."

"On a few occasions they've managed to get close enough to a seed to jack in. It's a deadly exercise. A promising young cypherteck had just enough time to download this data before she was killed."

Edie stared at the datacap, wondering what was on it. Trying not to wonder . . .

"Please, take a look," O'Mara said, holding out the cap. "We would be most interested in your interpretation."

"I don't work for Theron and I never will."

"Well then, do it as a favor to me. One cypherteck to another."

Edie took the cap. She couldn't *not* take it. A quick look wouldn't do any harm. And really, it was her choice what she told O'Mara about it afterward.

He gave a little bow of thanks as she left the room.

The children had gone—to bed, she hoped, as it was getting late. The deck was filling up and the noise level was on the rise. She remembered why she hated this sort of thing. Natesa had a perverse fondness for these social dos, and had dragged Edie along to a few at Crai Institute on Talas. Edie's primary objective was always to sneak out as soon as they were crowded enough that her presence would not be missed.

Natesa accosted her as she searched the room again for Finn. "Why were you talking to that man?"

"O'Mara? *You* introduced us."

"And I've just found out who he is—one of Theron's cronies." She glared at Edie through slitted, black-lined eyes. "What did he want?"

"Nothing that concerns you." Edie surreptitiously slipped the datacap into her pocket.

"How dare you scheme behind my back. Has Theron given the order to reassign you to Scarabaeus?"

So that's what she was concerned about. "Wouldn't you already know if he had?"

"Well, if he does give the order, he'll have to wait." She

lowered her voice, bringing her lips to Edie's ear. "I read your message about that rogue protein Chessell deleted from the error logs. What he did was unforgivable, even if he truly thought it didn't matter. Until this past year, I'd never worked with him before and I'm not sure I trust him any longer. There's bound to be more he's not telling me. You're going dirtside to find out what else he's not putting in his reports."

"I can investigate from here."

"No. I think you'll be more focused if you're actually there. And by the time you get back in a few days, the *Fortitude* will have left. Theron will have to send another transport. And by *then*, Prisca will be back on track and I'll have the order rescinded. You're going to Prisca, Edie. Tomorrow morning."

Edie's heart sank. This could mess with their escape plans. "What time tomorrow?"

"Report to the docking bay at oh-seven-hundred. And I suppose you'll have to bring that lag along with you."

Oh-seven-hundred . . . They should be gone by then. Edie played along. "Okay, I'll be there."

"You'll do a better job down there than Caleb Chessell, anyway. A fresh set of eyes. Best cypherteck in the galaxy— if you can't rescue Prisca from self-destruction, no one can." The edge of panic to her voice was unmistakable.

CHAPTER 19

Edie snuck out a side door and returned to her quarters, the datacap burning a hole in her pocket. She went straight to her console, plugged in the cap, and pressed her fingertips to the access port.

As the datastream flowed through her splinter, she expected to hear the music of Scarabaeus. Realized she'd been anticipating it, longing for it. Instead, she got a blast of foreign code that felt like an electric shock.

She concentrated on listening to the datastream. The song she recognized was here after all, choked by overlays of new code that astonished her with its complexity and impenetrability. It wasn't set up in tiers, the standard way to organize biocyph. Instead, it was concentrated into tight tangled balls wedged between the tiers and vibrating at such a high frequency that they buzzed—like knots of twine, she thought, using a visual metaphor that Eric O'Mara would understand. These tangles obscured much of the base datastream.

No cypherteck would program in this way . . . *could* program this way. Had the knots come from Scarabaeus itself, as O'Mara had speculated? Biocyph was self-programming, of course—that was how the BRATs functioned, adapting to perform simulations and calculations that were far beyond the capabilities of any human. But biocyph didn't invent new *ways* of programming. Not like this.

She delved deeper between the tiers.

Loose strings extruded from the nearest tangle, each wailing its own tune. She isolated one, hooked a glyph to it, and pulled herself along. The string was far more complex than she'd initially thought. Its surface bubbled with activity as it recognized the intrusion and poked at the glyph with a hundred wasp stings. A headache bloomed behind Edie's eyes.

She pushed on, cutting past the confusion, ignoring the persistent buzzing that grew louder as it drilled into her brain. Up ahead she felt the datastream thicken as she approached the tangle, ever more complex and angry.

Angry. The children would describe it that way.

Edie tugged at the knot, determined to unravel it, but to no avail. Up close, she could tell it wasn't integrated properly into the datastream. The loose tendrils were merged with the tiers, but the bulk of the tangle could not possibly be interacting much with the biocyph because it was so balled up. Whether or not these tangles were O'Mara's "emergent property," large parts of them were unlikely to be having a direct effect on the biocyph and therefore on the planet's evolution.

Edie jacked out before her headache became unbearable. She'd satisfied her curiosity, frustrating though the experience had been. Whatever was happening on Scarabaeus, she wouldn't learn anything more from this sim.

She still had four hours to kill before she was to meet Finn, Corinth, and Valari in Valari's room to make final preparations for their escape. She paced her room restlessly, nervous about what might go wrong. They still had to steal the neuroxin—a last-minute job that would be made easier by the fact that most of the ship's personnel were at the function. At the back of her mind, half formed plans about how they might have taken the children jostled for her attention. Natesa and Theron wouldn't get what they wanted from her, but she wouldn't get what she wanted, either.

But maybe there *was* something of value she could take with her . . .

Ten minutes later she was outside the lab hatch on Deck B. The lifts and corridors had been deserted—no one to question why she was running around the ship in a party dress holding a ratty old duffel bag. Now she drew out her crew key and hesitated. Her entry would be logged, but it was likely no one would check those logs until the morning—too late for repercussions. She snapped the hatch and stepped into the lab.

She moved through a maze of consoles, several of them lit as they worked on sims and other programs the tecks had left running overnight. In the darkened back room, orderly columns and rows of priceless biocyph modules lined the racks. She could fit two modules in the bag. Her imagination leapt ahead as she thought of what the Fringers could do with them. She'd heard there were maverick cyphertecks on the Fringe. Not Crib trained, not as good as she was, but skilled enough to make good use of the modules with or without her help.

With the crack out there, the Fringers didn't need her any more. With the leash cut, Finn didn't need her any more either—much as he might want her.

The children needed her. She'd always known that. Valari had refused to take them, and Edie had relented for Finn's sake . . . but there was another option. Finn had said he wouldn't leave her behind. But she could let him go. She could crush her ethical objections to Ardra, work dutifully for the Crib, and stand by the children, giving them the attention and love she'd never had.

Maybe, eventually, it would make up for what she'd done to Pris.

At the sound of footsteps near the door, Edie muttered a curse and slipped behind the racks. She'd foolishly left the main hatch open, assuming no one would be around. Peeking out, she saw Finn in the doorway. Edie moved slowly into the wedge of soft light that spilled in from the main lab, suddenly nervous, of all things, about the dress.

"You left in a hurry. I've been looking for you." His voice was a touch hoarse as he stared at her from the doorway, his gaze flickering over her body—mouth, breasts, dress, boots.

"You found me." When he didn't say more, didn't move or do anything but look at her, she said, "How are the plans coming along?"

"The *Molly Mei* was given permission to dock for repairs a few hours ago. They messed with the fuel mix to cause neutron leak, and they're asking for help with a valve recalibration. So far, so good."

Her heart raced as she anticipated sneaking on board and leaving the Crib forever. Her brain fought the idea. She couldn't do it . . . could she? Instead of voicing her ambivalence, she found herself talking about something else entirely.

"In case something goes wrong, in case we don't get away . . . You should know they're sending us dirtside early tomorrow morning. I mean, they're sending me. And they don't know about the leash, so—you as well." He didn't ask the obvious question, so she brought it up. "Unless you want to tell them the truth and avoid the trip."

"You convinced me Natesa would force me to leave and then have me killed."

Edie chewed her lip and nodded. "After what happened to Lukas, I think she might, if you left on a Crib ship. You'd be unprotected. On the Saeth ship you stand a chance."

"Then let's hope it all works out."

"Yes . . ."

He'd moved toward her, a few casual paces that she'd somehow failed to notice. Her fingers closed around a nearby strut and she backed up a step, half hiding behind the rack. She'd been closer to Finn on more than one occasion but this was different. There was a look of determination in his eyes that only added to her ambivalence. If she stayed behind . . . if she had the courage to stay behind, was it fair to let him believe this was the start of something when it was really the end?

"You look beautiful."

She soaked up his words for a few seconds. "There were supposed to be shoes . . ."

"The boots make you look like you."

"We made a deal once, remember? You comb your hair, I wear a dress."

He made a small grunt of apology and came to her. "I didn't comb my hair."

Edie pushed her fingers through his dark curls, still too short to really need a comb anyway. She urged his head lower—not that he needed encouragement—and then lost her nerve at the last moment, nose-to-nose with him and frozen with her lips parted. She breathed in time with him, allowing herself to feel the tension building between them, for the first time not needing to clamp down on it. He kissed her instead, his hands sliding around her, pulling her close.

Something was wrong. He was tense.

"What is it?" she asked.

He shook his head slowly. "Feels strange . . . not having you in my head."

"That's good, right?"

"Yeah." He slowly rolled his head from side to side. "I don't know. I got used to you."

"It wasn't *me*, not really. Just static interference from a malfunction in the receiver—"

"I got used to you," he repeated. He cupped her face between his hands and tilted her face upward. His thumbs lay across her cheekbones, warm points of pressure, and he kissed her again.

Lacing her fingers behind his neck, she responded aggressively, welcoming the groan from deep in his throat that signaled his surprise and pleasure. His hands were all over her skin and the racks clattered when he backed her up against them. It wasn't until he cupped her bottom to lift her onto the front rail of the racks, pressing between her thighs to show her where this was going, that she remembered a moment ago she'd been considering letting him go. She *had* to let him go . . .

Yet she was desperate for him. Her hands went to his belt, his went under her dress and he hooked aside the gusset of her panties.

His lips brushed her ear. "Is this what you want?"

She nodded quickly and pulled herself against him.

Giving in was easy. His hand was warm and firm on her thigh, and his other hand reached behind her to grab the rack for support. Around them, the vast metal lattice clinked in response to his rhythm. She should tell him she was going to stay behind. *Soon. Not now . . .*

A sudden wash of orgasm baffled her, as though her body had betrayed her. She turned her face into the crook of his shoulder as he leaned into her, crushing her in his arms. She wanted to imprint him on her memory—his warmth and strength and smell. His calm assurance, his determination, and most of all his unwavering support of her.

"Are you okay?" Finn slid his hand into her hair and tugged gently to make her look at him. He gave a smile that made her chest tighten. "I think I was a little rough."

"No . . . No, you weren't," she quickly said, because he looked like he was about to apologize.

Still, the metal rack dug into the backs of her thighs. She hadn't noticed it until now. He helped her hop down and she surreptitiously straightened her underwear. His hands rested lightly on her upper arms, his fingers stroking her skin.

"Let's find a bed and do this properly," he said.

That made her smile. "Was it not done properly?"

He groaned, his eyes glittering. "That's not what I meant. Take me back to your quarters."

"You're not allowed."

"There's no one around."

Damn, he was temptingly persistent. The tension built in a not altogether unpleasant way as he watched her steadily for a reaction and she stood there not knowing how to ask him to back down. But the idea of a repeat performance—especially when she knew he needed an emotional connection and whatever he thought might follow from that—terrified her. It was everything she wanted, had never had, could never have once they parted ways.

Her brief hesitation gave him his answer. Apparently he didn't need the leash to sense her mood. Still, he tried again.

"Come with me." Now he sounded like he knew she would refuse. When she shook her head, he lifted her chin with one finger and his intense gaze searched her face. "What are you not telling me?"

Words lodged in her throat, a plea for understanding that she couldn't voice. Once she said it, it would become true and she couldn't bear it being true.

He turned his head away with an impatient noise and stepped back, touching his temple reflexively. She realized he was listening to his Saeth chip.

"Corinth wants to meet. He's on his way here."

"Is something wrong?"

"Don't know. Come on." He took her hand and led her back into the main lab. "They'll know you've been here," he observed.

"Yes." That was something she hadn't considered. If she stayed, she'd have to explain herself to Security. And that reminded her of why she *had* come here. "Wait—the stock biocyph modules. I was thinking we could take a couple of them." She'd said *we*, not *you*. Her indecision was a fist squeezing her heart. How could she let him go, the only person who was on her side? How could she leave here, when she was the only person in the children's lives who was on their side?

Finn glanced back. "Risky. If anyone sees us carrying something—"

Corinth appeared at the hatch. "We've moved up the schedule. The *Molly Mei* has been ordered to leave immediately. We have twenty minutes at the most."

"Are they suspicious?" Finn asked.

"We don't know." He sounded urgent, breathless. "But there's nothing we can do to delay the ship's departure. We need to get to the infirmary for the neuroxin."

They ran to the lift, the modules forgotten. As they waited for the car, Corinth outlined the plan in low tones.

"There's just one dockmaster on duty. The *Molly Mei*'s navpilot Gutala will keep her busy in the control room while we sneak on board."

Edie was barely listening. Every time Corinth paused for breath, she drew in her breath—to tell them . . . *I'm not coming with you*. When the lift car arrived and they stepped inside, she noticed Finn looking at her. Something flickered in his eyes that made her think he knew what she was about to say.

"We have a clear path through the tool room on Deck F to the hangar," Corinth went on. "Valari's there now, keeping watch."

"Finn—" Edie began just as the car stopped its descent and the door opened at Deck C.

Corinth exited. Edie held back, and Finn stayed with her, frowning deeply. She wanted to tell them to forget the neuroxin, get to the hangar now, leave her here . . .

Corinth made a gesture toward the infirmary. "Hurry. We don't have a lot of time."

"Go with him," Finn said, guiding Edie out of the car. Then he glanced down the corridor in the opposite direction. Toward the children's dorm. "I'll get the kids."

Corinth froze. "What?"

"No, Finn, don't risk it," Edie said. "You two, get to the hangar. I'll stay with them." Her throat closed over. "I'll stay behind."

Finn ignored her. "They can get to the hangar unseen via the access tubes. I'll meet them there and bring them on board."

"Will they go with you?" Corinth asked. The question surprised Edie. Shouldn't Corinth be protesting this change in plans?

"The boy will. Maybe he can persuade the others, if I turn it into a game."

"It won't work," Edie said, terrified he was ruining his chance for escape because of his determination to do what *she* wanted. "The dorm will be guarded."

"I'll handle it."

He took off in the direction of the dorm, while Corinth went the other way. Edie clenched her fists and followed Corinth.

"This is crazy," she hissed. "Valari will refuse to take the children."

"If he shows up with them, she'll take them."

"Why are you letting him do this?"

"*Letting* him? He outranks me."

"There must be more to it than that. Valari outranks Finn. Shouldn't you be obeying her?"

"Truth is, I agree with you about the children. I did all along. This is what the Saeth do—we fight for what's right, regardless of a person's citizenship."

As they approached the infirmary, they slowed to a walk to avoid arousing suspicion. A couple of medics exited the foyer, finishing up a conversation. One of them walked off and the other went back inside.

"This way." Corinth turned abruptly left, down a narrow corridor leading directly to the offices of the infirmary. He used his crew key to open Dr Sternhagen's door. As a utility teck, he was permitted access to the room for cleaning and repairs.

"Valari's signaling us to move faster," he said. "Must be trouble in the hangar."

And Finn's decision to take the children would surely cause delays. Edie couldn't think about that. She had to do her part while he did his. She pointed to the cabinet where she'd seen the boxes of neuroxin implants a few days earlier, during her medical exam. Corinth examined the cabinet quickly.

"Locked, but no alarm," he said.

He pulled a device off his tool belt and stuck it over the plaz door lock. It whirred softly for a minute, rotating and clicking. Corinth tapped it sharply, then pulled on it, and the door popped open. He grabbed a box and stuck it in his inside jacket pocket, along with the device.

"Is Finn okay?" Edie said, feeling left out of the communication loop.

"He hasn't reported." That didn't sound good. "Wait . . . *shit*." He listened to his chip for a moment. "Valari says there are milits heading our way."

"Did we trigger an alarm?"

He thrust the box of implants at her. "Take this. Use the service lift and get to the hangar. I'll hold them off."

Edie stared at the box. This wasn't going to work. She couldn't let Corinth sacrifice himself.

"No. I'll talk my way out of it. You get out." Before he could protest, she added, "I was going to stay behind, anyway. I was going to tell Finn that I'd stay here with the children. I didn't know he'd go back for them at the last minute."

"You were going to stay? But I thought the two of you . . . ?" He left the rest unspoken.

"Yes." One word that said everything—and she was saying it to the wrong man. "Corinth, get out of here." She pushed him into the corridor.

"I won't make it to the hangar in time."

"I'm sorry. Maybe Finn and Valari can still get away. Just . . . go back to your quarters or to the party. Give me your crew key—I'll say I stole it." She grabbed it off him. "And tell Finn to leave. Tell him not to wait for the children. He should just leave."

Footsteps and voices approached. Edie backed into the office again. When she glanced over her shoulder, Corinth was gone.

Edie replaced the box and shut the cabinet door. The lock clicked back in place. Her mind whirred with possible excuses she could give for breaking into the office. Nothing seemed plausible. She was going to get into trouble for this.

As long as Finn got away, safe on a Saeth ship where Natesa couldn't touch him, it was worth it.

CHAPTER 20

"I wanted to find out what you did to Finn," Edie said. It was tough making up an excuse when she had no idea yet what had happened to Finn, the children, or Valari and her ship and crew. But this was the best she'd come up with. "He told me he was rendered unconscious during his medical exam. That's not usual. I came here looking for his records."

Natesa paced the doctor's office, regal in her green dress. She'd been seething with anger when she'd first been called to the room. Now she seemed taken aback by Edie's explanation, as if it was the last thing she'd expected to hear.

"You could have asked me or Dr Sternhagen, if you had any concerns."

"Okay, I'm asking you."

"To my knowledge his exam was entirely routine. What makes you think I'd take any interest at all in some meckie's medical exam?"

"He's not *some meckie*. He's the man you've threatened to kill if I don't behave."

"I've done no such thing. This is ridiculous, and beside the point. You were supposed to be wooing my guests. You're going dirtside early in the morning. You have serious work to do. Instead, you're using someone else's crew key to sneak about the ship." Natesa glared at the milit who flanked Edie. He'd been the one to find her in the office a few minutes earlier. "Have you arrested the worker to whom that key belongs?"

"Yes, ma'am," the milit replied. "He's a utility tech who recently transferred to the project. His use of the key outside his shift hours alerted Security."

"But I stole the key from him," Edie said. "He didn't do anything wrong."

Natesa was unmoved. "He's still at fault for being careless. Now, is there anything else you want to tell me? I don't like surprises, least of all from you. If not, I'd like to get back to my guests—"

Her commlink beeped with an incoming call. She extracted the device from under her sleeve and jabbed the switch.

"What is it?"

"Administrator, there's a report of a disturbance in the hangar."

"Why are you bothering me with this?"

"It's the children, ma'am. We found the children in an access tube leading to the loading dock, and they seem to think they're supposed to board that merchant ship, the one that docked for repairs."

Natesa's glare snapped to Edie, her face hardening with suspicion. Edie maintained a neutral expression but found it hard to breathe. Their entire escape plan was in ruins. And where was Finn?

"Impound that ship. Detain the crew. And take the children back to their dorm. I'll meet you there." Natesa eyed Edie a moment longer, as if unable to decide what to do with her. "If you're not going to make yourself useful at the function, return to your quarters and get some sleep. You leave at oh-seven-hundred." She walked toward the door, then pulled up beside Edie, standing a little too close for comfort. "If I find out this has anything to do with you . . ." She let the statement hang in the air, apparently unable to think of a suitably dire way to finish it. Then she stalked out.

Edie was given an unwelcome escort to Deck D. Once back in her room, she debated whether to try and contact Finn. She had, with luck, saved Corinth from serious charges. But if Finn had been caught near the hangar, there was no story convincing enough to save him. If he'd got away, and if Cat on board the *Molly Mei* could successfully play innocent, maybe the damage could be confined to Valari alone. If the children kept their mouths shut, no one would associate Finn with Valari or with the children's odd excursion.

One thing was certain—if Edie and Finn were going to escape, they'd have to start from scratch with a new plan.

An hour later, Edie could stand it no more. She had to find out what was going on. She took the lift down one deck and wandered through the meckies' quarters, hoping to find Finn. Many of the doors were open and the party seemed to have spread to this deck. It wasn't often that the Crib doled out free alcohol, and the workers were making the most of it. Conflicting music blared from two different sources. The deck swarmed with people in various stages of inebriation. A few of them were playing a raucous game of handball down the length of one narrow corridor.

Edie asked a series of random people where she could find Finn. Eventually she was told he shared a room with someone called Slake. Someone else told her Slake's room number, and she buzzed the door.

Finn snapped open the hatch. He looked relieved to see her—neither of them had been caught . . . yet. He moved aside to let her enter the room. The first thing she noticed was a semiconscious man on one of the bunks. He had apparently dressed for the party, with lime-green boots, a lopsided velvet top hat, and a matching jacket that lay open to reveal a bare chest carved with a variety of tattoos.

"Hey, Slake," Finn said. "Give us some privacy, will you?"

Slake moaned, his limbs twitching, but showed no other signs of life.

Finn prodded his leg. "We had a deal, buddy."

One bleary eye opened to give Edie the once-over. Then

he rolled off the bunk and staggered around for a while, hiccupping violently, before finally finding the door. Finn snapped it shut behind him. He sat on the other bunk and ran his hands through his hair. Edie took a quick look around at the mess, the piles of dirty clothes and scattered belongings. It really didn't seem fair that Finn had been sent down here, but he was probably used to far worse.

"They found the children," Edie said. "What happened?"

"I sent a service tom into Galeon's room with a message to take the kids to the loading dock. I could've snuck them on board from there, into the cargo hold, without being seen from the hangar. By the time I got down there, the dockmaster was getting suspicious of the *Molly Mei*'s delaying tactics. Then Corinth told us the two of you weren't going to make it."

"I told him to tell you to leave anyway, without the children."

He gave her a sideways look. "You mean, to leave without *you*?"

"That was your chance, Finn. That ship was the safest place for you."

"Doesn't matter anyway. The ship never left."

Edie bit her lip. "I know. I was with Natesa when she ordered it impounded." She couldn't shake the thought that Valari and Finn might have made it out if Valari hadn't waited for the children and for her and Corinth.

"So—what's the damage? Corinth is in the brig, that's all he told me." His voice was oddly flat. It wasn't like Finn to be discouraged. The soldier in him always had a contingency plan.

"I don't think he's in too much trouble. There's no reason for them to link me or Corinth to any of this. What about Galeon?"

"He knows I sent that tom, but the other kids don't. I don't think he'll tell."

"How can we find out what happened to Valari?"

Finn hesitated, taking in a deep breath, exhaling slowly.

"Her chip winked out a few minutes ago. Corinth can't reach her, either."

"What does that mean? Is she dead?"

"Not necessarily. If they've arrested her, she'd have switched it off to prevent them from tapping into it."

The hatch snapped open suddenly, and Slake stumbled inside with a stupid grin on his face. In the corridor beyond, people were shouting with excitement.

"Hey, there's been a fuckin' shootout in the hangar," Slake said. "C'mon, man, let's check it out!"

Edie started to rise, but Finn touched her arm.

"There's nothing we can do about it," he murmured.

Their lack of enthusiasm couldn't diminish Slake's, and he loped outside again to find out what was going on.

"You should get back," Finn said. "If they do connect me with this . . . if they come for me, I don't want you here."

"What about Valari and Cat?"

"We'll find out soon enough. Don't ask about it. Just stay out of it. I guess we'll be going dirtside, right? Maybe this will all blow over while we're on the surface."

Edie hoped it was true. She got up to leave. "I meant what I said about the children—I know you tried because of me, but it's too risky. Next time your chance comes, just take it." He opened his mouth and she knew what he was about to say, and preempted him. "I trust you to come back for me, Finn. Bring the cavalry if you want to—but first, you need to get safely away where Natesa can't follow you."

He looked like he was restraining himself from arguing with her. Instead, he stood and reached out to run his fingers down her bare arm. She shivered, wishing she could lock the door and go to him, even in this god-awful hovel. He kissed her—once, lightly, a quick brush of warm lips, as if sealing a promise—and she left.

CHAPTER 21

The skiff plummeted through the atmosphere and hit the storms. Edie clung to her harness and listened to the engines scream. She was seated close enough to the cockpit to hear the pilot's calm, professional voice and it was the only reassuring thing about the flight to Prisca's surface.

After the excitement of the previous evening, she'd been woken up three hours early by Natesa, still in the green party dress, and told to report to the hangar immediately because the schedule had been moved up. Natesa's reason was neither welcome nor entirely unexpected.

"The Weapons Research Division just sent the order to transfer you immediately into the custody of Captain Fox of the *Fortitude*, for reassignment to Scarabaeus. Obviously I cannot allow that. Theron seems to think he can pull apart Ardra at the seams. He'll never get away with it. I need time to sort this out while you're safely out of the way on Prisca."

So Theron was finally throwing his weight around and Natesa's chosen option was to hide Edie away. Unless Natesa's friends in high places really were as powerful as she seemed to think, she was putting her career in serious jeopardy.

Edie had given Finn one more chance to back out. After

all, he was only coming dirtside because no one knew the leash was cut.

"I'd rather keep an eye on you," was his response.

Now he sat three rows back with Winnie and two other meckies assigned to the mission. In truth, Edie was glad he wanted to come. She wanted to keep an eye on him, too—the farther he was from Natesa, the better. They'd exchanged a grim look as they entered the hangar and saw the *Molly Mei* in the bay next to the skiff, two milits at the main hatch and another patrolling the hangar. All they knew about what had happened last night was that the *Molly Mei*'s crew was confined inside the ship.

Sheeting rain outside the skiff's small windows made it impossible to see much of the compound as they landed on Prisca. Once they breached the barrier of the perimeter shield, the atmosphere cleared. Fifty meters from the landing pad stood the compound buildings—a cluster of half a dozen prefabs connected by walkways.

Before she had time to disembark, Caleb beeped her commlink from the lab building.

"New data coming in from the highlands north of our base camp," he said. "I need you to take a look."

"We just landed," Edie said. "Give me a minute, okay?"

"We don't have a lot of time. This is . . . It's some sort of meltdown. Like the biomass collapsed overnight, and it's spreading."

"What do you mean, *collapsed*?"

"I don't know. We can't get accurate data because of these storms. The survey team had to turn back and our aerial drones aren't much help. Maybe it's some sort of blight."

Some sort of blight? Caleb was still fooling himself that this wasn't a fundamental problem with the terraforming process, that it could be fixed.

"I'll be there soon."

Edie climbed down from the skiff. Local time was early afternoon, not that it was obvious with the sun obscured by the storm. Peering through the haze of the compound's shielding, she saw the vague silhouette of a sprawling mountain range rising up to the north, shrouded in low rain clouds. The compound itself was nestled in the foothills, and what vegetation she could see cowered under the gale-force winds.

Winnie stepped up beside her. "Jezus, I hate touching ground. Last time I was here was . . . let's see, ten months ago, setting up the shielding." She indicated a nearby shield generator, one of dozens lined up about ten meters apart around the perimeter of the compound. They projected the force field that kept the biocyph's lethal retroviruses—and the weather—at bay. "The lab's in the east wing. I'm sure Caleb's eager for you to check in."

Winnie went to help the meckies offload equipment brought down from the *Learo Dochais*. Finn was among them. They stacked crates onto pallets and hauled them into the nearest building. Edie followed the walkways to the lab. Inside, in a room half the size of the main lab on the *Learo Dochais* and packed with twice as much equipment, Caleb and three other tecks hunkered over consoles as holos wafted around their heads.

Caleb glanced up, stark-eyed and pale-faced in the middle of his personal hell—the end of Ardra. Without offering any greeting or bothering to introduce the other tecks, he waved her over to his console.

"Take a look at this. What the hell is going on?"

Edie glanced at the sims that Caleb flashed to the holoviz. This was even worse than she'd imagined. Caleb had been very creative with his updates and no one, not even Natesa, had dared to question his reports until now.

"Look at how erratic these biochemical pathways are," Edie said. "Your regulator code has raised the level of retroviral interference to the point where sims can't accurately predict the results. Those error logs we've been working on are always ten steps behind. Where's the raw data from the BRATs? When was the last time you actually jacked into one?"

"Until two days ago, one of us was out there every day," Caleb insisted. "The storms have kept us away. And now they present a physical threat, in this region anyway. The rain is washing away the degraded vegetation and topsoil on the mountainside, right down to the bedrock. We've orders from Natesa to get back out there, reprogram the BRATs manually if we have to."

"When will the weather clear up?"

"Not today. But this can't wait."

"Uh, have you looked out the window?"

"I mean it, Edie. Large areas surrounding the compound are already mash." His lips twitched on the word. "The nearest BRAT is about three klicks from here, due east. You need to get out there right now."

"When did *we* become *you*? You're not going?"

"I'm working on some urgent sims. Nothing you're qualified to handle."

This was new—instead of talking about security clearance, he was now talking about qualifications. Caleb was certainly more experienced with biocyph than Edie, but she knew she was better at interfacing with it. And experience didn't count for quite so much on Prisca, where the situation was novel.

She glanced at the holoviz again. "The degradation is irreversible. You know that."

"Yes, but if we can stop it now, the rest of the ecosystem may absorb the damage."

"Are you just making this up as you go along? These sims estimate thirty-two percent of the planet's biomass is either mash or well on the way to becoming mash within the next few days. Prisca isn't going to recover, Caleb. All we can do is try and figure out what went wrong."

"Which is why you're going out there. Take a biocyph module." He pointed to a crate in the corner that one of the meckies had brought in. "If the weather gets too dicey out there, you can at least get a download imprinted on the stock biocyph. It'll give me a better feel for the BRAT than this dry data."

"How do I get to the BRAT? The skiff?"

"No, there's nowhere for a ship to land halfway up a mountain. We have an amphibious skidder on standby."

Knee-deep slime, gray with swirls of green, sucked at Edie's boots. Her e-shield kept her legs dry but it didn't make trudging through the muck any easier. Rain fell steadily. Despite Caleb's insistence that they leave immediately, Winnie had refused to head out in the storm. They'd waited two hours for a window of relatively mild weather.

The BRAT seed was just up ahead, a three-meter-tall elongated dome buried in a natural indentation, shrouded in mist and drowning in mud that had run down the incline and become trapped.

Not really mud, Edie reminded herself, but a soupy mix of rotting biomatter. This was what an ecosystem turning to mash looked like. The cells of every living thing touched by the biocyph's ineffective and confused retroviruses were breaking down, destroying the structural integrity of foliage, wood, bacteria, worms, animals—everything—from the inside out. Only their e-shields protected the humans.

Up ahead, ton upon ton of twisted vegetation and broken branches stuck out of the mud that the rain washed downhill. Below them, the mud ran down into the valley in sluggish streams, coursing between boulders. They'd taken the skidder out of the valley and across several kilometers of rough terrain—she and Finn, Winnie driving, and a milit escort who introduced himself as Ramirez. For the first half hour, the compound behind them had been visible through the rain and fog as a diffuse light in the far distance. Now it had disappeared.

"This is a landslide waiting to happen," Finn said, plodding along beside Edie and carrying a biocyph module in one hand. His miserable expression showed what he thought of the field trip. They had to tackle the last few meters on foot.

"The compound's shielding will protect the buildings, won't it?" Edie asked.

"If it holds."

They both looked up the slope at what used to be a thriving forest, now a jumbled compost heap. What didn't turn to mash could still come sliding down once the root systems were compromised.

"Winnie," Edie called over her shoulder, "maybe you should send a couple of aerial drones into the hills to check out the stability of all that vegetation."

"They took recordings three days ago."

"Yeah, but it's changing fast."

Winnie shrugged and returned to the skidder, where the drones were stored. Ramirez continued after them, a few paces behind.

"Any other dangers out here?" Finn asked. She knew he was thinking back to Scarabaeus and the vicious slaters they'd encountered there.

"On land Caleb's team hasn't identified anything more advanced than flightless insects. Most of the biomass comes from mosses, cycads, ferns. The main danger here is to the environment, not to us."

They arrived at the BRAT, sliding the last few meters over the edge of a ridge to reach it. The mud was deeper here, reaching Edie's upper thighs. It was littered with half-rotten debris that swirled and bubbled around her like stew boiling in a pot. She waded over to the access port, reeled out a hardlink from her belt, and jacked into the BRAT.

She was used to listening to the datastream of Prisca's sims. Letting the real music of Prisca flood her splinter, direct from the source, was a different experience—louder, richer, and far more chaotic than she'd anticipated. She tried to attach a glyph to the datastream so she could follow it. The glyph wouldn't stick. It dissolved in the churning, discordant music that sounded to Edie like a thousand different tunes melded together, each out of sync with the rest.

The boosted biocyph had taken so many shortcuts in its calculations toward the Terran ideal that the retroviruses simply couldn't keep up. They were rewriting DNA code across the planet, always a step behind the next round of calculations, the next round of retroviruses. A hundred steps behind. It was as if nature had gone into shock, and the shockwaves were spreading. According to the latest data, this level of confusion and degradation was being repeated across many of the eight hundred BRATs scattered across the planet's surface.

Reconstructing the data into orderly tiers was a hopeless task. There was no saving Prisca, regardless of Natesa's determination and Caleb's ego-driven confidence.

Something caught her attention. A new tier, wedged between the others, complex and robust and humming like a well-greased engine. This was the regulator code that Caleb had installed. She noticed it not because it was unusual, but because it was familiar. And it was not Caleb's work.

She called him on her commlink.

"Have you begun the imprint yet?" he asked before she could say anything.

"Not yet." She had to raise her voice over the rain drumming on the BRAT's surface. "I found something interesting, though."

"What?" He sounded wary.

"The regulator code. You took this from Scarabaeus."

Silence for several seconds. Then, "I developed it from subroutines I found there, yes."

"Why have you been hiding that fact?"

She knew, of course. He wanted all the credit for his "innovative" code and with his next words he admitted as much.

"It's still *my* work. It took my skill to recognize it and extract it and modify it for Prisca. It's all my work."

"You could still have told Natesa . . . and me! This could be an important clue as to why Prisca is failing."

"She'd probably have forbidden me to use it. She wants nothing to do with Theron's work. And I couldn't tell Theron because then Natesa would have owed him another favor. She was already in the red for having me reassigned to her team only weeks after I joined his."

Up on the ridge, Ramirez edged closer and yelled, "Are we done yet? The wind's picking up. We need to leave ASAP."

"The storm is making this area unstable," Edie told Caleb. "We're heading back."

"No! It'll only take thirty minutes or so to download."

"I'm not risking four lives for such a pointless exercise."

Finn overheard. He'd been watching the mountainside as the rivulets of mud cascading toward them turned into turbulent streams. Now he turned and waded over to her, leaning in close to be heard. "Come on, we're leaving."

Edie jacked out of the BRAT. Caleb wasn't done.

"You're not leaving. I need that imprint. Nothing else I've tried is working."

"Nothing will work, Caleb. Just accept it."

"Edie!" It was Natesa on her commlink. Caleb must have called her to get some authority behind his demands. "I didn't send you down there to give up and do nothing. At the current rate of degradation, this is our last chance."

"Then take me to another BRAT where the weather's nicer."

"It will take half a day to get there on the skidder. The weather indicators are not showing a storm that's out of the ordinary."

"The storm itself is not the problem. We're halfway up a mountain whose entire face is about to slide down on top of us. We have to get back to the compound."

As she spoke, Finn was already dragging her back to the ridge, his hand clasped tightly around her wrist. She didn't resist, but it wasn't easy going. They were fighting the tide that tugged at them and the undercurrents that threatened to sweep them off their feet.

Ramirez was listening to rapid-fire instructions on his commlink. He looked nervously up the gray mountainside before turning back to slide down from the ridge. He landed right next to Edie and Finn in deep mud.

"My orders are to stay here for another half hour."

"Go right ahead," Edie said.

"Ma'am, get back to the seed," Ramirez said, fidgeting with his spur.

"Don't be stupid, Ramirez," Winnie called from above. "Natesa's not here. She doesn't know how dangerous it is."

Ramirez ignored Winnie, but there was a desperate look in his eyes as he sensed the other three—and his common sense—were against him. He was only a couple of meters away but hadn't raised his weapon—yet. "Ma'am, please do as she says. You," he told Finn, "move aside."

"We're leaving—*now*," Finn said, projecting an authority that Ramirez couldn't match.

Finn braced Edie's foot so she could clamber up the slope, and Winnie helped pull her up from above. Then the two of them hauled Finn onto the ridge, digging their toes into the rock for traction. They trudged toward the skidder. When Edie looked back, Ramirez was still standing there, staring at the black sky as though the heavens might tell him what to do. Then he gave up and followed them.

CHAPTER 22

The way Finn kept looking at Winnie, Edie could tell he wished he was in the driver's seat. Not that Winnie was doing a bad job in the appalling conditions, but it was a hair-raising ride. The skidder slid down the mountain, half the time carried along by the river of sludge, the rest of the time grinding against rock. The sheer wind slammed into them, never quite spinning them completely out of control. Edie's e-shield dulled the sting of the wind in her face, but she felt every jolt of the skidder. Ramirez sat up front with Winnie. Edie and Finn crouched in the back of the vehicle. Its sides were low enough that they were in danger of being pitched overboard.

Someone was yelling over the vehicle's comm. Winnie was too busy dodging boulders to notice. Edie hit the comm-link on her belt and redirected the message.

"This is Hueber at base camp. Can you hear me?" Edie vaguely recalled the name—one of the utility tecks on the ground team. "Where are you?"

"We're on the skidder, about a kilometer from base camp," Edie yelled over the howling wind.

"The landslide is right on us." The link crackled and died

for a second, then came back. ". . . four generators down, the rest struggling . . ."

Edie peered through the murk in the direction of the compound. It should be visible by now but she saw no lights. She dragged herself to the front of the skidder and leaned over to yell in Winnie's ear.

"Where's the compound?"

"It's out there. I'll find it," Winnie screamed through the wind.

"I think they're in trouble."

"More trouble than us?" She threw Edie a grim look.

Edie felt Finn's hand at the scruff of her jacket. "Get back here. Stay low."

She hunched down with him, her fingers wrapped around the railings. With her free hand she tapped her commlink, trying to reconnect to base camp.

"Hueber, are you there?"

The line spat and hissed. ". . . to evacuate . . . lose the perimeter . . ."

"It's the perimeter shield," Finn said. "Sounds like the storm has downed some of the generators. The others can compensate, but only so much."

If the shield failed, the entire compound would get washed away. Edie raised her head to search again for the lights of base camp. She saw something at last—a bobbing white glow. It wasn't the light that was bobbing. The raging river beneath them buffeted the skidder so violently that the misty gray world around them seemed to be shaking.

To her horror, Edie saw a sharp drop-off to their right. Winnie was no longer able to keep the skidder on anything resembling a straight path and she turned around suddenly, her face pale with terror.

"Jump! Jump!" she yelled over and over.

Ramirez looked around in panic, as if trying to figure out the danger. Finn reacted more instinctively. He reached out for Edie. They locked hands and clambered to the back of the vehicle. The skidder careened to the left, the engine screeching, and they were flung to the floor, but they kept a hold of each another. Then pulled themselves up and jumped blindly into the mud.

Edie slid along slick rock, her hands scrabbling for purchase. The skidder's taillights filled her vision. It careened down the incline and over the edge. It wasn't a deep drop-off, but the torrent of mud raged twice as fast, quickly carrying away the skidder. As she clung to a rough outcropping, Edie watched the skidder bob and spin in an impossible dance and finally crash into rocks. It upended and rolled down the mountainside.

She hadn't seen Winnie or Ramirez jump. There was no sign of them. She twisted her head to search for Finn, her mind still reeling from their dizzying leap. Then her commlink crackled.

". . . your ETA? . . . Tanning! Ramirez! . . . emergency evacuation!"

Edie fumbled for her commlink. By the time she had it, the line was dead again.

"The comm tower's down." Finn emerged out of the gray, a dark shadow in the rain. Visibility was so poor she hadn't seen him approach. He pointed to the compound in the distance. "I just watched its lights go out."

"Did Winnie and Ramirez jump out?"

"No. The skidder's gone. There's nothing we can do for them. Come on."

They clasped hands again and got moving, keeping to the rocks and the remaining islands of land where possible, and to the edges of the rivulets where the flow was slower and just about manageable. Edie kept her eyes on the compound lights. To one side, the landing pad was brightly lit and she could make out the shape of the skiff. The sound of an evacuation alarm reached her ears.

"They'll think we're dead," Edie said, suddenly aware of the very real possibility that they'd leave without her and Finn.

Finn moved faster, pulling her along now. Edie's legs ached from the effort of keeping her balance while bracing against the streaming mud, but she kept up. As they drew closer, the building outlines took form. On the near side of the compound, mud and rocks and uprooted vegetation crashed down the mountainside and hit the invisible shield. The debris piled up while the mud spewed out to the sides.

The shield hissed and flared. The ring of generators, visible only as a dotted line of green lights, had gaps here and there where the power had failed. More gaps appeared randomly as the generators died under the battering, one by one. At any moment the remaining generators would no longer be able to sustain a cohesive field . . .

A high-pitched siren wailed over the lower grunt of the evacuation alarm as the shield failed.

A wall of mud and debris crashed down, dousing most of the remaining lights. Instinctively, Edie and Finn pulled up and watched the disaster unfold. A long, low rumble vibrated through the air as a river of sludge rolled through the compound. Relentlessly the sludge surrounded and crushed the prefabs. They wilted, buckled, and ripped apart like wet cardboard, to be carried away on the black tide.

Edie checked her e-shield and saw Finn doing the same. There was still time to get to the skiff.

Together they looked across to the landing pad and saw the bobbing lights of the skiff. Half submerged in the deluge, it was attempting to take off.

"They're leaving!" Edie cried.

"We'll find emergency flares and call them back," Finn said. Edie didn't ask where they might find flares when most of the compound had already been swept away.

The skiff was being dragged along. The engines fired in a burst of light and it ascended, trailing rivulets of slime, belching smoke. It choked, banked sharply, and staggered. One engine blinked out. Edie heard the desperate whine of the other engine, a shocking addition to the sirens already wrenching the air. The skiff clipped a power generator on the edge of the compound, plunging it into near darkness. Only a few emergency lights remained, a sprinkling of glowing red hearth fires on those buildings that still survived.

The skiff nosedived into the side of the mountain. It turned a cartwheel, sparks flying, and the hull disintegrated. An explosion, painfully bright, agonizingly loud, swallowed up the remains of the vessel.

In shock, Edie turned to Finn. His face was a hard mask, lit gold by the fierce flames less than a hundred meters away. They had no way off the planet. They had no way of contacting the *Learo Dochais*. And, more than likely, they were considered dead.

Despite the catastrophic collapse of the compound, it was the safest place to be, at least for the next few minutes. The mudslide moved slower here, devouring buildings and clearing away ruins—but a couple of buildings, including the lab, still stood. Their buckled walls redirected the flow, leaving some areas above ground.

"We need to find a skidder," Finn said.

"And go where?"

"We'll find higher ground and wait for rescue."

The ship would send a rescue squad—when the storm passed, they would come looking for survivors . . . surely.

"There's a driveway on the other side of the lab, near the maintenance sheds," Edie said, drawing up a mental image of the map she'd once seen of the compound. "I think that's where they park the skidders."

When they got there, the sheds were gone. The driveway had been swept clean and now funneled the onslaught of mud flooding the compound. Only one skidder remained, caught up in debris from the buildings collapsing around it. It was on the far side of the driveway.

Finn surveyed the scene. "We need to get upstream." Trying to cross here would sweep them away before they could reach the other side.

They climbed over the prefab ruins to keep out of the worst

of the mud. At a loud cracking sound, Edie glanced over her shoulder. The lab building had finally succumbed. Its demise opened up the floodgates. The river rushed through, bringing with it crushed walls, walkways, and broken crates and furniture.

In seconds, that flood would cover the ruins they were on. Finn didn't waste time. He locked hands with Edie and pulled her into the river. They splashed and struggled across while the irresistible current washed them downstream and nearly past their only chance of survival. They threw themselves at the skidder and grabbed it, pulling themselves over the side. The mud sheared off their e-shields, leaving them clean.

Finn took the driver's seat. He brutally kicked at a cabinet that had fallen and trapped the skidder in place. When the cabinet finally slid off, the skidder floated free. Finn switched on the engine, taking control.

"What about the crash?" Edie had to shout to be heard. "There might be survivors."

Finn nodded and steered the skidder toward the area where the skiff had come down, vainly sweeping its headlights back and forth. There was nothing but mud and slime burbling past, to be replaced by more mud and more slime.

After a few more minutes of searching, Finn turned the skidder and gunned the engine, heading away from the remains of the compound. Of those killed in the crash, Edie had known only Caleb. She hadn't known him well, she hadn't liked him, and he hadn't liked her. A part of her recognized that, numb as she felt now, his death would hit her later. If the children were her past, he might have been her future—his arrogance and ego, his desperation to maintain the illusion that he could continue to fulfill whatever impossibilities the Crib required of him.

Buffeted by the currents, the small craft rode the river that cascaded along the valley floor. Finn maintained as much control as he could, dodging flotsam. Edie held on to the rails of the skidder and concentrated on keeping her balance.

After twenty minutes of working cross-stream, they began to escape the collapsing region and followed the river down through the widening valley. The sides of the valley seemed to be melting inward as organic sludge rolled downhill to join the river. Eventually the mud became shallow enough for the skidder to gain traction.

Finn drove like he had a plan, but there didn't seem to be any stable higher ground around. Still, the worst of the danger was over.

"I don't think we'll make it," Edie said. She meant their e-shields. It was unlikely they'd last until the *Learo Dochais* sent a rescue vessel. Even a few seconds' exposure to the retroviruses on Prisca would kill them.

"No, we won't."

Edie couldn't believe the finality of his statement. She'd expected him to come up with a plan, or at least give her hope that he was working on something.

He looked over at her. "You took me to hell and back once before. Can you do it again?"

Edie's mind was blank. Then the last image in her brain came back to her—the map of the compound. She pieced together the rest of what she remembered, zooming out. The local area, the topology of the mountain, the little dot that marked the location of the BRAT. The valley, the coast, the ocean. And another little dot . . .

"The skyhook. It's operational, right?"

He grinned. "They've done a couple of test runs. Where's the ocean platform in relation to here?"

"I don't know exactly, but this valley runs right to the coast, which runs north–south. The platform's a hundred meters offshore. It's out there somewhere."

Three hours after arriving at the coast, they still searched in vain for the skyhook platform. Edie only had an approximate idea of where exactly along the coast it was—probably twenty klicks or so in one direction or the other. So they'd pulled the skidder into the water and set out south, keeping parallel to the shoreline and a hundred meters out. Edie kept her eyes on the ocean, dark under a moonless night sky, searching for their sign of hope.

The night was silent, the ocean calm but for the steady hammering of rain disturbing the surface. It was starting to look like they'd gone the wrong way.

"How's our fuel?" she said. A pointless question because she knew Finn was watching it.

"We have enough to turn around, get back to where we started, and go about the same distance in the other direction." He scanned the horizon intently. "You want to turn around now?"

It was pure guesswork—the platform might be up ahead. But they'd never know if they chose this moment to reverse direction. They could miss it altogether and still be sitting here on the water when their e-shields died and Prisca's retroviruses invaded their bodies.

She did not want to die on this disastrous world.

"Your decision," she said.

"Then let's keep going."

A few minutes later, he looked over at her and said, "There's something I didn't tell you. The shootout in the hangar . . . there's a rumor that some of the *Molly Mei*'s crew was killed. A man—must be the navpilot Ganesh—and a woman."

"Valari?" That would explain why Finn had lost contact with her.

"I don't know any details. I heard it was crew, and Valari wasn't crew."

Edie's throat tightened. "Not Cat. She can survive anything." She stared at the skidder's headlight reflections dancing on the black water. The weight of another death was almost too much to bear. "There's something you should know, too," she said. "After what happened here, I suspect Colonel Theron will get his way. I'll be transferred to Scarabaeus. And this time, you're not coming with me. Natesa had petitioned for your freedom. Then you need to find your own way out of here."

He didn't say anything and the silence stretched out between them. Then, suddenly, he turned the skidder hard to port. Edie peered into the darkness and saw what he had seen—a faint unnatural glow on the water up ahead. The skyhook platform.

Finn moored the skidder alongside a narrow pier jutting out from the platform's vast scaffolding. They left the skidder and climbed a long ladder off the pier, up into the structure. Edie felt much safer with that distance between her and the water. Finn seemed to know where he was going— he'd worked on the skyhook from the other end, so he must know his way around, more or less. As she followed him, her energy sapped away and her legs became heavy. She thought about the people who had died on that skiff, and about Winnie and Ramirez. Cat might be dead, too. And Prisca—this world would soon be nothing but a rock covered in a rotten skin.

They arrived at the control room, which had its own comm uplink. Finn went to the console and called the *Learo Dochais*. Voices washed around Edie as she waited at the door. Finn told them to activate the skyhook and someone on the other end seemed to be protesting.

Then came the harsh authoritative tone she recognized— Natesa, taking control.

Two minutes later, Finn and Edie were in the climber. Its small central cabin was the only area suitable for passengers. On either side of the cabin were matching bins, flanking it like wings, each built to carry tons of crops—crops that Prisca would never produce now.

As Edie sat on the floor in the corner of the cabin, she heard Finn talking to a meckie on the *Learo Dochais*, who told him how to disconnect the bins. No point taking those up the nanoribbon with them. Then Finn sealed the cabin and adjusted the environmentals so they could switch off their e-shields. The climber gave a gentle lurch and began its ascent.

Finn slid down the wall of the cabin beside her. "Always wanted to ride one of these."

His everyday comment had the instantaneous effect of making Edie relax. She leaned against him and they rode in silence. The cabin had one narrow strip window, high up on the side. Edie had no sense of how fast they traveled because the gravplating kept the gravity constant. The dark cloudy sky outside merged into black space and stars. The long haul to the ship had just begun.

CHAPTER 23

A rescue raft that returned to the site the next day found no survivors. The entire base camp was washed away, the surroundings drowned in rotten sludge as the biocyph continued to decompose any remaining organic matter. Farther afield, aerial drones transmitted data showing that, across the planet, the ecosystem was quickly degrading.

Edie sat on a bunk in the infirmary waiting for Dr Sternhagen to give her the all-clear. Finn had already been dismissed. Neither of them had been told much, so now Edie listened to the medics talking among themselves. She learned that Natesa had locked herself in her office for hours, answering no one, and then had explosive verbal altercations with Captains Lachesis and Fox. Natesa had a PR disaster on her hands and her career might not survive the next few days. Edie was not inclined to sympathize.

People talked about memorial services for the twelve people who died on the planet and whispered about the future of Ardra.

"Are they shutting down the project?" Aila asked Edie in hushed tones when she visited the classroom that morning. "Natesa flat out denies it, but everyone's saying . . ."

"No one's told me anything," Edie said. That wasn't quite

true. She'd been told that Natesa's career depended on this planet. And that if the planet failed, the project wouldn't get a second chance.

Edie watched the children go through the previous day's error logs, the last Caleb had made. Aila said she was trying to keep things normal for them. But one way or another, everything was going to change. She wanted to get Galeon alone and find out what he had told the other children—or anyone else—about their little adventure in the access tubes. A suitable moment didn't come up, and he gave no sign that he thought she was involved.

By late morning she told Aila she was going back to her quarters. As she stepped out of the lift on Deck D, a milit waited—a young man with the same powerful soldier's build as Finn.

"Ms Sha'nim, Lieutenant Vlissides. I've been ordered to guard your quarters."

Her heart pounded. Now what was going on? She walked down the corridor toward her door. "What do you mean? My quarters, or me?"

"You. I've been asked to guard you."

"Am I in danger?"

"Uh, no, ma'am. There's some concern about keeping track of your whereabouts," he said vaguely.

"So Natesa sends an *officer* to guard me? Are all the enlisted men still hung over from the party the other night?"

"Administrator Natesa didn't send me, ma'am. The order comes from Colonel Theron."

Edie couldn't keep track of the pecking order on this ship. "So you're one of Theron's men? How did you get on board?"

"I'm under Crib Central's authority. They sent a few of us to escort the VIPs. Right now, Central is listening to Colonel Theron. So you could say I'm one of his men."

She knew what was going on. Natesa had sent Edie dirtside to evade Theron's previous orders. Now Theron wanted to keep track of her as Ardra fell apart, to make sure Natesa didn't send her off somewhere else on the ship that was coming to pick up the workers.

Edie snapped open her hatch. "Do you know if the VIPs have left? I haven't seen them around."

"The *Fortitude* left early this morning."

"Okay, thanks."

He assumed his post in the corridor and she shut the door on him. She didn't feel like sleeping. She'd slept for hours in the skyhook climber, though she didn't know about Finn. She didn't want to go to the lab and no one told her to. She knew she should write a report on what happened down there, but there had been no official debriefing yet.

When she heard Vlissides talking curtly to someone in the corridor half an hour later, she moved closer to listen. She recognized Finn's voice and snapped open the hatch.

"Let him in, Lieutenant. He's a friend of mine."

"My orders are to minimize your contact with the crew."

"Finn and I just survived hell together on that planet. Give us a break."

Vlissides cleared his throat. "I'll have to ask you to keep it brief."

Finn entered the room and Edie shut Vlissides out. Finn drew her into the bedroom, farther away from the hatch.

"Valari was killed in the shootout," he said.

"Jezus . . . I'm sorry." She was relieved about Cat, heartbroken for Finn. "What happened?"

"The milits moved in to arrest the crew and things got ugly. That's all I know." He spanned his forehead with his hand for a moment. She'd never seen him look so unsure of himself. It couldn't just be because of Valari. "Most of the work on the lower decks has stopped. It's pretty much official that the project is done for. They might release the *Molly Mei* at some point. And if not, Central's sending a transport vessel to pick up most of the workers. It'll arrive in a week or so."

"I heard about that. You need to be on board one of those ships." She'd told him not to come to Scarabaeus—and was determined to show him that she meant it even though it ripped her up inside.

A fleeting frown crossed his face and she realized the source of his uncertainty. He wanted to get off this ship as much as she wanted him to . . . which made this sound like goodbye.

"If *Molly Mei* isn't released, if Cat and Corinth are arrested and transferred, they'll be counting on me to get them out."

No point arguing in the face of Finn's sense of duty. "Maybe I can help you there. Theron doesn't care about that crew. Maybe I can make a deal—I'll go willingly to Scarabaeus if he clears all charges." She jerked her head in the direction of the main hatch, and Vlissides. "He clearly has some support on this ship."

"Thanks."

She still couldn't quite believe she was having this conversation—that he was agreeing to going separate ways.

"I'm sure Theron already knows what's going on," Edie said. "He's probably already dispatched a ship to pick me up. The truth is . . . I think I want to go back to Scarabaeus. Caleb used its regulator code on Prisca, and it should have worked. It should've been enough to overcome the contamination and the accelerated evolution. There's something *more* on Scarabaeus. Something else is in control." This was nothing Finn was interested in. She just wanted him to understand why it interested her so much.

"What about the children? Do you still want them saved?" he asked.

"I don't want you to risk yourself for them."

"There will come a time when I can rally forces. I'll keep it on the agenda."

Edie felt an overwhelming sadness. Finn was leaving her life soon, perhaps forever. She was abandoning the children to an unknown future with the Crib. And she was going to work for Theron, which she'd sworn she'd never do.

"Keep me on the agenda, too," she said.

He pulled her into his arms, fiercely. "Edie . . . Forget about that damn planet. I'll get you out of here when I leave. Somehow. Come with me." His voice was choked with emotion.

She shook her head into his shoulder. *No.* It wouldn't work—not now. They were guarding her too closely, and he knew it. It was on the tip of her tongue to ask him to stay. She knew he would, if she said the words. No one else knew the leash was cut—they'd let him stay to ensure her cooperation. That's the way it had always been.

Which was why she had to put a stop to it. He didn't deserve to be treated as a bargaining chip.

"It's okay," she said. "You can leave me behind. I know you'll come back for me." But she wasn't sure, not anymore. Not now his departure was so real and so soon. A thousand doubts crept in and some part of her recognized it was mostly her own fear of being abandoned again. Her mother, Lukas, even Natesa, who had implicitly promised so much by taking Edie in as a bewildered love-starved child, and delivered nothing.

And with that recognition came an even stronger determination to not abandon the children.

Edie kissed him with the same intensity as he'd shown her a moment earlier. She gave a mental finger to Vlissides's pointless request to *keep it brief.* Why the hell couldn't she, for once, be with the person she wanted to be with, do what she wanted to do, feel something real like any normal person—pretend, just for a while, that the Crib didn't control her life, and her future?

She was so eager to get her hands under his clothes that she didn't identify a nearby sound as anything other than boots scraping the deck as Finn maneuvered her toward the bed. Then something fell with a clatter and she spun around to face Galeon sliding out of the access panel. His face was red.

"Is that what this was?" he yelled at Finn. "Was this the top secret mission? Some stupid love thing?"

"Galeon—" Edie slid from Finn's arms and stepped forward to touch Galeon's shoulder reassuringly. He shied away from her, interested only in Finn. "Calm down. You don't understand."

Galeon seemed to think he understood all too well. "I heard you both. After all my help, you're going to run off . . . and this was all a stupid . . . stupid . . ." He sputtered on his rage, then gave up. He pulled something from his pocket and threw it at Finn. The little pouch opened in midair and tiny pegs flew out. They hit Finn in the chest before scattering on the deck. "I don't want that!"

Lieutenant Vlissides was in the doorway. He must have heard the yelling. Now he looked confused as hell. "How . . . ? What's the kid doing here?"

Edie looked reflexively at the open access panel and Vlissides followed her gaze, comprehension dawning on his face.

"I'll have to report this," Vlissides said. "You, come here."

He reached for Galeon, but the boy darted out of reach. Edie stepped between him and Vlissides.

"Let him go," she said wearily. "He hasn't done anything wrong."

Vlissides reconsidered for a second, which gave Galeon time to shimmy back into the access tube. By the time Vlissides changed his mind again and leapt after him, Galeon was gone.

"He just likes to visit me sometimes," Edie said. "It's not like I can stop him."

Vlissides was shaking his head. "This is damn irregular." He looked at Finn as though expecting an alternative explanation.

Finn didn't have one. "I think I'll leave."

He brushed his fingers down her arm as he walked past Edie. She forced a smile, her heart in her throat as she contemplated what damage a disillusioned seven-year-old might do.

When Edie was summoned to Natesa's office an hour later, it became immediately clear that this wasn't the Ardra debriefing she'd been expecting. Natesa's red-rimmed eyes looked like they were propped open by stims. Her hair was messily pulled back, her face devoid of makeup. What remained of her composure seemed to take great effort to maintain. Her state told Edie all she needed to know—with Prisca ruined and most of the team dead, Natesa's career was over. All she had left was Edie. And she wasn't happy with her protégée.

Two different holos hovered over her desk, their edges interacting confusingly. In contrast to their lazy spin, the desk was scattered with datacaps, signifying Natesa's frantic search for hope amid the depressing data.

When Edie entered the room, Natesa looked up and the lines of weariness on her face distorted until her rage was like a physical presence in the room. "What were you doing in the lab out of hours?"

So, Galeon had talked. And Natesa probably still had just enough power left on this ship to take out her anger on Finn. Edie's thoughts raced as she put together a story that would clear him.

"Running a few extra tests," she said. "It's no big deal."

"No big deal? We found a sabotaged module, scrubbed clean. Do you have any idea how much that piece of equipment was worth?"

A lot. But there was no way they'd know what she'd used it for. In any case, it was too late. The crack was out there and the Fringe worlds were already using it.

Natesa's assistant Darian poked his head around the door. "Colonel Theron's on the line."

Natesa gripped the edge of her desk. "Not now."

"He says it's urgent."

"I said, *not* now!"

Darian retreated from the office.

"Where were we?" Natesa said with a modicum of control. "Theft and conspiracy. Sabotaging millions of creds worth of CCU property—that's a life sentence, even if I can't prove treason. All this on top of the charges relating to your pirate adventure last year. I could have you executed."

"You wouldn't."

"Don't be so sure. I wash my hands of you, Edie. You've betrayed me one too many times."

Edie felt a shiver of fear. She'd got away with a lot in her life only because Natesa needed her. After the disaster on Prisca, maybe all Natesa needed was a scapegoat.

Darian dared to interrupt again, looking miserable as he did so. "Administrator, Captain Lachesis demands that you comply with Colonel Theron's request to take his call."

"Lachesis should mind his own business," Natesa snapped, waving Darian away without taking her eyes off Edie. "What tests were you running?"

Her face grew harder with each passing second that Edie failed to respond. She hit her commlink, not to talk to Theron but to call one of her guards.

"Have you arrested Finn yet?"

"We're handling that now, ma'am," came the response.

"Put him in the brig."

Edie drew an anxious breath. "Finn had nothing to do with this."

"That's not what Galeon says. He's been ranting about some top secret project . . ." Natesa tumbled over her own words. "You sabotaged Prisca. I know you did! And then—"

"I did not sab—"

"And then you planned to escape on the *Molly Mei*. And kidnap the children! That's why you were in Sternhagen's office. Stealing neuroxin."

Truth and fiction all mixed up together—Edie didn't know where to begin. "I told you why I was in her office."

"For Finn's records. Yes, yes, I know." Natesa's eyes held a wild gleam. "We found the damaged lock. You were stealing neuroxin. Finn is going to the firing squad for this. As for you—"

Edie's chest burned with panic. "Finn was not involved. It was Valari Zael." Blame it on the dead woman. She felt awful doing it. "She was some kind of eco-rad from the Fringe who infiltrated the project. She said she wanted to save the children." May as well fall on her sword. She wasn't going to be under Natesa's influence much longer. "She talked me into stealing neuroxin for them."

"Talked you into it?" Natesa was aghast. "She talked you into kidnapping children?"

"I was helping to *save* them. Look what happened to Pris. If you can't protect those kids, you don't deserve to have them."

"*You* did that to Pris! *You* put her in a coma, damaged her interface, ruined her chances of becoming the cypherteck she was meant to be."

"Yes I did, and this was how I tried to put it right. Valari promised them good homes on the Fringe." Edie was fantasizing now, describing what she had dreamed for them. "They could just be normal kids instead of having the fate of the galaxy weighing down their shoulders."

"I don't believe this. And don't try and tell me that lag of yours didn't play a part. From the moment you made us retrieve him from that freezer, I knew he'd manipulated you."

"You don't know anything." It was Edie who had influenced Finn—first the cryptoglyph, then the children.

Natesa shook with rage. "This is the end of the line for you, Edie. As soon as—"

Someone rapped on the door and opened it without waiting for permission. Lieutenant Vlissides entered with Darian fluttering around him in vain protest. Behind them, four more milts were gathered in the waiting area.

"You don't have permission to be here, Lieutenant. What's going on?" Natesa demanded, striding across the room to claim her space.

"Ma'am, Colonel Theron has ordered that Ms Sha'nim be transferred to my custody. Under the authority of the Weapons Research Division, I'm commandeering the *Molly Mei* and immediately escorting her to Scarabaeus."

"Absolutely not." Natesa's defiance was a frozen mask, covering what Edie sensed was blind panic. "Ms Sha'nim is being detained for questioning on serious matters of conspiracy. You won't be leaving with her today."

"Colonel Theron's orders came through the correct legal channels."

"I don't care what the orders are. She's not leaving this ship. And you!" she yelled at the milits outside the door, all of whom were from the *Learo Dochais*. "You're under Captain Lachesis's command, not the lieutenant's or the colonel's." She hit her commlink. "Captain, I need assistance in my office."

"If this is about the transfer, I'm sorry but the colonel's orders stand," came Lachesis's reply. "The children are also being transferred to the *Molly Mei*."

Natesa gaped and Darian made incoherent noises of distress.

Natesa finally managed to splutter an apoplectic response. "This . . . no! Not my daughter. This is not going to happen." She grabbed Edie's arm. "No one from my team leaves this ship."

Vlissides looked at Natesa's hand. "Let her go, ma'am, or I will make you let her go."

"Who the hell do you think you are? Why are you even on this ship? Theron's men have no authority here."

Someone pushed through the hubbub—Captain Lachesis. Natesa turned to him with relief.

"Jeremy, please sort out this nonsense."

"The orders are clear, Liv."

"But Pris is my daughter!" she screamed. "Why are they taking her? I forbid it!"

"Considering the failure of Project Ardra and the uncertainty of your position on the team, Theron has approval from the Weapons Research Division at Crib Central to transfer the cyphertecks to his custody. Pris is a Crib ward, not your daughter."

Natesa's eyes went hollow with anguish. "Please, Jeremy, you have to stop this."

"I wish I could. But unlike you, I'm not prepared to risk my career by disobeying orders."

He nodded to Vlissides, who stepped up to remove Natesa's hand from Edie's arm. Natesa was so surprised that she didn't protest. Then she recovered her senses and swung an arm at Lachesis, connecting with the side of his head.

"How dare you! How could you?"

She whirled around and went for Edie next. Edie blocked Natesa's flailing limbs but couldn't handle the sheer aggression behind Natesa's attack. Natesa grabbed a handful of her hair and tugged her backward. The milits rushed in and disentangled Natesa from Edie.

"Lieutenant, hold her in her quarters until further notice." Lachesis looked embarrassed as he gave the order.

Natesa gave a final horrified cry as she was dragged away.

CHAPTER 24

From the compact observation deck on the *Molly Mei*, Edie watched the new crew board. Lieutenant Vlissides, taking command of the ship, strode across the hangar deep in conversation with an officer whom Edie recognized as the *Learo Dochais*'s second navpilot. The first had been killed in the skiff crash on Prisca.

Two junior milits and one engie were the only other crew coming with them. Edie had pleaded with Vlissides to have Aila Vernet transferred as well. She was the closest thing the children had to a caring adult—but Theron didn't care about such things and Vlissides was carrying out his orders to the letter.

Which meant that Finn was being transferred as well. When Edie saw him enter the hangar, cuffed, flanked by two milits, she ran from the observation deck and arrived at the main hatch just as Vlissides boarded.

"Finn isn't coming. I managed to cut the leash—he can stay. He has to stay." With Natesa locked up for the time being, he was safe from her. Safe enough to leave on the transport ship that Central had sent for the workers.

"My orders are to bring him along," Vlissides said, unmoved. Theron didn't know about the leash being cut, so he'd included Finn in the transfer order. And Vlissides didn't seem to know how to think for himself on the matter.

"But I cut the leash! Let me talk to Theron."

"He's halfway to Scarabaeus and blacked out. We'll be doing the same. No comms in or out, emergencies excepted."

"At least take off the cuffs. There's no reason for him to be in the brig."

"The ship has no brig as such. Crew cabins with extra locks. It's not that bad."

"Please don't lock him up. He won't cause trouble."

Vlissides shrugged, like it was out of his hands. "We dock at Falls Station in thirteen days—three days before our final destination—to drop off the prisoners. Maybe you can persuade Theron to change his mind by then and release your friend with them."

"What prisoners?"

"Captain Lachesis is taking advantage of the *Molly Mei*'s departure to clean up his own ship." Vlissides indicated a small group just entering the hangar. Several milits escorted two more men to the *Molly Mei*—Corinth, who looked relieved, and Achaiah, who evidently recognized Edie but then warily avoided her gaze. "I agreed to take them with us—on my conditions. Feels like I'm commanding a prison ship. They stay under lock and key, including a woman from the original crew."

That was Cat. With the children already sequestered in a four-man cabin, and now Cat and Finn coming on board, Edie felt marginally better about this exodus. She was escaping Natesa, and everything associated with Ardra, for good. She spared a thought for her former boss, wondering how she must feel with her life's work in shambles, her first protégée reassigned, and her would-be young daughter taken away. Then she worried about Pris. She had no idea how the girl felt about Natesa, but she knew what being motherless felt like.

"I'll need you to oversee the kids during the trip," Vlissides said, urging Edie back inside.

"I just want you to know that I don't agree with bringing them along."

"It's my understanding you don't agree with much of anything when it comes to Crib affairs." Vlissides somehow managed to make the accusation sound eminently polite. "Anyway, they're here and I can't spare my crew for babysitting. You'll be sharing their cabin—please keep them confined for departure."

Edie would rather have hung around so she could talk to Finn, to explain what was going on, but Vlissides wanted her out of the way while the prisoners were processed and taken to cabins.

The small ship felt cramped and dark in comparison to the *Learo Dochais*, although everything was spotless and tidy. This was an older vessel, a typical merchant ship built on the Fringe with all the associated jury-rigged fits and quirks, and without any of the sparkle she was accustomed to. It was also a Saeth ship, unbeknownst to its new Crib crew. As Edie walked down its narrow corridors, it occurred to her that the Saeth might want their ship back. Corinth and Finn might not have the means right now, but there were other Saeth out in the Reach. Were they keeping track of the *Molly Mei*? Would they tail it to Scarabaeus?

The cabin she was to share with the children held two bunk beds, its own bathroom, and a decent number of closets—not that they had much to put in them. Still, it seemed a tiny living space for four active, inquisitive children. They'd already messed it up, tossing around bedclothes and pillows to relieve their boredom. Galeon was drawing stick figures on the porthole using a thick green marker. He looked up long enough to scowl at Edie, then went back to his masterpiece. Pris was on a bunk fiddling with a palmet while the other two girls had squeezed themselves under the second bunk where they whispered back and forth to each other.

Edie went to Pris, who sat hunched over and trembling. "Are you okay?"

Pris nodded and sniffed. She looked so forlorn that Edie

sat and put her arm around the girl's shoulders. She'd not anticipated this moment in her mind, the moment when she'd meet the child she injured. With luck, Pris didn't know the details of what had happened that night.

"I can't do it anymore," Pris said quietly.

"Do what?"

"I'm no good in the datastream. I can't fix things. My head's all messed up."

"That's not true. Your head is fine. It's your wet-teck interface. I'm sure they can repair it."

Pris shook her head. "No, it's no good. Nothing feels right anymore."

Resentment bubbled to the surface as Edie thought about how these children had been raised, believing their only purpose was to serve the Crib as cyphertecks. And now, when one of them could no longer perform adequately, she was left with nothing.

"There are other things you can do, you know."

"Like what? Ms Natesa always said I have to do my duty." How familiar was that refrain.

"Is that what you call her?"

Pris looked away and mumbled, "She wants me to call her Mother."

"Why don't you?"

"It's not fair to the others."

"Where are we?" Galeon called out suddenly. "Where are we going?"

"We're on the *Molly Mei*," Edie said. "We're going to a planet called Scarabaeus."

A few hours into the journey, with the ship in nodespace, Edie ventured out to find food. The crew apparently had no notion of the children's schedule. Edie had kept them occupied with toons and games, but that only lasted so long. They were hungry and tired and cranky, and Edie wasn't much better.

She searched for the galley through a maze of mismatched

corridors and annexes. It was strange to think that Cat and Finn were nearby in these locked rooms, isolated from contact. Maybe Vlissides would relax his strict confinement rules later, if everyone behaved.

A milit rushed past her yelling into his commlink for assistance. Something about prisoners brawling. Edie didn't need to hear more to guess who was involved. Someone had put Finn and Achaiah in close quarters—a very bad idea.

She followed the milit around the corner. Up ahead, one hatch was wide open and a second milit hovered in the doorway. He beckoned urgently.

"Private Gleick, get over here!"

Edie could hear yelling and the sounds of a scuffle, and from Achaiah's indignant cries she could tell who was winning. Vlissides approached at a jog from the other direction. Before he got there, Achaiah was suddenly thrown out of the cabin and hurled against the opposite bulkhead. He slid down, winded. Blood ran down a gash on his cheekbone.

Vlissides marched up to the hatch. Edie dodged around Gleick to join him. Finn stood in the center of the room absently nursing reddened knuckles. He looked otherwise unharmed, which was to be expected—the infojack stood no chance against a Saeth.

"I'll talk to him," Edie said before Vlissides did anything stupid.

At the sound of her voice, Finn looked up at her. His expression of desperation and lethal fury sent a chill through her. What the hell was going on? Was this simple revenge, even though the leash was now cut?

"Lock him in," Vlissides told Gleick. To Edie he growled, "Thought you said he'd cause no trouble."

"I'll find out what happened," Edie said. "Please let me talk to him."

"Not now. He stays here to cool off." Vlissides gave Achaiah a quick look. "Gleick, take this one to the infirmary and patch him up. Then I guess you'll have to review the bunking arrangements."

* * *

Confused and frustrated, Edie remembered her mission to find food and retraced her steps. She came face-to-face with Galeon.

"What are you doing here?"

"I followed you. Everyone's very hungry."

"I know. Come with me. We'll find something to eat."

The galley, when she finally found it, was little more than a kitchenette with one table and two long benches. The ship clearly wasn't intended to carry more than about six people, and right now it had over a dozen on board. Their difficult encounter on the *Learo Dochais* seemingly forgotten for now, she and Galeon companionably gathered up ration packs and heated them in dishes. They found a couple of trays and returned to their cabin carrying the five meals between them. Sitting in rows on the lower bunks, everyone dug in.

"That was Finn," Galeon said through a mouthful of noodles. "I heard Finn yelling."

"You're right," Edie said. "He's here, but he's not coming with us all the way." At least, she hoped not.

Pris picked pieces of rehydrated meat out of her soup and made a neat pile out of them on her napkin. "Ms Natesa's very angry with him. He's a nuisance."

"Is that what she told you?" Edie asked.

"Yes. But she sorted it out."

Edie swallowed and put down her fork. "What d'you mean?"

"She said it was all sorted out and she could get rid of him any time she liked." Pris's innocent words hid a host of sickening possibilities.

"When was this?"

"A few days ago when I was in the infirmary. I heard her talking to someone. I didn't see who it was."

Surely that didn't matter now, Edie told herself. Natesa was locked up on the *Learo Dochais*, and, in any case, Finn was by the minute farther and farther from her reach. Still, she couldn't help worrying. Natesa was unstable enough now to do anything.

With a sixteen-day journey ahead of them, the last thing Edie wanted on her hands were four bored and irritable children. The only ship's entertainment caps suitable for kids were a handful of toons. She rationed them to one a day to make them last. Because of their hasty departure, the children had brought nothing with them but a change of clothes. Being unused to packing, they'd managed to screw that up. Galeon had brought three spare tees but no clean underwear. Hanna and Raena were devastated because they'd forgotten their hair ties. Edie felt like she was taking a crash course in parenting as she tried to deal with each disaster as it cropped up.

Vlissides relented and allowed them to leave the cabin and stretch their legs for a couple of hours a day, and to eat in the galley. It wasn't enough to keep them happy. Edie knew their options on the *Learo Dochais* hadn't been much better, but they'd been less restless there. It soon became painfully obvious that the children missed the ten or twelve hours a day they used to spend in the classroom, riding the datastream.

She had one solution for that, and by the third day she was ready to try it. She took O'Mara's datacap from her tool belt and gave it to them.

"I thought Prisca was dead. We couldn't fix it fast enough," Pris said.

"That wasn't our fault," Galeon said indignantly.

"No, it wasn't your fault," Edie said. "This isn't from Prisca. It's a sim from Scarabaeus, the planet we're going to visit."

Much as she disapproved of their involvement, she was curious about what they'd make of the sim. In any case, they needed some sort of primer on Scarabaeus. They were going to be working for Theron, regardless of Edie's objections.

The children gathered around the console as Edie uploaded

the sim. They used their hardlinks to jack in, eager for a new datastream to explore. Before Edie had the chance to join them, an intraship call came through from Vlissides.

"Meet me on the bridge. We could have a problem on our hands."

Edie left the children to the sim and went to the bridge, a glorified cockpit with only one seat—the navpilot's—and two standing consoles behind it. Vlissides was alone, in the navpilot's seat, which he spun around to face Edie.

"I've been talking to Captain Lachesis," he said. "The man has a strange idea of what constitutes an emergency, but I thought you'd want to know. Liv Natesa called on some friends in Central and they're sending a ship for her. She intends to follow us and demand we hand over the children. I doubt it'll work, but it'll sure make a scene. The last thing the colonel wants is to draw attention to that planet."

"Why? Because he has nefarious plans for it?"

"Well," he drawled, "I don't know about that. Anyway, she has no legal standing, but I get the feeling that's not going to stop her. "

"What do you plan to do about it?"

"She's a few days behind us, probably won't catch up until we reach the planet. Colonel Theron's ship has the man-power and firepower to handle whatever she's brought with her. I'm not worried. Like I said, the only problem is a pos-sible security breach if she decides to kick up a fuss."

"There could be another problem—not that you Crib drones even care—but I think Finn could be in danger. Natesa wants him dead."

"What's he to her?"

"Nothing. He's nothing at all. She'd kill him to spite me."

"She won't get the chance."

"I'm not so sure. One of the kids overheard something—I think she's already arranged it. I don't know how. Maybe she's paid one of your men here to kill him." Edie hoped she didn't sound so paranoid that he'd completely dismiss her concerns.

"I assure you, that's not possible."

"Then maybe she organized an assassin on Falls Station. Listen, I just want to talk to him. Find out what he knows. I don't think that brawl with Achaiah was a disagreement over who got the top bunk."

Vlissides relented. "Okay, but I'm putting a guard on the door."

Private Gleick let Edie into Finn's cabin. She found him playing cards with his new roommate, Corinth. They were a picture of grimness. Finn couldn't even manage a smile, but he did look somewhat relieved to see her. He pushed back his chair and stood.

"When do we get off this boat?" he asked.

"About ten days, if I can get permission from Theron. I'm not allowed to contact him until he reaches Scarabaeus." She hesitated at the door, acutely conscious that both Gleick and Corinth were unwelcome on the scene. "What happened the other day?"

Finn rubbed his hand over his face in a gesture of exhaustion. "That day when they knocked me out . . . Achaiah told me your boss offered to cut his sentence if he did a little job for her. He thought he was there to cut the leash. Instead, she had him make a new link to the bomb in my head. She has the detonator. She taps in the code and I'm dead."

CHAPTER 25

"No . . ." Edie wrapped her arms around her ribs as if to prop herself up as the blood drained from her head. So this was how Natesa had planned her revenge. When she felt Edie had stepped far enough out of line, she'd planned to kill Finn with the push of a button.

"I checked out his chip," Corinth said. "The infojack was telling the truth. He hacked the receiver and locked it to a commlink."

"What's the range?" Edie asked.

"Same as a regular commlink—a few hundred thousand klicks."

"Why didn't she use it already? She could've triggered it before we left Prisca's system." And Edie would never have known why it happened.

"I don't know," Finn said. "I don't know what her plan is, or was."

"Wait . . ." Edie replayed the events of her last few minutes on the *Learo Dochais*. "Lachesis confined her to quarters because she got a little hysterical about the transfer orders. I think she was stuck there a few days. Maybe she didn't have the detonator with her."

"This Achaiah sounds like a real sweetheart," Corinth said.

Finn began to pace. "I knew he was hiding something when they put him in here with me. Didn't take much to make him talk."

"We always knew Achaiah had the morality of a nematode," Edie said.

"I'll say this for him—he had just enough conscience left to feel guilty about it."

"Can he undo it?"

"He claims no. The detonator's at her end. As long as this bomb is in my skull . . ." Finn stopped pacing. "Maybe nothing will come of it. The Reach is wide and I fully intend to stay out of her way."

Edie bit her lip. "One problem. She's following us to Scarabaeus."

Both men were instantly alert.

"She wants to take the children back," Edie said. "Specifically Pris, I suppose."

"How long do I have?" Finn asked.

"We're a few days ahead of her."

"Doesn't mean much if we don't know how fast her ship is," Corinth said.

Finn moved to sit on the bunk. "Damn. This is a fucking bad way to die."

"That's not going to happen, Finn. Vlissides will have to let you leave at Falls Station, regardless of Theron's orders. Once I tell him about this—"

"She could be waiting for him at Falls," Corinth observed.

"Then what do we do?" Her voice was thin, wavering with fear. She looked from Corinth to Finn, hoping one of them had an idea.

Finn did. "Put me back in cryo."

Every ship had at least one cryo capsule on board for medical emergencies. At least, the reputable ships did. The *Molly Mei* was from the Fringe, and Fringe ships weren't necessarily reputable. Nevertheless, Lieutenant Vlissides, who agreed to their plan for what he called *logistical* reasons, confirmed with the ship's databank that there was indeed one cryo capsule and it was in the cargo hold.

The only person on board with medic training was Finn himself. As he checked over the capsule in a musty corner of the hold, Edie struggled for some final words to say. Her voice was as frozen as her feet, and she could neither speak nor go to him.

Vlissides had also agreed, at last, to drop off Finn at Falls Station with the prisoners. He wasn't interested in Natesa's charges against Finn—she'd never formalized them anyway—and the only charge on Corinth's file was failure to keep his crew key on his person, a relatively minor security breach. As far as Vlissides was concerned, both men could go free at Falls.

Corinth, whose cover as a utility teck was still intact, volunteered to take charge of the capsule on Falls until Finn could be safely defrosted.

What all this meant to Edie was that Finn had less reason than ever to come back for her. Natesa's career might never recover from this crisis, and in any case she'd washed her hands of Edie, but Edie still had a contract to work off for the Crib. All Natesa had to do was give the detonator to someone close to Edie, and if Finn ever did return . . . he'd be killed instantly and at a distance. He'd have to stay away.

For some perverse reason, she wished Cat was here with her. The woman could be impossible, but she was a friend. The only real friend left in Edie's life now.

Finn finished his checks and kicked off his boots. He didn't seem inclined to talk, anyway. She knew how hard this must be for him—to make himself helpless in the face of his enemy. He climbed into the capsule and slipped his arm through the cuff. It wasn't until he lay back and hit the switch to close the lid that Edie was able to move. She looked through the window of the capsule and locked eyes with him until his eyelids drooped and closed.

Too late now to say the things she needed to say.

* * *

"We're starving," Raena said as soon as Edie returned to the cabin.

"Where have you *been*?" Hanna whined.

Edie had been gone almost two hours, completely forgetting both the children and the sim she'd left with them. Emotionally exhausted, she didn't have the energy to deal with their neediness. Fortunately, Galeon had something more important to discuss.

"There's someone in there." He pointed to the console.

Edie blinked, baffled by the incongruous statement. "Someone?"

"Someone very angry."

"Not someone," Pris said. "*Pieces* of someone. And not really angry. More like . . . confused and broken."

"Okay, what are you talking about?" Edie said.

"All those little bunched up feelings that are clogging everything up," Pris said.

"You mean the knots of code sitting between the tiers of the datastream?"

Pris gave her a strange look. The children didn't interpret the datastream like she did—she had to remember that. Aila had said they personified it, and that's exactly what they were doing here.

Edie tried again. "Can you tell me what the pieces are doing?"

"I think they're broken and they want to be fixed," Pris said.

"That would make the biocyph happy again," Galeon pointed out. "You know, it's forty-seven minutes past supper time."

"Should we fix it?" Hanna asked eagerly. Fixing glitches was, of course, all they knew how to do.

"No . . . no," Edie said distractedly. "Uh, let's get your supper, okay? We'll figure it all out in the morning."

She needed time to process this. She was fairly sure the knots of code had little coherent effect on the biocyph itself.

But it must be doing something if the children could decipher it well enough to describe its "moods."

Whatever it was, it was one more thing drawing her back to Scarabaeus.

A sim only ever provided a fraction of the information to be gleaned from an active BRAT. A sim was a recording of the biocyph at a particular moment in time. You could run it backward or forward, but what you were seeing then was an extrapolated best guess as to what the biocyph had done in the past, or would do in the future. The sim from Scarabaeus was only a tantalizing glimpse of what was really going on.

The children were fascinated.

"When we get to Scarabaeus, can we jack into a BRAT for real?" Pris asked. "We want to meet Macky."

Macky was the name they'd given the "someone" in the sim. This was a new experience for them, and they were hooked. They spent hours each day running the sim, exploring the many moods of Macky, talking about "him" as if he were a real person who had somehow wandered into their datastream and was flailing about, sick or injured, unable to comprehend his environment.

"You won't be going to the surface of the planet," Edie said. "I'm sorry, it's too dangerous. But if we can find a way to download more sims like this one, you can look at those."

The sim kept them amused, which made Edie's life easier. Pris worked hard by herself to regain the function she'd lost when her wet-teck overloaded. When she couldn't quite keep up with the other children, they learned to adapt their strategies to accommodate her limits. Galeon seemed to have forgotten or forgiven his altercation with Edie and Finn, and was disappointed Finn wasn't around.

"Do you have my Pegasaw pegs?" he asked one day.

"No. You threw them away."

"I wish I had them back. Now I only have the board and it's no use without pegs."

"Perhaps you can make some more."

"If I tell Finn I'm sorry, maybe he'd make me some more."

"He can't do that right now. I'm sure he knows you're sorry," she said, and he brightened a little.

It was so easy to forgive a child anything.

Each day that passed brought the *Molly Mei* one day closer to Falls Station. One day closer to saying goodbye to Finn. Except that she couldn't say goodbye to a man who couldn't see or hear or touch her.

She'd made her choice. She would stand by the children, and that had to be enough.

On the eleventh day, Lieutenant Vlissides had sobering news.

"We've lost contact with Colonel Theron. He arrived at Scarabaeus six days ago and since then we've had four daily hails from his ship, the *Plantagenet*. Then . . . nothing for the past thirty hours. Central hasn't heard from them either."

"Could there be trouble in the system?"

"I doubt it. No one knows that planet even exists. Probably just a problem with the commsat. But I'm canceling our detour to Falls Station. We can't afford a four-day delay. We'll go directly to Scarabaeus instead. Our ETA is about twenty-eight hours."

"What about Finn and the others?"

"That will have to wait. After we transfer you and the children to the *Plantagenet*, we'll go back to Falls and drop them off. Can't imagine the colonel will be anything but pleased when we arrive early."

Being woken up by sirens was unpleasant at the best of times. The accompanying screams of terrified children wasn't exactly a welcome twist. Edie stumbled out of bed. On the bunk above hers, Pris was sitting up—the only one not making any noise. Galeon, on the other top bunk, was shouting questions and seemed more angry than scared. The screams came from the two younger girls, sharing the lower bunk.

"See if you can calm them down," Edie told Pris. "I'll find out what's happening."

Edie pulled on her boots, snapped the hatch, and headed toward the bridge. Private Gleick rushed past in the other direction, ignoring her. She couldn't fail to notice his sense of urgency. She ran to the bridge. Through the open hatch, she glimpsed the hurried gestures of the crew as they punched consoles and exchanged curt questions and responses. Their manner reeked of a dire emergency. Vlissides paced the deck from one console to another.

"What's going on?" she called out.

As if in response, the ship lurched sharply. Edie grabbed a panel on the bulkhead to keep her balance. The gravplating took a moment to stabilize.

"We're crashing into the planet, that's what's going on," the engie screamed from his post behind the navpilot's seat.

Edie went onto the bridge. Vlissides had stopped at one of the workstations, his expression serious but not panicked.

"No sign of the *Plantagenet* when we came through the jump node a few hours ago." He barely glanced at Edie as he studied garish readouts and flashing telltales. "Then, as soon as we fell into low orbit around Scarabaeus, our nav guidance went haywire. We're spiraling downward, can't escape the gravity well."

"Can I help?" Edie said, certain she could not.

He looked at her now. "Seems trouble follows you everywhere." There was a resignation to his voice. "Is there something on that planet that could do this? I heard whispers that Theron was talking about an intelligence, crazy as it sounds. Well, *something* took over the commsat and used it to fuck up our systems."

Or someone. After hearing the way the children talked about that sim, Edie was prepared to entertain the idea of an intelligence. But it hadn't evolved on Scarabaeus, she was sure of that. Those tangles of code weren't O'Mara's so-called emergent property. They were superimposed on the datastream—and badly. It was the work of a hacker, a trick of some sort. It had to be. They were being played. Now the game had become dangerous.

Before she could voice her theory, the ship listed again and Edie was thrown against a railing on the walkway. It jammed painfully into her back.

The junior milit—an op-teck and Vlissides's fourth crew member—called from the other side of the bridge. "Sir! I've found the *Plantagenet*."

Vlissides covered the five strides to cross the bridge by grabbing onto railings and seats as the *Molly Mei* continued to roll and tilt. The op-teck showed Vlissides her holoviz while Edie peered over their shoulders from her vantage point on the walkway. The display, an aerial landscape captured by a drone, zoomed in on a rocky landscape. Scattered across a wide area were smoldering pieces of wreckage.

"Damn. I'm guessing the same thing happened to them," Vlissides said. "The commsat's hijacked, so like us, they couldn't even send out a distress call. No sign of their lifepods—must've happened fast."

"We've lost stabilizers!" yelled the engie. He turned frantically to Vlissides. "Once we hit atmo, the gravplating won't hold."

"How long?"

"If we can't pull out of this . . . fifteen minutes."

"Too late to eject the lifepods into space, then. We'll have to hit the dirt in them."

That was bad news. The stats for a lifepod surviving reentry and a hard landing weren't good—the pods did a much better job sustaining life in space.

Vlissides punched a series of commands into the console. The high-pitched siren changed to a lower, repeating horn. Edie had heard that before. "All hands, abandon ship. Five minutes." He pointed at the engie. "Program the lifepods to land as close as possible to the crash site. We'll rendezvous there and look for survivors from the *Plantagenet*."

The engie nodded, wild-eyed, and left.

Vlissides hit his commlink. "Gleick, get the prisoners into lifepods." He closed his hands around Edie's shoulders. His skin felt clammy against the thin fabric of her tee. "You're responsible for getting the children to the lifepods. " He indicated a side corridor outside the bridge. "Can you do that?"

"Yes, of course. What about Finn?"

"I'll send someone to fetch the cryo capsule."

"Please . . . please don't leave him behind."

"Get the children!"

She hurried out while Vlissides gave more orders. Back in the cabin, the children were already pulling on sweaters and boots over their PJs. Despite a sheltered upbringing, their instincts for detecting impending disaster were fully functional.

She herded them through the corridors to the lifepod bay. A small crowd had already gathered there. The engie, still checking the pods. Gleick, guarding Achaiah and Corinth. And—

"Cat!" Edie was irrationally pleased to see her. The emotion was wildly out of place considering the situation.

"Who the hell are all these kids?" Cat said, shrinking against the bulkhead to put some distance between them and herself.

"Can you get them into a pod for me?" Edie said as the op-teck came running toward them from the bridge and started ordering people into pods. Vlissides and the navpilot would no doubt remain on the bridge until the last moment.

So who was going back for Finn?

CHAPTER 26

Edie slipped away. She wasn't about to let Finn die, helpless and unaware. Rushing into the cargo hold, she found it abandoned and blissfully quiet. That didn't last. The ship shuddered and the engines made a terrifyingly unfamiliar whine.

There was no one here to rescue Finn. No one had been sent—or whomever Vlissides had sent had ignored the order. The cryo capsule glowed green in the far corner of the hold. Surrounding it was a jumble of dislodged crates and equipment, some broken apart by the tumbling ship.

Edie gave a cry of frustration as she pushed through the rubble. She couldn't possibly clear a path for the capsule and drag it out in time. Once the ship hit atmo, it would be too late to eject the lifepods.

There was nothing to do but try. Her hands fumbled at the brackets that held the capsule to the bulkhead. They released abruptly, and the frozen coffin slid a few meters along the deck until it crashed into a wall of crates. Edie climbed over it, dropped to the other side, and began to push.

Her efforts were close to futile. The capsule was impossibly heavy and it caught on every damned ridge of the gravplating. She needed a gravlift or a pallet. Panic rose in her throat as she looked around for something she could use.

Precious seconds ticked by. Edie returned to the cryo capsule and tried again. She pulled from the front this time, tugging upward on the leading edge to help the capsule over the ridges.

A second pair of hands was suddenly beside hers. Tiny, white-knuckled hands.

"Galeon! Get back to the lifepod!"

"Pull harder! We can't leave him."

"I won't leave him. But you have to go back."

She released the capsule and grabbed Galeon's arms to wrench him away. He fell onto his backside on the deck. She hauled him up and pushed him in the direction of the hatch.

"Go on!"

Galeon clambered back to the capsule. "Get him out of there. Wake him up!" He pounded on the window, as if Finn might hear.

To do that safely would take an hour or more. "We don't have time."

"Wake him up! Wake him up!" Galeon was near hysterical, his cheeks smeared with tears.

He was right. Rapid emergence from cryosleep was dangerous, but it was Finn's only chance. They'd never get this bulky capsule to the lifepods in time, even with more help.

Edie pulled up the capsule's holoviz to access the controls. The screen showed clear instructions on how to manually wake up the occupant, along with the recommended timeframe. She hit the switch to pump warm plasma into Finn's blood, to replace the cryo fluids. Ignoring the warning beeps, she cranked it to max and then flipped open the catches around the lid. It slid aside, frustratingly slowly.

Vlissides's voice came over the shipwide comm. "Six minutes until we hit atmo. Report immediately to the lifepods."

She wanted to scream back at him that she needed help. Why had no one come to look for them? Surely they wouldn't leave a child behind.

"Hurry!" Galeon pushed on the lid's edge. "Why hasn't he woken up yet?"

"It takes time."

Too much time. The readout showed Finn's plasma replacement was less than two-thirds complete and his heart rate was deathly slow.

Edie took hold of Galeon's shoulders and crouched to his level. "Listen to me, Galeon. You have to go to the lifepods. I'll get Finn out." He shook his head emphatically. She tried a different tack. "I need you to find someone to help me. Get back up there and send someone."

"*You* find someone. I'm not leaving him."

Leaning into the cryo capsule, he pulled on Finn's shoulders in a futile effort to haul him up. Finn remained unconscious, but Edie thought she saw his eyes move behind the lids. The plasma replacement was up to eighty percent. She touched his hand—it was ice cold. But his upper arm was merely cool, his face almost warm. His heart rate was up a little, too.

An automated voice over the shipwide announced a five-minute warning.

"We have to get him out of this," Edie said. "Help me tip it."

Galeon followed her actions, hooking his little fingers under the side of the capsule, and together they lifted the edge to tilt it. Finn's body rolled to the side of the chamber.

"That's it. Just a little more . . ."

Edie wedged her shoulder against the side and gave it a hard shove. It tilted a few more degrees, and Finn rolled out. Galeon dropped his end and ran over, calling Finn's name. Edie lowered her end more carefully, not wanting to damage the capsule while it was still attached to Finn. He lay sprawled facedown on the deck and connected to the capsule by an umbilical cord of wires and tubes running into the cuff on his forearm.

"Finn, wake up, wake up, wake up!" Galeon yelled as he tugged on the leg of Finn's pants.

Edie leaned into the empty capsule and found the bag of IV fluid attached to the other end of Finn's cuff. She peeled it off the inside chamber, complete with the tiny pump clipped to the edge. The monitoring wires were not portable—she ripped those out.

She fell to her knees next to Galeon and jammed the IV bag into Finn's belt. Then she lifted Finn's arm over her shoulder and dragged him into a half-sitting position. His body was twisted awkwardly.

"Finn—get up. Move!"

She squeezed his trapezius muscle as hard as she could, her fingernails digging into his cool skin. The pain elicited a groan and he attempted to pull away. Edie kept a firm hold of him.

"Get up, Finn. The ship's going down. We have to get out of here."

He shook his head slowly, then sharply, as if to wake himself up. Leaning heavily on Edie, he pulled himself to his feet . . . and lost his balance. He collapsed to the deck. She helped him up again and kept up a string of encouraging words while Galeon echoed her in his high-pitched voice.

They made it a few meters toward the hatch before he fell to the deck again. Over the shipwide came a three-minute warning. They would never make it.

A shadow crossed the light spilling in through the hatch.

"Hey! Help us!" Edie yelled.

Whomever it was backed up and came inside. It wasn't one of the crew.

"Achaiah . . ."

He stepped into the cargo hold, his pale blue eyes glowing in the emergency lighting.

"The captain sent me to look for you." He grinned charmingly. "Said he wouldn't let me on a lifepod unless I came back with you."

"Well, you found us. Are you going to help?"

"You and the boy, that's who he told me to find."

"Help me with Finn."

Achaiah cocked his head slowly, as if that course of action hadn't crossed his mind.

"Damn it, Achaiah, we had to freeze him because of that

detonator you made for Natesa. This is your fault. You owe him!" When Achaiah didn't move, she felt despair close in. "Then take Galeon. Get him to safety."

Galeon tilted his pale face to her, his brow set stubbornly. Edie looked from him to Achaiah, waiting for some response. Something flickered across Achaiah's face. It might have been remorse. Edie found the man incomprehensible. He'd done despicable things without ever giving a thought to the people he hurt, and he'd also shown moments of compassion. Those two sides seemed to war within him now.

To her relief, he stepped forward and grabbed Finn's arm. Edie took the other and together they hauled him up. Finn had enough wits about him to get his legs moving so they could drag him out.

As the *Molly Mei* hurtled into the upper atmosphere, the gravplating destabilized. It switched on and off randomly, making them lurch and stumble. Galeon ran ahead, stopping frequently for them to catch up. Whenever Finn fell, Achaiah helped him up. The calm, impersonal voice on the shipwide gave them two minutes, and then, as they turned into the last corridor, one minute.

Galeon bounded ahead. "This way—hurry!"

They passed the bridge hatch. Vlissides backed out, reluctant to leave. He spun around at their approach.

"Where the fuck were you?"

"You said you'd send someone for Finn. Where were they?"

"I sent Private Isaacson."

"Well, no one came." Private Isaacson, the op-teck, had apparently chosen to disobey that order in the confusion.

"Come on." Vlissides swung Galeon into his arms and ran the last twenty meters to the lifepod bay, where two pods stood open. One was empty, while the other held the rest of Vlissides's crew. A third pod had been ejected, and a quick headcount told Edie that Cat, Corinth, and the four children must be aboard. Cat must be overjoyed at that arrangement.

An explosion ripped through the ship. Edie lost contact

with Finn and tumbled out of control as the grav switched off, then slammed to the deck as it came back on. With a terrific wrenching sound, part of the corridor caved in and the bulkheads ripped open. Smoke filled the air.

Vlissides was at her side in seconds. "Explosion in the engine room. The altitude stabilizers can't handle the strain."

When he tried to help her, she pushed him away. "Help me with Finn."

He didn't waste time arguing. Finn was nearby, unconscious again. They dragged him the last few meters to the empty lifepod and maneuvered him inside.

"Strap yourselves in." Vlissides turned to the other pod, the one with his crew. "Isaacson, eject," he told his op-teck, and snapped shut the hatch.

As Edie strapped in Galeon, she realized what was wrong. "Where's Achaiah?"

They both looked back down the corridor. Achaiah was on the deck, his legs trapped by a twisted piece of plazalloy paneling.

Vlissides wavered. He looked at Edie, turned back to look at Achaiah, looked at Edie again. She knew they were both thinking the same thing.

Is he worth it?

She loathed Achaiah. She'd never forgive him. But . . .

She stepped out of the pod, her body making the decision before her mind caught up. She and Vlissides ran back to Achaiah. While she lifted up the paneling, Vlissides pulled him out. His legs were a mangled bloody mess. Vlissides lifted him over his shoulders and staggered down the corridor. Edie supported him as best she could as the ship squealed and shook and began to break apart.

They sealed themselves in the pod and it lit up under its own power. A holoviz bloomed out of a console near the hatch. The pod shimmied and jarred, and then the display showed it falling away from the ship.

The lifepod had a med brace, little more than a strap to secure a patient to the floor. They had two unconscious patients before them. They'd just risked their lives for Achaiah, but he was in a bad way, bleeding heavily from gashes in his legs and other wounds in his torso that Edie hadn't seen until Vlissides pulled open his shirt. His chest was a jumble of blood and bone that Galeon couldn't stop staring at. Finn was pale and motionless and still had poisonous cryo fluids in his blood, but his chances in the next few minutes were better. Weren't they? Edie had no hope of being objective about the decision. She hurried to secure Finn.

"Strap in!" Vlissides yelled over the whine of the pod's thrusters.

Edie took a seat next to Galeon and pulled the harness over her shoulders. Vlissides braced himself on the floor and tried to attend to Achaiah's wounds. The pod performed a series of near somersaults, throwing both men around until its trajectory finally stabilized.

Edie slipped out of her harness then, trying not to look at Achaiah's twisted body, and checked Finn's IV. He was breathing shallowly. Still alive. She buckled up again.

The lifepod screamed through the atmosphere, shaking like a popcorn popper. But all of the warning lights stayed green. She knew Achaiah was dead when Vlissides stopped what he was doing, hauled himself onto the seat beside her, and strapped himself in.

CHAPTER 27

The lifepods weren't sophisticated vessels—they were supposed to float around in space providing life support and basic medical aid until a ship picked them up. Dirtside, they had minimal functional capabilities as land vehicles. Between them, Vlissides and Edie figured out how to deflate the landing balloons and deploy the wheels. It was only when he started moving around that Edie noticed Vlissides was injured. One ankle was swelling up from a bad sprain and he'd wrenched his shoulders at some point during the landing. He most likely had a lot of other bruises that he wasn't complaining about.

The tiny pod windows showed a late-afternoon vista of desolate, rocky plains in all directions. The scope showed more of the same.

They had nowhere to go and a corpse to dispose of.

The medkit thoughtfully included a body bag. Edie sent Galeon into the impossibly small head and told him not to come out until he'd washed every smudge off his skin *and* his clothes. Then she and Vlissides put Achaiah inside the bag, sealed it, and pulled the tab that released its refrigerant chemicals. Edie would just as soon have left the body bag outside. She thought it best not to say so aloud. Instead, she helped Vlissides empty out the storage bins under the seats and they wrestled the body bag in there.

Vlissides slapped a patch on his ankle to reduce the swelling, and insisted he was fine.

The pods had been programmed to land close to each other. Whether any other pods had survived the landing or were in the vicinity, they didn't know. Edie had no luck raising anyone on the comm. The signal had to bounce off the commsat and its relays, and the commsat was apparently under the planet's control. Right now, it didn't work. As for rescue . . . any ship that parked in orbit was likely to suffer the same fate as the *Plantagenet* and the *Molly Mei*.

Edie concentrated on more immediate problems. Her major concern was Finn, now plugged into the onboard med-teck unit. It diagnosed cryo sickness and suggested various drugs, which she found in the medkit. He slipped in and out of consciousness, and she couldn't tell how much he understood when she explained what had happened. She didn't mention the real fear—that Natesa might arrive within hours with the ability to kill him remotely, in an instant, soon after she entered the system.

Galeon was as restless and impatient as any seven-year-old confined to an area the size of a couple of double beds.

"When can we go outside? I want to talk to Macky."

He was impossible to subdue until Edie found him something to do—reading a holo of the pod's instructions in order to find out what every single switch and light meant. She heated him a serve from the breakfast rations and he happily delved into the task. She saw him slide a suspicious glance only once toward the seats where the body bag was stored.

Two hours after landing, the sound of a voice on the comm was a welcome relief. It was Cat. She and Corinth had accurately predicted the direction of Edie's lifepod and driven theirs sufficiently close so that site-to-site communication between the vehicles was possible.

"Rough landing," Cat reported. "Our pod was damaged but the kids are okay, other than some scrapes and bruises and so much bloody screaming I'm ready to murder them all." Edie could hear the frightened children crying in the background.

"What about the other pod?"

"It's on my scope two klicks due east, in rocky terrain. Completely dead, by the way."

At that, Vlissides took over the comm. "Are you sure?"

"Uh, yeah. I know how to read my scope. Who is this?"

"Lieutenant Vlissides, commander of the *Molly Mei*. I don't believe we actually met."

"Your loss. And just because you commandeered a ship doesn't make you its commander. You milits killed the commander of the *Molly Mei*."

Vlissides gave Edie a *Who the hell does she think she is?* look, but persevered. "Let's deal with the issues at hand. You should send a search party."

"Great idea. Which little girl should I take with me while Corinth watches the others?"

"Don't be—" He cut himself off. Edie could see his frustration rising. He might be a Crib officer, but here no one was likely to follow his orders. "The kids will be all right by themselves for a while," he finally said.

"Actually, we shouldn't be wandering around outside," Edie said. "According to Theron, this planet actively resists attempts to explore it. E-shields won't protect you. In any case, it's almost dark and you're still limping."

Vlissides looked at her, horrified. "That's my crew out there. They could still be alive. Not to mention possible survivors at the *Plantagenet*'s crash site."

Edie gave what she hoped was a nod of understanding. "Let's start with a rendezvous. Cat, can we meet you halfway?"

"I've burned through the wheel rims on this thing. I think you'll have to come to me."

Driving was something else for Galeon to get interested in. Edie let him scrutinize the instructional holoviz until he pronounced himself an expert. Vlissides was clearly no teck, and actually seemed to appreciate the boy's help. Together they figured out the steering controls and exterior spotlights.

By the time they were ready to go, Finn had improved to the point of being able to sit up. His breathing was less labored, though he was still disturbingly pale and listless.

They trundled toward Cat's pod, a green dot on the scope, cutting a meandering path to avoid pits and boulders because Vlissides wasn't sure how much the vehicle could handle. The pod had landed in a shallow ravine, so the way out was uphill. After an hour's bumpy ride, Edie took over the driving. They rounded the crest and a new landscape was revealed.

Galeon saw it first. Edie was too busy negotiating obstacles and checking the scope and the nav chart to ensure they were on course for the other pod.

"Look, it's Macky!" He ran from one window to the next for the best view.

A couple of kilometers in the distance, dozens of enormous dark structures rose up from the ground. Their isolated location, surrounded by near-barren plains, convinced her this was the site of a BRAT—but this was nothing like what she'd encountered a year ago. Tight clusters of terraced pyramids and mounds were pierced by spires that spiraled a hundred meters or more into the indigo sky.

Edie stopped the vehicle and drew in her breath. Her immediate reaction sent a chill through her. *It doesn't look natural.* A year ago, every BRAT on the planet had become enclosed in a matted dome of vegetation, a megabiosis several kilometers in diameter, created by mutated biocyph caught in a feedback loop. When she and the rovers had climbed into the depths of one of these domes, she'd seen the amazing results of that distorted evolution. As bizarre and unique as the megabiosis had looked at first glance, everything she'd encountered seemed to belong to Scarabaeus.

Flora and fauna fitted together and functioned in harmony as an ecosystem should.

The irregular structures ahead, while clearly organic, looked like a living city of skyscrapers. A man-made city.

At her side, Vlissides let out a low whistle. "Well, that is fucking weird."

Galeon tugged at Finn's arm to get him to stand. "Take a look. You have to see this!"

Finn struggled onto one of the seats with a view out the window. He planted his bare feet on the floor to steady himself, and looked out.

"Let's go there," Galeon said. "I know Macky wants to meet us properly."

"Not tonight," Edie said. Not ever. Scarabaeus had claimed too many lives. "Anyway, we have to meet up with Cat's pod. Don't you want to see the girls and make sure everyone's okay?"

Galeon shrugged and acquiesced. "Suppose so."

"It's over there." Vlissides pointed out a side window.

Edie saw the pod's light a few hundred meters away, and headed for it.

The two pods mated in the dark, side by side to create a habitat. The children were settled down in one, catching up on sleep after their alarming early morning start. Finn was hooked up to drugs and oxygen. In a proper medfac they'd have engineered nanoteck to repair his damaged lungs. Their equipment here was far more basic. Keeping infection at bay was the main priority while Finn's body healed itself.

"In the morning I intend to check the third pod wreckage for survivors." Vlissides was adamant about it.

Edie's heart felt heavy but she nodded. It was surely hopeless.

"No sign of wreckage from the *Molly Mei*," Cat said from her seat up front, where she manned the scope. "But it probably came down hundreds of klicks from here. It could be anywhere."

"We have to warn other ships somehow," Edie said. "Tell them not to link to the commsat when they approach the planet."

Corinth had an idea about that. "We can set up a signal from the pod's comm system. A ship will only pick it up if it's pretty much directly overhead, but it's better than nothing."

Cat agreed, and they set to work creating a repeating message for the pods to broadcast. Vlissides wisely stayed out of the way. Meanwhile, Edie took stock of their supplies. Dirtside, oxygen and solar power weren't going to be a problem, so food and water were the limiting factors. With five adults and four children, she estimated they could last about thirty days if they were careful, perhaps longer if they found a clean water supply.

Thirty days was plenty of time for a rescue ship to come. Crib Central was already aware of the *Plantagenet*'s sudden disappearance, and now the *Molly Mei* had vanished as well. Help was surely already on the way—if they could outwit whatever controlled the commsat.

And Natesa was on the way, too.

They had pulled stowaway bunks out of the walls in preparation for the night. Edie knelt by Finn's bunk and compulsively checked his vitals for the fourth time that hour. She caught him watching her, his eyes gleaming in the reflected light of the med-teck over his head. His breath rasped in and out, his bare chest the only part of him that moved.

"How do you feel?"

"Like I'm drowning."

"Do you remember what I told you—about what happened?"

"The *Molly Mei* crashed when . . . something took control of the commsat and screwed up its navigation." He'd been more aware than she'd thought at the time.

"And Natesa. She's coming."

He nodded. "I remember."

Her fingers fluttered to the beetle inlay at her throat in a nervous gesture. "If you have any ideas . . ."

"Other than you pleading for my life?"

"Well, the commsat's out, or at least not under our control. Her ship will probably crash, too."

"Not before she's had a chance to use that detonator."

"Even if I could talk to her, I don't think she'll listen. She wants to punish me." She drew a deep breath and tried to think positive. "Or maybe she's forgotten all about you and me. She wants Pris back. Maybe she's just coming for the children."

"We'll see. At least, you'll see. I guess I won't know what hit me."

Nights on Scarabaeus were short—only six hours long. As soon as dawn broke, Vlissides made preparations to leave for the other lifepod. He ignored Edie's warnings. Despite nothing showing up on the scopes all night, she wasn't sure it was safe. She'd seen those images of the huge slaters Theron's team had encountered. This was a big planet—maybe there were no slaters in this area. That didn't mean there might not be other dangers. She'd witnessed firsthand the innovative ways Scarabaeus had developed to protect itself. Judging from the appearance of the city ahead, the planet had developed a few new tricks since then.

To Edie and Cat's surprise, out of some sort of sense of honor, Corinth volunteered to go with Vlissides. Even Corinth didn't seem too happy about it. Vlissides was grateful for the support. He strapped on the spur he'd been wearing when they abandoned ship—their only weapon. They both clipped on topped-up e-shields and went out the airlock, Vlissides limping badly.

Edie couldn't stop them from doing what they felt they needed to do, but she spent long anxious minutes watching them on the scope—two green dots moving away from the habitat toward the dense shrub and rocks that surrounded the crashed pod. It showed up as a faint heat blur. At least the weather was good—windy, but mild and dry. The scopes showed the landscape was desert as far as they could read.

Megabioses formed by drawing in biomass from surrounding areas over the years, leaving the land barren.

"An unlikely couple, huh?" Cat said, coming over to watch the scope with Edie. "I can't believe Corinth went with him."

"It was the decent thing to do."

"Yeah. Decent. That's Corinth."

Edie took a good look at Cat's dreamy smile. "Are you two . . . ? Jezus, Cat, you're a fast worker."

At the sound of squabbling from the next pod, Edie went to sort out the children. She assigned them jobs—Hanna and Raena to tidy up, Galeon to organize rations for the next two meals, and Pris to divide up the blankets, toiletries, and clothes in the supply lockers. They were all desperate to go outside. Edie was just as determined to keep them safely in.

Finn lay in a corner, barely moving. She couldn't tell when he was conscious and when he wasn't. While she checked the med-teck, she heard Vlissides report that they'd reached the lifepod.

"It's broken open, burnt up." A few minutes later he added, "Strange. No sign of bodies."

"Are any of the supplies salvageable?" Cat asked.

"We're still looking. I doubt it."

Something on the wide scope caught Edie's eye as she joined Cat. "Guys, there's something moving at the edge of the city."

"Could you be more precise?" Vlissides said.

"I can't make it out on the cams but the scope shows activity, a ripple of movement." Her gut churned while she tried to keep her voice calm.

The ripple on the scope started to spread and move out from the city. The scope picked up heat differentials and movement, displaying the result as a sim on a real-time holoviz. For an actual visual, Edie checked the externally mounted cams—and on full zoom they showed only a dark, indistinct flurry.

"What the fuck is that?" Cat said.

"Can you see anything yet?" Edie asked the men.

"Nothing. But we're a good thousand meters from the city, aren't we?" Corinth said.

"Still, I think you should get back."

"We'll be done here in twenty minutes," Vlissides said curtly.

Whatever it was on the scope, it seemed to coalesce into a more distinct mass. Then it moved again—this time in a very definite direction.

"It's moving toward you." Edie heard the urgency in her voice. "Heading toward the crash site."

"Corinth, are you seeing anything?" Vlissides didn't sound convinced.

"Uh . . . yeah, something's out there," Corinth said. His commlink crackled as if he was moving or climbing. "Way in the distance."

"It knows you're here." Edie wiped sweaty palms against her thighs. She wasn't even sure what she meant by "it"— only that it was unlikely to be friendly. "You need to head back—now!"

She was relieved to hear Vlissides agree. She had no authority over him but she trusted him to at least act rationally. She watched the scope as whatever it was moved closer to the crash site. The comm filled with the sound of the men's heavy breathing and shouting as they ran. Two minutes later, the cams picked them up as they cleared the shrub and headed for the habitat.

A single black shape appeared behind them, creeping low to the ground. Then another.

"Ohhhh . . . Oh, shit," Cat said.

Edie glanced at the scope. Most of the creatures still headed toward the crash site. A few isolated ones had broken away to follow the retreating men. From their size and appearance, even at this distance, Edie knew what they were— the ferocious slaters that Theron's team had encountered.

As Edie watched, Vlissides turned and raised his spur.

"Don't fire at them!" Edie yelled over the comm, surprised

when Vlissides obeyed and kept running with a pronounced limp. "Keep moving. *Faster!*"

It had taken them almost an hour to walk out there, taking it slow because of Vlissides's injuries. The zoomed-in cams gave a false impression of how much ground they were gaining. They were a good ten minutes from the habitat. Vlissides looked unsteady on his feet, though he managed to keep up with Corinth. Every dozen paces or so, he stumbled and even fell a couple of times.

"They're in trouble." It was Finn, leaning on the back of her seat. His breathing sounded better, but his face was strained. He wore only the canvas pants he'd gone into cryosleep with.

"I can see that. I told Vlissides not to fire but that doesn't mean they won't be attacked."

"Or that he'll be able to resist firing," Cat said.

"Close that hatch." Edie pointed to the airlock between the two pods. "I don't want the children to see anything."

Finn did so, moving stiffly as though every muscle ached. Then he came back to watch the cams again. Vlissides and Corinth were halfway to the habitat, the slaters staying apace fifty meters behind them. Edie was sure the creatures could move faster if they wanted to. For some reason they held back.

The scope showed the bad news—the remaining slaters turned from the crash site, as one mass, and proceeded after the fleeing humans. Their pace was much faster, as if they were hurrying to catch up. Edie waited for the inevitable images from the cams. A minute passed, another ten seconds, and then she saw them—a nightmarish onslaught of black creatures crawling through the undergrowth. Their black carapaces gleamed in the sun.

Vlissides's bad ankle had caught up with him and he'd fallen behind.

"We have to help them." Edie turned to Finn, waiting for him to come up with a solution.

"What do you suggest?"

"I don't know. Think of something!"

Finn shook his head, like he knew it was hopeless. "Can we move the pod closer?"

"We don't have time. Took us fifteen minutes to get the wheels out and put it in driving mode yesterday. And unless we disconnect the other pod, it'll be real slow going. And we can't leave the children behind."

"Do we have any more weapons?"

"No, nothing," Edie said.

But Finn looked anyway—he was a soldier, after all—and found a flare gun. "Maybe they're scared of bright lights," he said grimly.

"You have no boots. You can barely stand . . ."

"Someone has to go out there." He glanced at Cat, who looked like she was going to be sick.

Vlissides stumbled again and fell. Edie held her breath as a slater crept toward him. He rolled over and onto his knees, aimed his spur and fired. The creature exploded in a gush of milky blood. It spurted over him and slid off his e-shield.

The slaters veered away from Vlissides and descended on Corinth in a swarm. Cat let out a cry of helplessness.

Corinth's e-shield could only take so much. Under the combined attack and weight of so many creatures, it would eventually fail. There was no point warning Vlissides not to fire now. He couldn't override his instincts and training. He sprayed the slaters with bullets, killing a few, scaring off the rest long enough for Corinth to drag himself up.

A shrill clicking sound carried to the habitat, muted by the bulkheads but chilling all the same. And with it, sounds from the children in the next pod. They didn't have access to the cam feeds, but the slaters were close enough now to be seen with the naked eye. Edie heard excited chatter mixed with startled cries and whimpers as the children began to realize something terrible was going on outside.

The men were still a hundred meters from the habitat, and the slaters were closing the gap again.

Finn loaded the flare gun. "Let's see if this distracts them."

Cat handed him an e-shield from the cabinet near the hatch. He clipped it on, shut himself in the airlock and opened the outer hatch.

Edie heard the gunfire and watched through the driver's window as the flare arced upward, a mere glint in the sunlight. It descended into the spires of the city. Some of the slaters did wander off course, perhaps distracted by the sound more than the sight. But it didn't stop the relentless onslaught. A slater pounced on Vlissides, who was now several meters behind Corinth, and brought him down. He kicked out, rolled away, and got back on his feet, staggering on his bad ankle. The slater tried again, and this time it took Vlissides longer to free himself. He wasn't going to make it to the habitat.

Edie ran to the airlock and yelled through the hatch. "Finn, get back inside!" They had to seal the habitat.

Instead, Finn stepped out through the main hatch and shambled forward, moving quickly but stiffly. It was an incongruous gait for a man whose nakedness from the waist up showed off his powerful muscles. He crossed fifty meters of ground before aiming the flare gun directly into the seething wave of black behind Vlissides. He fired. The flare lacked the impact of a bullet, but it was enough to open up a hole in the ranks. The slaters shrieked and tumbled over each other. Finn quickly reloaded and fired again. Each shot only gained Vlissides a second, but every one counted. His e-shield was still intact. He still had a chance.

Two slaters put on a burst of speed and brought Vlissides down. He fired indiscriminately, hitting them more by accident. His legs were twisted badly beneath him and he failed to get up. Instead he crawled, pulling himself along on his elbows, stopping to shoot and keep the slaters at bay until they were on him again and he couldn't maneuver to use the weapon. It was hard to tell exactly when his e-shield failed, but suddenly there was a lot of blood on the ground.

Finn staggered forward, loading and firing the flare gun

on the move. Several flares landed near Vlissides, and the mass of slaters retreated from the pool of light and heat.

When Finn reached Vlissides' still form, he knelt over the milit, almost collapsing. The slaters inched forward again. Edie caught her breath. There was no way Finn could carry the unmoving milit and evade the slaters.

But Finn stood up again, Vlissides's spur on his wrist, and slowly retreated. Even from her vantage point in the pod she could see his anger and defeat. There was nothing left to do for Vlissides. Finn turned his attention to the slaters that had once again overtaken Corinth, firing with more control and precision than the panicking milit had been able to achieve. He ran to the injured man and helped him up. Corinth's e-shield was intact but its power must have been almost drained—it hadn't fully protected him, and his legs had been crushed. Finn dragged him along.

The creatures that the shots and flares had scattered were back in pursuit. Two or three leapt forward every so often to launch a new attack, forcing Finn to stop and deal with them while Corinth clung helplessly to him.

In the next pod, the children screamed and banged on the door.

"Cat . . . please, go to the children," Edie said.

Cat tore her eyes away from the grisly scene and slipped into the other pod. She seemed grateful for the distraction.

There had to be something Edie could do. If this planet truly knew her, she was the only one who could stop the attack.

She went into the airlock, breathing deeply and slowly as it cycled. The outer hatch opened and she faced Scarabaeus without an e-shield, without defenses or weapons.

CHAPTER 28

The slaters had no eyes, but they had sensed the humans at the crash site, sensed them running away—and now they sensed Edie as she stepped onto the hard, dry earth. A group of three broke away from the main crowd and skittered toward her. She walked out quickly, before she could change her mind, and waited for the attack she knew would come.

"Edie, get back!" She had never heard such anguish in Finn's voice. He was barely thirty meters away—she could see the horror in his eyes.

"I'm okay. Scarabaeus knows me. Remember?"

A year ago, she and Finn had escaped the vicious jungle after she programmed the biocyph to recognize and ignore their biopatterns. If that programming was still intact—and she was staking her life on the hope that it was—then once the cyphviruses sampled her again, they'd transmit the information to the nearest BRAT and it would give the command to leave her alone. Just like last time.

A slater rushed forward and reared up in front of her, exposing its churning jaws. Edie stood her ground. The slater snapped forward and she flung up her bare arm protectively. Pain seared through her as the slater latched on and knocked her to the ground.

It took ten seconds, maybe more. Longer than she'd expected, anyway. The slater let go with a hiss. It turned around in a slow circle, as if confused, then wandered off.

Edie didn't want to look at her mangled arm. She forced her legs to move and ran over to Finn and Corinth. The slaters on and around them dropped away at her approach. As a group, the creatures calmed and slowed down, the clicking sounds diminishing. They meandered about the area as if they'd forgotten what they were doing there.

Finn got to his feet, still holding on to Corinth, and Edie propped him up on the other side. They went back to the habitat, moving as fast as they could—which wasn't very fast at all. Finn was obviously exhausted, his breathing disturbingly rough. Corinth had lost the use of his legs, and Edie's arm burned like a thousand razor blade cuts where the slater had sampled her flesh.

They stumbled through the airlock and sealed themselves in. The children's hysteria had turned to sobs. Edie heard Cat's low words of comfort through the dividing hatch and started to go to them.

Finn was helping Corinth onto a bunk. He pointed to her arm. "Let's clean that up first."

Edie glanced at her gaping wound, feeling strangely detached at the sight. Was this really part of her body? Nevertheless, Finn was right. The children didn't need to see that much blood and ripped flesh up close.

"You help Corinth. I can deal with this," she said.

A bandage would do, for now at least. While Finn got Corinth comfortable and organized the med-teck unit to scan his legs, Edie found tubes of saline and medigel. She rinsed off the blood and the slater's slimy saliva, then squirted on medigel. That was enough to seal the wound. She quickly wrapped her arm in bandages to hide the gash from young eyes.

The children were desolate and just sitting around. Edie didn't want to think about what they could have seen through the window. Hanna was in Cat's lap, clinging, with her arms tightly wrapped around her neck. Cat looked uncomfortable but was coping well.

"Corinth is okay," Edie said. She meant he was alive. His legs were another matter.

Galeon put his head around the doorway to see what was going on in the other pod. He was pale with shock but putting on a brave front. "What's wrong with Finn?"

"He's just very tired because he came out of cryosleep too quickly."

"I think the lieutenant is dead. Those things got him."

"Yes, they did."

"They hurt your arm." Galeon stared at Edie's bandaged arm. "It was all covered in blood. I saw it."

"I'll be fine, too." Her arm did feel better, thanks to the analgesic in the medigel. She recalled something Theron had said—that the slaters had toxic mucus. She needed to get back to that medkit and do some blood work.

"Why are there monsters here?" Raena asked. She was huddled on a bunk, hugging her knees.

Pris put her arm around the younger girl's shoulders. "They're not monsters. Everything on this world is made by Macky. The creatures are part of Macky. They only hurt Edie accidentally. They won't hurt us."

Edie wasn't so sure of that, but she was grateful for Pris's calming words.

"What's going to happen now?" Galeon asked.

"I don't know. We'll talk about it and decide what to do next."

"I know what to do next," Pris said. "We have to go out there." She pointed at the city. "We have to find Macky and talk to him."

Edie's analysis of her own blood showed elevated levels of neuroxin byproducts. The biocyph in her cells broke down neuroxin as soon as it entered her system, so those elevated levels told her exactly what the "toxin" in the slaters' mucus was—neuroxin, or something so similar her body didn't distinguish. She'd given Scarabaeus the template for the drug when she'd used her implant to kill Haller on her last visit to the planet. The biocyph machinery had figured out a way to create organisms that could synthesize a near-perfect copy. And so neuroxin had ended up as part of the slaters' physiology.

"So the planet recognized you," Finn said when she showed him the results. "Shouldn't it recognize me, too?"

"Not through an e-shield. You'd have to turn it off. But not when the slaters are around. They'd have to bite you before they recognized you, and this bite would be fatal to any non-Talasi."

Most of the slaters had retreated from the area. Every so often one crept around outside the habitat, no longer displaying aggressive behavior. Perhaps this was a normal part of their routine. Edie had observed other fauna, too—several species of flying insects, including one that looked like a bright-red miniature dragonfly, and a curious spiky tailless lizard that occasionally popped up from underground warrens to cause a brief frenzy among the slaters. Through the rest of the morning, Edie kept the children occupied with watching for new creatures. They took turns operating the external cams to get a closer look.

This was not an ecosystem that fitted together well. Why would it be? The biocyph marched to its own rhythm. It could create and mold genomes on a daily basis, any way it wanted. The question was—what was driving it? Edie had to find the answer.

Corinth slept soundly, drugged up on painkillers and wrapped in splints. At least the e-shield had kept the toxic mucus away. Cat checked the comm system obsessively for any sign that the commsat was functional again. Edie sat down beside Finn and handed him a heated ration pack.

"I'm going to walk down to the city and jack into the BRAT seed," she told him.

If she'd expected a negative reaction, she didn't get it. "What do you think you'll find?"

"What I *hope* to find is whatever has taken over the bio-cyph. The gross morphological changes in that city—and presumably in all of the organisms across the planet—can only be accounted for by a major change in the target ideal of the BRATs. Theron was convinced the biocyph grew so complex it evolved sentience. The children keep talking about a personality. It seems impossible, but—"

Finn held up a hand to stop her, and she realized she'd been babbling about stuff he couldn't possibly care about. "Maybe you should just ask it how the hell we can get off this planet. Preferably before Natesa shows up." Finn glanced through the open dividing hatch to where the children were amusing themselves with the cams. "I don't want to drop dead in front of them," he said.

Edie didn't know what to say. Her heart clenched when-ever she thought of what must be going through Finn's head. She refused to even think of how she would feel if he died.

"Maybe there's something Scarabaeus can do about that, too," she said finally. "It controls the commsat. Maybe it could block the signal from her detonator. Achaiah said it's basically a commlink."

"At that range, the commlink doesn't need a satellite."

Edie nodded, feeling wretched. "At least we can find out if she's even out there. Maybe she'll crash before she knows what hit her."

"If she has her finger on that detonator, then I hope so. Take the spur."

"I think that's a bad idea."

"I wouldn't let any of my men go out there unarmed." Per-haps he was referring to Vlissides, who had let Corinth do just that.

"I'm not one of your men. And you're not in charge here."

He smiled unexpectedly. "You're right. This is your world. Do what you have to."

Without her e-shield, Edie's every sense was alive to Scara-baeus. As she left the habitat behind, her boots crunched on the parched earth, kicking up the occasional smooth pebble that told her this was a dry riverbed. The dust smelled clean. No hint of fresh greenery or rotting vegetation. The biocyph had used up almost every gram of biomass in the vicinity and channeled it all into the city. The low shrubs that appeared as she drew closer to the city were little more than awkward clots of brown sticks, the life drained out of them.

Every five minutes she checked in with Cat, wishing it were Finn on the other end of the line. Every minute drew him closer to possible death. She pushed that unbearable thought from her mind.

The living city loomed larger in the distance. The ground became rockier, forcing her to slow down as she climbed over small boulders and traipsed up and down inclines. Here a few things grew—mosses and ferns entwined with a slender thorny vine. A year ago, the vegetation in the megabiosis jungle had been translucent, probably fungal and parasitic, not photosynthetic. Now there were green plants. Delicate blue flowers on impossibly long stalks sprouted from the moss. Edie plucked one to examine it closer, and realized it wasn't a true flower at all, just a complex structure of folded pigmented fronds. No stamen or petals. Yet it had fooled her at first glance.

She heard the occasional buzz and chirp of insects. There was no further sign of the slaters, but she no longer feared them. Nothing here would harm her.

A new sound emerged on the edge of her awareness, growing louder with each step. The rush of water. She smelled it, too—fresh and slightly metallic. As she climbed to the top of a particularly large hillock, the view on the other side took her breath away. A lake had formed in a natural crater. Its banks were lush with reeds and taller plants that looked almost like trees, but not quite. Branches fanned outward from central disks, bending in graceful curves to trail needlelike leaves in the water. Everything had a primeval appearance, harking back to the way this world had looked when she'd first visited it eight years ago. Yet it was all a little odd. True woody trees, like flowers, represented a stage of evolution too advanced for this world. Instead, Edie saw ancient species masquerading as more modern Terran analogs.

Or perhaps she was seeing what she wanted to see. When she'd discovered what had happened to Scarabaeus, the mutated disaster her kill-code had wrought, she'd wanted to repair the damage and had failed. Now, in this oasis anyway, something beautiful had evolved out of that mess.

She was tempted to linger at the lake, but the city beckoned. That was where the BRAT seed lay hidden. If she was to talk to Scarabaeus, she needed to find it. She reported briefly to Cat before moving on, skirting the banks of the lake to get back on course.

The afternoon shadows of the towering structures ahead grew longer. The largest structures were dozens of meters wide at the base, rising up from an undergrowth of ridged folds. Smaller versions were dotted around the larger ones, some malformed and lumpy, others elegant and smooth, filling every cubic meter. Edie wondered how she would ever penetrate the dense growths until she drew nearer and realized the ridges covering the ground were hollow and pierced all over with large holes ripped in the sides, like irregular windows. This was a system of tunnels, tall enough for her to stand up in.

Half an hour after leaving the habitat, she entered the outskirts of the city and her perspective changed. Details became clearer. Each structure was created from a vast rib cage of organic scaffolding that defined its shape—rounded bulges, terraced and truncated pyramids, twisted spires. These "bones" were entwined with dozens of other species—slabs of glistening fleshy moss dappled with lichen, delicate vines, multicolored funguses, and patches of brightly colored buds.

Everything twined together into clotted masses and the air hummed with the rustling and chirping of animals. Creatures clambered in and out of pockets in the scaffolding— much smaller than the slaters, many of them resembled insects but with soft, amphibianlike flesh that bulged out from between the ribs of their exoskeletons. They looked like they'd been turned inside out.

Edie waded into the undergrowth. It first clustered around her with trembling tendrils and then pulled back. The ferny growths had thick translucent stems that reminded her of the vines she and Finn had battled a year ago. Their movement was controlled by the ebb and flow of the fluid within them.

She could've camped on the edge of the city for a week, happily logging species and observing interrelationships. Finding the BRAT and persuading it—or whatever it was that controlled it—to return control of the commsat to humans seemed like a mundane task when confronted with this awe-inspiring, living city. But the BRAT was the priority.

There was no way of knowing where to start or which was the quickest route to the seed, so she stepped into the nearest tunnel. Its pale, damp inner walls felt sleek under her hand, like satin. Running under the surface of the walls was a network of tubules, barely visible because they were as pale as the lining of the tunnel. Edie laid her palm flat over the tubules and felt the ripple of fluid flowing through them.

The humidity was noticeably higher, although the perforations in the walls made the tunnel feel airy and light. She moved forward. Ahead, the tunnel branched into two.

Without warning, the left side of the branch began to collapse. A dark substance flowed into the tubules like poisoned blood through veins and capillaries, and the tunnel crumpled in on itself. Edie resisted the urge to turn and run. She took the other branch, which remained untouched, and continued on.

At every intersection, all tunnels but one caved in as she approached. The veins of side passages turned black, threatening to do the same, so Edie stayed out of them. She knew she was being driven in one direction. Was this sentience, or nothing more than the reflexes of a Venus flytrap?

Heading deeper into the organic city, the tunnels darkened as the sheer volume of vegetation outside blocked the sunlight. The veins in the tunnel walls glowed with soft purple phosphorescence, lighting the way. As she rounded a corner, the tunnel widened ahead. Beyond that was a wall of patchy light.

Edie approached the end of the tunnel slowly and allowed her eyes to adjust. Only when she stood on the very edge, at the top of a gently sloping ramp, did she realize she was looking into a vast cavern. Its curved walls were created from the same scaffolding as she'd seen outside. Thick curtains of semi-opaque resin dangled from ceiling to floor. It looked like partially dried sap, and divided the cavern into random smaller chambers. Suspended in these syrupy stalactites were irregular patches of phosphorescent cells. More cells covered the uneven floor in a haphazard, lumpy mosaic, glued together with matted twine. Some cells glowed with soft violet light while others lay dormant, exuding a pearly gray sheen.

Edie felt like she was on the stage of an amphitheater. No, it was the other way around. This was the exhibition and she was the audience.

Hiding in the center of the dome, draped in garlands of glistening sap, the metal casing of the BRAT was just visible. The cavern's overwhelming size rendered it trivially small, but clearly it was intended to be the focal point. Soft folds of lush pink moss cascaded around its base like a flower in bloom.

The children would love this. That thought popped into Edie's mind as she looked around the cavern in awe. To them, this was the true face of Macky—beauty and whimsy, with plenty of nooks to explore.

Pulsing beneath the matted floor and twisting behind the walls were the same glowing tubules from the tunnels. They were thicker here and formed raised channels. Edie stepped out of the tunnel, careful to walk between the veins. Dodging the sticky resin drapes or pushing them gently aside to clear the way, she approached the BRAT. The ground under her feet vibrated in anticipation.

CHAPTER 29

Edie climbed onto the mossy petals to reach the access port of the BRAT, and used the softlink in her fingers to jack in.

The datastream rushed across her splinter. Resisting the urge to pull away, she kept her focus steady. The cacophony was a hundred orchestras, each playing a different symphony. Each time she managed to decipher a familiar cadence, the surrounding music drowned it out. Yet each thread of music held a vague familiarity—all stemming from the song she recognized. Overlaid on that foundation was the same tangled code she'd found in the isolated sim, and it buzzed with the same unsettling intensity. It didn't have complete control. It didn't control the main subroutines at all. It redirected and molded aspects of the biocyph's calculations—a drumbeat that tried to make everything else play in time, even while its own rhythm was unsteady.

Someone or something had injected that code and imprinted that beat. Edie let the beat trickle through her splinter, searching for a hint of where it came from. It wasn't the work of a cypherteck. She would've recognized that. Maybe an infojack had planted a worm or a virus, but why? Edie could only imagine—and nothing she imagined was good. Scarabaeus had demonstrated aggressive wildlife and malicious intent when it killed Theron's entire crew and most of the *Molly Mei*'s as well.

Yet it had also created a peaceful oasis, whimsical little creatures, soaring spires, and this beautiful cavern.

Edie felt dizzy from the effort of keeping the datastream in some semblance of order in her splinter. She closed her eyes and sank to the ground, leaning against the cold metal casing of the seed. For a moment, her mind relaxed as she lost concentration. That's when she noticed the knots of code untangling, as if it, too, was relaxing. The knots unraveled and laid themselves across the datastream and melded with it. The threads began to weave together, each riff and beat gradually coming into line, until in one swift, final moment, a new song of Scarabaeus coalesced into a perfect form.

Gasping at the beauty of the music, Edie was compelled to listen. The melodies flowed through her mind like a narcotic, blanking out rational thought.

—*Beautiful, isn't it?*

Edie opened her eyes and looked around for the source of the voice. There was no one there.

—*I did this. Do you like it?*

The words were in her head, flowing through the music. A million questions came to mind.

"Parts of it are beautiful," she replied honestly. She spoke the words aloud as well as transmitting them down the link.

The melodies fractured, the beat strayed like a skipped heartbeat, and the knots of code tightened and tangled until they were as dense as they'd been before.

—*Sometimes it all comes together, but I can only hold it for a moment. I need your help, Edie.*

"Who are you?"

—*You call me . . . Scarabaeus.*

"How do you know my name, and the name I invented for this world?"

—*I know you, Edie Sha'nim.*

It didn't make sense. Biocyph didn't use names. She'd never used names while jacked into the BRATs on this world.

Biocyph didn't speak Linguish—the standard language used across the Reach—either. There had to be a prankster on the other end of the line. Well, she'd play along—for now.

"Why do you need my help?"

—You know biocyph. You can show me what I'm doing wrong. In here, all alone, I can't think straight. I can't tell my voice from the echoes.

"That doesn't explain why you're killing people. The slaters may have acted on instinct, but *you* took control of the commsat and crashed two ships."

—We both know what kind of people were on those ships. They came to steal from me. They tried to interfere with me, but I fought them off.

She started to wonder if whoever was talking to her was even sane. Regardless of how this deception was being carried out, the entity, or whatever it was, managed to sound perfectly earnest. Edie pushed aside her uneasiness for now.

"What makes you think I can help you control this ecosystem?"

—You created it. If you can't help me, no one can.

"What will you do for me in return?"

Another hesitation. Edie's suspicions twinged as she waited.

—I offer you the chance to create a glorious new world with me, Edie. Why would you ask for anything in return?

There was a time when she'd wanted nothing more than to fix Scarabaeus, to make it whole and peaceful again. That time was past. There were people on this planet. Friends and innocent children. They were more important than this.

"Your offer is intriguing," she lied, "but I need your help, too. There are survivors on the planet, in a habitat nearby. They need access to the commsat so they can call for help. And when that help comes, the ship needs safe passage."

Another hesitation. When the voice returned, it seemed distracted, aloof.

—These things don't concern me. You've no idea how it feels to have an entire planet's blood running through your veins. To design new life, to start the heartbeat of a delicate animal, to build entire cities. Together we can rebuild this world exactly as we want it. We will control it all. We will create something so beautiful, you'll never want to leave.

Her spine tingled, and she was unable to decide if the idea was sinister or bizarrely tempting.

"I'm not sure it can be controlled."

—You can do it. We can. Disarm the security protocols on your splinter and I will show you.

"I won't agree to anything until you restore the commsat and my friends are safe—inside and outside the habitat."

—I can't control the slaters' innate behavior.

"Then change it. Look at the instructions I programmed into the biocyph a year ago. I convinced the wildlife and the retroviruses to leave *me* alone."

—That's why I need you. You, of all people, understand this stuff.

"You claim you're Scarabaeus—the whole planet. Now you talk as if you're a low-grade amateur hacker. Which is it?"

Yet another pause before the response came.

—I am the evolved awareness of Scarabaeus. I am your creation, Edie. I thought I could do it alone, but I can't. Help me.

"Like I said, put that commsat back online and stop killing people. Then I'll consider it."

—Very well. The commsat is functioning again—for now. There is a ship approaching. I will allow it through. You can send your friends away on it.

Edie went cold. "Who? Can you talk to them?"

—I seem unable to talk to anyone without a biocyph link. I'm not even sure I am using words. You may be the only person who can hear me.

She realized there was some truth to that. She was communicating through the biocyph, hearing it as a voice the same way she heard the tiers as music. It wasn't like a regular commlink. If she wasn't experiencing it right now, she probably wouldn't have believed it was even possible.

She didn't have time to be amazed. She hit her commlink.

"Cat, the commsat is back up and there's a ship out there. Is it Natesa?"

Cat answered a few seconds later. "Edie, where are you? The scope is barely picking up your signal."

"I'm deep inside the city. I'm fine. Just . . . please, find out who's on that ship."

"Okay. Stand by."

Edie jumped back into the datastream. "I'm returning to the habitat for a while."

—*I would prefer that you stay.*

"I'll come back. Maybe we can figure out a way to hook up a remote patch through a commlink, so we can talk any time.

—*Talking won't change anything. I need to show you the glory of this world.*

Edie felt an uncomfortable tickle in her mind. The tangles of code unraveled, sending out strands to tap at the matrix of her splinter. There was a cohesive intelligence behind the intrusion. Could it invade her if it wanted to? The tapping was cautious, not insistent, but definitely deliberate. If she didn't let it in, would it become more forceful?

"I'm not ready," she said. "I need rest and food. I need to make sure my friends are okay."

She pulled her fingers free from the port without waiting for a response. The datastream dissolved, leaving behind a killer headache to remind her how much concentration the interaction had required.

As she emerged from the city, Cat called. "The ship isn't responding to hails, which makes me think it's not Fleet. It's squawking an ident from Port Trivane. I sent out our distress call. Don't know if it got through because now the commsat's dead again."

Trivane . . . the science station O'Mara had mentioned. Probably the nearest port to Prisca, and the logical place for Natesa to contract a ship to bring her to Scarabaeus.

Cat winced as Edie pulled apart the med-teck unit.

"We have another one in the other lifepod," Edie reminded her.

"You mean our backup. Now we have no backup."

"This is important. I need to keep in contact with Scarabaeus and I don't want to spend all my time out there in its lair."

She reached into the guts of the unit and pulled out a wafer of biocyph matrix—a slice of plaz the size of a small belt buckle. Before Cat could protest again, she took it into the other pod, where Finn fiddled with a commlink and a receiver taken from the pod's console. He'd pried open the receiver to make use of its port and power traces.

Beside him, Galeon sat on the floor intent on his own project. Finn had shown him how to make a new set of Pegasaw pegs from wire and pieces of colored food wrapping. The pair of them were fast friends again.

Edie handed Finn the biocyph wafer. "Do your Saeth magic."

The intention was to convert a commlink into a biocyph conduit. The idea of a remote biocyph communication interface was nothing new, but in this case they had to create one from salvaged parts.

"Any news on that ship?" Finn said as he got to work.

"The commsat's still down."

"But it's Natesa, right?"

"I think so." It had to be. Any other ship would've responded to their hails and reassured them that rescue was near. Natesa was acting outside the Crib's jurisdiction, running silent, formulating her plan to take back the children— or Pris, at least.

"We need the commsat back up," Finn said. "There's a chance the Saeth could make it here before the Crib."

A slim chance. Scarabaeus was nearer to the Fringe than it was to Crib Central, but Central must've been aware of something wrong on Scarabaeus for several days now, ever since the *Plantagenet* went down. It had a head start.

"If the Saeth do get here first," Edie said, "we can still save the children from Natesa."

"You still want to take them—without a supply of neuroxin?"

She shook her head miserably. "No, you're right. We can't risk their lives."

What about her life? Would she take the chance and escape, knowing she'd have to steal neuroxin again in a few months or return to Talasi herself, tail between her legs, and beg for it?

She left Finn working on the devices and went back to the other pod to organize a meal.

"It's my turn to do that." Pris had joined her.

"Let's both do it."

As they sorted through packets of pro-bars and freeze-dried fruit, Pris kept looking through the open hatch to watch Finn work.

"Is he still sick?"

"He's almost better. He'll be fine."

"He's not fine. My m— Natesa did something to him, didn't she?"

Edie kept her eyes focused on the food. She didn't want to be responsible for causing any disillusionment in Pris. "Why do you say that?"

"I told you, I heard her talking. She said he was a bad man. Galeon told us the stories he told him. I don't think he's so bad."

"He's not. He's a good man." She managed a smile. "What stories?"

"About when he was a little boy. The big house he grew up in, in the middle of fields of barleat, with trees to climb and a river. Did you know he had a dog who could fish?"

"Yes, I heard about that." Edie's throat tightened.

"So why does Natesa want to kill him?" Pris asked quietly.

Disillusionment be damned. Edie couldn't invent a comforting lie. "It's not because of who Finn is. It's because of who Natesa is. Finn is important to me, so she knows she can use him to control me. Ever since I was your age, she's controlled my life—or tried to."

"Isn't that what parents do?"

"I don't know." Edie shook her head. "Like you, I never had parents. Maybe she tried to be my mother, but implanting things in my body, isolating me, training me for one purpose, using me to further her career . . . I don't think that's what real mothers do."

Pris helped in silence for a while.

"Natesa used to tell me about you," she said at last.

"She did?"

"She said you were talented, the very best, and she was proud of you. But that you didn't believe in what you were doing. She tried to make you believe, but you wouldn't. She said you wanted something else—she didn't know what. The Talasi were cruel to you. She rescued you, but it wasn't enough."

"She's right. It wasn't enough. What I wanted was the chance to choose which way to go." Edie looked at Pris, at the wan face and troubled eyes she recognized so well. Her younger self. "What do *you* want, Pris?"

Pris shrugged, then thought about it for a moment. "I think I want that house. The trees and fields and the river with flat guppy. Someone to show me how to do stuff, like Finn is showing Galeon how to make that game."

That all sounded pretty good to Edie, too. Normal kid stuff. Something these children would never have as Crib wards and invaluable cyphertecks.

"What about Natesa? She wants to adopt you. We think she's on that ship in orbit, coming for you."

"I still prefer a house and a dog. And real parents for all of us."

CHAPTER 30

Edie stared at the creature on her pillow. Spindly legs, curled antennae poking out from a spiral head. A polished carapace, turquoise and black, gleaming under the habitat's night lights. Its head was tilted whimsically to one side.

She rubbed her eyes and took it between her fingers. It was hard and cold, made of plazalloy wires and bits of paper wrap.

Finn had made this, a gift for her. A parting gift? In a panic, she threw off her blanket and got up. The pod murmured with the children's light breathing. She rushed to the other pod, where Cat and Corinth dozed on bunks, and hit the scopes to search for him.

"He walked out about an hour ago," Corinth said from his bunk. He hadn't been sleeping after all.

"But why?"

"Said he wanted to take a look around. He took a comm-link."

Edie hit the comm switch on the driver's console. No response. She checked the scopes. A green dot that represented Finn's body heat moved slowly and apparently randomly across an area on the near side of the city. He had no boots . . . Why would he go out there in bare feet? What the hell was he doing?

A warm breeze lifted Edie's hair as she clambered over moss-covered rocks, feeling her way in the diffuse violet light coming from the nearby city where the spires were lit with spiraling phosphorescent channels. She retraced her steps from the day before, over the ridge leading to the oasis. It was where the scope had shown Finn's last position.

The rippling water gleamed with reflected light. Edie heard the occasional scuffle of creatures moving about in the dense greenery draped over the banks. Otherwise it was silent and perfectly serene. Irresistibly inviting. Exquisite, the way all of Scarabaeus was supposed to be.

A few meters from the bank, the water's surface broke and Finn emerged, swimming away from her. His arms flashed silver with each slow, powerful stroke. Edie noticed his pants lying crumpled on the bank, the commlink clipped to the belt. So that was why he hadn't answered. She sat and watched Finn turn at the far bank and swim back.

When he was halfway, he saw her. He stopped and stood up. His skin glistened in the strange light. The water lapped against his shoulders as he regarded her, motionless.

Her fingers had already worked her boots loose. She wriggled out of her pants, then got to her feet, her toes curling in the cool moss. Finn had started to wade toward her. When she stepped out of her underpants and pulled her tee over her head, he was still again, watching her.

Cautiously negotiating the steep bank, she walked to the edge and slipped into the water. The lake bed was gritty under her feet. A couple of steps in, the water was already up to her waist—cool, but not unpleasantly so. Warmth from the previous day's sunshine lingered, taking the edge off.

Finn waited for her as she waded out. The water crept up her rib cage and under her breasts, tickling like a lover's fingers. She stopped a couple of meters in front of him.

"You don't have an e-shield," she said, noticing the lack of a shield's aura around him.

"The slaters dispersed so I figured it was safe enough." By now, something must have sampled his DNA—the brush of a plant frond, the bite of an insect—and the planet knew who he was. "I decided to check out the lay of the land," he said. "Following my instincts, I guess. You didn't mention this place."

"It's beautiful, isn't it?" She was looking at him when she said it.

Finn slapped the water. "It's good to get dirtside for a change. Too much time on stations and ships—you can forget what living is supposed to be."

Natesa could send death at any moment. A pointless death, on her whim. Involuntarily, Edie looked up at the night sky, as if she might see it coming. Finn followed her gaze for a moment, then sank back in the water.

"I couldn't die in that tin can."

So he really thought this was the end. His certainty forced her to face it, too.

"I didn't want you to die alone," she said, almost choking on the words. Then she grew angry. Facing it didn't mean accepting it. "There's still a chance . . . If she would just talk to us, I could make her stop. I'll do whatever it takes, whatever she wants. I'll tell her that I'll go to CCU and plead with them to give Ardra another chance. That's all she really wants—to leave her mark on the Reach. If she lets you live, I'll help her do that. I'll figure out how to make Ardra work eventually, no matter how many worlds it ruins along the way."

"You'd destroy the galaxy to save me?"

She smiled at him through her tears. He made it all sound so tragically romantic. To her it was just unbearably tragic.

"I would. Even if you left me behind. You *should* leave me behind. Everything you want is out there—your home and family, the Saeth, the Fringers you swore to help. That's where you should be. Not tangled up in my life."

"Maybe that's true. It doesn't matter now." He moved closer to push strands of damp hair off her forehead. "You were the first person I trusted in a long time. I know I tested you. You never wavered. You were always on my side—I don't know why. But I love you for it."

Why did those words that should have made her joyful sound like a deathbed confession? She couldn't bear to remember that he was a condemned man. That this would soon be over. Natesa would take the children. Edie would go back to the Crib. They'd send more men to this planet to probe it, abuse it, most likely destroy it. There was no one left on her side.

And Finn would die here, in her arms.

"I wish I could take you home with me," he said. "Just . . . *home*. Someplace where you don't feel used or hunted, where you don't feel you have to save the galaxy, or someone else's kids, or even me. I want to know who you are when it's just you and me."

His intensity made it hard for her to breathe. She slid into his arms and his finger trailed down her cheek and across her lips.

"Now I don't have time," he said.

"Pretend that you do."

Finn kissed her and the bad thoughts fled. His lips were confident, demanding. His hands were tentative, as if he feared he might be dragged away from her at any moment. Edie wrapped herself around him, melding skin to skin. Everywhere they touched, his heat soaked into her. Everywhere else, cool water.

Weightless, they glided through the water. Lifting her onto the sloping bank, Finn slid his weight over her in a single smooth movement. She still sensed his hesitation. Before he could change his mind, she wrestled him onto his back and drew him inside her as she straddled his hips. In the ethereal light, her hands looked unnaturally pale, his darker skin richly luminous and shimmering with violet-tinged water drops. With her palms pressed to the hard muscle of his chest, she felt his heart beating—racing, as if to outrun its fate.

This world had killed so many. Lying on the lake's bank with Finn, their limbs loosely tangled, her thoughts turned morbid. He, too, waited to die here, this time through someone else's murderous intent.

She imagined the slaters finding his body and ripping apart the flesh, as they had no doubt done to the bodies from the crash sites, and as their smaller ancestors had done to the rover team that died here a year ago . . . Zeke, the cheerful op-teck injured by Rackham's flash bomb, and five serfs, all devoured by slaters when their e-shields failed. The hapless Kristos, buried alive and crushed by a particularly persistent carnivorous plant.

And Haller, the *Hoi*'s unstable, sleazy XO. There was a man she avoided thinking about when at all possible. Unlike the others, he'd been entombed by the slithering vines of the jungle and taken apart, piece by piece. Under the control of retroviruses, the vines had performed the delicate task of vivisecting Haller over the course of several hours, until she'd killed him out of mercy with her neuroxin implant.

What else was this world capable of?

—I can feel it inside me, thinking my thoughts . . .

She shuddered as Haller's dying words came back to her. Finn's arms closed tighter around her, his hand stroking her back as if he thought she might be cold. She wasn't cold. She was unnerved by the memory of Haller's slow, messy death as the biocyph invaded his brain.

Invaded him, cracked open his skull . . .

—I'm thinking its thoughts . . .

Edie bolted upright, her blood turned to ice. *Haller was here.* He wasn't dead at all. His consciousness had been absorbed into the biocyph as it invaded his brain.

It made sense. Everything she'd seen here had the unnatural touch of a human about it, too much high-level order and not enough basic organisms. The creepy, impossible conversation through the biocyph link. It knew her name. It knew what a human being was, a ship, a commsat. It knew she had created Scarabaeus with the kill-code. She'd been talking to Haller, what was left of him—or rather, what he had become.

"What is it?" Finn's hand rested on her shoulder blade, where he must have felt her heart thumping against her ribs.

A second realization hit, even more overwhelming than the first. "Finn, I think Scarabaeus can help you."

He sat up beside her. "What?"

"Remember Haller? The jungle dissected him while keeping him alive. Perhaps it could remove the bomb from your skull without damaging you." Something stopped her from telling him the full extent of her realization. She stuck with the part that really mattered. "The bomb is integrated into your splinter, and the splinter is biocyph. That's something the planet can understand and manipulate . . . and destroy."

She got to her feet and grabbed his hand to pull him up. She had to get back to the cavern and talk to Scarabaeus. To *Haller*. That part she couldn't tell Finn. He would never put his life in Haller's hands. The two men had hated each other, and for generally good reasons.

They scrambled into their clothes. Finn, who had only pants to put on, watched her finish dressing. She got the feeling he was humoring her, that he'd rather stay right here on the riverbank and wait it out.

"It might work," she said breathlessly. "A wet-teck interface can't be extracted from the cortex, but this is different. You only have a sliver of it in your head. The way the jungle dealt with Haller's body and brain—so precise and delicate . . . It might work."

She started up the bank, pausing when Finn did not follow.

"Finn, please. This is your only chance."

"Brain surgery performed by plants. That's my only chance?"

"Just come with me."

He did, without further protests. They ran to the city's edge, Finn apparently immune to the discomfort of traveling barefoot over rocky ground. Edie found the tunnel where she'd entered before.

"This way."

As they jogged through the twists and turns, Edie spoke her thoughts aloud, hoping to reassure him.

"These aren't really plants. This entire place is one being. One creature. One consciousness. It has autonomous functions, like the instinctive reactions of the wildlife to intrusions and the everyday calculations that keep it evolving. And it has a thinking, creative component that plans ahead and molds the evolution according to its desires."

That part was Haller, she now knew. He'd spent the last year learning how to control the biocyph—not very successfully, but certainly well enough to confound Theron's team.

"Why would it help me?" Finn said.

"Because it wants my help."

That was going to be the tricky part—persuading Haller to help Finn, to not kill him. Haller would demand a price. Edie would agree to it. She'd help him turn this world into whatever he wanted. What did it matter now? In the future, humans were sure to try again to tame Scarabaeus—let them try. Finn would be alive and safe and free.

They entered the cavern. Phosphorescent patterns spun in greeting across the floor and along the stalactites. The retroviruses of Scarabaeus could taste her presence, and the planet was evidently pleased at her return.

"Jezus . . ." Finn looked around, marveling.

Edie pushed through to the BRAT. She'd left the jury-rigged biocyph commlink back at the pod, so she reeled out a hardlink and jacked in.

—*I have been waiting.*

"I'm here to make a deal, Haller," she sent down the link, not speaking aloud. She'd debated whether to let Haller know that she knew who he was. Their relationship when he was a man had been tense at best, and sometimes abusive. But maintaining the deception would only waste time.

—A deal? What I offer you is so immense, so gratifying, it will be its own reward.

"No games. I know it's you. I don't care why you pretended otherwise—"

—I'm not the same as I used to be. But I didn't know if you would see that.

Fair enough. She'd detested Haller the man, and he knew it.

"Well, I'm here and I'm prepared to work with you. I need more from you than the joy of experiencing your planet-sized brain. I've brought Finn with me—he's unshielded, so you know he's here." Finn wandered around the chambers of the cavern, coming in and out of Edie's view as he examined everything with a critical eye.

—Edie, I've no interest in deals. I could take you by force if I chose.

She doubted that. "What use would that be? I'm a cypherteck. Biocyph is my playground, not yours. If you force me, I'll overpower you."

—Perhaps. You will give your cooperation once you realize the wonders we can create together.

"I'll do what you want, but here's what I want. Remove the bomb from Finn's brain. It's integrated into his biocyph splinter."

—What makes you think I'm capable of that?

"Scarabaeus pulled you apart cell by cell in order to merge with you. The biocyph knows how to do that. You just need to guide it so it knows when to stop. If you succeed, if he survives, I'll help you."

—You'll help me?

She could sense Haller thinking it through.

—Edie, helping me is not enough. You must merge with me completely. I will take your body as Scarabaeus took mine. Your mind will integrate with the planet's biocyph and you will join me. We will be Scarabaeus. It's the only way to take complete control over this world.

Edie felt sick as visions of Haller's grisly demise—his physical demise, anyway—came back to her. *I don't want to control this world,* her mind screamed. She wanted Finn to be safe. She wanted him to rejoin his friends and restart his life.

To get what she wanted, she had to give Haller everything.

Huddled against the BRAT seed, she found herself staring at her hands. This is what she would lose—skin, muscle, bone, but so much more. What would remain? Only the memory of what it felt like to touch another human. Would she even recognize herself?

There wasn't time for philosophical pondering. Just as he'd done a year ago, Haller offered her an escape from the Crib. Perhaps, if she merged with Scarabaeus, she could even save it from the Crib's interference. That, and Finn's life, would have to be enough.

"I'll agree to merge with you," she sent to Haller.

—You will be amazed. Together we—

"But only if Finn survives," she broke in. "And you need to hurry. Natesa's on the way with a detonator to kill him at any moment."

—Natesa! That woman will not cease trying to steal you from me until she's dead.

Edie felt Haller's attention fading. She called him back, desperately.

"Don't destroy her ship, Haller. There are innocents on board. Save Finn from her, and then she won't matter. She won't have power over me anymore."

The entire cavern vibrated in frustrated anger. Finn came over, alarmed.

"It's okay," she told him. "I've arranged it." Finn looked confused, and she felt guilty about deceiving him. If she was going to set him free, it had to start now—she had to give him the freedom to make the decision even knowing what it involved. "Finn, the consciousness of the planet—it's John Haller. His mind merged with the biocyph."

"And you trust him?" Finn seemed more amazed by that than he did by the idea of a planet with a mind.

"Yes, because I promised to help *him* if it works—and he really wants my help. He won't harm you."

She kept the rest from him, knowing he'd refuse if he knew the cost. If he knew, he'd sacrifice himself for her, just as she'd chosen to sacrifice herself for him.

Finn didn't look any happier, but to Edie's relief he nodded. "He can't kill me any more dead than Natesa will."

"Haller." She spoke aloud now, as well as through the link. "He's ready."

—Tell him to return to the chamber where he just was.

Edie cut the link and walked between the resin drapes at one side of the BRAT, beckoning for Finn to follow. The small chamber looked much like any other, its walls dripping with sticky fluid. The ground under Finn's feet opened up. Instinctively, Edie backed away.

"Don't be afraid," she said, only because she was terrified.

As Finn was knocked to his knees, a milky, shimmering mass erupted from the disturbed ground and engulfed him. Hundreds of vines snaked around his body and lifted him up spread-eagled. She caught a split-second glimpse of his face—his trusting gaze locked with hers—before the column of vines raised him higher still. More vines dropped from the ceiling of the chamber and locked together to create a sturdy, twisted stalk as wide as the BRAT itself and three times taller. Finn's body was suspended halfway up the column.

Thin filaments crept up the vines, their sensitive tips searching for a hold. They swarmed around Finn's head and encased it. His body convulsed once, and he was still.

Edie crawled back to the BRAT over uneven, shifting ground, and pressed her fingers to the access port.

"Haller, don't hurt him." Hot tears burned her eyes.

—I remember your wasted feelings for this man. After you merge, you'll realize that individuals are irrelevant.

Finn was now completely cocooned. The vines writhed around him, grotesque fingers prodding and manipulating while the fine tendrils invaded his body to latch onto the biocyph.

Edie sank to the spongy ground outside Finn's chamber and waited.

CHAPTER 31

It seemed like hours later that she was distracted by sounds
in the distance—laughter and shouting drawing nearer. It
couldn't be . . .

Through the strands of dried sap, Edie saw Galeon rush
into the cavern. The other children followed, eyes wide with
joyous wonder. They still wore their PJs along with an assortment of adult-sized clothes from the meager lifepod supplies.

"Macky!" Galeon headed straight for the BRAT, almost
tripping over himself on the soft uneven ground.

Edie could do little more than scramble to her feet and
watch the children in horror. Why were they here? The slaters could have attacked them. Then she saw they wore no
e-shields.

Edie grabbed Galeon, and he winced as she dug her fingers into his wrist harder than she'd intended. "What are you
doing here? Where's your e-shield?"

"Macky asked us to come. He said it was safe."

"*Asked* you? How?"

"We've been talking to him."

Galeon pointed to Pris, who was running her hands over
the velvety surface of a phosphorescent cell suspended in a

resin stalactite. Strapped to her arm was the biocyph comm-link.

Edie should have predicted this—the children's curiosity for Macky was insatiable. "You weren't supposed to use that," she said.

"Well, we did. Then Cat and Corinth fell asleep and we snuck out." Sneaking out was, of course, Galeon's forte.

"Macky needs our help," Pris said.

"Give me the commlink."

Pris unstrapped the device and handed it to Edie without objecting. She gave Edie a beatific smile and went on to explore the next chamber. The other two girls were out of sight, although she could hear them.

Edie hit Cat's callsign on her regular commlink. Oddly, she got no response, as if the link could not connect. That had to be bad news. As she walked through the chambers, trying to keep track of the excited children, she pressed her fingers to the port on the biocyph wafer attached to the commlink, to gain a remote connection to the BRAT.

"Haller, what did you tell the children?"

His reply came through the datastream.

—*Ah, the children. They contacted me several hours ago. At first I thought it was a trick, but they are so guileless.*

Edie was filled with fear for them. And for Finn, who was now a helpless hostage.

"What did you tell them? If you've made any kind of deal—"

—*They wanted to meet me.*

"In the middle of the night?"

—*Dawn is breaking. Don't worry. I ensured their safety from the retroviruses and slaters. They told me who they are. Talasi cyphertecks, like you. They even showed me what they can do, as far as the link would allow. I realized I need their help with this procedure. I would like them to jack in.*

"No. Never."

—*This surgery is trickier than I had anticipated.*

Was he about to blackmail her? His transformation to planethood did not seem to have changed his personality much. What if he liked what he saw when the children jacked in, and wanted them to merge with him? She doubted it would take much to persuade them to go "willingly."

"Don't touch them, Haller. They're innocent pawns of the Crib."

—*I have already touched them, and I think you'll be pleased.*

"What do you mean?"

—*They had the same defect as you. A design flaw. I corrected it.*

"You cured their neuroxin dependence?"

—*Yes. I have released retroviruses to repair the biocyph in their cells and destroy the remaining neuroxin in their implants.*

"Then they're free . . ." Edie murmured.

And so was she. She looked down at her hand, the one that had grabbed Galeon, her touch a vector of transmission. The retroviruses would work on her the same way. They were free from their homeworld. No longer reliant on the Crib to provide them with neuroxin. Their future was theirs to make . . . if she could keep the past, in the form of Natesa, from catching up with them.

Galeon tugged at her sleeve. "Is Finn in there?" He pointed to the column of vines in the nearby chamber.

"Yes. Macky's helping him."

"Macky wants us all to help," Pris called. She was at the BRAT, already jacked in. Beside her sat Hanna and Raena, jacked in as well.

Before Edie could stop him, Galeon hurried over to join them. Frozen by indecision, Edie stayed where she was. Did she have a right to stop them? She'd taken it upon herself to plan their future, destroy their past—hoping, at least, to remove them from the Crib and this life of endless datastreams. Yet they loved it. They'd anticipated meeting Macky for days.

And Haller had cured them. Why would he bother doing that if he intended to merge with them? Perhaps it was safe enough. Edie spoke to Haller again using the remote link.

"Please don't harm them." She couldn't think of anything else to say.

—*I will not harm them. Ahh . . . they are indeed unique.*

She didn't trust him. At the very least, she had to supervise the connection. She found space next to the children, who were crowded around the multi-access port, and reached over to jack in with them. As the datastream rushed into her splinter, she blocked it immediately. She didn't want to be distracted, didn't want to be tempted. She would simply observe, not interact, and make sure Haller didn't make a move to merge with the children.

The children sat quietly, eyes glazed over in concentration. Edie watched their glyphs tumble into diamond formation around the datastream. Haller directed them to the complex tiers he'd set up to monitor Scarabaeus's infiltration of Finn's brain. Haller had given the instructions, but it was the autonomous biocyph doing the work. Edie had programmed it not to harm Finn, and it recognized the bomb in his head as harmful. Prehensile tendrils had drilled into his skull, each one branching a hundred times into microscopic filaments that could be perfectly controlled to physically maneuver the bomb and disassemble his splinter's biocyph strand.

Whether or not the children's help was really required, Edie could see that they enabled the surgery to proceed faster. They were trained to iron out blips in the datastream. Now, as feedback from Finn's splinter flowed through the tiers, they kept it note-perfect with their usual efficiency, helping to extract the splinter without damaging the neural pathways of his brain.

At the same time, their glyphs were drawn to the tangles of code they'd named Macky in the sim, which Edie now knew represented the intelligence and personality of Haller. This was what was missing from Prisca, the reason Scarabaeus thrived while it died. The tendrils that delved deep into the datastream, fully integrated, were his intelligence. The remaining parts, the knots, were his personality—his human drives and desires that were largely incompatible with the biocyph, but nevertheless affected its evolution indirectly. Haller wanted her to help integrate that part of himself, so he could fully control the planet.

—*What's this?*

Edie was drawn back to Haller. He was probing something in Finn's splinter.

—*This belongs to me. It belongs to Scarabaeus.*

The cryptoglyph.

"Yes. I found it last time I was here."

—*Why?*

"I realized I could use it to unlock the Fringe-world BRATs." Haller should understand that. As a rover, he'd helped the Fringe worlds in the same way, although his fixes had been temporary.

—*Did you succeed?*

"Yes. The Fringe is free."

—*Then I will take it back.*

He extracted it in an instant. Edie was suddenly uneasy at the thought of Haller having access to a powerful BRAT master key.

"What are you going to do with it?"

—*Watch.*

While the children finished filtering the datastream that was operating on Finn, Haller directed Edie elsewhere. He had begun to assemble the knots of code, tagging them with a delivery vector. That could only mean he intended to send the data somewhere. The code was already present in every BRAT across the planet. Where else could he send it?

—*This is what I truly want,* he said. *To replicate myself across the Reach. Every terraformed world will become sentient like Scarabaeus. I'll finally have someone to talk to.*

Blasting the Reach with code that could affect BRATs was no easy task. The BRATs were usually shut off from outside data, keeping themselves isolated to a single planet.

But Haller had the cryptoglyph now. He could bypass that security and turn any world into an intelligent entity.

Not just intelligent, but brimming with Haller's charming personality. He'd killed people here. What might happen when his violent and unpredictable self controlled every inhabited planet in the Reach? Had she just saved the Fringe worlds from ecological disaster only to see them destroyed by Haller's whimsical desires and ambition? How long could humans survive with Haller in charge?

"Why didn't you tell me this before?"

—I wasn't sure if you'd approve of my grand ambition. I've been working for months on a way to deliver the transmission but I lack the skills. I'd almost given up. Then you returned to Scarabaeus and I knew you could help me if you merged. But now I have this cryptoglyph . . . perhaps I don't need you.

What did that mean for Finn?

"Maybe you do," Edie said, thinking fast. "What you don't know is that BRATs across the Reach are failing. The older Central worlds are rife with famine. The Fringe worlds will suffer the same fate eventually. If you take control of the BRATs, you may be able to prevent this disaster and save everyone." That much was possibly true, and if it had been anyone else . . . But she didn't trust Haller to be responsible with that colossal power. "We need to get this right, Haller. You will need my help."

—Perhaps. I admit I was greatly anticipating merging with you.

She raced back along the datastream to check the progress with Finn. She was desperate to go into the adjacent chamber and physically look at him. Instead, all she had was the datastream that poured through the children's diamond glyph formation, and it showed her that Scarabaeus was still teasing apart the delicate biocyph matrix and bomb from his cortex.

There was something she could do to stop Haller—deactivate the commsat. She jacked out and hit Cat's callsign.

This time, she got through. The planet didn't have ears—she could talk to Cat without him hearing.

It was clear that her call woke Cat up. Before she could say anything, Cat started panicking. "Where are the kids? Shit . . . Where are they?"

"Relax, Cat. They're with me and they're safe. Listen, is the commsat active?" She waited while Cat checked.

"Not right now."

"It has to be destroyed."

"Uh . . . how? And why?"

"The intelligence controlling Scarabaeus is Haller."

"John Haller? Our John Haller?"

"Yes. I'll explain later. He plans to send out a blast of data that will integrate itself . . . *him*self . . . into every BRAT on the Fringe."

"That can't be good."

"Right now he's playing nice and removing the bomb from Finn's head, so I'm not voicing my objections. Presumably at some point he's going to activate the commsat. I'll try and delay him sending the blast. But as soon as I give you the word that Finn is safe, and the commsat is up, you need to get the message out to the Crib or the Saeth, anyone with a cannon on their ship, to come and destroy that commsat."

"Understood."

"You are a crappy babysitter, by the way."

"I know. I guess I'm not cut out for—"

Cat stopped suddenly. When she spoke again, all humor was gone from her voice.

"A sleek little ship just did a flyover. When I say little, I mean a fucking awesome Trailblazer class-A model about ten times the size of a skiff but just as maneuverable in atmo. Shit. That has to be Natesa. She must've homed in on the lifepods."

Edie moved closer to the tunnel entrance, her heart racing. "Is she landing?"

"Yes. It's coming around to land. Right next to the city. How come she didn't check out this habitat first?"

"My guess is that whatever she did to Finn's chip serves as a locator. She knows he's in here. What I don't understand is why hasn't she already triggered the detonator?"

"Maybe she wants to be sure you're watching. My scope's showing three people entering the tunnel. She's on her way in."

"And I can't stop her."

"I don't know if I can help, Edie." Cat sounded desperate. She went through her options, muttering to herself. "If I go out there, I'll be eaten alive. Even if I don't . . . it's a half-hour walk, maybe a ten-minute run. I can drive over, but it'll take a while to prep the vehicle. Our one spur is empty and Corinth can't even get up to piss. I've got nothing."

"It's okay. I'll figure a way out. I just want to get Finn to safety."

It wasn't okay, not at all. Edie had no idea how to stop Natesa and her reinforcements from killing Finn and taking the children.

Opening the remote biocyph link, she spoke to Haller. "Natesa's here. She could walk in at any moment."

—*Let her come. I can crush her easily.*

"No. You have to be careful. No doubt she'll have her finger on the detonator. If you want me to merge with you, keeping Finn alive is all that matters."

—*Then I hope she behaves herself.*

Edie could do nothing but wait. It seemed like forever before she heard voices approaching down the tunnel. It had taken Natesa a long time to find her way in, or perhaps she was being a lot more cautious than Edie had been.

Edie moved back toward the children and braced herself to confront the woman who still controlled Finn's life, even if Edie's fate lay elsewhere.

CHAPTER 32

Natesa strode into the cavern, exuding confidence and purpose. She stopped just inside the chamber and her silhouette was framed by the arch of the tunnel as she stood there, hands on hips, looking like she'd just walked on stage and expected everyone to applaud. On her heels were two men armed with rifles and spurs. Not milits, but hired mercs. Proof that this trip wasn't authorized by the Crib.

Natesa glared at Edie as she made her approach, but even she couldn't help being distracted by the sights. She looked around quickly, in awe. Her mercs held back, ignoring the scenery. Their focus was on the woman who'd hired them to protect her.

Natesa noticed the children, partially hidden by the growths filling the cavern. She picked her way toward them, forcing Edie to back up farther, only to stop again when she saw what they were doing.

"What's going on?"

"They're communicating with the biocyph." Edie's gaze swept over Natesa's tailored jacket and flight suit, searching for the detonator that would kill Finn. "Just as you taught them to do," she added sarcastically.

The children remained in their huddled group. The girls'

attention was now on Natesa. Galeon moved away, gravitating toward Finn's chamber. He sought to protect his friend.

Natesa followed him and peered up at the cocoon where Finn's body was nestled a few meters off the ground. "So, there he is. Is he dead?"

Galeon bravely strode up to Natesa and stopped a few paces in front of her, hands on his hips. "He's not dead. We helped him. *You* leave him alone!"

"Pris," Natesa said, stepping back and raising her voice. "You're coming with me. It's time to go."

Pris didn't move. Galeon looked over his shoulder at her, then back to Natesa. "She doesn't want to go with you."

"She's my daughter. She's coming with me.'

"She told us you want to kill Finn, and he's our friend."

"Wretched child," Natesa mumbled, and turned her glare on Edie, who had edged closer. Natesa held up one hand to reveal a small device in her palm. "He's quite correct, however. This detonator is linked to the bomb in your lag's head."

"Don't hurt him!" Galeon rushed Natesa, his arms outstretched. Edie lunged after him and grabbed him around the waist just before he reached her.

Natesa snatched back her hand, her eyes gleaming. "All I want is Pris. My men will enforce my wishes, but I'd rather things went smoothly."

"What about the other children?" Edie said. "Who's coming for them?"

"I understand there's a fleet of Crib ships on the way. The children will be quite safe in that habitat outside until then. They will be taken back to work, and you will be arrested and shipped off to the nastiest prison camp I can find."

While Natesa talked, Edie surreptitiously linked to the biocyph commlink on her belt and silently questioned Haller.

"How much longer do you need?"

—*Almost done. The children's work is complete. Is that Natesa?*

With her e-shield on, Natesa was indistinguishable to

Haller from any other human. And he had no ears to hear their conversation.

"Yes, and she has the detonator. Don't do anything to alarm her."

—*Very well. But if anyone starts shooting in here, I have little control over the instinctive retaliation that will follow.*

"Pris," Natesa called sweetly. "Come, my darling. I'm here to take you home."

Pris pushed herself to her feet, a little unsteadily. "Where? The *Learo Dochais*?"

"No, we don't work there anymore. I'll find us a new home, somewhere just as nice."

"But it wasn't very nice. No house, no river, no dogs or trees."

"Trees?" Natesa turned a quizzical look on Edie. "What have you told her?"

"They just want to be kids, Natesa."

"What would you know?"

Edie's anger rose in a heated rush of blood. "How can you ask that? I know exactly how they feel. I understand the lure of the datastream. I know why they've submitted to you and want to please you. I understand the feeling of being used. I know why, in the end, they will rebel against you. Asking one of them to call you Mother won't change that. She sees through you, as I did."

Edie stopped, terrified she'd pushed Natesa too far. The woman was shaking. The children watched, wide-eyed.

Edie fumbled for her link to Haller, but Natesa saw the movement.

"Don't!" Natesa said, waving the detonator about.

Edie froze.

"Mother, no!"

Pris's plaintive cry was the only thing that could reach Natesa. Her eyes flicked to her would-be daughter and she hesitated. She gave a quick signal to the mercs, and they approached Edie, moving awkwardly through the resin.

"Take that from her," Natesa ordered.

The mercs descended on Edie. One captured her arms while the other yanked the device off her belt and handed it to Natesa.

"What's this?" She recognized the biocyph component. "Do you use this to control the so-called intelligence on this planet?"

"I've no control over the planet." Edie struggled against the merc, who was immovable.

"Well, something is controlling it," Natesa said. "We arrived in the system to find a dead commsat, two crashed ships on the surface, a mere handful of survivors. It looks like Theron's grand project has ended the same way as mine. Except that I survived."

She tossed the commlink aside, flicking her wrist sharply to eject it through her e-shield barrier. Then she gave a quick signal to the merc holding Edie to release her.

"Take Pris back to the ship," Natesa told him.

"Let them all leave," Edie said. "If you care about them at all, don't let them see this."

Natesa considered for a moment. "Very well. Take them."

The merc looked from one child to another, as if deciding how best to round them up. He assessed Galeon as the difficult one and went for him. Galeon was having none of it. He dodged the merc with a furious squall, but there was nowhere to run. The merc captured him easily.

"Galeon, it's okay. Go with him," Edie said, trying to sound reassuring. "All of you."

"We don't want to leave Macky," Pris said. "We just fixed everything and now we have to go?"

"Yes, I'm sorry. But it's not safe in here."

The younger girls traipsed out ahead of the merc, who carried a struggling Galeon, defiant to the last. Pris went along, too. Miserably.

Edie faced Natesa across the chamber, hope drained. "Why all the drama? You could've killed Finn an hour ago from orbit."

"I wanted the satisfaction of watching him die. As far as

I'm concerned, he should've been executed as a traitor when he was first captured. He's been on borrowed time for five years, and in that time he's caused immeasurable damage. He's turned you against me, against everything I taught you. If I dig deep enough, I'm sure I'll find his hand guiding you to sabotage Prisca using that module you hijacked."

She was wrong in every respect. Edie had started turning away long before she met Finn, and it was she who'd persuaded him to join her cause and help the Fringers. But Edie couldn't explain that now, didn't know what she could say to calm Natesa down and save Finn when the woman was so determined to carry out the sentence she thought he deserved.

Edie's gaze was glued to the detonator in Natesa's hand, the hand that she raised higher with each irate word, as if building to a climax. Edie watched helplessly, every instinct telling her to pounce.

"You disappoint me." Natesa's voice shook with emotion. "You threw away everything, and I will never understand why."

Edie gave in to her instinct, her last remaining hope for Finn. She launched herself at Natesa, fixated on Natesa's left hand. A sharp pain lanced through her injured forearm. The force of her attack knocked Natesa backward. Her hands closed around Natesa's wrist, slippery and staticky because of the e-shield. She slammed Natesa's arm on the ground as they both fell, flinging the detonator from her hand. It skittered away a few meters.

Edie scampered after it on hands and knees, kicking out at Natesa's attempt to grab her legs. Something was wrong with her arm. It buckled beneath her, spurting blood. Her mind backtracked a few seconds and she realized she'd heard a shot. She glanced back to see the remaining merc pointing a spur at her, a deadly rifle held in his other hand. He had aimed to wound, not to kill.

But now he would pay for firing his weapon. A tremor swept through the cavern, and the curtains of sap quivered.

The ground vibrated and ruptured, and thick leathery stalks studded with bulbous nodules rose up from the crevices. Edie was thrown onto her back. Her arm throbbed with pain.

The shimmying, swaying stalactites broke apart in places to send flailing braids through the air. The merc fired repeatedly into the gummy resin, his explosive rifle bullets splattering it everywhere. The subterranean stalks snaked toward him, the fronds at their tips curling into speckled fingers. The stalks, riddled with nodules, had glowing veins that supported and moved them. Now black fluid pumped through the veins and the nodules erupted into serrated spikes.

Natesa was yelling something but the merc's screams and weaponsfire drowned her out. The coiled, grasping fingers tangled around the merc's legs and pulled him down, twisting his body into grotesque postures as he struggled. With a hiss, his e-shield was knocked out.

The spikes buried themselves in exposed flesh and spurted milky sap that mingled with blood in pink streaks. The merc spasmed, gasping for breath as the spikes plunged into his body. Neuroxin . . . those spikes were poisoning him. Encased and immobilized, the merc was swallowed up by the ground.

To Edie's horror, in the chaos, the column of vines holding Finn started to wilt and collapse.

Pain from her reopened wound overwhelmed her and she feared blacking out. She struggled to her knees, only to be thrown onto her belly as shuddering waves rocked the cavern. She focused on the detonator. A hand reached to grab it—it took her another second to realize it wasn't her hand. Natesa had got there first.

But Natesa could not escape the reaction rippling across the floor. The gashes that cracked open the ground spread toward her, and more prehensile stalks unfolded from within. Natesa held up the detonator in what might have been a triumphant gesture, but from the look on her face she knew the merc's fate would soon be hers.

Edie expected a threat. Instead, she got a plea.

"Save me. Tell it to stop."

Edie managed to get to her knees, one hand clutching her forearm to stem the flow of blood. She couldn't make it stop, but she had to make Natesa stop.

"Throw me the detonator and I'll try," she bluffed.

Sticky claws clamped around Natesa's boots and slithered up her legs. The e-shield, for as long as it lasted, would prevent her from feeling much, but seeing herself being devoured was quite enough to terrify her.

Edie held her breath, hoping beyond reason that Natesa would show Finn mercy in her final moments.

Natesa pressed the trigger.

At the sound of the muffled explosion, Edie whirled around, her eyes seeking out Finn in the tangled nest of vines that had collapsed into a mushy heap. The few remaining vines encasing him unraveled and spilled him out in a puddle of milky fluid. He lay curled up on the ground, fine tendrils still buried in his flesh. A bloody patch extended from his temple all the way around one side of his scalp.

Edie ran to him and fell to her knees beside his body, pressed her palms to his chest, refusing to believe, numb to the truth. She heard Natesa's strangled gasps, smelled the sharp earthy scent from the crushed vines, felt the stinging fire in her arm . . .

Finn's heart thumped under her hands.

Edie opened her senses to hope. To the singe of burned vegetation amid the ruined vines where the bomb had exploded, the living tendrils pulsing under Finn's flesh, and, finally, the slow rise and fall of his chest. Haller had removed the bomb in time and it had detonated nearby. She pressed her ear to Finn's chest to reassure herself of his heartbeat. It was slow but steady. His skin was cool and damp and smeared with sap.

The thrashing and churning calmed down. The fissures in the ground pressed together. Natesa was gone.

Edie retrieved the biocyph commlink, clipped it to her belt, and jacked in.

—He will live.

"Thank you."

—The children taught me a great deal.

"Such as?"

—The way they work together, that diamond formation that funnels and controls the datastream . . . I have never seen anything so elegant and powerful, and so I copied its structure. Imagine how I might multiply my processing power by joining with other worlds using this formation!

Edie didn't want to ask why he would want to multiply his processing power. As she wiped blood from Finn's face, the tips of the tendrils withdrew from his skin with popping noises. He stirred, barely conscious.

"Haller, I'm going to help Finn out of here and then I'll come back and merge with you, like I promised. Don't send out that blast until I get back."

—Hurry. I can't wait long.

She added impatience to the growing list of Haller's personality flaws. This was not the kind of all-powerful entity that humanity could count on. With no possibility of destroying the commsat any time soon, merging with Haller in order to destroy him was Edie's only option.

Her mind focused only on the immediate task—get Finn to safety—so she wouldn't have to think about what was to come afterward.

She leaned over Finn again and gently shook his shoulders. "Wake up. We're leaving."

His eyes flickered open and he groaned.

"You're alive, Finn. You're free."

CHAPTER 33

Finn was coming around slowly. Too slowly. As Edie was wondering how she was going to get him out, she heard someone running through the tunnel. Cat appeared at the chamber's entrance. She looked around quickly, as if expecting danger.

"Where's Natesa? What happened?"

"She's dead. Help me with Finn."

Cat came over, giving the chamber another once-over as if she couldn't quite believe what she was seeing.

"The bomb?" she asked.

"It's gone."

"Sorry I missed the show. Got here as fast as I could. Sprinted all the way. Seems those monsters weren't hungry today. Are you okay?" She squatted and turned over Edie's injured arm. "What's that stuff?"

Edie's arm hurt a lot less than before. Tendrils had invaded the wound, bubbling beneath the flesh.

"It's healing me."

"We have med-teck for that. Is he okay?" Cat nodded at Finn.

"He will be."

"Then let's go. I've got a fancy ship waiting outside for you, and four frightened kids."

Edie's heart leapt. "You have Natesa's ship?"

"Yup. Can't wait to fly that beauty."

"Where's the merc?"

"Locked in the cargo hold." Cat grinned. "He had his hands full with Galeon and wasn't paying attention."

"Haller cured their neuroxin dependence. We can save them after all."

"Fantastic. We just have to collect Corinth from the habitat and we're all saved."

All but Edie.

She didn't tell Cat what she intended until they'd helped Finn all the way out and had him resting on a bunk on the ship and pumped full of pain meds.

"You're going *back*?" was Cat's incredulous response.

"Haller is still in there, and I have to destroy him."

"Can't we just bomb the site or something?"

"He's in every BRAT on the planet. We don't have a thousand bombs. We don't even have one. And we don't have time."

"So you're going to—what did you call it? *Merge* with the planet? What the hell does that mean, anyway?"

"You don't want to know." That was suddenly the hardest part of all—that Finn would know what she'd suffered. Unlike Cat, he'd seen exactly what had happened to Haller when Scarabaeus had taken him.

"What am I supposed to tell Finn?" Cat asked.

Edie would tell him a thousand things if she could. "Tell him . . . Tell him I went to complete the mission."

"And you're sure this is the only way?"

"Yes."

"How about I tell him you love him?"

Edie nodded and tried to smile as she pulled Cat into a quick embrace.

"Jezus, he's going to kill me when he wakes up and finds out I let you go," Cat said.

"Just get out of here before the Crib arrives. Do me a favor—a big one. Find good homes for the children." She couldn't bring herself to say goodbye to them.

"I will."

"And stay out of trouble."

"Can't promise that."

Edie pressed her lips to Finn's one last time before she left.

She returned to the central chamber, her heart thumping in fear of what was to come. She couldn't shake the image of Haller strung up in the jungle, his body in shreds as he was slowly digested alive. Would that happen to her, too?

There was just enough room to sit comfortably at the foot of the BRAT and jack in with a hardlink. She knew she wouldn't be comfortable for long.

The datastream flowed through her splinter. First the familiar refrains of Scarabaeus, the song she knew well. Then came the complex, tangled beat of Haller's overlaid intelligence. The song pressed against her, but her mind resisted. The vines moved around her and tickled her skin.

—The transition was painful and terrifying for me. Unlike you, I didn't understand what was happening. I was in shock for many weeks afterward.

"Let me get used to it," Edie said. "Take it slow."

—Clear your mind. It will go easier for you. Let go of the past. You have a glorious future now.

"This isn't easy."

—You have to trust me.

John Haller was not a man she trusted. She was here now, doing this, because she didn't trust him—neither the man nor the planetary intelligence.

She filed through the security protocols in her splinter, the walls of code that kept outsiders safely out. Pris had managed to break through that barrier to jolt Finn. Haller didn't have the skills for it, and Scarabaeus wouldn't do it by force. She had to make the decision.

She shut them down.

Her right arm twitched as tendrils burrowed into her flesh again. They weren't just healing now. They had found the path of least resistance to her splinter. They sent microscopic extensions into the implanted biocyph wires that extended from her fingertips to her spine and from there to the wet-teck interface in her cerebral cortex. The biocyph of the planet was hooked into her now. She didn't know if the hardlink was still in place—it was no longer necessary.

The organic material surrounding her had physically hooked into her, too. Her limbs were trapped by vines, her body encased. She opened her eyes to a squirming nightmarish cocoon—a brief look was all she could stand.

Something slick and warm wrapped around her throat. Unable to move, she was helpless to fight it. Panic set in as she imagined suffocating. She didn't want it this way. She wanted to disconnect from her body before Scarabaeus devoured it.

The skin of her throat prickled. It wasn't painful, not yet. But she'd seen Haller's fate. She knew what was to come. Tendrils had already invaded her wounded arm, and now she felt them gain entry above her sternum. They were drawn to the beetle inlay, she realized. Like the cryptoglyph, it was something else she'd taken from Scarabaeus, and the planet recognized it. The DNA in the dried husk was the only pure thing from this planet that was untouched by the Crib's biocyph or by Haller's meddling.

Her flesh ripped. Now the pain was sharp. Warm blood trickled down between her breasts. Scarabaeus had reclaimed the beetle.

She tried to block out the physical and concentrated on the mental—the link—but still she resisted the datastream. She allowed it no farther than the surface tiers of her splinter.

—Edie, you must give in. Scarabaeus refuses to harm you, so it must be your decision.

"Give me a moment. I'll give you my mind, Haller, but leave my body until I don't care anymore. Don't make me suffer what you suffered."

—Don't be scared.

A new song flooded the datastream. It washed through

her, an ocean of sound. Edie skimmed the surface, feeling the currents tug at her mind.

The transition would be easier for her after all, not harder. She understood the ebb and flow of the datastream because her wet-teck interface had spent ten years reorganizing her brain. She would bleed into the biocyph, mentally and physically, lose her sense of self, forget this life and feel no regrets. All she had to do was give herself to Scarabaeus. She could already feel her mind seeping into the datastream. Here, finally, she could truly become what she was meant to be . . .

She relented and sank into the multi-tiered mesh. The physical structures of the chamber and the living city that Haller had spent a year building, so human in concept, held no more interest for Edie. She heard DNA and chemical re-actions, cellular organelles, physiology, blood and sap. Felt the pulses of a billion beating hearts. The temptation to become part of this song overwhelmed her.

Her splinter buckled under the flood. It hardly mattered if it got damaged. Haller wanted her brain and her training, not her wet-teck.

Haller . . . she had to destroy Haller. She wasn't here to become one with the planet. She was here to demolish the very structure of the biocyph in order to obliterate Haller, and herself along with him. It would take a simple kill-code. She'd done it before. Only this time, she'd do it right.

First, she had to stop his transmission blast. She searched for the delivery vector he'd been assembling. It was ready to go, complete with cryptoglyph, and he'd put the commsat back online. She was almost too late . . .

She stalled for time. "Haller, wait. Let me check this before you send it. You don't know what you're doing. You need my help."

No answer.

Edie quickly examined the code packaged for transmis-sion, expecting to find the knots that she'd come to think of as Haller's combined intelligence and personality. The knots were there, but they were shrinking. The datastream was being pushed through a four-pointed filter. A diamond formation.

The children had been here.

As the knots hit the filter, parts of the tangle unwound and slid seamlessly between the tiers of the datastream. The rest—fractured pieces and tight nubs that could not be untangled—broke off and floated free and dissolved.

Edie pulled back to view the process from a distance. In a matter of minutes, it would be complete. From the children's descriptions of the sim they'd played with, she identified the broken bits as Haller's personality. His desires, his emotions, his petty human concerns—all this was being sloughed off. What remained was his raw intelligence, and this part was being integrated into the datastream. The children had treated Haller's presence in the datastream like an error log, and had fixed it by removing those parts that would not integrate.

The delivery vector was set to launch in just a few seconds. As she watched Haller unravel, she considered what the transmission would mean to the Fringe worlds. She'd had her first taste of what a planet-sized consciousness was like, and she recognized its potential. With Haller dissolving away, all that was left in the transmission was the integrated intelligence along with the cryptoglyph that enabled the BRATs on other planets to absorb the new data.

She had only seconds to make a decision. She'd already unlocked the Fringe-world BRATs and destroyed the extortion racket that held the Crib together, but she couldn't prevent the inevitable failure of the biocyph that maintained those planets. Was this consciousness the answer? It had successfully managed Scarabaeus's ecosystem. Now devoid of Haller's human foibles and destructive tendencies, could it manage the ecosystem of an entire galaxy?

She did nothing. Haller . . . No, Scarabaeus—the planet, not the man—released the blast of data to the commsat, which transmitted it into the nearby node at the speed of light. From there it would travel at impossible speeds through nodespace, and spread across the Reach. It was unstoppable.

"Haller, are you there? Talk to me."

She kept checking, every few minutes, but she couldn't find him. She'd intended to destroy Scarabaeus from within, taking out Haller in the process, but instead the children had selectively destroyed Haller and there was no need to worry about the impartial sentience that remained. Edie could hear its song clearly now, a cold, bright, complex music that sounded . . . *felt* perfect. She *felt* its affinity for life and knew the worlds it was now in contact with were safe.

She felt its affinity for her, too. It recognized parts of her in its deepest, oldest coding, and it wanted her. She could still merge, if she chose.

Her cocoon shook so violently that her joints popped and she was jolted back to physical reality. The vines were slick against her skin, and repulsive. She struggled to not feel sickened by what would happen to her body if she merged. *When* she merged. She wanted it as much as Scarabaeus did.

She buried herself deep in the datastream, drowning in the anticipation of joining with the planet's consciousness. Her destiny lay here, and she wouldn't fight it.

Now something grappled with her, clutched at her. The physical conversion was beginning. In a short while the pain wouldn't matter anymore. Sensations of the flesh would be irrelevant. Her life would become the datastream. She welcomed it.

Fingers of vines curled around her wrist, her arm, gnawing at her newly healed wound. The jolt of pain knocked her out of the datastream. The vines were warm, hard against her bones—not cool and moist as they'd been before. Edie forced open her eyes. A creamy blur of movement writhed around her and it took a moment to focus.

She saw dark hazel eyes, clenched teeth, a creased brow. She tried to pull away but strong arms encircled her and ripped her free from her nest.

She tumbled to the ground, tangled up in vines and tendrils and someone else's limbs. Fiery pinpoints of pain blazed across her arm and throat and skull as the tendrils were yanked out of her body. Scarabaeus vanished from her mind, suddenly and completely. She dragged air into her lungs and it was agonizing, like taking the first breath after leaving the womb. She mustered enough strength to thrash out at her captor.

"Don't fight me." The compelling voice brought to mind visions of loving hands stroking her skin . . .

. . . and less pleasant memories of fear and frustration and anger, a terrifying maelstrom of human interactions. She didn't want that. She wanted the safe familiarity of the datastream that she could control and sculpt.

—*Don't take me away . . .*

She sent the message down the link. But the link was gone. Her human body felt heavy and useless. Some part of her recognized that she had to speak the words out loud.

"Don't . . ."

She was maneuvered upright and hauled to her feet. She could hardly make her legs work.

"Edie, you're coming with me."

CHAPTER 34

Finn's voice pulled her back again, and Edie held on while the world shook around them. He pulled her to her feet, his arm around her waist, and dragged her over the shifting ground that spewed jets of sap and bore acrid limbs of leathery stalks.

The tunnel seemed too far away. The mosaic of cells that formed the ground started to break apart. The walls of the cavern crumpled inward in tremendous waves, crushing the resin sheets that fell in shards like icicles. The air filled with wrenching, snapping sounds and a putrid sweet smell.

Edie waited for the inevitable—for the ground to swallow them up—but that didn't happen.

She jacked into the biocyph commlink and was hit with a screaming torrent.

—*You can't leave. I'll kill you! You belong here with me.*

This was Haller, not Scarabaeus. Somehow he'd hidden the last vestiges of his awareness from her while she'd been distracted by her impending ascension to planethood. Now, as he fractured and dissolved in a scream of fury, he was taking the physical world with him.

But Haller couldn't kill her, it seemed. Every time the flattened spiky stalks rose up to capture, they were sucked back under by an unseen force. Vines descended from the ceiling to knock them down, and then retreated, flopping uselessly. She'd programmed Scarabaeus not to harm her and Finn, and despite Haller's efforts it still protected them. Nevertheless, the chamber quickly disintegrated around them. Before much longer, they'd be trapped by the sticky debris.

Finn locked hands with her, wrist to wrist, and pulled her along.

—Edie, what's happening? Please, I need you! Help me. Save me.

Haller's cries tore through her.

"I have to go back . . ." Her reaction was instinctive. She'd promised to merge, prepared herself for it and accepted it, been seduced by the datastream to the point of longing for it. This planet was hers. She had birthed Scarabaeus, and now it needed her.

She pulled away but Finn was relentless. He yanked her close and grabbed her upper arms, forcing her to face him. Half his skull was still bleeding and bruised.

"I won't leave you behind, Edie. You don't belong here."

His words made no sense. She had to stay, didn't she? "This is the only place I belong. It needs me."

"I need you. I won't let you choose *this* over me." His face was distorted by raw pain.

She'd chosen him before—his life over the chance to salvage Scarabaeus. Once again, Scarabaeus beckoned and she had to turn away. Finn's grip on her was real and honest and the only thing she truly wanted. She'd choose life with Finn—complex, painful, joyful, human life.

They turned again to the tunnel entrance, only meters away. A formless mass of tangled vines and resin and sap rose up before them. It morphed into limbs and torso and head. Its arms reached out toward them and twisted in supplication. A gaping misshapen mouth opened up in the head and grimaced in a wordless plea.

They darted around it and more creatures emerged from

the ground and walls. A chorus of wide-mouthed pleas and thrashing limbs.

Edie stumbled out of the cavern with Finn. The tunnel was just as unstable. Its walls shook and crumpled. From outside came a great wrenching sound, growing louder as they drew nearer. Ahead, something fell from above and crushed the tunnel, blocking the way.

They scrambled through a jagged hole torn in the wall, emerging into bright daylight amid the spires of the city, where there was no firm footing. The spires toppled as the caverns beneath them collapsed.

Clear ground was only minutes away. They dodged falling debris and kept moving. Finn never let go of her, pulling her along to match his relentless pace.

They slid down the last embankment and ran over flat rocky ground, leaving behind the chaos of collapsing structures—Haller's death throes. Only then did they see the black swarm approaching. Hundreds of slaters clambered over the low rocks.

Finn slowed to a walk and unlimbered a rifle from his back. She recognized it as having belonged to Natesa's merc.

"No," Edie said. "I don't think they'll harm us."

He glanced at her, clearly not quite believing. She wasn't sure she believed it, either, but in any case, one rifle was no use. If the slaters attacked, there was nothing they could do.

The habitat was a glint of silver in the distance. The ship was gone.

"Cat was right here . . ." Finn said.

That ship had been their only ride off the planet. Had Cat seen the city collapsing and given up on them?

"Crib ships will come," she said, her heart sinking.

Not Natesa, not Theron, but some other faceless 'crat with new plans for Edie . . . and no plans for Finn.

"We should get back to the habitat," Finn said. There was nowhere else to go.

The slaters were close enough that she could see their busy jaws working under their carapaces. They circled Edie and Finn, blocking their way. As one, the creatures reared onto their hind legs, clicking their jaws and waving their forelimbs. Edie pressed her back to Finn's chest, feeling his arm slide around her protectively. He threw down the rifle, perhaps thinking that was the reason for the aggressive stance. It didn't help. The slaters slowly closed the circle.

Edie fumbled for the biocyph commlink, but it was gone, torn from her belt somewhere back in the chamber.

Then the city behind them grew calm. The slaters dropped, spun around, and started to squawk and sway.

"What happened?" Finn asked.

"It's Haller. Or rather, it's the end of Haller. He's finally gone. Scarabaeus has full control now."

"Is that a good thing?"

"Yes."

They watched the slaters warily, neither wanting to take the first step into the fray.

"They won't harm us," Edie said again, hoping that by saying the words she could believe them.

She walked forward, tugging Finn along behind her. The slaters scuttled out of the way, left and right, and they pressed on. The sea of black parted for them. The slaters moved off in small groups, chattering and squabbling among themselves, and the way was clear. Edie glanced over her shoulder to watch many of the creatures scurrying toward the city. Its structures stood silent under the noon sun, its silhouette broken and changed after the recent upheaval.

A small shape rose up behind the city. Edie's mind jumped from one horror to the next—some flying creature left over from Haller's imagination?

"It's Cat," Finn said.

The ship came right at them, tipping its sleek wings to acknowledge them.

Finn turned to Edie with a rare smile. "We'll make it."

CHAPTER 35

"Finn really did almost kill me." Cat cut an indignant glare in Finn's direction before turning back to the nav console. "Then right after he left to find you, those evil beetles swarmed the ship. I was worried they'd damage it so I had to take off and circle."

They punched through the atmosphere and into space. In Natesa's fancy ship that Cat was so thrilled to be flying, the jump node was only four hours away. No sign yet of any Crib ships, but they had to be on the way.

"The commsat came back up while you were in there," Cat said.

"I know. Scarabaeus used it to blast the Reach."

"Well, I uploaded a beacon to it—basically, a firm suggestion to any ship that shows up with a cannon to destroy it. But the beacon kept winking out."

"Scarabaeus controls the commsat. It's not going to tolerate a message inviting its own destruction."

"The Crib will destroy it anyway, once they figure out it's linked to all the other Fringe worlds," Corinth said. He was sprawled on a seat at the back of the cockpit, one leg out of action and the other still heavily strapped. "That's the sort of shit that freaks out the Crib. That loss of power."

"Are you kidding?" Cat said. "This shit is freaking *me* out!"

Corinth grinned at her appreciatively. "Point is, they'll blow up the commsat and bomb the planet if they feel like it."

"Maybe not." Edie had already worked through the options in her head. "Set up a scrambled link so I can talk to someone at CCU. Contact Eric O'Mara," she said in a flash of inspiration. He was the one person who might listen to her. "What the Crib has to realize is that what's happened on the Fringe is a solution for them, too. If the Crib allows Scarabaeus to transmit its sentience to the Central planets, it can bring those ecosystems back under control. No more famine. No need for another hairbrained scheme like Ardra to feed the masses."

Corinth's dubious expression was starting to look a little more inspired.

Galeon poked his head into the cockpit. "We made food for everyone." The children had been left in the galley, shaken but unharmed after their adventure.

Finn helped Corinth out, with Galeon tailing them and chattering about the noodle-and-cereal faces Hanna and Raena had labored over. Edie waited for Cat while she checked the autopilot.

"How long to the Fringe?" Edie asked her.

"Five days to the border, another week to Fairbairn."

"We're going to Fairbairn?"

"Yes. You know, before she was killed, Valari had already asked me to look into finding homes for the children."

That was a surprise. "She was really against the idea of taking them."

Cat shrugged. "Well, that's what she did. Anyway, I followed up on her contacts so we have somewhere to start. She also told me Finn might need some persuading to return home."

"I got that impression too."

"Fairbairn was neutral in the Reach Conflicts, Valari told me. Pretty much sold out to the Crib to keep the peace.

Finn's family was in the public eye. Everyone knew he left to fight against the Crib. He disgraced them."

"Will they welcome him back?"

"Valari thinks so. The problem is that Finn doesn't want them to do so at the expense of their reputation. He could go home a hero if he wanted to."

"I don't think that's a hat he's comfortable wearing."

"What about you?"

Edie thought about it for a full second. "No. And not just because I hate speeches. So, will you stay with us?"

"Absolutely. As long as you let me keep the ship. I've already christened it *Ezekiel*. Come on, let's eat."

They joined the others in the galley.

"Edie!" Galeon had a salt cracker in one hand and a small shiny object in the other—the beetle sculpted from scrap. "Finn made this for you. I helped with the feelers."

She'd forgotten about Finn's farewell gift. "The feelers are the best part."

"I found it in the lifepod right before we left to visit Macky."

"Thanks for thinking to pick it up." She slipped the beetle in her pocket.

"Finn said he'll get me a puppy."

Finn swallowed a mouthful of soup and pointed his spoon at the boy. "Is that really what I said?"

"Well, you said a pet. A spider would be okay, I guess."

The younger girls fell about in giggles over the merits of that idea. Edie went to Pris, who was preparing something at the counter.

"Is Ms Natesa dead?" Pris asked, too quietly to be heard by the others over the animated conversation.

"Yes. It's not your fault. You know that, right?" Edie said, worried Pris would accept the blame.

Pris gave a small smile and nodded. She handed Edie a plate of food. Trees cut from flatbread, flowers made from dried fruit, and a noodle river running along the bottom. At the river's edge sat a salt cracker house.

"I know it's silly, but the younger ones thought it was fun to make pictures."

"It's perfect. Thank you." Edie sat down and took a moment to just watch them all. She found herself smiling. When she looked at Finn, he was smiling at her. She picked up a fork and tucked into the food.

Edie awoke to the sound of the shower running and the sight of Finn's silhouette behind the frosted plaz screen. She'd collapsed on the bed in her cabin and slept solidly. Her hair was slightly damp from her own shower, so she must have been asleep a few hours.

Curling up on her side, she waited for him. When he emerged, towel around his hips, she noticed new bruises and scrapes on his shoulders and ribs, the consequences of doing battle without an e-shield. She had a few of her own, too.

"Go back to sleep," he said.

"I'm okay. How long was I out?"

"Five hours. We've jumped twice already."

He palmed a switch by the window to dissolve the shutter. She got up and went to him, standing near enough that their bare arms brushed, and together they watched the nonsensical patterns of nodespace energy that the human eye and brain interpreted as chaotic ribbons of light lashing against black velvet.

"Are you okay with returning home?" she asked him.

He let out his breath slowly. "For now. But there's work to be done, even if the fighting's over. That strange planet of yours has given the Fringe worlds something to talk to each other about. We have an alliance to build. We'll do it right this time."

"First, we need to drop off that merc as soon as we can. And somehow I have to persuade Cat to return this ship. Doesn't feel right to steal it just because it was Natesa who commissioned it."

"She's going to love that idea," he said dryly.

They watched nodespace in silence for a while.

"Why did you come back for me?" she asked at last.

"I told you I wouldn't leave you behind."

"But I was trying to . . . you know, save the galaxy. Cat explained that to you, right?"

"Yeah," he drawled. He turned to her, tucked a strand of her hair behind her ear. "Just didn't seem like a fair trade to me."

She leaned against him. "Finn," she whispered, "I only wanted to save the galaxy because you were in it."

His laughed softly. "Galaxy saved. Mission accomplished. What do you want next?"

"I want you. In a bed, for once."

She kissed him, rising on her toes as his hands swept down her back. She pressed against him but he broke the kiss, his brow furrowed.

"If you want me so bad, why did you fight me when I came for you?"

She pulled back and sighed and stared out the window again. "I was too far gone, barely aware of you. I was so tempted to merge with Scarabaeus. The world would've been *mine*."

"Without your emotions and memories, you wouldn't be you anymore."

"It didn't matter. I just wanted to let go of life and become part of something bigger."

He tilted her chin with a finger and his eyes narrowed as he searched hers. "You don't know life yet, Edie. You don't know what you'd be letting go."

A lump came to her throat at the tender look he gave her. Nothing she was leaving behind meant much to her, but it was all she'd ever known. She'd relied on that familiarity for a sense of safety. Yet the only place she'd felt truly safe was with Finn.

"Will you show me?"

"I intend to."

THE CRITICALLY ACCLAIMED
SOLDIER SON TRILOGY FROM
NEW YORK TIMES BESTSELLING AUTHOR

ROBIN HOBB

SHAMAN'S CROSSING
978-0-06-075828-8

Nevare Burvelle was destined from birth to be a soldier in service of the King of Gernia. Now he must face a forest-dwelling folk who will not submit easily to a king's tyranny and they possess a powerful sorcery that threatens to claim Nevare Burvelle's soul and devastate his world.

FOREST MAGE
978-0-06-075829-5

Freed from the Speck magic that infected him, Nevare Burvelle is journeying home to Widevale, anticipating a tender reunion with his fiancée, Carsina. But his nights are haunted by grim visions of treachery, and his days are tormented by a strange side-effect of the plague that shames his family and repulses the lady of his heart.

RENEGADE'S MAGIC
978-0-06-075830-1

Nevare Burvelle stands wrongly accused of unspeakable crimes, including murder. Suddenly an outcast and a fugitive, he remains hostage to the Speck magic that shackles him to a savage alter ego who would destroy everything Nevare holds dear.

JOCELYNN DRAKE'S

NEW YORK TIMES BESTSELLING
DARK DAYS NOVELS

NIGHTWALKER
978-0-06-154277-0

For centuries Mira has been a nightwalker—an unstoppable enforcer for a mysterious organization that manipulates earth-shaking events from the darkest shadows. But the foe she now faces is human: the vampire hunter called Danaus, who has already destroyed so many undead.

DAYHUNTER
978-0-06-154283-1

Mira and her unlikely ally Danaus have come to Venice, home of the nightwalker rulers. But there is no safety in the ancient city and Danaus, the only creature she dares trust, is some-thing more than the man he claims to be...

DAWNBREAKER
978-0-06-154288-6

Destiny draws Mira and Danaus toward an apocalyptic confrontation with the *naturi* at Machu Picchu. Once the *naturi* are unchained, blood, chaos, and horror will reign supreme on Earth. But all is not lost as a rogue enemy princess can change the balance of power and turn the dread tide.

PRAY FOR DAWN
978-0-06-185180-3

Mira and Danaus—vampire and vampire slayer—must unite to prevent the annihilation of their separate races when the slaying of a senator's daughter threatens to expose Mira to the light of day.

Visit www.AuthorTracker.com for exclusive information on your favorite HarperCollins authors.

JD 0510

HARPER VOYAGER
TRADE PAPERBACKS

WEREWOLF SMACKDOWN
by Mario Acevedo
978-0-06-156718-6

LORD OF LIGHT
by Roger Zelazny
978-0-06-056723-1

THE GREAT BOOK OF AMBER
by Roger Zelazny
978-0-380-80906-6

BRAINS
by Robin Becker
978-0-06-197405-2

SWORDS & DARK MAGIC
Edited by Jonathan Strahan and Lou Anders
978-0-06-172381-0

THE CHILD THIEF
by Brom
978-0-06-167134-0

Z IS FOR ZOMBIE
An Illustrated Guide to the End of the World
by Adam-Troy Castro and Johnny Atomic
978-0-06-199185-1